Praise for *New York Times* bestselling author

LINDA HOWARD

"You can't read just one Linda Howard!"
—*New York Times* bestselling author Catherine Coulter

"Linda Howard writes with power, stunning sensuality
and a storytelling ability unmatched in the romance genre.
Every book is a treasure for the reader to savor again and again."
—*New York Times* bestselling author Iris Johansen

"This master storyteller takes our breath away."
—*RT Book Reviews*

Praise for *USA TODAY* bestselling author Marie Force

"This book starts out strong and keeps getting better. Marie Force
is one of those authors that will be on my must-read list in the future."
—*The Romance Studio* on *Fatal Affair*

"The author makes the reader part of the action,
effortlessly weaving the world of politics and murder
in which the characters come alive on the pages.
The plot was addictive and scandalous with so many family secrets....
Drama, passion, suspense—*Fatal Affair* has it all!"
—*Book Junkie*

"Marie Force's second novel in the Fatal series is an outstanding
romantic suspense in its own right; that it follows the
fantastic first installment only sweetens the read."
—*RT Book Reviews*, 4 ½ stars, on *Fatal Justice*

LINDA HOWARD

— AND —

MARIE FORCE

LETHAL ATTRACTION

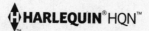

Recycling programs
for this product may
not exist in your area.

ISBN-13: 978-0-373-77823-2

LETHAL ATTRACTION

Copyright © 2013 by Harlequin Books S.A.

The publisher acknowledges the copyright holders of the individual works as follows:

AGAINST THE RULES
Copyright © 1983 by Linda Howington

FATAL AFFAIR
Copyright © 2010 by Marie Sullivan Force

This edition published by arrangement with Harlequin Books S.A.

For questions and comments about the quality of this book, please contact us at CustomerService@Harlequin.com.

Printed in U.S.A.

AGAINST THE RULES

LINDA HOWARD

CHAPTER 1

Cathryn wearily dropped her travel bag at her feet and looked around the air terminal for a familiar face, any familiar face. Houston's Intercontinental Airport was crowded with holiday travelers over the long Memorial Day weekend, and after being pushed both backward and forward by people hurrying to make connecting flights, Cathryn stepped back out of the worst of the crunch, using her foot to push the travel bag along. Her flight hadn't been early, so why wasn't someone there to meet her? This was her first visit home in almost three years, so surely Monica could have—

"Cat."

The irritated thought was never finished; it was interrupted by a husky growl in her ear and two hard hands curving around her slim waist, turning her around and pulling her against a lean male body. She had a startled, fleeting glimpse of unreadable dark eyes before they were covered by drooping lids and long black lashes; then he was too close, and her lips, parted in surprise, were caught by the warmth of his mouth. Two seconds, three...the kiss lingered, became deeper, his tongue moving in to take sensual possession. An instant before she recovered herself enough to protest, he released her from the kiss and stepped back.

"You shouldn't do that!" she snapped, her pale cheeks becoming warm with color as she noticed several people watching them and grinning.

Rule Jackson thumbed his battered black hat farther back

on his head and regarded her with calm amusement, the same sort of look he'd given her when she was an awkward twelve-year-old, all long arms and legs. "I thought we'd both enjoy it," he drawled, leaning down to pick up her bag. "Is this all?"

"No," she said, glaring at him.

"It figures."

He turned and made his way over to the luggage claim area, and Cathryn followed him, fuming inwardly at his manner but determined not to let him see it. She was twenty-five now, not a scared kid of seventeen; she would *not* let him intimidate her. She was his employer. He was only the ranch foreman, not the omnipotent devil her adolescent imagination had painted him. He might still have Monica and Ricky under his spell, but Monica was no longer her guardian and couldn't command her obedience. Cathryn wondered with well-hidden fury if Monica had deliberately sent Rule to meet her, with the knowledge that she hated him.

Unconsciously watching his lean body as he stretched and claimed the lone suitcase with her name tag on it, Cathryn shut off the rest of the violent thoughts that flooded her mind. Seeing Rule had always done that to her, driven her out of control and made her do things she would never have done except in the heat of temper. I hate him, she thought, the words whispering through her mind, but still her eyes moved over the width of his shoulders and down the long, powerful legs as she remembered....

He brought the suitcase to where she stood and one straight black eyebrow arched questioningly. After making her feel that she had imposed on him by having more than one piece of luggage, he grunted, "Not planning on a long visit, are you?"

"No," she replied, keeping her voice flat, expressionless. She had never stayed long at the ranch, not since that summer when she had been seventeen.

"It's about time you thought about coming home for good," he said.

"There's no reason for me to."

His dark eyes glinted at her from under the brim of his hat, but he didn't say anything, and when he turned and began threading his way through the groups of people Cathryn followed him without saying anything either. Sometimes she thought that communication between her and Rule was impossible, but at other times it seemed that no words were necessary. She didn't understand him, but she knew him, knew his pride, his toughness, his damned black temper that was no less frightening for being controlled. She had grown up knowing that Rule Jackson was a dangerous man; her formative years had been dominated by him.

He led her out of the air terminal and across the pavement to the area where private aircraft were kept, his long legs eating up the distance without effort; but Cathryn wasn't used to keeping up with his strides and she refused to trot after him like a dog on a leash. She maintained her own pace, keeping him in sight, and at last he stopped beside a blue-and-white twin-engined Cessna, opening the cargo door and storing her bags inside, then looking around impatiently for her. "Hurry it up," he called, seeing that she was still some distance away.

Cathryn ignored him. He put his hands on his hips and waited for her, his booted feet braced in an arrogant stance that came naturally to him. When she reached him he didn't say a word; he merely pulled the door open and turned back to her, catching her around the waist and lifting her easily into the plane. She moved to the copilot's seat and Rule swung himself into the pilot's seat, then closed the door and tossed his hat onto the seat behind him, raking his lean fingers through his hair before reaching for the headset. Cathryn watched him, her expression revealing nothing, but she couldn't help remembering the vitality of that thick dark hair, the way it had curled around her fingers....

He glanced at her and caught her watching him. She didn't look guiltily away but held her gaze, knowing that the still blankness of her face gave away nothing.

"Do you like what you see?" he taunted softly, letting the headset dangle from his fingers.

"Why did Monica send you?" she asked flatly, ignoring his question and attacking with one of her own.

"Monica didn't send me. You've forgotten; *I* run the ranch, not Monica." His dark eyes rested on her, waiting for her to flare up at him and shout that she owned the ranch, not he, but Cathryn had learned well how to hide her thoughts. She kept her face blank, her gaze unwavering.

"Exactly. I'd have thought you were too busy to waste time fetching me."

"I wanted to talk to you before you got to the ranch; this seemed like a perfect opportunity."

"So talk."

"Let's get airborne first."

Flying in a small plane was no novelty to her. From her birth she had been accustomed to flying, since a plane was considered essential to a rancher. She sat back in the seat and stretched her cramped muscles, sore from the long flight from Chicago. Big jets screamed as they came in for landings or lifted off, but Rule was unruffled as he talked to the tower and taxied to a clear strip. In only minutes they were up and skimming westward, Houston shimmering in the spring heat to the south of them. The earth beneath had the rich green hue of new grass, and Cathryn drank in the sight of it. Whenever she came for a visit she had to force herself to leave, and it always left an ache for months, as if something vital had been torn from her. She loved this land, loved the ranch, but she had survived these years only by keeping to her self-imposed exile.

"Talk," she said shortly, trying to stem the memories.

"I want you to stay this time," he said, and Cathryn felt as if he had punched her in the stomach.

Stay? Didn't he, of all people, know how impossible that was for her? She slid a quick sideways glance at him and found him frowning intently at the horizon. For a moment her eyes lingered on the strong profile before she jerked her head forward again.

"No comment?" he asked.

"It's impossible."

"Is that it? You're not even going to ask why?"

"Will I like the answer?"

"No." He shrugged. "But it's not something you can avoid."

"Then tell me."

"Ricky's back again; she's drinking a lot, running out of control. She's been doing some wild things, and people are talking."

"She's a grown woman. I can't control her," said Cathryn coldly, though it made her furious to think of Ricky dragging the Donahue name in the dirt.

"I think you can. Monica can't, but we both know that Monica doesn't have much mothering instinct. On the other hand, since your last birthday you control the ranch, which makes Ricky dependent on you." He turned his head to pin her to the seat with his dark hawk's eyes. "I know you don't like her, but she's your stepsister and she's using the Donahue name again."

"Again?" Cathryn sniped. "After two divorces, why bother to change names?" Rule was right: she didn't like Ricky, never had. Her stepsister, two years her senior, had the temperament of a Tasmanian devil. Then she slanted a mocking look at him. "You told me that *you* run the ranch."

"I do," he replied so softly that the hair on the back of her neck rose. "But I don't own it. The ranch is your home, Cat. It's time you settled down to that fact."

"Don't lecture me, Rule Jackson. My home is in Chicago now—"

"Your husband's dead," he interrupted brutally. "There's nothing there for you and you know it. What do you have? An empty apartment and a boring job?"

"I like my job; besides, I don't have to work."

"Yes, you do, because you'd go crazy sitting in that empty apartment with nothing to do. So your husband left you a little money. It'll be gone in five years, and I won't let you drain the ranch dry to finance that place."

"It's my ranch!" she pointed out shortly.

"It was also your father's, and he loved it. Because of him, I won't let you throw it away."

Cathryn lifted her chin, struggling to keep her composure. That was a low blow and he knew it. He glanced at her again and continued. "The situation with Ricky is getting worse. I can't handle it and do my job too. I need help, Cat, and you're the logical person."

"I can't stay," she said, but for once her uncertainty was evident in her voice. She disliked Ricky, but, on the other hand, she didn't hate her. Ricky was a pain and a problem, yet there had been times when they were younger when they had giggled together like ordinary teenagers. And as Rule had pointed out, Ricky was using the Donahue name, having taken it as her own when Cathryn's father had married Monica, though it had never been made legal.

"I'll try to arrange a leave of absence." Cathryn heard herself giving in, and in belated self-protection tacked on, "But it won't be permanent. I'm used to living in a big city now, and I enjoy things that can't be found on a ranch." That much was true; she did enjoy the activities that went on nonstop in a large city, but she would give them up without a qualm if she felt that she could have a peaceful life on the ranch.

"You used to love the ranch," he said.

"That was used to."

He said nothing else, and after a moment Cathryn leaned her head back and closed her eyes. She recognized her complete trust in Rule's capabilities as a pilot, and the knowledge was bitter but inescapable. She would trust him with her life, but nothing else.

Even with her eyes closed she was so aware of his presence beside her that she felt as if she were being burned by the heat of his body. She could smell the heady male scent of him, hear his steady breathing. Whenever he moved the nerves in her body tingled. God, she thought in despair. Would she never forget that day? Did he have to shadow her entire life, ruling her with his mere presence? He had even haunted her marriage, forcing her to lie to her own husband.

She drifted into a light doze, a drifting state halfway between awareness and sleep, and she found that she could recall with perfect clarity all that she knew about Rule Jackson. She had known of him her entire life. His father had been a neighbor, a fellow rancher with a small but prospering spread, and Rule had worked the ranch with his father from the time he was old enough to sit a horse; but he was eleven years older and had seemed a grown man to her instead of the boy he had been.

Even as a child Cathryn had known that there was scandal attached to the name of Rule Jackson. He was known as "that wild Jackson boy," and older girls giggled when discussing him. But he was only a boy, a neighbor, and Cathryn liked him. He never paid much attention to her whenever she saw him, but when he did talk to her, he was kind and able to coax her out of her shyness; Rule was good with young animals, even human ones. Some said that he was better suited for the company of animals, but, for whatever reason, he had a rare touch with horses and dogs.

When Cathryn was eight her world changed. It had also been a time of change for Rule. The same year that her mother died, leaving Cathryn stunned and withdrawn, solemn beyond her years, Rule was drafted. He was nineteen when he got off the plane in Saigon. By the time he returned three years later, nothing was the same.

Ward Donahue had remarried to a darkly beautiful woman from New Orleans. From the first Cathryn didn't quite like Monica. For her father's sake she hid her feelings and did her best to get along with Monica, establishing an uneasy truce. Each of them walked softly around the other. It wasn't that Monica was the stereotypical wicked stepmother; she simply wasn't a motherly woman, not even to her own daughter, Ricky. Monica liked bright lights and dancing, and from the first she didn't fit in with the hardworking ranch life. She tried, for Ward's sake. That was the one thing Cathryn never doubted, that Monica loved her father. For that reason she and Monica existed in mutual if unenthusiastic peace.

The upheaval in Rule's life had been even greater. He had survived Vietnam, but sometimes it seemed as if only his body had returned. His dark, laughing eyes no longer laughed; they watched and brooded. His body was scarred with wounds that had healed, but the mental wounds he had suffered had changed him forever. He never talked about it. He seldom talked at all. He kept to himself and watched people with those hard, expressionless eyes, and soon he became an outcast.

He drank a lot, sitting alone and steadily downing the alcohol, his face closed and stony. Naturally he became even more attractive to women than he had been before. Some women couldn't resist the aura of danger that clung to him like an invisible cloak. They dreamed of being the magic one who could comfort him, heal him and take him away from the nightmare he still lived.

He was involved in one scandal after another. His father threw him out of the house and no one else would hire him, the ranchers and merchants banding together to rid the neighborhood of him. Somehow he still found money for whiskey, and he sometimes disappeared for days, leading people to speculate that he had crawled off somewhere and died. But he always turned up like a bad penny, a bit thinner, more haggard, but always there.

It was inevitable that the hostility against him would escalate into violence; he had been involved with too many women, snarled at too many men. Ward Donahue found him one day lying sprawled in a ditch on the outskirts of town. Rule was battered from the punishment a group of men had decided was his due, and so thin that his bones shone white through his skin. Still silent and intent, his dark eyes glittered up at his rescuer with grim defiance even though he was unable to stand. Without a word Ward lifted the younger man in his arms as if he were a child and placed him in the pickup, taking him to the ranch to be cared for. A week later Rule crawled painfully onto a horse and rode with Ward about the ranch, performing the hard but necessary chore of riding fence, repairing broken fencing and rounding up strays. He was in such pain for the first few days that sweat poured from his body whenever he moved, yet he continued with grim determination.

He stopped drinking and began eating normal meals again. He grew stronger and gained weight, both from the food and from the hard physical work he was doing. He never talked about what had happened. The other ranch hands left him strictly alone except for what contact was necessary during work, but Rule was uncommunicative at the best of times. He worked and he ate and he slept, and whatever Ward Donahue asked of him he would have accomplished or died in the effort.

The affection and trust between the two men was evident; no one was surprised when Rule was made foreman after the previous foreman left for another job in Oklahoma. As Ward said to anyone who would listen, Rule had an instinct for horses and cattle, and Ward trusted him. By that time the ranch hands had become used to working with him and the transition was a peaceful one.

Shortly afterward Ward died of a massive stroke. Cathryn and Ricky were at school at the time, and Cathryn could still remember her surprise when Rule came to take her out of class. He led her outside and there told her of her father's death, and he held her in his arms while she cried the violent tears of fresh grief, his lean callused hand smoothing back her heavy mahogany red hair. She had been slightly afraid of him, but now she clung to him, instinctively comforted by his steely strength. Her father had trusted him, so how could she do less?

Because of that tentative trust, Cathryn felt doubly betrayed when Rule began to act as if he owned the ranch. No one could take her father's place. How dare he even try? But more and more Rule took his meals at the ranch house. He finally moved in completely, settling himself in the corner guest-room that overlooked the stables and bunkhouse. It was particularly galling that Monica made no effort to assert herself; she let Rule have his way in anything concerning the ranch. She was a woman who automatically leaned on whatever man was handy, and certainly she was no match for Rule. Looking back, Cathryn realized now that Monica had been utterly lost when it came to ranch matters, yet she had no other home for herself and Ricky, so she had been locked into a life that was alien to her, totally unable to handle a man like Rule, who was both determined and dangerous.

Cathryn was bitterly resentful of Rule's takeover. Ward had literally picked him up out of the gutter and stood him on his feet, held him up until he could stand on his own, and this was how he was repaid, by Rule moving in and taking over.

The ranch was Cathryn's, with Monica appointed as her legal guardian, but Cathryn had no voice in the running of it. Without exception the men went to Rule for their orders, despite everything Cathryn could do. She tried to do plenty. Losing her father had shocked her out of her shyness, and she fought for her ranch with the ferocity of the uninformed young, disobeying Rule at every turn. At that stage of her life Ricky had been a willing accomplice. Ricky was always willing to break rules, any rules. But no matter what she did, Cathryn always felt that she was no more irritating to Rule than a mosquito he could casually brush aside.

When he decided to branch out into horse breeding, Monica provided the capital over Cathryn's vociferous opposition, dipping without argument into the funds set aside for the girls' college educations. Whatever Rule wanted, he got. He had the Bar D under his thumb...for the time being. Cathryn lay awake at night and thought ahead with relish to the day when she would be of age, savoring in her mind the words she would say when she fired Rule Jackson.

Rule even extended his domination to her personal life. When she was fifteen she accepted a date with an eighteen-year-old boy to attend a dance. Rule found out about it and called the boy, quietly informing him that Cathryn wasn't old enough yet to date. When Cathryn discovered what he had done she lost her temper, goaded into action and recklessness.

Without thinking, she hit him, her palm slamming across his face with a force that numbed her arm.

He didn't speak. His dark eyes narrowed; then, with the swiftness of a snake lashing out, he grabbed her arm and hauled her upstairs. Cathryn kicked and scratched and yelled every inch of the way, but it was a useless effort. He handled her with ease, his strength so much greater than hers that she was as helpless as an infant. Once they reached her room, he jerked her jeans down and sat on the bed, pulled her across his lap and gave her the spanking of her life. At fifteen Cathryn had just begun shaping from adolescence into the rounder form of womanhood, and the embarrassment she suffered had in some ways been worse than the pain inflicted by his callused palm. When he let her go she scrambled to her feet and repaired her clothing, her face twisted with fury.

"You're asking me to treat you like a woman," he said, his voice low and even. "But you're just a kid and I treated you like a kid. Don't push me until you're old enough to handle it."

Cathryn whirled and went flying down the stairs in search of Monica, her cheeks still wet with tears as she screamed that he should be fired, *now*.

Monica laughed in her face. "Don't be silly, Cathryn," she said sharply. "We need Rule...*I* need Rule."

Behind her Cathryn heard Rule quietly laughing and felt his hand stroke her tumbled mahogany-red hair. "Just settle down, wildcat; you can't get rid of me that easily."

Cathryn had jerked her head away from his touch, but he had been right. She hadn't been able to get rid of him. Ten years later he was still running the ranch and it was she who had left, fleeing from her own home in panic that he would reduce her to the position of mindless supplicant, with no more will of her own than the horses he so easily mastered.

"Are you asleep?" he asked now, drawing her back to the present, and Cathryn opened her eyes.

"No."

"Then talk to me," he demanded. Though she wasn't looking, she could visualize his sensually formed mouth moving as he said the words. She had never forgotten anything about him, from the slow way he talked to the dark, slightly hoarse tone of his voice, as if his vocal cords were rusty from lack of use. He gave her a swift glance. "Tell me about your husband."

Cathryn was startled, her dark eyes widening. "You met him several times. What would you want to know about David?"

"A lot of things," he murmured easily. "Such as if he asked you why you weren't a virgin when he married you."

Bitter, furious, Cathryn choked back the words that tumbled to her lips. What could she say that he wouldn't use against her? It's none of your business? He would only reply that it was more his business than it was any other man's, considering that he had been the one responsible for the loss of her virginity.

She tried not to look at him, but against her will she turned to him, her eyes wide and vulnerable. "He never asked," she finally said in a quiet voice. Rule's profile was etched starkly against the blueness of the sky, and her heart lurched; it brought painfully, vividly to mind that summer day when he had bent over her with the hot molten sun and brazen sky behind him, outlining him like a graven image. Her body tightened automatically in remembered response and she tore her gaze away from him before he turned and saw the rawness of her pain mirrored in her eyes.

"I would have asked," he rasped.

"David was a gentleman," she said pointedly.

"Meaning I'm not?"

"You know the answer to that as well as I do. No, you're not a gentleman. You're not gentle in any way."

"I was gentle with you once," he replied, his dark eyes moving over her with slow relish, tracing the curves of her breasts and hips and thighs. Again the hot tightening of her body warned her that she wasn't indifferent to this man, had never been, and pain bloomed in her.

"I don't want to talk about it!" As soon as the words left her mouth she wished they could be unsaid. The ragged panic in her tone made it evident to anyone with normal intelligence that she couldn't treat that long-ago incident with the indifference that the years should have brought, and Rule was more intelligent and intuitive than most. His next words proved it.

"You can't run forever. You're not a kid now, Cat; you're a woman."

Oh, she knew that! He had made her a woman when she was seventeen, and the image of him had tormented her since, even intruded between her and her husband and cheated David out of the devotion that had been his due, though she would have died rather than let him guess that her response to him hadn't been all it should have been. Nor could she tell Rule how deeply he had affected her life with what to him could have been only a casual coupling.

"I didn't run away," she denied. "I went to college, which is entirely different."

"And came home on visits as seldom as you could," he said with harsh sarcasm. "Did you think I'd attack you every time I saw you? I knew you were too young. Hell, I didn't mean for it to happen anyway, and I was going to make damned sure the opportunity never came up again, at least until you were older and had a better idea of what it was about."

"I knew what sex was!" she defied, not wanting him to

guess how totally unprepared she had been for the reality of it, but her effort was useless.

"You knew what it was, but not what it was like." The hard, stark truth of his words silenced her, and after a minute he said grimly, "You weren't ready for that, were you?"

She drew a shuddering breath, wishing she had pretended to be asleep. Rule was like a blooded stallion: when he got the bit between his teeth there was no stopping him. "No," she admitted raggedly. "Especially not with you."

A hard smile curved his grim mouth. "And I took it easy on you. You really would have been scared out of your dainty little pants if I'd let myself go the way I wanted to."

Twisting agony in her midsection made her lash out at him, hoping futilely that she could hurt him as he had hurt her. "I didn't want you! I didn't—"

"You wanted it," he interrupted harshly. "You were in a redheaded temper and fighting me just for the sake of fighting, but you wanted it. You didn't try to get away from me. You lit into me and tried to hurt me in any way you could, and somewhere along the line all that temper turned into wanting and you were wrapped around me like a vine."

Cathryn winced away from the memory. "I don't want to talk about it!"

Without warning he erupted into fury, into that deadly temper that smart people learned how to avoid. "Well, that's just too damned bad," he snarled thickly, switching the controls to automatic pilot and reaching for her.

She made an instinctive, useless effort to ward off his hands, and he brushed her fingers away with laughable ease. His fingers bit into her upper arms as he hauled her out of her seat until she was lying sprawled against him. His mouth was hard, hot, well remembered, the taste of him as familiar as if she'd never gone away. Her slim hands curled into fists and beat ineffectively at his shoulders, but despite her efforts at resistance she found that nothing had changed, nothing at all. A hot swell of sensual excitement made her heart beat faster, made her breath come in panting gasps, her entire body quiver. She wanted him. Oh, damn him, how she wanted him! Some curious chemistry in her makeup made her respond to him like a flower to sunlight, twisting, seeking, even though she knew he was no good for her.

His tongue probed slowly into her mouth and her hands ceased their beating to suddenly clasp his shoulders, feeling the hard muscles under her palms with instant delight. Pleasure was filling her, pleasure comprised of the taste and feel and smell of him, the slightly rough slide of his cheek against hers, the intimacy of his tongue on hers that vividly recalled a hot summer day when no clothing had been between them.

His anger was gone, turned into desire that glittered plainly in his dark eyes when he lifted his mouth just the fraction of an inch necessary to demand, "Did you ever forget what it was like?"

Her hands slipped up to his head, trying to pull him across that delicious, intolerable tiny space to her own mouth, but he resisted and her fingers wrapped in his silky, vibrant dark hair. "Rule," she muttered huskily.

"Did you?" he insisted, and drew his head back when she tried to raise her own to allow her mouth to cling to his.

It didn't matter; he knew anyway. How could he not know? One touch and she melted against him. "No, I never forgot," she admitted in a whisper of sound that slid away into nothing as at last his mouth came down and crushed hers and she drank again of the sweet-tart freshness of him.

It was no surprise when she felt his long fingers close over her breast, then slide restlessly down her ribs. The thin silk of her sleeveless summer dress was no barrier to the heat of his hand, and she felt burned as his touch sleeked down her body to stop at her knee, then began a slow, stroking journey up her thigh, lifting her skirt, exposing her long legs. Then abruptly he halted, shuddering with the effort it cost him, and he removed his hand from her leg. "This is no place for making love," he whispered hoarsely, lifting his mouth from hers and sliding his kisses to her ear. "It's a miracle we haven't already crashed. But I can wait until we're home."

Her lashes lifted to reveal dazed, slumberous dark eyes, and he gave her another hard kiss, then shifted her back into her own seat. Still breathing hard, he checked their position, then wiped the sweat from his forehead and turned back to her. "Now we know where we stand," he said with grim satisfaction.

Cathryn jerked herself erect and turned her head to stare out at the sweeping ranchland below. Fool! she berated herself. Stupid fool! Now he knew just how powerful the weapon he had against her was, and she had no illusion that he would hesitate to use it. It wasn't fair that his desire for her didn't leave him as vulnerable as she was, but the basic fact was that his desire was simply that, desire, without any of the accompanying emotions or needs that she felt, while the mere sound of his voice submerged her into so many boiling needs and feelings that she had no hope of sorting them out and understanding them. He was so deeply associated with all the crises and milestones of her life that even while she hated and feared him, he was so much a part of her that she couldn't fire him, couldn't kick him out of her life. He was as addictive as a drug, using his lean, hard-muscled body and educated hands to keep his women under control.

I won't be one of his women! Cathryn vowed fiercely, clenching her fists. He had no morals, no sense of shame. After all her father had done for him, as soon as Ward was in the grave, Rule had taken over. Nor was that enough. He had to have the ranch and Ward's daughter too. In that moment Cathryn decided not to stay, to return to Chicago as soon as the holiday was over. Ricky's problems were not hers. If Rule didn't like the way things were, he was free to seek employment elsewhere.

Then they were circling over the sprawling, two-story frame house to signal their arrival to the ranch, and Rule banked the plane sharply to the left to line up with the small runway. She felt stunned at how little time it had taken to reach the ranch, but a glance at her watch told her that more time had elapsed than she'd thought. How long had she been wrapped in Rule's arms? And how long had she been lost in her thoughts? When she was with him everything else seemed to fade out of her awareness.

A dusty red pickup came bouncing across the field to meet them as Rule took the plane in for a smooth, shallow landing; they touched down so lightly that there was scarcely a bump. Cathryn found herself looking at his hands, strong and brown and competent whether they were flying a plane, mastering a fractious horse or soothing a flighty woman. She remembered those hands on her body, and tried not to.

CHAPTER 2

As Cathryn went up the three steps to the porch that ran the width of the house she was surprised that Monica didn't come out to greet her. Ricky didn't come out, either, but she hadn't really expected Ricky. Monica, on the other hand, had always at least kept up appearances and made a big show of affection when David was alive and visited with her. She opened the screen door and went into the cool dimness; Rule was right behind her with her luggage. "Where's Monica?" she asked.

He started up the stairs. "God only knows," he grunted, and Cathryn followed him with rising irritation. She caught him as he opened the door of the bedroom that had always been hers and went inside to drop the bags by the bed.

"What do you mean by that?" she demanded.

He shrugged. "Monica ranges far and wide these days. She's never been too keen on the ranch anyway. You can't blame her for hunting her own amusements." He turned to leave and Cathryn followed him again.

"Where are you going?" she asked sharply.

He turned back to her with exaggerated patience. "I've got work to do. Did you have anything else in mind?" His eyes strayed to the bedroom door, then back to her, and Cathryn set her jaw.

"I had finding Monica in mind."

"She'll show up before dark. I noticed that the station wagon is gone, and she hates driving after dark, so she'll be here by then unless she has an accident."

"You're so concerned!" Cathryn lashed out.

"Should I be? I'm a rancher, not a chaperon."

"Correction: you're a ranch *foreman*."

For a moment his eyes flared with temper; then he damped it down. "You're right, and as the foreman I have work to do. Are you going to stay here and sulk, or are you going to change clothes and come with me? There've been a lot of changes since the last time you were here. I thought you might be interested, *boss*." He stressed the last word slightly, his eyes mocking her. He was the boss, and he knew it; he had been for so many years that many of the ranch hands had been hired since Ward's death and had no loyalty to a Donahue, only to Rule Jackson.

She wavered for a moment, torn between her reluctance to spend any time in his company and her interest in the ranch. The years she had spent away had been an exile and she had suffered every day, longing for the vast spaces and the clean smell of the earth. She wanted to see the land, reacquaint herself with the things that had marked her earliest days. "I'll go change," she said quietly.

"I'll wait for you at the stables," he said, then let his eyes drift down the length of her. "Unless you'd like some company while you change?"

Her fierce "No!" was automatic, and he didn't act as if he had expected any other answer. He shrugged and went down the stairs. Cathryn returned to her room and closed the door, then twisted her arms up behind herself to unzip the dress and take it off. For a moment she thought of Rule helping her with the zipper; then she shivered and wrenched her mind away from the treacherous idea. She had to hurry. Rule's patience had a time limit.

She didn't bother to unpack. She had always left most of her jeans and shirts there at the ranch. In Chicago she wore chic designer jeans; on the ranch she wore faded, worn jeans that were limp from use. She sometimes felt that when she changed clothes, she changed personalities. The chic, polished wife of David Ashe again became Cathryn Donahue, raised with the wind in her hair. As she stamped her feet into her boots and reached for the tan hat that she had worn for years, she became aware of a sense of belonging. She pushed the thought away, but pleasurable anticipation remained with her as she ran down the stairs and made her way out to the stables, pausing in the kitchen to greet the cook, Lorna Ingram. She was friendly enough with Lorna, but was aware that the woman looked on Rule as her employer and that that precluded any closeness between them.

Rule was waiting for her with outward patience, though his big-boned chestnut nudged him in the back and shifted nervously behind him. He also held the reins to a long-legged gray gelding, a horse Cathryn didn't remember having seen before. Having been around horses all of her life she had no fear of them and rubbed the animal's nose naturally, letting him learn the smell of her while she talked to him. "Hi, fella, you're a stranger to me. How long have you been here?"

"A couple of years," answered Rule, tossing the reins to her. "He's a good horse, no bad habits, even-tempered. Not like Redman here," he added ruefully as the chestnut nudged him again, this time with enough force to shove him forward several steps. He swung up into the saddle without offering to help Cathryn, a gesture she would have refused anyway. She was far from helpless on a horse. She mounted and urged the gray into a trot to catch up with Rule, who hadn't waited.

They rode past the stables, and Cathryn admired the neat paddocks and barns, several of which hadn't been there during her last visit. Money on the hoof either grazed without paying attention to them or sent soft, curious nickers their way.

Playful, long-legged foals romped over the sweet spring grass. Rule lifted his gloved hand to point out a structure. "That's the new foaling barn. Want to take a look at it?"

She nodded and they swung the horses' heads in that direction. "There's only one mare due right now," he said. "We're just waiting on her. The last few weeks have been busy, but we have a break now."

The stalls in the foaling barn were airy and spacious and scrupulously clean; as Rule had said, there was only one occupant now. There in the middle of a large box stall stood a mare in a posture of such utter weariness that Cathryn smiled in sympathy. When Rule held out his hand and clicked his tongue, the mare walked to him with a heavy tread and pushed her head over the stall to be petted. He obliged her, talking to her with that special crooning note in his voice that soothed even the most nervous of animals. When she had been younger Cathryn had tried to duplicate the tone and its effect, but without result.

"We're one of the best horse-breeding farms in the state now," Rule said without any evidence of pride, simply stating fact. "Buyers are coming from every state, even Hawaii."

When they resumed their ride Rule didn't say much, letting Cathryn see for herself the changes that had been made. She was also silent, but she knew that the operation she saw was well run. The fences and paddocks were in excellent shape; the animals were healthy and spirited with no signs of ill-use; the buildings were strong and clean and wore fresh coats of paint. The bunkhouse had been added to and modernized. To her surprise, she also noticed several small cottages to the rear of the ranch house, some distance away but within a comfortable range. She pointed to them. "Are those houses?"

He grunted an affirmative answer. "Several of the hands are married. I had to do something or have some good men a long way off if I needed them during the night." He slanted a dark glance at her, but Cathryn had no objection to the houses; it seemed a logical move to her. Even if she had an objection she wouldn't have voiced it, not wanting to start an argument with him. Not that Rule argued. He simply stated his position and backed it up. Without looking at him she was aware of the power of his body, his long, steely-muscled legs that controlled half-ton horses with ease, the dark-fire gaze that made people back away.

"Want to ride out and see the cattle?" he asked, and without waiting for her answer headed out, leaving Cathryn to follow or not. She followed, keeping the gray's head just even with the chestnut's shoulder. It was a brisk ride to the west pasture where the white-faced Herefords were grazing, and it made her predict ruefully that she would regret all of this in the morning. Her muscles weren't used to so much activity.

The herd was small—astonishingly so. She said as much to Rule, and he drawled, "We're not in the cattle business anymore. What we raise is for our own use mostly. We're horse breeders now."

Stunned, Cathryn stared at him for a moment, then shouted, "What do you mean? This is a cattle ranch! Who gave you the authority to get rid of the cattle?"

"I don't need anyone to 'give' me any authority," he replied sharply. "We were losing money on the cattle, so I changed operations. If you had been here, I'd have talked it over with you, but you didn't care enough to visit."

"That's not true!" she yelled. "You know why I didn't visit more often! You know it's because of—" She cut herself off abruptly, sick with emotion but still stopping short of admitting her weakness to him.

He waited, but she said nothing else and he turned Redman's head back to the east. The sun was dipping low, but they kept to a leisurely pace, not talking. What was there to say? Cathryn paid no attention to their exact location until Rule reined in his horse at the top of a gentle rise and she looked down to see the river and a clump of trees, the wide sheltered area where she had swum naked that hot July day, and the grassy bank where Rule had made love to her. Though aware that he was watching her with sharp intensity, she couldn't prevent the healthy color from leaving her cheeks. "Damn you," she said in a shaky voice, leaving it at that, but she knew that he would catch her meaning.

He removed his hat and raked his fingers through his hair. "What are you so upset about? I'm not going to attack you, for heaven's sake. We're going to walk the horses down there and let them have some water, that's all. Come on."

Now the color flamed into her cheeks and she seethed at how easily he had made her make a fool of herself. She took a tight hold on her self-control and followed him down the slope to the river with no hint of her agitation showing on her face, but every inch of her body remembered.

It was here that he had found her skinny-dipping and harshly ordered her out of the water, threatening to haul her out if she didn't leave it willingly. She had stomped out of the river, outraged at his high-handed attitude, and waded right into battle without once considering the possible consequences of attacking a man while she was totally nude. What had happened had been more her fault than Rule's, she admitted now with more maturity than she had been capable of eight years earlier. He had tried to hold her off and soothe her out of her temper, but his hands had slipped over her bare wet flesh, and he was all man, so blatantly virile that his masculinity was like a flashing neon sign to every woman who saw him. When he ground his mouth harshly against hers, stopping her screams of fury, she had changed in one heart-stopping instant from white-hot fury to the dark blaze of desire. She had no idea how to control her own responses or exactly what responses she was arousing in him, but he had demonstrated the last point in the most explicit way possible.

When he dismounted to let his horse drink, Cathryn followed suit. He noticed the slight stiffness of her movements and said, "You're going to be sore if you don't get a rubdown. I'll take care of you when we get back."

She stiffened at the thought of him massaging her legs and refused the offer more abruptly than she'd meant to. "Thanks, but I can manage it myself."

He shrugged. "It's your pain."

Somehow his easy acceptance of her refusal irritated her even further, and she glared at him as they remounted and began the ride back to the house. Now that he had mentioned it, she was aware of her steadily increasing soreness with every yard they covered. Only pride kept her from requesting that they slow the pace, and her jaw was rigidly set when they finally reached the stables.

He swung out of the saddle and was beside her before she could kick her feet out of the stirrups. Without a word he reached up and clasped her waist, carefully lifting her down, and she knew that he realized just exactly how uncomfortable she was. She muttered her thanks and moved away from him.

"Go on up to the house and tell Lorna I'll be ready to eat in about half an hour," he ordered. "Hurry, or you won't have time to get the horse smell off beforehand."

That thought loosened her stiff muscles, and it wasn't until she was going into the house that she thought to be irritated at the fact that mealtimes had to conform to his schedule. She hesitated, then remembered that, after all, he did the work around there, so it was only fair that he have hot meals. On the heels of that thought came the idea that he could always

eat with the other hands; no one had invited him into the
main house. He hadn't waited for an invitation, she thought,
then sighed, and dutifully passed along his message to Lorna,
who smiled and nodded.

Neither Monica nor Ricky presented themselves, so she
dashed up the stairs and took a fast shower. Meals on the ranch
weren't formal, but she changed into a sleeveless cotton dress
rather than jeans, and carefully applied her makeup, driven by
some deeply buried feminine instinct that she was hesitant to
examine too closely. As she was brushing her dark mahogany-
red hair into a smooth bell that curved against her shoulders,
a brief knock sounded on the door, which promptly opened
to admit her stepsister.

Her first thought was that Ricky's last marriage must have
been a rough one. The dark hair was lustrous, the dainty body
slim and firm, but there was a febrile tenseness about her, and
lines of discontent were fanning out from the corners of her
eyes and lips. Ricky was a lovely, exotic woman, a younger
version of Monica, with her ripe mouth and slanted hazel eyes,
her golden-hued skin. The effect of that beauty, however, was
ruined by the petulance of her expression.

"Welcome home," she purred, lifting a graceful hand,
which held a glass with two inches of amber liquid in the
bottom. "Sorry I wasn't here to greet you, but I forgot that
today was the big day. I'm sure Rule took good care of you."
She took a healthy swallow of her drink and gave Cathryn a
twisted, malicious grin. "But then, Rule always takes good
care of his women, doesn't he? All of them."

Suddenly, uneasily, Cathryn wondered if Ricky somehow knew about that day by the river. It was difficult to tell;
Ricky's normal style of conversation tended to be vicious,
springing from her own discontent and internal fears. For

the time being Cathryn decided to ignore the insinuations in Ricky's tone and words, and greeted her normally.

"It's nice to be home again after so long. Things have changed, haven't they? I almost wouldn't have recognized the place."

"Oh, yesss," Ricky drawled, letting the "yes" linger on a sibilant whisper. "Rule's the boss, didn't you know? He has everything going his way; everybody jumps when he says jump. He's not the outcast anymore, sister dear. He's an up-standing—and outstanding—member of our little community, and he runs this place with an iron fist. Or he *almost* does." She winked at Cathryn. "He doesn't have me under his thumb yet. I know what he's up to."

Determined not to react or ask Ricky what she meant, knowing that in her half-drunken state any sensible conver-sation was impossible, Cathryn took Ricky's arm and gently but firmly steered her to the stairs. "Lorna should have din-ner on the table by now. I'm starving!"

As they left the room, Rule approached them and his hard mouth tightened when he saw the glass in Ricky's hand. With-out a word he reached out and relieved her of it. For a moment Ricky looked up at him with a kind of tense, pleading fear; then she visibly mastered herself and trailed a fingertip down his shirtfront, tracing a path from button to button. "You're so masterful," she purred. "No wonder you can have your pick of women. I was just telling Cathryn about them...your women, I mean." She gave him a sweetly poisonous smile and continued down the stairs, satisfaction evident in the sway of her slim, graceful body.

Rule swore softly under his breath while Cathryn stood there trying to understand what Ricky was getting at and why it was making Rule angry. There was the possibility that Ricky was getting at nothing. She loved to say upsetting things just for the joy of watching the stir. But just worrying about it wouldn't give her any answers. She turned to Rule and asked him directly, "What's she getting at?"

He didn't answer for a moment. Instead he sniffed suspiciously at the contents of the glass he held, then tossed the remainder of the drink back in one swallow. A terrible grimace twisted his features. "God," he choked, his voice strained. "How did I ever drink this stuff?"

Cathryn almost laughed aloud. From the day her father had carried him home, Rule had refused to drink liquor, even beer. His surprised reaction now was somehow endearing, as if he had revealed a hidden part of himself to her. He looked up and caught her grin, and she was startled when his hard fingers slid under her hair and clasped the back of her neck. "Are you laughing at me?" he demanded, his voice soft. "Don't you know that can be dangerous?"

She knew better than most just how dangerous Rule could be, but she wasn't frightened now. An odd exhilaration made her blood tumble through her veins and she tilted her head back to look at him. "I'm not afraid of you, big man," she said in both taunt and invitation—an invitation she hadn't meant to issue, but one that came so naturally that she had voiced it almost before the thought was completed. A second too late, she tried to cover her mistake by throwing in hastily, "Tell me what Ricky meant—"

"Damn Ricky," he growled as his fingers tightened on her neck a split second before his mouth closed on hers. Cathryn was surprised by the gentle quality of the kiss. Her lips softened and parted easily under the persuasive pressure and movements of his. He made a rough sound in his throat and turned her more fully into his arms, pressing her to him, his hand sliding down her back to her hips and arching her into the power of his loins and thighs. Her fingers clenched on his shirt sleeves in response to the heated pleasure that flared deeply within her. She was vividly aware of his male attraction, and everything that was female within her strained to answer the primitive call of his nature. It had never been like this with any other man; she had begun to realize that it never would be, that this was something unique for her. David hadn't stood a chance against the dark magic that Rule practiced so effortlessly.

The thought of David was a lifeline to grasp, something to pull her mind away from the sensual whirlpool he was drawing her into. She tore her lips away from his with a gasp but was unable to move from his arms. It wasn't that he held her captive, but that she lacked the strength to push him away. Instead she let her body lie against him while she rested her head on his shoulder, inhaling the aphrodisiac of his warm male scent.

"It's good," he muttered huskily, bending his head to bite at the delicate earlobe bared by the tilt of her head. "You're not a kid now, Cat."

What did that mean? she wondered with a flash of panic. That he no longer saw any need to keep away from her? Was he warning her that he wouldn't try to keep their relationship platonic? And who was she trying to kid? Their relationship hadn't been platonic in years, even though they had never made love since that day by the river.

From somewhere she dredged up enough strength to pull away from him and lift her head proudly. "No, I'm not a kid. I've learned how to say no to unwanted advances."

"Then mine must be wanted, because you sure as hell didn't say no," he taunted softly, moving his body in such a way that she was eased to the head of the stairs. So that was how a cow felt when being gently but inexorably herded to wherever a cowboy wanted, she thought on a slightly hysterical note. She took a deep breath and briskly composed herself, which was just as well, because suddenly Monica appeared at the foot of the stairs.

"Cathryn, Rule, whatever is keeping you?"

That was Monica—not even a greeting, though it had been almost three years since she'd last seen her stepdaughter. Cathryn didn't object to Monica's remoteness. At least it was honest. She went down the stairs with Rule close behind her, his hand resting casually on the small of her back.

The table wasn't formal. After a long, hot day on the ranch a man wanted a meal, not a social occasion. Cathryn's decision to wear a dress had been an unusual one, but now she noticed that Ricky had also elected to leave off her jeans and instead wore a white gauze dress that wouldn't have been out of place at a party. She knew instinctively that Ricky didn't have a date that night, so she had to be dressing up for Rule's benefit.

Cathryn's eyes strayed to Rule as he sat in the chair where Ward Donahue had always sat. For the first time she noticed that he had changed into dark brown cords and a crisp white shirt, with the cuffs unbuttoned and rolled back to reveal brawny tanned forearms. Her breath caught as she watched him, examined the features that had so often occupied her dreams. His hair was thick and as silky as a child's, with only a hint of curl; both his hair and eyes were that precise, peculiar shade that was neither black nor brown, but a color that she could define only as dark. His forehead was broad, his brows straight and heavy over a thin, high-bridged nose that flared into spirited nostrils. His lips were chiseled, sensual, but capable of compressing into a grim line or twisting into an enraged snarl. His broad shoulders strained at the white cloth that covered them, while in the open neck of the shirt she could see the beginnings of the virile curls that decorated his chest and arrowed down his abdomen. She knew all of that about him, knew exactly the texture of that hair beneath her fingers....

Slowly she became aware of the amusement in his eyes and she realized that she had been staring openly, practically eating him with her eyes. She flushed and fidgeted nervously with her fork, not daring to look at either Monica or Ricky for fear they had also noticed.

"How was the flight?" Monica asked trivially, but Cathryn was grateful to her and latched onto the gambit eagerly.

"Crowded, but on time, for once. I didn't ask if you had to wait," she said to Rule, deliberately making the effort to converse with him and demonstrate that she wasn't disturbed at having been caught staring at him.

He shrugged and started to say something, but Ricky broke in with a harsh, bitter laugh. "It didn't bother him any," she sniped. "He left yesterday afternoon and spent the night in Houston to make certain he didn't miss you. Nothing's too good for the little queen of the Bar D, is it, Rule?"

His dark face had that closed, stony look that Cathryn always associated with the painful days when he had first come to the ranch, and she had to clench her fists to quell the sudden, powerful urge to protect him. If any man was less in need of protection than Rule Jackson, he was one tough customer indeed. Rule proved that by giving Ricky a smile that was nothing more than a baring of his teeth as he agreed with seeming ease. "That's right. I'm here to give her whatever she wants, whenever she wants it."

Monica said coolly, "For God's sake, can't we have one meal without the two of you sniping at each other? Ricky, try acting your age, which is twenty-seven, instead of seven."

In the small silence that followed, Monica continued with a statement that must have seemed completely innocent to her, but which hit Cathryn with all the power of a jackhammer. "Rule says that you've come home to stay, Cathryn."

Cathryn shot a furious look at Rule, which he met blandly,

but the denial that was on her lips was never voiced as Ricky dropped her fork with a clatter. All heads turned to her; she was white, shaking. "You bastard," she said thinly, glaring at Rule with pure venom in her eyes. "All of these years, as long as Mother had control of the ranch, you've mooned around her and sweet-talked her into doing anything you wanted, but now that Cathryn's twenty-five and has taken over legal control, you drop Mother as if she's nothing more than yesterday's laundry! You used her! You didn't want her or me eith—"

Rule leaned back in his chair, his eyes flat and unreadable. He didn't say anything, just watched and waited, and Cathryn had a sudden impression of a cougar flattening out on a limb, waiting for an unsuspecting lamb to walk beneath it. Ricky must have sensed danger too, because her voice halted in midword.

Monica glared at her daughter and said icily, "You don't know what you're talking about! With your track record in romance, how can you have the gall to either criticize or advise anyone else?"

Ricky turned wildly to her mother. "How can you keep on defending him?" she cried. "Can't you see what he's doing? He should've married you years ago, but he put you off and waited until *she* came of age! He knew she would be taking over the ranch! Didn't you?" she spat, whirling to face Rule.

Cathryn had had enough. Trembling with temper, she discarded her hold on good manners and slammed her silverware down on the table while she struggled to organize the red-hot words in her mind into coherent sentences.

Rule had no such difficulty. He shoved his plate back and got to his feet. Ice dripped from his tone as he said, "There's never been the slightest possibility that I'd marry Monica." He left on that brutal note, his booted feet taking long strides that carried him out of the room before anyone else could add to the fire.

Cathryn glanced at Monica. Her stepmother was white except for the round spots of artificial color that dotted her cheekbones. Monica snapped harshly, "Congratulations, Ricky! You've managed to ruin another meal."

Cathryn demanded in rising anger, "What was the meaning of that scene?"

Ricky propped her elbows gracefully on the table and folded her hands under her chin in an angelic posture, regaining her poise though, like Monica, she was pale. "Surely you're not as dense as that," she mocked. She looked definitely pleased with herself, her red lips curling up in a wicked little smile. "There's no use in pretending that you don't know how Rule has used Mother all these years. But lately...lately he's realized that you're of age, conveniently widowed, and can have full control over the ranch whenever you decide to take an interest. Mother's of no use to him now; she no longer holds the purse strings. It's a simple case of off with the old, on with the new."

Cathryn gave her a withering look. "You're twisted!"

"And you're a fool!"

"I'd certainly be one if I took anything you said at face value!" Cathryn shot back. "I don't know what you've got against Rule. Maybe you're just soured on men—"

"That's right!" Ricky shrilled. "Throw it up to me because I'm divorced!"

Cathryn wanted to pull her own hair in frustration. She knew Ricky well enough to recognize a play for sympathy, but she also knew that when the spirit moved her, Ricky didn't adhere too closely to the truth. For some reason Ricky was trying to make Rule appear in the worst light imaginable, and the thought irritated her. Rule had enough black marks against him without someone manufacturing false ones. The area had never forgotten how he had acted when he returned from Vietnam, and as far as she knew he had never been reconciled with his father. Mr. Jackson died a few years ago, but Rule had never mentioned that fact in her hearing, so she supposed that the strain between him and his father had still existed at the time of Mr. Jackson's death.

Unwilling to examine her motives more closely, merely acknowledging the surface desire to set Ricky back on her heels, Cathryn said, "Rule did ask me to stay, but, after all, this is my home, isn't it? There's nothing to keep me in Chicago now that David is dead." With that parting shot she got to her feet and left the room, though with considerably more grace than Rule had exhibited.

She started to go to her room, because she was feeling the effects of travel and her long ride. Her stiff muscles, forgotten during the heat of battle, renewed their appeal for her attention, and she winced slightly as she crossed to the stairs. Pausing with one foot on the first step, she decided to find Rule first, prompted by some vague urge to see him. She didn't know why that should be when she had spent years avoiding him, but she didn't stop to analyze her thoughts and emotions. It was one thing for her to rip up at him; it was something else entirely for anyone else to take that liberty! She let herself out by the front door and walked around the house, directing her steps to the foaling barn. Where else would Rule be but checking on one of his precious horses?

The familiar smells of hay and horses, liniment and leather greeted her as she entered the barn and walked the dark length of the aisle to the pool of light that revealed two men standing before the stall of the pregnant mare. Rule turned as she emerged into the light. "Cat, this is Floyd Stoddard, our foaling man. Floyd, meet Cathryn Ashe."

Floyd was a compact, powerfully built man with leathery

skin and thinning brown hair. He acknowledged the introduction by nodding his head and drawling, "Ma'am," in a soft
voice totally at odds with his appearance.

Cathryn made a more conventional greeting, but there was
no chance for further conversation. Rule said briefly, "Tell
me if anything happens," and took her arm. She found herself
being led away, out of the circle of light and into the darkness of the barn. She didn't have good night vision, and she
stumbled uncertainly, not trusting her footing.

A low chuckle sounded above her head and she felt herself
pulled closely against a hard, warm body. "Still can't see in
the dark, can you? Don't worry, I won't let you run into anything. Just hold on to me."

She didn't have to hold on to him. He was doing enough
holding for the both of them. To make conversation she said,
"Will the mare foal soon?"

"Probably tonight, after everything quiets down. Mares are
usually shy. They wait until they think no one's around, so
Travis will have to be really quiet and not let her hear him."
Amusement in his voice, he said, "Like all females, they're
contrary."

Resentment on behalf of her sex flared briefly, but she
controlled it. She realized that he was teasing her, hoping to
make her react hotly, thereby giving him a perfect reason for
kissing her again—if he even needed a reason. When had he
ever let a little thing like having a reason stop him from doing
anything he wanted? Instead she said mildly, "You'd probably be contrary, too, if you were faced with labor and birth."

"Honey, I'd be more than contrary. I'd be downright surprised!"

They laughed together as they left the barn and began the
walk back to the house. She could see now by the faint light
of the rising moon, but he kept his arm around her waist and

she didn't protest. A silent moment went by before he murmured, "Are you very sore?"

"Sore enough. Got any liniment I can use?"

"I'll bring a bottle to your room," he promised. "How long did you tough it out with Monica and Ricky?"

"Not long," she admitted. "I didn't finish eating, either."

Silence fell again and wasn't broken until they had neared the house. His hold on her tightened until his fingers bit into the soft skin at her waist.

"Cat."

She stopped and looked up at him. His face was completely shadowed by his hat, but she could feel the intensity of his gaze. "Monica isn't my mistress," he said on a softly exhaled breath. "She never has been, though not for lack of opportunity. Your father was too good a friend for me to jump into bed with his widow."

Apparently the same restriction didn't apply to Ward's daughter, she thought, stunned into momentary speechlessness by his bold statement. For a moment she simply stared at him in the dim, silvery light as she stood there with her face tilted up to his. Finally she whispered, "Why bother to explain to me?"

"Because you believed it, damn you!"

Stunned again, she wondered if she had automatically accepted, without really thinking about it, that Rule had been Monica's lover. Certainly that was what Ricky had been getting at earlier, but something in Cathryn violently rejected the very thought. On the other hand, she instinctively shied away from handing him a vote of confidence. Torn between the two, she merely said, "Everything pointed to it. I can see why Ricky is so convinced. Whatever you wanted, you only had to mention it to Monica and she made sure you got the money to do it."

"The only money I ever got from Monica was for the ranch!" he snapped. "Ward trusted me to run this ranch for him, and his death didn't change that."

"I know that. You've worked for this ranch as hard— harder—than any man would for his own spread." Obeying another instinct, she put her hand on his chest, spreading her fingers and feeling the warm, hard flesh beneath the material of his shirt. "I resented you, Rule. I admit it. When Dad first died it seemed like you were bulling in and taking over everything that had been his. You took the ranch, you moved into his house, you organized everything about our lives. Was it so impossible to think that you might have taken over his wife, too?" God, why had she said that? She didn't even believe it, yet she felt driven to somehow lash out at him.

He went rigid and his breath hissed between his teeth. "I'd like to turn you over my knee for that!"

"As you've said several times, I'm all grown up now, so I wouldn't advise it. I won't take being treated like a child," she warned, her spine stiffening as she remembered that long-ago incident.

"So you want me to treat you like a woman, then?" he ground out.

"No. I want you to treat me like what I am…" She paused, then spat out, "Your employer!"

"You've been that for years," he pointed out harshly. "But that didn't stop me from spanking you, and it didn't stop me from making love to you."

Realizing the futility of standing there arguing with him, Cathryn jerked away and started for the house. She had taken only a few steps when long fingers closed over her arm and pulled her to a halt. "Are you always going to run when I mention making love?" His words were like blows to her nervous system, and she quivered in his grip, fighting the storm of mingled dread and anticipation that confused her.

"You didn't run that day by the river," he reminded her cruelly. "You were ready and you liked it, despite it being your first time. You remind me of a mare that's nervous and not quite broken, kicking your heels at a stallion, but all you need is a little calming down."

"Don't you compare me to a mare!" The furious words burst out of her throat and she was no longer confused; she was clearheaded and angry.

"That's what you've always brought to mind—a long-legged little filly with big dark eyes, too skittish to stand under a friendly hand. I don't think you've changed all that much. You're still long legged, you've still got big dark eyes, and you're still skittish. I've always liked chestnut horses," he said, his voice sliding so low that it was almost a growl. "And I've always meant to have me a redheaded woman."

Sheer rage vibrated through her slender body, and for a moment she was incapable of answering. When she was finally able to speak, her voice was hoarse and shaking with the force of her temper. "Well, it won't be me! I suggest you go find yourself a chestnut *mare*.... That's more your type!"

He was laughing at her. She could hear the low rumbling sound in his chest. She raised her clenched fist to hit him, and he moved with lightning reflexes, catching her delicate fist in his big, hard palm and holding it. She tried to jerk away, but he pulled her inexorably closer until she was close enough that their bodies just touched. He bent his head until his breath feathered warmly over her lips, and with the lightest of contacts he let his mouth move against hers as he said, "You're the one, all right. You're my redheaded woman. God knows I've waited long enough for you."

"No—" she began, only to have her automatic protest cut

short as he moved forward the tiny bit that was needed to firm the contact between their mouths. She shivered and stood still under his kiss. Since that morning when he had kissed her at the airport it seemed that she had done nothing but let him kiss her whenever he pleased, a situation that she had never even dreamed would develop. With a shock she realized that his behavior all day had been distinctly loverlike, and for the first time she wondered what lay behind his actions.

Her lack of response irritated him and he drew her roughly nearer, his mouth demanding more and more until she gave a muffled groan of pain as her muscles protested against the handling she was receiving. Immediately his arms relaxed and he raised his head. "I forgot," he admitted huskily. "We'd better go in and get you taken care of before I forget again."

Cathryn started to protest that she could take care of herself but bit the words back, afraid of prolonging the situation. With counterfeit docility she suffered the possessive arm that lay around her waist as they entered the house. There was no sign of either Monica or Ricky, for which she was profoundly grateful, as Rule went up the stairs with her, his arm still around her. She could imagine the comments either of them would have been likely to make and which she felt oddly incapable of handling just then.

Rule unsettled her; he always had. She had thought herself mature enough now to face him with calm indifference, only to find that where he was concerned she was far from indifferent. She hated him, she fiercely resented him, and underneath all of that lay the burning physical awareness that had haunted her during her marriage to David and made her feel as if she were being unfaithful…to Rule, not her own husband! It was stupid. She had sincerely loved David and suffered after his death, and yet… She had always been aware that, while David could take her to the moon, Rule had made her reach the stars.

To her surprise Rule left her at her bedroom door and continued down the hall to his own room. Not questioning her good luck, Cathryn quickly entered her room and closed the door. She longed for a soak in a tub of hot water to ease her protesting muscles, but the only bathroom with a full tub, instead of a shower stall, was down the hall between Rule's bedroom and Monica's, and she didn't want to risk an encounter with either of them. Sighing in regret, she began unbuttoning her dress. She had slipped three of the buttons loose when a brief hard knock on the door, a knock which preceded Rule by only a split second, had her whirling around in a startled movement that made her wince with pain.

"Sorry about that," Rule muttered. "Here's the liniment."

She reached out for the bottle of clear liquid and saw his eyes drop to the unbuttoned neckline of her dress. In instantaneous reaction she felt her breasts tighten and grow heated in that bitter, uncontrolled response she had to him. She drew a ragged, protesting breath, and his eyes lifted slowly to her face. His pupils were dilated, his skin taut as he sensed, like a wild animal, the way it was with her. For a moment she thought that he was going to heed the primal call; then, with a stifled curse, he shoved the bottle into her hand.

"I can wait," he said, and left as abruptly as he had entered.

Cathryn felt as if her legs were going to collapse beneath her and she moved to the bed, sinking gratefully onto the white chenille bedspread. If that wasn't a close call, she didn't know what was!

After carefully rubbing her legs and buttocks with the pungent liniment, she put on her nightgown and crawled stiffly into bed, but despite her weariness she was unable to sleep.

Everything that had been said that day drifted through her tired mind with maddening persistence.

Rule. Everything came back to him. Cathryn thought she knew enough about men in general, and Rule in particular, to recognize passion, and Rule did nothing to hide his arousal when he kissed her. But Rule was a complicated man, and she didn't feel that he was motivated solely by simple lust. He was like an iceberg only allowing a small bit to show. He kept most of himself submerged, hidden from view, and she could only guess at his motives. Was it the ranch? Was Ricky right after all in her assessment? Was he trying to make the ranch legally his by marrying the owner?

She drew her thoughts up sharply. Married! What made her think that Rule would ever consider marriage? She was beginning to understand that he could control her easily enough by other means, and the realization was sharply humiliating. Unless he did want the ranch legally...? He was a man with a dark past; who could guess at the importance of the ranch to him? She could well imagine that to him it represented his salvation, both physically and emotionally.

Whatever happened, she didn't want to let herself become embroiled with him. And whatever his motive, she was certain that she wouldn't be able to shield herself from harm. She was so frighteningly vulnerable to him....

CHAPTER 3

Cathryn had intended to get up early, but her intentions weren't strong enough to do the job and it was after ten when she rolled over groggily and pushed her hair out of her face to peer at the clock. She yawned and stretched, cutting the motion short with a wince of pain. Easing gingerly out of the bed, she decided that she wasn't as sore as she had feared she would be, but she was still sore enough. As Rule would have been out of the house for hours by now, she felt safely able to have that hot bath, and she gathered up her clothes, then beat a path to the bathroom.

An hour later she felt considerably better, though still stiff. She rubbed the liniment into her muscles again, then decided to ignore the pain. Despite the night's uncomfortable beginning, the long sleep had completely refreshed her and her dark eyes were sparkling, her cheeks delicately pink. Her hair was pulled back on each side with a matching pair of tortoiseshell combs, giving her the look of a teenager. For a moment as she looked in the mirror she had a disturbing sense of looking into the past, as if the reflection she saw was that of the young girl she had been on a hot summer day, gleefully planning on a ride to the river. Had she smiled that way? she wondered as her lips curved in a faint smile of secret anticipation. Anticipation of what?

She studied the face in the mirror, searching for an answer. The delicate features revealed nothing; she saw only the elusive smile, a certain mystery in the dark eyes. Her coloring was unusual, inherited directly from her father; dark fire in her hair, a shade neither red nor brown but with the sheen of mahogany; dark eyes, not as dark as Rule's, but a soft deep brown. Her skin, thankfully, had no freckles. She could tan lightly, but had never been able to acquire a deep tan. What else was there? What else would attract a man's attention? Her nose was straight and dainty, but not classical. Her mouth looked vulnerable, sensitive; her facial bones were delicate, finely drawn. Fairly tall, slender and long-legged, with narrow hips, a slim waist and rather nice, round breasts. She didn't have voluptuous curves, but she did have the long, clean lines of good breeding and a certain grace of movement. Rule had compared her to a long-legged filly. And Rule had always wanted a red-haired woman.

No great beauty, the young woman in the mirror, but passable.

Passable enough to hold Rule Jackson's interest?

Stop it! she told herself fiercely, turning away from the mirror. She didn't want to hold his interest! She couldn't handle him and she knew it. If she had any sense at all she'd take herself back to Chicago, continue her rather boring job and forget the nagging, incessant ache for the home where she had grown up. But this was her home, and perhaps she didn't have any sense. She knew every plank in this old house, had never forgotten anything about it, and she wanted to stay there.

She went downstairs to the kitchen. Lorna turned from the stove as she entered and gave her a friendly smile. "Have a good sleep?"

"Marvelous," Cathryn sighed. "I haven't slept this late in years."

"Rule said you were worn out," said Lorna comfortably. "You've lost some weight, too, since your last visit. Are you ready for breakfast?"

"It's almost lunchtime, so I think I'll wait. Where is everyone?"

"Monica is still asleep; Ricky went out with the men today."

Cathryn lifted her eyebrows questioningly, and Lorna shrugged. She was a big-boned woman in her late forties or early fifties, her brown hair showing no trace of gray, and her pleasantly unremarkable features revealed only contentment with her life. Acceptance was in her eyes as she said slowly, "Ricky's having a rough time right now."

"In what way?" Cathryn asked. It was true that Ricky seemed even more highly strung than before, as if she were only barely under control.

Again Lorna shrugged. "I expect she woke up one day and realized that she doesn't have what she wanted, and she panicked. What has she done with her life? Wasted it. She has no husband, no children, nothing of any importance that she can say belongs to her. The only thing she's ever really had is her looks, and they haven't gotten her the man she wanted."

"She's been married twice," said Cathryn.

"But not to Rule."

Shocked, Cathryn sat silently, trying to follow Lorna's reasoning. Rule? And Ricky? Ricky had always alternated wildly between rebelling against Rule and following him with slavish devotion, while Rule had always treated her with stoic tolerance. Was that the basis for Ricky's sudden outbreak of hostility? Was that why she didn't want Cathryn to stay? Once again Cathryn had the uneasy thought that somehow Ricky knew that Rule had made love to her when she was seventeen. It was impossible, but yet…

It was all impossible. Ricky couldn't be in love with Rule. Cathryn had known what it was to love, and she could see none of the signs in Ricky, no gentling, no caring. Her reactions to Rule were a mixture of fear and hostility that bor-

dered on actual hate; that, too, Cathryn understood all too
well. How many years had she stayed away because of those
same feelings?

Agitated, she felt a sudden, powerful need to be alone for a
while, so she said, "Does Wallace's Drugstore still stay open
on Sundays?"

Lorna nodded. "Are you thinking of driving into town?"

"If no one else needs the car, I will."

"Nobody that I know of, and even if they did there's other
means of going," Lorna said practically. "Would you mind
picking up a few things?"

"I'll be glad to," Cathryn replied. "But to be on the safe
side, write everything down. No matter how careful I try to
be, I always forget one item unless I have a list, and it's usually the most-needed thing that I forget."

With a chuckle Lorna pulled open a drawer and extracted
a notepad from which she tore the top sheet. She handed it
to Cathryn. "It's already done. I'm guilty of the same thing,
so I always write things down as I think of them. Let me get
some money from Rule's desk."

"No, I have enough," Cathryn protested, looking at the
list of items. It was mostly first-aid things such as alcohol and
bandages, nothing very expensive. Besides, anything bought
for the ranch was her responsibility.

"All right, but keep the sales receipt. Taxes."

Cathryn nodded. "Do you know where the keys to the
station wagon are?"

"Usually in the ignition, unless Rule took them out this
morning to keep Ricky from disappearing as she sometimes
does. If he did, then they'll be in his pocket, but since Ricky
went with them he wouldn't have had any reason for taking
the keys."

Cathryn made a face at that information and went upstairs

to get her purse. Was Ricky so bad that it was necessary to hide the car keys from her? And what if someone else needed the car? But then, Lorna and Monica would make arrangements beforehand if they needed the car, and in any medical emergency Rule could be located quickly enough. The plane would be faster than a car anyway.

She was in luck. The keys were still dangling from the ignition. She opened the door and slid behind the wheel, looking forward to her little trip.

The station wagon wasn't a new model and it had a rather battered appearance, but the engine caught immediately and hummed with steady precision. Like everything else on the ranch, it was kept in good mechanical condition, another indication of Rule's excellent management. There was no way she could fault him on that score.

She felt pride in the way the ranch looked as she drove down the dusty road that led to the highway. It wasn't a huge ranch or a rich one, though it had done well enough. She knew that Rule had brought new life into it with his horses, though it had been a comfortable place before that. But now the land had the well-tended look that only devotion and hard work could bring.

The town was small, but Cathryn supposed it had everything required by civilization. It was as familiar to her as her own face, never changing much despite the passage of time. San Antonio was the nearest large city, almost eighty miles distant, but to someone used to Texas distances, that didn't seem like a long trip. No one felt denied by the undemanding tenor of life in Uvalde County.

Probably the last scandal in memory was the last one Rule had figured in, Cathryn thought absently as she parked the station wagon against the curb, joining the lineup of dusty pickups and assorted cars. She could hear the jukebox inside, and a smile lit her face as memories washed over her. How many Sunday afternoons had she spent here as a teenager? The pharmacy was located in the back of the building. The front was occupied by a booming hamburger business. Red-topped stools lined the counter and several booths marched down the opposite wall, while a few small tables were scattered about the remaining space. The stools and booths were crowded, while the tables remained empty, always the last to be filled. A quick glance around told her that the majority of the customers were teenagers, just as it had always been, though there were enough adults on hand to keep youthful enthusiasms under control.

She went back to the pharmacy and began gathering the items on Lorna's list, wanting to do that first; then she intended to reward herself with a huge milk shake. The pile in her arms kept growing and became unmanageable; she looked around for a shopping basket and her gaze was met by a young woman her own age who was studying her curiously.

"Cathryn? Cathryn Donahue?" the woman asked hesitantly.

As soon as she spoke Cathryn placed her voice. "Wanda Gifford!"

"Wanda Wallace now. I married Rick Wallace."

Cathryn remembered him. He was the son of the owner of the drugstore and a year or so older than she and Wanda. "And I'm Cathryn Ashe."

"Yes. I heard about your husband's death. I'm sorry, Cathryn."

Cathryn murmured an acknowledgement of the polite phrase as Wanda moved to take some of the precariously balanced things out of her arms, then swiftly changed the subject, still feeling unable to discuss David's death calmly. "Do you have any children?"

"Two, and that's enough. Both boys, and both monsters."

Wanda smiled wryly. "Rick asked me if I wanted to try for a girl next time, and I told him that if there was a next time we'd have a parting of the ways. Good Lord, what if I had another boy?" But in spite of her words she was laughing, and Cathryn had a moment of gentle envy. She and David had discussed having children, but put it off in favor of a few years alone; then they had learned of David's illness and he had refused to burden her with a child to raise alone. She didn't understand how he could have imagined that his child would ever be a burden to her, but she had always thought that making a baby should be a mutual decision, so she hadn't pressured him. He had been under enough pressure, knowing that his life was slipping away.

Wanda led the way to the nearest table and dumped everything onto the shiny surface. "Have a seat and let me buy you a soft drink to welcome you home. Rule told us that you're home to stay this time."

Slowly Cathryn sank into an empty chair. "When did he say that?" she asked, wondering if she looked as cornered as she felt.

"Two weeks ago. He said you'd be home for Memorial Day weekend." Wanda went behind the counter to get two glasses brimming with ice and fill them with fountain cola from the machine installed there.

So Rule had let it be known two weeks ago that she was coming home to stay? Cathryn mused. That was when she had called to let Monica know that she was coming home for a visit. Just like that, Rule had decided that she'd stay this time and had spread the news. Wouldn't he be surprised when she got on that plane tomorrow?

"Here you go," said Wanda, sliding the frosted glass in front of her.

Cathryn leaned over to take an appreciative sip of the

strong, icy drink, sharp as only fountain cola could be. "Rule's changed a lot over the years," she murmured, not certain just why she said it, but wanting for some reason to hear someone else's opinion of him. Perhaps he wasn't out of the ordinary; perhaps it was her own perception of him that was at fault.

"In some ways he has, in some he hasn't," said Wanda. "He's not wild anymore, but you get the feeling he's just as dangerous as he always was. He's more controlled now. But the way most folks think about him has changed. Rule knows ranching and he's a fair boss. He's president of the Local C.A., you know. Of course, to some people he'll always be as wild as a mink."

Cathryn managed to hide her surprise at that information. In some parts of the West, the Cattlemen's Association was the inner circle of the elite; in other parts, such as here, it was a working group of not-so-big ranchers who tried to help each other. Still, she was stunned that Rule had been elected president, because he wasn't even a ranch owner. That, more than anything, was a measure of his move from scandalous-ness to respectability.

She gossiped with Wanda for the better part of an hour and noticed that Ricky's name wasn't mentioned at all, an indi-cation of how completely Ricky had alienated the local peo-ple. Had Wanda been on friendly terms with the other young woman, she would have asked after her, even if it had been only a day or two since she had seen her.

Cathryn finally noticed the time and began gathering up the items she had scattered over the table. Wanda helped her manage them and walked with her back to the cash register, where her father-in-law checked Cathryn out. "We still have a dance every Saturday night," Wanda said, her friendly eyes smiling. "Why don't you come next time? Rule will bring you if you don't feel like coming on your own, but there's plenty of men who'd like to see you walk in without an escort, especially without Rule."

Cathryn laughed, remembering the Saturday night dances that were such an integral part of the county social life. Most of the marriages and at least a few of the pregnancies of the last fifteen years had gotten their start at the Saturday night dances. "Thanks for reminding me. I'll think about it, though I don't think Rule would thank you for volunteering him for escort duty."

"Try him!" was Wanda's laughing advice.

"No, thanks," muttered Cathryn to herself as she left the coolness of the pharmacy and the heat of the cloudless Texas day hit her in the face. She had no intention of being there for the next dance, anyway. She'd be on that plane in less than twenty-four hours, and by the next Saturday she would be safe in her Chicago apartment, away from the dangers and temptations of Rule Jackson.

She opened the car door and dropped her purchases onto the seat, but stood for a moment allowing the interior of the car to cool somewhat before she got in.

"Cathryn! By God, I thought it was you! Heard you were back!"

She turned curiously and a grin widened her mouth as a tall, lanky man with white hair and sun-browned skin loped along the sidewalk to reach her. "Mr. Vernon! It's nice to see you again!"

Paul Vernon reached her and enfolded her in a hug that lifted her off the ground. He had been her father's best friend, and she had carried on the tradition with his son, Kyle. To Paul Vernon's disappointment the friendship between the two had never matured into romance; but he had always had a soft spot in his heart for Cathryn and she returned the affection, in some ways liking the older man more than she had Kyle.

He replaced her on the ground and turned to beckon another man forward. Cathryn knew him at once as a newcomer, even though she had been away for years. The man who removed his hat politely and nodded at her wasn't dressed in quite the manner a local would have dressed. His jeans were a little too new; his hat wasn't a hat that had been on the range.

Mr. Vernon's introduction confirmed her guess. "Cathryn, this is Ira Morris. He's in the region looking at some livestock and horses; he owns a spread in Kansas. Ira, this is Cathryn Donahue…sorry, but I can't remember your married name. Cathryn is from the Bar D."

"Bar D?" asked Mr. Morris. "Isn't that Rule Jackson's spread?"

"That's right; you'll have to see him if it's horses you want. He's got the best quarter-horse farm in the state."

Mr. Morris was impatient. He barely contained his restlessness when Paul Vernon seemed content to linger and chat for a while. Cathryn was in sympathy with his impatience, because she was burning with fury and it was taking a great deal of self-control to hide it from Mr. Vernon. At last he said good-bye and admonished her to come visit soon. She promised to do so and quickly got into the car before he could continue the conversation.

She started the car and slammed it into gear with violent temper; not in years had she been so consumed with white-hot rage. The last time had been that day by the river, but there wouldn't be the same ending this time. She wasn't a naive teenager who hadn't any idea of how to control a man or handle her own desires now. She was a woman, and he had encroached on her home territory. Rule Jackson's spread, indeed! Was that how people thought of the Bar D now? Maybe Rule thought it was his, too; maybe he considered himself so much in control that there was no way she could dislodge him. If so, he'd find out soon that *she* was a Donahue of the Bar D and a Jackson just didn't belong!

The first wave of anger had passed by the time she reached the ranch, but her resolve hadn't faded. First she took her purchases in to Lorna, knowing that the woman would have seen her arrival from the kitchen window. That guess was proved correct when she opened the door and saw Lorna standing at the sink while she peeled potatoes, looking out the window so as not to miss any activity in the yard. Cathryn placed the paper bag on the table and said, "Here are the things. Have you seen Rule?"

"He came in for lunch," said Lorna placidly. "But he could be anywhere now. Someone in the stables should be able to tell you where he's gone."

"Thanks," said Cathryn, and retraced her steps, moving with her free-swinging stride to the stables, her feet kicking up tiny clouds of dust with every step.

The cool dimness of the stable was a welcome change from the bright sun, the smell of horses and ammonia as familiar as ever. She squinted, trying to adjust her eyes to the dimness, and made out two figures several stalls down. In a few seconds she recognized Rule, though the other man was a stranger.

Before she could speak Rule held out his hand. "Here's the boss lady," he said, still with his hand held out to her, and she was so surprised by his words that she stepped into reach of that hand and it curved around her waist, drawing her close to his heat and strength. "Cat, meet Lewis Stovall, the foreman. I don't think you've been here since he was hired. Lewis, this is Cathryn Donahue."

Lewis Stovall merely nodded and touched his hat, but his silence wasn't prompted by shyness. His face was as hard and watchful as Rule's, his eyes narrowed and waiting. Cathryn felt uneasily that Lewis Stovall was a man with secrets locked inside, just as Rule was, a man who had lived hard and dangerously and who bore the scars of that life. But...he was the foreman? Just what did that make Rule? King of the mountain?

She wasn't in the mood for small talk, so she returned the greeting that she had received, a brief nod of the head. It was enough. His attention wasn't on her; he was listening to Rule's instructions, his head slightly dipped as if he were considering every word he heard. Rule was brief to the point of terseness, a characteristic of his conversations with everyone. Except with herself, Cathryn realized suddenly. Not that Rule could ever be termed talkative, but he did talk more to her than he did to anyone else. From the day he had told her of her father's death, he had talked to her. At first it had been as if he had to force himself to communicate, but soon he had been teasing her in his rusty, growling voice, aggravating her out of her grief.

Lewis nodded to her again and left them, his tall body graceful as he moved away. Rule turned her back toward the entrance, his hand still on the small of her back. "I came up to the house at lunchtime to take you with me for the rest of the day, but you had already gone. Where did you go?"

It was typical of him that he hadn't asked Lorna. "To Wallace's drugstore," she answered automatically. The warm pressure of his hand was draining away her resolve, making her forget why she was so angry. Taking a deep breath, she stepped away from his touch and faced him. "Did you say that Lewis is the foreman?" she asked.

"That's right," he said, pushing his hat back a little and watching her with his dark, unreadable eyes. She sensed the waiting in him, the tension.

She said sweetly, "Well, if he's the foreman, then I don't need you any longer, do I? You gave away your own job."

His hand shot out and caught her arm, pulling her back into the circle of his special heat and smell. His mouth was a grim line as he shook her slightly. "I needed help, and Lewis is a good man. If you care so much, then maybe you'd better stay around and do a share of the work too. Ward had a foreman to help him, and that was without the added work of the horses, so don't turn bitchy on me. While you were tucked up in bed, I was up at two o'clock this morning with a mare in foal, so I'm not in the mood to put up with any of your tantrums right now. Is that clear?"

"All right, so you needed help," she admitted grudgingly. She hated to acknowledge the logic of his words, but he was right. However, that didn't have anything to do with what she had heard in town. "I'll concede that. But can you tell me why the Bar D is known as Rule Jackson's spread?" Her voice rose sharply on the last words and temper made color flare hotly in her cheeks.

His jaw was set like granite. "Maybe because you haven't cared enough to stay around and remind people that this is Donahue land," he snapped. "I've never forgotten who this ranch belongs to, but sometimes I think I'm the only one who does remember. I know very well that this is all yours, little boss lady. Is that what you wanted to hear from me? Damn it, I've got work to do, so why don't you get out of my way?"

"I'm not stopping you!"

He swore under his breath and stalked away, his temper evident in the set of his broad shoulders. Cathryn stood there with her fists clenched, fighting the urge to launch herself at him and pound on him with her fists as she had done once before. At last she stormed into the house and was on the way to her room when she met Ricky.

"Why didn't you tell me you were going into town?" demanded Ricky petulantly.

"You weren't here, for one thing, and for another you've never been that crazy about Wallace's Drugstore," replied

Cathryn wryly. She looked at her stepsister and saw the brit-
tleness of her control, the shaking of her hands. Impulsively
she asked, "Ricky, why are you doing this to yourself?"

For a moment Ricky looked outraged; then her shoulders
slumped and she gave a defeated little shrug. "What would you
know about it? You've always been the darling of the house,
the one who belonged. I could call myself a Donahue, but I've
never really been one, have I? You noticed who the ranch was
left to, didn't you? What did I get? Nothing!"

Ricky's particular brand of illogic defeated Cathryn; evidently it made no difference to her that Ward Donahue hadn't
been her father, while he had been Cathryn's. She shook her
head and tried again. "I couldn't have made you feel unwelcome, because I haven't even been here!"

"You didn't have to be here!" Ricky lashed out, her small
face twisting with fury. "You own this ranch, so you have a
weapon to hold over Rule!"

Rule. It always came back to Rule. He was the dominant
male in his territory and everything revolved around him.
She hadn't meant to say it, but the words left her mouth involuntarily. "You're paranoid about Rule! He told me that he's
never been involved with Monica."

"Oh, did he?" Ricky's slanted hazel eyes brightened suspiciously; then she turned away before Cathryn could decide
whether the brightness had been caused by tears. "Are you really gullible enough to believe him? Haven't you learned yet
that he won't let anything stand between him and this ranch?
God! I can't tell you how often I've prayed that this damned
place would burn to the ground!" She brushed roughly past
Cathryn and bolted down the stairs, leaving Cathryn standing there mired in a combination of pity and anger.

She would be a fool to believe anything Ricky said; it was
obvious that the other woman was emotionally unstable. On

the other hand, Cathryn remembered clearly the way Rule had doggedly followed her father's instructions when he had first come to the ranch, working when his body was weak and wracked with pain, his eyes reflecting the wary but devoted look of a battered animal that had finally met with kindness rather than kicks. He too had been emotionally unstable at that time; it was possible that the ranch had assumed an irrational importance to him.

Cathryn shook her head. She was thinking like an amateur psychiatrist, and she had enough trouble sorting out her own thoughts and emotions without taking on someone like Rule. He certainly wasn't uncertain about anything now. If there was anyone on this earth who knew what he wanted, it was Rule Jackson. She was simply letting Ricky's paranoia cloud her own thinking.

All afternoon Cathryn thought of what she had said to Rule earlier, and reluctantly she came to the conclusion that she would have to apologize. No one could ever accuse him of not working, of not putting the ranch first. Whatever his reason, he had driven himself past the point where lesser men would have broken, not for his personal gain but for the good of the ranch. Facing it squarely, she admitted that she had been wrong and had flared into rage out of sheer, petty jealousy, striking out at him for cherishing the same land that she loved so deeply. She was wrong, and she felt small.

When he finally came in to wash before dinner her heart tightened painfully at the sight of him. His face was taut with weariness, his clothing soaked in sweat and overlaid with a thick coat of dust that was turning to mud on his body, evidence that he was no shirker when it came to work. She stopped him before he went up the stairs, placing her slim hand on his dirty sleeve.

"I'm sorry for the way I acted this afternoon," she said

directly, meeting his flinty gaze without flinching. "I was wrong, and I apologize. This ranch would never have made it without you, and I...I suppose I envy you."

He looked down at her, his face blank and hard. Then he took off his sweat-stained hat, wiping his sleeve across his moist face and leaving a brown smear of mud behind. "At least you're not totally blind," he snapped, pulling his arm from her touch and taking the stairs two at a time, his lithe body moving easily, as though weariness were a stranger to him.

Cathryn sighed, torn between wry laughter and the anger that he so easily provoked. Had she really thought that he would be gracious? As long as he was angry no apology she could make would pacify him.

Dinner was a silent meal. Monica was quiet, Ricky sullen. Rule wasn't a conversationalist at any time, but at least he did justice to the hot meal Lorna had provided for him. As soon as he was finished he excused himself and disappeared into the study, closing the door with a thud. Ricky looked up and shrugged. "Well, that's a normal evening. Exciting, isn't it? You're used to a big city, to entertainment. You'll go crazy here."

"I've always liked a quiet life," replied Cathryn, not looking up from the peach cobbler she was destroying with delicate greed. "David and I weren't the life of the town." They really hadn't had much time together, she reminded herself painfully. She was glad they had spent it learning to know each other, rather than wasting the precious time they'd had in socializing.

It was still early, but she felt tired. Lorna cleared away the dishes and stacked them in the dishwasher; Monica went upstairs to her bedroom to watch television in privacy. After sulking for a few minutes Ricky flounced upstairs to her own room.

Left on her own, Cathryn didn't linger. On an impulse she opened the door of the study to tell Rule good-night, but paused with the words unsaid when she saw him sprawled back in the oversized chair, sound asleep, his booted feet propped up on the desk. Papers scattered on the desk indicated his intention to work, but he hadn't been able to fight off sleep any longer. Again that funny wrenching of her heart caught at her as she watched him.

Vaguely annoyed with herself, she started to back out of the room when his eyes snapped open and he stared at her. "Cat," he said huskily, his voice rough with sleep. "Come here."

Even as her feet carried her into the room, she wondered at her own obedience to that drowsy voice. He swung his feet to the floor and stood up, his hand going out to close around her wrist and pull her close to him. Before she could guess his intent, his mouth was warm on hers, moving hungrily, demanding her submission. A ripple of unwilling pleasure moved up her spine and her lips parted, allowed him to deepen the kiss.

"Let's go to bed," he muttered against her mouth.

For a moment Cathryn sagged against him, her body more than willing; then awareness snapped her eyes open and she pushed belatedly at his heavy shoulders.

"Now, wait a minute! I'm not going to—"

"I've waited long enough," he interrupted, brushing his lips against hers again.

"That's tough! You can just keep on waiting!"

He laughed wryly, sliding his hands down to her hips and pulling her solidly against the power of his loins, letting her feel his arousal. "That's my girl. Fight me to the bitter end. Go on up to bed, Cat. I've got a lot of work to do before I can turn in."

Confused by his dismissal, Cathryn found herself out of the room before she knew what was happening. What *was* happening? Rule wasn't a man to deny himself...unless it concerned the ranch. Of course, she told herself in amusement. He had work to do. Everything else could wait. And that was just fine with her!

She went into the kitchen to tell Lorna good-night, just catching the cook before she went to her own two-rooms-and-a-bath quarters at the rear of the house, converted specifically for her use when Rule had hired her. Then Cathryn climbed the stairs, wincing at the pain in her legs with each step. Another leisurely bath loosened her muscles a bit and she didn't bother with the liniment, though she knew that she would regret it in the morning.

After opening the curtains to let in the moonlight, she tossed her robe over the back of the rocking chair that sat placidly in the corner, then turned out the light and crawled into the familiar bed with a sense of homecoming, of belonging. There was no other place on earth where she felt so peaceful and complete, no other place where she was so relaxed.

But, relaxed or not, she couldn't sleep. She moved restlessly onto her side, her mind turning inexorably to Rule. So he'd waited long enough, had he? Was there no limit to that natural arrogance of his? If he thought she was going to trot obediently to bed and wait for him...

Was that what he had meant? Her eyes popped open. Surely not. Not with both Monica and Ricky just down the hall. She tried to remember exactly what he had said. Something about her going on to bed because it would be a while before he could turn in. What did that have to do with her? Nothing. Nothing at all. Unless...unless he meant to come to her later.

Of course not, she reassured herself. He knew that she wouldn't let him do that, and he wouldn't risk raising a ruckus. She closed her eyes again, trying to ignore the nagging thought that Rule would risk anything to get what he wanted.

She dozed, but came suddenly awake to the knowledge that she wasn't alone. Quickly she turned her head to see the man standing beside her bed, removing his shirt. Her breath strangled in her throat and her heartbeat accelerated, making her body feel warm and flushed, making the thin nightgown she wore seem suddenly restrictive. She gasped for breath, struggling for words as he shrugged out of his shirt and tossed it aside. The colorless moonlight fell across him, starkly illuminating his lean, muscled torso, but leaving his face concealed in darkness. But she knew him, knew the look and smell and heat of him. Vivid images of a hot summer day and his black outline against the brazen sky as he covered her washed over her, swamping her senses with oddly mingled panic and longing. He *had* dared, after all.

"What are you doing?" she was finally able to choke as he removed his boots and socks, then stood to unfasten his belt.

"Undressing," he explained in a low rasp, his voice flat and inexorable. In further, unneeded explanation he said, "I'm sleeping here tonight."

That wasn't what she had meant. She had been asking if he had lost his senses, but Cathryn felt as if all the breath had left her body. She was unable to make a protest, unable to order him to leave. After a long pause while he seemed to wait for her objection, one that didn't come, he chuckled. "Or rather, I'm staying with you tonight, but I doubt we'll be doing much sleeping."

An automatic refusal rose to her lips but remained unsaid; somehow the words wouldn't come, halted by the hot life that flooded into her stunned body, by the wild slamming of her heart against her ribs. She sat up, her eyes locked on his moon-silvered body. She heard the sibilant whisper of a zipper sliding down; then he slid out of his jeans. His hard body was

muscled, powerful, his masculinity a potent, visible threat…
or was it a promise?

The heat in Cathryn began to throb maddeningly and she
held out a hand that beckoned even as she warned in a whisper.
"Don't come near me! I'll scream!" But the lack of conviction
in her words was evident even to herself. Oh, Lord, she wanted
him so badly! As he had pointed out to her so often, she was
a woman now and she no longer feared his sexual power, but
rather wanted to cling to him and warm herself with his fire.

He knew. He sat down on the bed beside her and cupped
her cheek in his hard, callused palm. Even in the colorless
moonlight she could feel the heat of his gaze as it wandered
over her body. "Are you, Cat?" he asked, his voice so low
that it was almost without sound. "Are you going to scream?"

Her mouth was too dry to allow speech; she swallowed,
yet still she was able to manage only a faint admission. "No."

He drew a deep, shuddering breath into his lungs and the
hand on her face trembled. "God, sweetheart, if you've ever
wanted to slap a man for what he was thinking of doing,
now's your chance," he said roughly, his voice shaking with
the force of his desire.

The unsteadiness of his words told her how affected he was
by her nearness and the quiet intimacy of her bedroom. That
reassured her, gave her the courage to reach out and put her
hand on his chest, feeling the rough curl of dark hair against
her palm and the sleek warmth of his skin where the hair
ended, the taut, tiny buds of his nipples. The sound that rumbled in his throat could have been a growl, but her heightened
senses recognized it for what it was—a rough purr of pleasure.

She leaned closer, seeking the delicious male scent of him.
"Are you going to do everything you're thinking about?" she
asked, her voice shaking.

He was sliding closer too, moving in to nuzzle his mouth

against the base of her throat where the skin was throbbing with the pounding of her pulse, his lips feeling the frantic rhythm and increasing it with his touch. "I couldn't," he murmured, his mouth moving against that delicate spot. "I'd kill myself if I tried to live up to those particular fantasies."

Cathryn shuddered with the liquid desire that flooded her and she twined her arms around his shoulders, trembling with a need that she couldn't deny even though she couldn't understand it. This was a mistake, and she knew it, but for now the primitive joy she was drowning in was more than worth the price she would have to pay when sanity returned. She allowed him to stretch her out on the bed and take her in his arms, his nakedness scorching her flesh through the flimsy fabric of her gown. Her head tilted back in invitation and Rule laughed quietly, then gave her what she wanted, his mouth coming down and taking control of hers, parting her lips for the invasion of his tongue.

She could have died content in that moment, delirious with the pleasure of his kisses, but soon the contentment was gone and kisses weren't enough. She twisted restlessly in his arms, seeking more. Again he knew; he sensed the exact moment when she was ready for increased intimacy. His hand went to the neckline of her gown and she went still with anticipation, hardly daring to breathe as she felt his lean fingers deftly slipping open its buttoned top. Her breasts began to throb, and she arched, seeking his touch. He satisfied her need immediately, his hand sliding in to cup and fondle the rich, sensitive mounds, his rough palm seeming to delight in the softness of her.

The groan that followed was his, an inarticulate sound of hunger. His hands pulled at the nightgown with rough urgency and moved it from her shoulders, baring her breasts to the moonlight. His mouth left hers and slid down her body;

then his tongue snaked out to capture a taut nipple and draw it into the searing moistness of his mouth. Cathryn gave a strangled cry at the wildfire that leaped along her nerves; then she arched herself into his powerful body, her hands clenching on his shoulders.

He reached down to her ankles and slid his fingers beneath the hem of the gown, then made a reverse journey, a journey that took the hem upward. There was no protest. She was burning, aching, ready for him. She lifted her hips to aid him and he bunched the cloth about her waist, but that was as far as it got. With a hoarse, shaking sound he covered her, kneeing her thighs apart, and Cathryn went still, waiting.

"Look at me," he demanded hoarsely.

Unable to do otherwise, she obeyed him, her eyes locked with his. His face was taut with primitive hunger, releasing the answering hunger in her body that she had tried—and failed—for so many years to conquer. The probing of his maleness found her moist and yielding, and he took her easily, sliding his hands beneath her bottom to lift her into his possessive thrust. Electric pleasure shuddered through her and she gave a faint, gasping cry. This was wilder, hotter than anything she had experienced before. Her eyes began to slide shut and he shook her insistently, whispering from between his clenched teeth, "Look at me!"

Helplessly she did so, her body his as he began to move. Nothing she had known had prepared her for this, for the wildly surging pleasure that didn't wait but almost immediately swept away her control, carrying her swiftly to the peak. He held her tightly to his chest until she was limp beneath him; then he gently lowered her to the pillow. "Greedy," he said in a low, tender drawl. "I know just how you feel. It's been too long, and I can't hold back either."

Still stunned by the force of her ecstasy, she was totally

overwhelmed by his passion and need. Nothing made any sense; nothing mattered but the strength of his driving body. She clung to him with the frail tenacity of a slender vine wrapped around a sturdy oak, cradling him within her silky embrace until he too surrendered to pleasure and cried out hoarsely.

Long minutes later he stirred, lifting his heavy weight onto the support of his elbows. He kissed her mouth and eyes, feathering kisses along her lids until they lifted and darkness met darkness, hers soft and vulnerable, his sharp with undisguised triumph. "That took the edge off," he growled, his voice rough and low and vibrant. "But that was a long way from the end of it."

He proved it, making love to her this time with patience and an absorbing tenderness that was even more devastating than his rampaging lust. There was no way she could resist him, no way she even wanted to try. This too had a sense of homecoming, a completion that she had lacked, a satisfaction that she had longed for and tried to deny. Tomorrow she would regret this, but for tonight she had the wild joy of being in his arms.

CHAPTER 4

When the sensual storm had passed he didn't leave her, didn't roll away to fall into isolated sleep; he kept her a willing captive beneath him, his long fingers threaded into her hair on each side of her head as he began a siege of kisses. He didn't speak. His lips feathered kisses over her entire face, slowly, lightly, feeling the contours of her features with his mouth. His tongue teased at her skin, stealing tastes. She made no protest; she didn't even try to resist the erotic appeal of his exploring mouth. She let herself be absorbed in his sexual magic, in the tremors that started anew, feeling them grow stronger as she tightened her hold on him. They were both prisoners, she of his confining, muscled weight, he of the strong, silky bonds of her arms and legs.

When he freed a long, muscular arm and stretched it out to snap on the bedside lamp, she murmured an inarticulate protest at the intrusion of light. The silvery moon magic had wrapped them in a comforting aura of unreality, but the soft glow of the lamp created new shadows, illuminated things that had previously been hidden, and concealed expressions that had been brought out by the stark colorless light of the moon. One thing that couldn't be concealed was the hard male triumph written on the dark face above her. Cathryn became aware of a blooming regret as she began to admit the folly of the night's actions. There were a lot of things she didn't understand, and Rule himself was the largest enigma, a complicated man turned in on himself, but she did know that the hot sensuality between them had only made their situation more complex.

He trapped her face between his hands, his thumbs under her delicate chin as he gently forced her to look at him. "Well?" he growled, his raspy voice sinking into a rumble. He was so close that his warm breath touched her lips, and automatically she parted them in an effort to recapture his heady taste. A shudder of reaction rolled through her, eliciting an answering ripple in the strong body that pressed over her.

She swallowed, trying to gather her thoughts into some sort of coherency, not certain what he was asking, or why. She wanted to give him a controlled, bland response, but there was no control to be found, only raw, unvarnished emotions and uncertainties. Her throat was tight with anxiety as she blurted, "Is this an effort to keep your job as ranch manager?"

His shadowy eyes narrowed until only gleaming slits remained; he didn't reply. His thumbs exerted just enough pressure to raise her chin and he settled more heavily against her, fitting his mouth to hers with sensual precision. Hot tingles twitched into life beneath her skin and she joined the kiss, meeting him with teeth and tongue and lips. Why not? she reasoned fuzzily. It was too late to even try to stifle her responses to him. Rule was an exciting lover on such a basic, primary level that responding to him was as compelling a need as breathing.

At last he lifted his mouth enough to let an answer whisper between them. "This doesn't concern the ranch," he murmured, his lips so close to hers that they brushed hers lightly when he spoke. "This is between us, and nothing else even begins to matter." Suddenly his voice thickened and he said harshly, "Damn you, Cat, when you married David Ashe I was so mad I could have torn him apart. But I knew it wasn't over between us, so I let you go for then, and I waited. He died, and I waited. You've finally come home, and this time I won't let you get away. This time you won't run away to some other man."

Under the lashing fury in his voice she instantly retaliated, digging her fingers into the thick strands of his hair and holding him as he held her. "You make it sound as if there was a commitment between us!" she snapped. "There was nothing besides a stupid, hot-tempered teenager and a man who couldn't control himself. Nothing else!"

"And now?" he mocked. "What excuse do you have for now?"

"Do I need an excuse?"

"Maybe you do, for yourself. Maybe you're still not able to admit that, like it or not, we're a pair. Do you think that hiding your head in the sand will change anything?"

Cathryn shook her head blindly. He was asking for more than she was ready to give. She couldn't say that she loved Rule; she could only admit to herself that the strength of the physical attraction she felt for him was undeniable. To admit to more was to give herself up to his influence, and too many questions and uncertainties remained for her to allow that to happen.

His eyes glinted down at her; then he smiled slowly, a dangerous smile that alarmed her. "Let's see if you feel the same way in the morning," he drawled, and began moving against her in a compelling caress.

Hours later only the barest graying of the horizon signaled the approach of dawn, the room darker than ever because clouds had moved in to cover the moon. A light rain began to spatter against the window with a metallic rhythm. Cathryn stirred in the warm cocoon created by the sheet and Rule's radiant body heat, aware that he had lifted his head and was listening to the rain. With a sigh he dropped his head back onto the pillow.

"It's morning," he muttered, his dark voice flowing over her. The arm beneath her head tensed and he became a darker shadow against the blackness of the room, leaning over her, drawing her beneath him. His hips pressed against hers, his desire for her obviously aroused, and his powerful legs parted hers to allow the intimate contact.

Her breath caught at this renewed evidence of his virility. "Again?" she whispered into the warm hollow of his throat. They had gotten very little sleep during the night and her body ached from the demands he had made on her, though he had been nothing but tender. Surprisingly, she was more relaxed and physically content than she had thought possible. During the long hours of the night it had been impossible to keep even a mental distance. They had been as one, moved together as one, explored and stroked and experimented with the other's responses, until now she knew his body as well as she knew her own. She gasped helplessly as he took her, and his low chuckle fanned the hair at her temple.

"Yes," he rasped, the words so low she could barely hear them. "Again."

Afterward she fell into a heavy sleep, undisturbed by his departure from the bed. He bent over her to tuck the sheet about her bare shoulders; then he smoothed the tangle of dark red hair away from her face. She didn't stir. He pulled on his jeans, then gathered the rest of his clothing and left to return to his own room to shower and dress for a day of wet, muddy work.

Cathryn slept on, and though Lorna was curious as the hours wore away, she didn't wake Cathryn. At almost noon Monica came down and disappeared without a word, taking the station wagon and leaving in a spray of water. Ricky sulked for a while, then brightened when one of the hands got into the pickup. Ricky dashed across the muddy yard and climbed into the cab of the truck with him. It didn't matter to her where she went.

The steady rain continued, a welcome rain, but one that was still a mess to work in. Rule returned for a late lunch, his weariness evident only in the tautness of the skin over his cheekbones. Lorna saw and understood the faint smile of satisfaction that curved his hard mouth when she casually mentioned that Cathryn was still asleep. He cast a speculative look at the ceiling, then rejected temptation and ate his lunch before returning to his chores.

The rain had the effect of a sedative on Cathryn, soothing her into long, deep sleep. She woke feeling marvelously rested, stretching lazily and becoming aware of the soreness of her body. She lay drowsily for a moment, remembering when Rule had turned her over on her stomach during the night and straddled her legs, firmly massaging her thighs and buttocks, whispering to her teasingly that if she had let him do that from the beginning, she wouldn't have gotten nearly so sore.

Other remembrances drifted over her and a tiny smile of contentment touched her lips as she felt the caress of the sheets on her bare body. Her sensations were heightened, her skin more than usually sensitive. She was still smiling as she sat up cautiously; then her eyes fell on the bedside clock and the smile faded abruptly. Two-thirty? But her flight back to Chicago was at three!

She scrambled out of bed, ignoring the protests of her muscles. Her feet tangled in the nightgown that Rule had finally tossed aside during the night and she kicked it impatiently out of the way. After jerking on her terry robe and tying it about her, she left her room and ran down the stairs, erupting into the kitchen so swiftly that Lorna dropped the spoon she was using. "Lorna! Where's Rule?"

Lorna took a deep breath and retrieved her spoon from the bowl of cake batter. "There's no telling. He could be anywhere."

"But my flight is in half an hour!"

"No way you can make it now," said Lorna calmly. "The best thing you can do is to call the airline and see if you can get on a later flight."

That was so sensible, and her predicament was so unalterable, that Cathryn sighed and relaxed. "Why didn't I think of that instead of running wild?" she asked ruefully, then went to the study to carry out Lorna's suggestion.

The study had once been her father's domain, but Rule had long since taken it over, to the extent that his masculine scent seemed to linger in the room. The papers on the desk were in his handwriting; the letters were addressed to him. Cathryn sat down in the leather chair and had the uneasy sensation of sitting on his lap. She pushed the thought away and reached for the phone.

It was as she had expected. The later flight that day was booked, but there was plenty of space on the red-eye flight. Knowing that she had no choice, she booked a reservation and resigned herself to a sleepless night. At least sleeping as late as she had would help, she thought; then she remembered why she had slept so late and her mouth tightened.

She couldn't place all the blame on Rule. She had responded to him so strongly that she could deny it neither to herself nor to him. She had never been a woman inclined to casual affairs, which was one reason why she had been so upset years ago when he had first made love to her, one reason why she had avoided him for so long. Knowing David, loving him and being his wife, being with him as he slipped into death had given her maturity and inner strength. She had thought that she would be able to keep Rule at a distance now, but last night had proven to her once and for all that she had no resistance to him. If she stayed she would be in his bed—or he in hers—whenever he had the urge. It was a clear-cut situation: If she wanted to maintain her moral standards, she would have to stay away from Rule Jackson. Returning to Chicago was her only option, regardless of her halfhearted promise to stay.

Her stomach was growling hungrily, but she disregarded it in her haste to leave the ranch. She went upstairs to shower, then put on full battle makeup and subdued her dark red hair by pulling it back with a tortoiseshell clasp. She dressed in sensible dark brown linen slacks and a white cotton blouse, slipped her feet into comfortable cork-soled shoes, and swiftly packed her suitcase and tote bag. Taking them downstairs, she entered the kitchen and told Lorna, "I managed to get on the red-eye flight. Now I have to find Rule and talk him into flying me to Houston."

"If you can't find him," said Lorna placidly, "maybe Lewis can take you. He has a pilot's license, too."

That was the most welcome news Cathryn had heard all day. She donned a too-large slicker and jammed the matching yellow cap over her head, taking them from the assortment that hung in the small utility room just off the kitchen. The rain wasn't heavy, but it was steady, and the ground seemed like one big puddle as she picked her way down to the stables. The ranch hand she found there wasn't full of good news. A group of cattle had broken through the fencing in the far western pasture, and both Rule and Lewis Stovall were there helping to round up the cattle and repair the fencing, which looked like a long job. Cathryn sighed; she wanted to leave now. Specifically, she wanted to leave before she had to face Rule again. He didn't want her to go, and she doubted her ability to resist him if he got the opportunity to argue with her face to face. There was also the possibility that Rule would flatly refuse to take her to Houston. Lewis Stovall might help her, unless Rule ordered him not to, so she wanted to ask him when Rule wasn't around. Now it seemed that she wouldn't have the chance.

She didn't relish the thought of a long drive, but it seemed her only alternative now. She looked at the ranch hand. "I have to get to Houston," she said firmly. "Can you drive me?"

The man looked startled, and he pushed his hat back on his head while he thought. "I'd be glad to," he finally said, "but there's no way right now. Mrs. Donahue is gone in the wagon, and Rule has the keys to his pickup in his pocket. He doesn't leave them in the ignition."

Cathryn knew he was referring to the dark blue pickup that she had noticed before, and she hadn't even considered using it. Her heart sank at the news that Monica had taken the station wagon. "What about the other truck?" she prodded. It was aging and not very comfortable, but it was transportation.

The man shook his head. "Rule sent Foster into town to pick up more fencing. We'll have to wait until he gets back and gets the fencing unloaded."

Cathryn nodded her understanding and left the man to his work, but she wanted to scream in frustration as she made her way back to the house. By the time Monica returned it would probably be too late to make the drive, and the same thing went for the pickup. Not only that, by then Rule would probably be back.

Her last supposition was right on the money. Several hours later, as the last light was falling, helped by the clouds and light rain that lingered on, Rule came in the back door. Cathryn was sitting at the kitchen table with Lorna, feeling safer in company, and she watched as he removed his slicker and hung it up, then brushed the excess water from his dripping hat. His movements as he leaned down to remove his muddy boots were slow with fatigue. An odd pang hit her as she realized that he hadn't had the benefit of sleeping late. For the past two nights he had managed to get very little sleep and the strain was telling on him.

"Give me half an hour," he muttered to Lorna as he passed her in his stockinged feet. He cast a searing look at Cathryn, all the more effective for the fatigue that lined his face. "Come with me," he ordered shortly.

Bracing herself, Cathryn got to her feet and followed him. As they passed her luggage where it sat in the hallway, Rule leaned down and scooped it up, taking it with him on his way up the stairs. Behind him Cathryn said softly, "You're wasting your time. The bags go right back down."

He didn't answer, merely opened the door to her bedroom and tossed the bags inside with fine disregard for their safety. Then he wrapped his long fingers around her delicate wrist and pulled her after him down the hallway to his room. Even when he was tired she was no match for his strength, so she didn't waste any energy in trying to jerk away. He opened the door and ushered her into his bedroom, which was in almost total darkness because the last of the feeble daylight had gone. Without turning on the light he closed the door and reached for her, folding her against him and kissing her with an angry hunger that belied his obvious weariness.

Cathryn put her arms around his waist and kissed him in return, almost weeping with the knowledge that she didn't dare stay with him. Her senses were swamped by him, by the taste of his mouth, the feel of his hard body against her, the damp smell of his skin and hair and clothing. He released her and snapped on the overhead light, moving away as he spoke.

"I'm not taking you to Houston," he said grimly.

"Of course not. You're too tired," she said with outward calm. "But Lewis can—"

"No, Lewis can't. No one will take you to Houston if they want to keep working on the Bar D," he snapped. "I made that clear to all of them. Damn it, Cat, that very first day, when I picked you up, you told me you'd stay!" He began to unbutton his shirt, shrugging it away from his powerful shoulders and tossing it aside.

Cathryn sat down on the bed and clasped her fingers tightly together as she fought for control. At last she said, "I only said maybe I'd stay. And don't bother with threatening me or any of the hands, because you know I can leave tomorrow, if not tonight."

He nodded his head. "Maybe, if Monica comes back tonight. But she's afraid to drive at night, and since she's not here by now I don't expect her back until tomorrow. Then you'll have to get to the station wagon before I put it out of commission."

Control was forgotten and she leaped to her feet, her eyes narrowing with temper. "I won't be kept here like a prisoner!" she shouted.

"I don't want it that way either!" he yelled back, rounding on her. "But I told you that I won't let you run away from me again, and I meant it. Hell, woman, didn't last night tell you anything?"

"It told me it's been a while since you had a woman!" she flared.

"Don't kid yourself!"

Silence fell and Cathryn admitted uneasily that he could have a woman whenever he wanted one—a particularly unpalatable thought. When she said nothing else he unfastened his belt and jeans and pushed them down, stripping off his socks in the same movement and stepping away from the pile of clothing, as unconcerned about his nudity as if she hadn't been in the room. But then, weren't they as familiar with each other as a man and woman could be? Cathryn eyed the tall, vital body with secret hunger, then turned her gaze away before he could read the expression in her eyes.

He gathered up clean clothing and tossed it into her arms. She caught it automatically, holding his clothes to her. After a few moments he muttered, "Give it a chance, Cat. Stay here. Call your boss tomorrow and tell him that you quit."

"I can't do that," she said quietly.

He erupted again. "Damn it, why not? What's stopping you?"

"You are."

He closed his eyes and she could have sworn that he was snarling under his breath. An unwanted smile tried to break over her lips, but she subdued it. How had Wanda described him? Still dangerous but controlled? It was a safe bet that no one knew as well as she did just how volcanic Rule really was. Finally he opened his eyes and glared at her, the dark irises gleaming with angry frustration. "Ricky got to you. You believe her."

"No!" she burst out, unable to control her reaction. He didn't understand and she couldn't tell him, couldn't say that she was afraid to trust him on such an intimate level. He was asking for more than just sex…and she didn't feel capable of dealing with either scenario. She was afraid of him, afraid of how he could hurt her if she let her guard down. Rule could destroy her, because he could get closer to her than anyone else ever had or would.

"Then *what?*" he roared. "Tell me! Tell me what I have to do to get you to stay here! You've put it all on my shoulders, so tell me exactly what you want me to do."

Cathryn considered him, standing there furious and naked and so magnetically masculine that she wanted to drop the clothing that she held to her breast and run to him, wrap her arms around him and bury her face in the curly dark hair that decorated his muscular chest. How much she wanted to stay! This was her home, and she wanted to be here. Yet she couldn't handle Rule...unless she had his cooperation. An idea glimmered, and she didn't stop to consider it. She simply blurted out, "No sex."

He looked staggered, as if she had suggested that he had to give up breathing. Then he swore aloud, scowling at her. "Do you really think that's possible?"

"It will have to be," she assured him. "At least until I decide if...if..."

"If?" he prodded.

"If I can stay permanently," she finished, thinking swiftly that there had to be some way she could maneuver him into promising to behave himself. "I'm not looking for an affair. I'm not a casual woman and I never have been."

"We can't be 'just friends,'" he said savagely. "I want you, and I've never been good at self-denial. It was bad enough when you were married, but now it'll be damned near impossible. When are you going to face up to what the real situation is?"

Cathryn ignored him, determined to press her point. She sensed that he was off-balance, and it was such an unusual circumstance that she was loath to let the opportunity pass. "I'm not asking for a vow of celibacy from you," she retorted. "Only that you leave *me* alone until I've decided." Even as she said the words she felt furious at the mere thought that he would go to another woman. Just let him dare!

His jaw was like a chunk of granite. "And if you decide to stay?"

Her dark eyes went wide as she realized what such a decision would mean. If she stayed she would be Rule Jackson's woman. She wouldn't be able to hold him off forever with the shield that she was "trying to decide." He would want a definite answer before long, and now she fully understood that what she had conceived as a delaying tactic had become a trap. She could stay, or she could go, but if she stayed she would be his. She looked at him, standing there as naked and powerful as some ancient god, and pain twisted her insides. Could she really leave him?

She lifted her chin and answered him evenly, using all her woman's courage in the effort. "If I stay, then I accept your terms."

He didn't relax. "I want you to call tomorrow and quit your job."

"But if I decide to leave—"

"You don't need a job. This ranch can support you."

"I don't want to bleed the ranch."

"Damn it, Cat, I said I'll support you!" he snarled. "Just leave it alone for now. Will you quit the job or not?"

"Be reasonable—" she began to plead, knowing that it was a hopeless request. He cut her short with a slashing movement of his hand.

"Quit…the…job," he ordered from between clenched teeth. "That's the deal. You'll stay if I keep my hands to myself. All right, I'll go along with that if you'll quit your job. We both have to give in."

She saw his muscles quiver and knew that if she said no, his control would be gone. Rule had compromised his position and he would go no further. Either she quit her job or he would keep her on the ranch by any means at his disposal. It seemed to her that she could be either a willing prisoner or an unwilling one, but she gave in on the job in order to keep her advantage in other areas. "All right. I'll quit the job." Even as she promised, she felt lost, as if she had severed her last tie to Chicago and her life with David, as if she had turned her back on his memory.

He sighed and ran his hand roughly through his dark hair. "Lorna's holding dinner," he muttered, taking his clothes from her. "I'll take a fast shower and be right down."

As he opened the door Cathryn leaped across the room and slammed it shut, jerking it out of his hand. He gave her a startled look, and she hissed at him, "You're naked!"

He gave her a tired half smile. "I know. I usually shower this way."

"But someone will see you!"

"Honey, Monica isn't here, Lorna is downstairs, and Ricky hasn't come in from the stables yet. You're the only one who can see me, and I don't have anything to hide from you, do I?" The smile changed from tired to mocking as he opened the door again and sauntered down the hall. Cathryn followed him, so exasperated that she wanted to punch him, but she wasn't that foolish.

After dinner Rule promptly went to bed and Cathryn found herself alone with Ricky, a far from comfortable companion. First she turned on the television and flipped from one channel to the next; then she turned the set off and flopped down on the couch. Cathryn did her best to continue reading the article she had started, but she was completely unbalanced when Ricky said nastily, "Shouldn't you go tuck him in?"

Cathryn jumped, then looked away as she felt her face heat up. "Who?" she managed to say, but her voice wasn't quite steady.

Ricky smiled and stretched her legs, crossing them at the ankle. "Who?" she mimicked sweetly. "It's hard to believe you're really that dumb. Do you think I don't know where he slept last night? But you've got to give Rule credit. When he wants something, he goes after it. He wants this ranch and he's using you to get it, but he's so great in bed that you can't see beyond that, can you?"

"I see a lot of things, including your jealousy," Cathryn snapped. Anger had leaped to life in her, and she wasn't about to deny that Rule had made love to her, if that was what Ricky was trying to provoke her into saying.

Ricky laughed. "That's right, keep your head in the clouds. You haven't been able to think straight since he gave you your first taste of sex when you were seventeen. Did you think I didn't know? I rode up in time to see him help you put your clothes back on. You've been running scared since then; but now you're old enough that you're not scared, and you've been remembering, haven't you? Lord, Cathryn, he's got a reputation that puts those stud horses of his to shame. Doesn't it bother you to be just one on a long list?"

Eyeing her narrowly, Cathryn said, "I can't decide if you hate him or if you're jealous because he doesn't pay any attention to you."

To Cathryn's surprise, color flooded hotly into Ricky's cheeks, and this time it was the other woman who looked away. After a moment Ricky said thickly, "Don't believe me, I don't care. Let him use you the way he's used Mother all these years. Just remember, nothing and no one is as important to him as this ranch, and he'll do whatever he has to do to keep it. Ask him," she dared, jeering. "See if you can get him to talk about it. Ask him what Vietnam did to him and why he holds on to the ranch with a death grip. Ask him about the nightmares, why he spends some nights just walking around the ranch."

Cathryn was stunned. She hadn't thought that he was still troubled by memories of the war. Ricky laughed again, regaining her composure. "You don't know him at all! You've been away for years. You don't know anything about what went on here while you were gone. Be a fool. It doesn't matter to me!" She got up and left the room, and Cathryn heard her running up the stairs.

She sat there, disturbed by the things Ricky had said. She had thought them herself, in part, wondering what motivated Rule. She thought wearily that she would probably go crazy wondering what went on in Rule's mind. Did he want her for herself or because of the ranch? And even if she asked him straight out, could she believe what he told her? She could only make up her mind for herself, using her instincts. At least she had bought time for herself, time free of the sensual pressure he could so easily bring to bear. All she had to do was not let Ricky goad her into some reckless action.

Cathryn woke before dawn and lay awake, unable to sleep again, and soon rosy fingers began piercing through the purple patches of cloud that still remained from the day before. The house began to resound with the familiar, comforting sounds of Lorna preparing breakfast, and soon she heard Rule's heart-stopping tread as he walked past her door and went down the stairs. She threw the sheet back and hurriedly dressed in jeans and an emerald-green knit pullover shirt, then ran barefoot down the stairs. For reasons that she didn't want to examine too closely, she needed to see Rule before he left the house for the day, just to see him…to make certain that he didn't look as tired as he had the day before.

He was sprawled at the kitchen table with a steaming cup of coffee before him when she entered, and both he and Lorna looked up in surprise. "I thought I'd have an early breakfast," she said serenely, moving to set herself a place at the table and pour a cup of coffee.

After that initial look of surprise, Lorna returned placidly to her cooking. "Eggs or waffles?" she asked.

"One egg, scrambled," said Cathryn as she checked the big homemade biscuits in the oven. They were a perfect golden brown and she took them out, transferring them deftly to a napkin-lined straw basket and setting the fragrant mount in front of Rule. While Lorna was finishing the scrambled eggs, Cathryn also transferred the plate of bacon and sausages to the table and slipped into a chair beside Rule, taking advantage of Lorna's turned back to lean over and plant a quick kiss under his ear. She couldn't have said why she did that, either, but the effect was pleasing. Rule shuddered wildly and Cathryn grinned, absurdly pleased that he was so ticklish in that particular spot. It made him seem so much more vulnerable… and, as he had said, he didn't have anything to hide from her.

The fuming dark glance he turned on her promised retribution, but the look lingered on her smiling face and slowly the threat faded from his expression.

Lorna set their plates before them and took her own place across the table. Conversation was nonexistent for a few minutes as they went through their own ritual of salting and peppering and arranging their food exactly as they preferred. Then Lorna asked a question about the sale, and though Rule's replies were characteristically brief, Cathryn managed to learn that he had scheduled a horse sale in three weeks and that it was turning out to be a large event. Over the years he had developed a solid reputation as a horsebreeder and more people were coming to the sale than he had originally anticipated. Lorna was beaming with pride—a pride that Rule didn't allow himself to show.

"Is there anything I can do to help?" asked Cathryn. "Groom the horses, clean out the stables, whatever?"

"Have you made that phone call yet?" Rule growled.

"No. The switchboard doesn't open until nine." She smiled

at him with mock sweetness, intent on fully enjoying her opportunity to have him under control.

Lorna looked confused, and Cathryn explained, "I'm quitting my job and staying here, at least for the time being. I haven't made a permanent decision yet." She tacked that last on for Rule's benefit, just in case he was thinking he had already won the war.

"My, that'll be nice, having you in the house for good," said Lorna.

After breakfast Cathryn realized that Rule hadn't answered her question about helping and she followed him outside, stepping on his heels like a determined little bulldog and almost tripping him. He turned on her and planted his fists on his hips, every inch the dominating male. "Well?" he barked.

"Is there anything I can do to help?" she repeated patiently, planting her own fists on her hips in duplication of his stance and tilting her jaw at him.

For a moment he looked as if he were going to explode with frustration; then the iron control she usually saw on his face returned and he even gave her a crooked smile. "Yes, there is. After you make that phone call, take the truck into town and pick up our order of feed supplements. And we'll need more fencing. Foster didn't get enough yesterday." He told her how much fencing to get and dug into his pocket for the keys to his pickup.

As she took the keys, he cupped her chin in his hand and turned her face up to his. "I'm relying on you to be here when I get back," he said, a hint of warning in his voice.

Irritated that he didn't trust her, Cathryn glared at him. "I know. I will be," she replied stiffly. "I'm not a liar."

He nodded and released her chin. Without another word he walked away, and she watched his tall form for a minute before she returned to the house, vaguely irritated that he hadn't even kissed her. That was what she had wanted; it was silly now to be disappointed that he was following her orders. Taking that as an indication of how deeply she had already fallen under his spell, she firmly pushed aside her disappointment.

Promptly at nine she sat down before the phone and chewed on her lips, uncertain in the face of the step she was taking. In a way Rule was asking her to choose between himself and David—an unfair choice, as David was dead. And he had been a very special person. Cathryn knew that a part of her devotion would always be David's...but he was gone, and Rule was very much alive. He was asking her to leave the home that she had shared with her husband, to leave behind everything. Yet she had promised, and if she broke that promise she would have to leave the ranch today, before Rule returned. She couldn't do that. Not now, not after that night spent in his arms. She had to know for certain how she felt—and how he felt—or she would regret it for the rest of her life. Picking up the receiver, she dialed.

Ten minutes later she was unemployed. Now that she had done it she was almost in a panic. It wasn't money; she really had no money worries. While talking to her supervisor she had suddenly had the thought that only people in love made such sacrifices. She didn't want to love Rule Jackson, didn't want to let herself get that vulnerable until she was certain in her own mind that she could trust him. She didn't think that Rule had ever been involved with Monica, despite Ricky's tales to the contrary. There was just no sense of intimacy between Rule and Monica, nothing in their behavior that would indicate even a *past* relationship. That was obviously pure mischief making on Ricky's part, something that she excelled in.

No, what Cathryn wasn't certain about was Rule's motive for pursuing her. She wanted desperately to believe that he wanted her simply for herself, but the fact remained that he was extremely possessive of the ranch. He had taken it over, made it his, and she had no doubt that he would fight with whatever weapons he had to in order to keep the ranch. He controlled the ranch, but she legally owned it, and it might be constantly on his mind that she could sell it at any time and his control would be ended. He had denied being concerned with the ranch at all, but the doubt remained in her mind.

If he was so interested in her, why hadn't he made an effort to contact her at some point since David's death? It hadn't been until she came for a visit, indicating a renewed interest in the ranch, that he had suddenly become so smitten with her.

As she drove his truck into town the issue nagged at her. Her entire decision hinged on that one matter. If she trusted him, if she believed that he wanted her as a man wanted a woman, with no other considerations involved, then she would stay with him in whatever capacity he wanted. On the other hand, she refused to let him manipulate her with sex. He was an extremely dominating, virile man. Sex was one of the weapons he could use against her, clouding her senses with the sensual need he aroused simply by touching her. She knew of no way she could reach her decision except by simply being with him, hoping to learn enough about him despite his iron control to be able to say that she trusted him.

CHAPTER 5

Franklin's Feed Store was the only one in town, so Cathryn had no doubt that she was in the right place as she backed up to the loading dock. She had gone to school with Alva Franklin, the owner's daughter, and she grinned as she remembered the day Alva had pushed her older sister Regina into a mud puddle. Alva had been a little devil. She was still smiling as she went up the back steps into the musty atmosphere of the building.

She didn't recognize the man who came over to take her order, but it had been eight years since she had spent any time at all on the ranch, and he was obviously one of the people who had moved into the region since then.

However, the man eyed her doubtfully when she told him what she wanted. "The Bar D order?" he asked warily. "I don't believe I know you, ma'am. What did you say your name is?"

Cathryn stifled a laugh. "My name is Cathryn Donahue… Ashe," she added as an afterthought, guilt-stricken as she realized that she had almost forgotten her married name. It seemed as if David were being pushed away as if he had never existed, and she didn't want that to happen. She hadn't even protested when Rule had introduced her to Lewis Stovall by her maiden name, letting herself slip back into the identity of Cathryn Donahue and under the domination of her ranch manager. But not now, she thought grimly.

She finished her explanation, but the man still stood uncertainly.

"I own the Bar D."

"Mr. Jackson—" began the man.

"Is my ranch manager," she finished smoothly for him. "I understand that you don't recognize me, and I'm grateful that you're so careful with the orders. However, Mr. Franklin knows me, if you want to verify my identity with him."

He did, and went in search of the store owner. Cathryn waited patiently, not at all put out by his caution. It would be chaos if just anyone was allowed to sign a load slip and have a load of feed charged to any ranch at random. It was only a few minutes before the man returned with Ormond Franklin close behind him. Mr. Franklin peered at her through his glasses; then his gaze settled on her hair and he said, "Why, hello, Cathryn. I heard you were back in town." He nodded to his employee. "Go ahead and load the order, Todd."

"It's good to see you again, Mr. Franklin," said Cathryn pleasantly. "I arrived on Saturday. I had only intended to stay for the holiday, but now it looks as though I'll be here for a longer time."

He smiled so widely that she wondered why her news should be so pleasing. "Well, now, that's good news. Glad to hear that you're taking the ranch over. Never did like that Rule Jackson. Got rid of him, did you? Fine, fine. He's nothing but trouble. I've always thought your pa made a bad mistake in taking on trouble the way he did with Jackson. He was wild enough before he went to Vietnam, but after he came back he was pure crazy."

Cathryn could feel her mouth fall open as she stared at him, stunned. He had made so many fantastic assumptions that she didn't know where to start. But why should Mr. Franklin hold such a grudge against Rule? Then memory stirred and she had a clear vision of Regina Franklin's pretty, sulky face, remembered also that the girl had had a reputation for chasing men she would have done better to avoid. One of those men had been Rule Jackson, and, being the man he was, he had made no effort to hide it.

She made an effort to be reasonable. Mindful of Mr. Franklin's grudge against Rule—even if his daughter had been equally responsible—she said mildly, "I couldn't begin to run the ranch by myself, Mr. Franklin. Rule has done a fantastic job; the ranch looks better now than it did even when Dad was alive. I have no reason to fire him."

"No reason?" he asked incredulously, his brows gathering over the bridge of his glasses. "His morals are reason enough for a lot of decent people around here. There's a lot of people who haven't forgotten the way he acted when he came back from overseas. Why, in your own house you've got to watch him like a hawk or that stepsister of yours—"

"Mr. Franklin, I can understand why you dislike Rule, given the circumstances," interrupted Cathryn, suddenly and fiercely angry at his persistent attack on Rule and at the way he had linked Rule with Ricky. She refused to listen to any more of that. She went straight to the heart of the matter with her counterattack. "But Rule and your daughter were both very young and confused, and that was all a long time ago. Rule was in no way solely responsible for that scandal."

Mr. Franklin turned a dusky red with fury, and he spat from between clenched teeth, "Not responsible? How can you stand there and say that? He forced himself on my girl, then refused to stand by her. Why, she couldn't hold her head up in this town. She had to leave, and he walks around as if he never did anything wrong in his life!"

She hesitated, wondering if he had twisted his own guilt around to rest on Rule because he couldn't face the possibility that his own rigidity had been responsible for driving his daughter away. She didn't want to hurt him, but there was one thing she couldn't let pass, and she said coldly, "Rule Jackson has never forced a woman in his life. He's never had to. I was young, but I can remember the way girls chased him from the time he could even think of growing a beard. After he got out of the army it was even worse. You can think what you like, but I'd advise you not to say things like that out loud unless you want a charge of slander brought against you!"

Their raised voices had gathered the attention of everyone in the feed store, but that didn't stop Mr. Franklin. His gray hair almost stood on end as he shouted, "If that's the way you feel, Miss Donahue, then I suggest you buy your feed from someone else! Your daddy would never have said something like that to me!"

"The name is Mrs. Ashe, and I think my dad would be proud of me! He believed in Rule when no one else did, and it's a good thing he did, because the ranch would have gone under years ago without Rule Jackson!" She was boiling now, and she stomped down the steps to where Todd was waiting, bug-eyed, with the ticket for her signature. She scribbled her name across the bottom of it and crawled under the steering wheel of the pickup. Her foot was heavy with temper and the vehicle shot away from the loading dock, bucking under the demand she was making of it.

Shaking with temper, Cathryn drove only a block and pulled over to calm herself. Fencing…she couldn't forget the fencing, she reminded herself, drawing in a deep breath. Her hands were trembling violently and her heart was pounding, her body wet with perspiration. She felt as if she had been in a physical free-for-all rather than an argument. Catching a glimpse of her hair in the rearview mirror she startled herself by giving a shaky giggle. Did the color of one's hair really have anything to do with temper?

She regretted the scene with Franklin now. It would have been bad enough if there hadn't been any witnesses, but with

so many people standing around the argument would be repeated verbatim all over town before dark. But she couldn't
let anyone talk about Rule like that!

"God, I'm really getting a bad case of it," she moaned to
herself. Rule needed protection about as much as a prowling
panther did, but she had leaped to his defense as if he were
nothing more than a helpless cub. It was just one more measure of the hold he had on her. He had always seemed larger
than life, outsized in both his reputation and his domination
of her. As a child she had been frightened and awed by him; as
a teenager she had bitterly, wildly resented his authority; but
now, as a woman, she was so drawn to his rampant masculinity that she felt as if she were battling for her own existence.

After several minutes she made a U-turn and drove down
the street to the building-supply store. She had no trouble
there. Not only had she known everyone employed there all
of her life, but Rule had called in an addition to the order he
had given her. When everything was loaded the bed of the
pickup was riding low on the springs, so she drove carefully
back to the ranch, mindful of the heavy load she was hauling.

It was a beautiful day, with everything fresh and sweet and
green after the needed rain of the day before, and Cathryn took
her time, trying to calm herself completely before she reached
the ranch. She didn't quite succeed. Rule was waiting in the
yard for her when she drove up, and she remembered that he
hadn't fully trusted her to return. As she thought of the battle
she had fought on his behalf, resentment welled up in her and
her temper surged back in full force. She got out of the truck,
slammed the door and yelled at him, "I told you I'd be back!"

He stalked up to her and took her arm, hauling her with
him to the house. "I need those supplies right away," he gritted. "That's why I'm here. Now rein in that temper of yours
before I put you over my knee right here in front of the men."

Right then she needed nothing more than a chance to work off the energy her temper had raised, and she welcomed the prospect of a fight. "Any time you feel ready, big man," she challenged between her teeth. "After what I've been through this morning, I could take on five of you!"

He pulled her up the steps and she stumbled, only to be rescued by his hard grip on her arm. "Ouch!" she snapped. "You're jerking my arm out of its socket!"

He began swearing softly under his breath as he opened the kitchen door and ushered her inside. Lorna looked up from her permanent station in front of the window, a flicker of amusement in her serene eyes as she continued without pause in her preparation of a beef casserole that Rule was fond of.

Rule sat Cathryn forcibly in one of the chairs, but she bounded out of it like a rubber ball, her fists clenched. With one big hand on her chest he returned her to the chair and held her there. "What in the *hell* is wrong with you?" he growled softly in the almost crooning tone he used when he was about to lose his own temper.

He would hear about it anyway, so Cathryn thrust her chin out at him belligerently and told him herself. "I got in an argument! We have to buy our feed somewhere else now."

His hand dropped away from her chest and he stared at her in disbelief. "Do you mean," he whispered, "that I've managed to do business with Ormond Franklin all these years without having a flare-up, and in one trip you've wrecked all of that?"

Her lip curled, but she didn't tell him the details of the argument. "So we'll go to Wisdom to buy our feed," she said, naming the nearest town.

"That's twenty miles farther, an additional forty miles round trip. Damn it, Cat!"

"Then we'll drive that extra forty miles!" she shouted. "Let me remind you that this is still my ranch, Rule Jackson, and after what Mr. Franklin said I wouldn't buy another sack of feed from him even if the next feed store was a hundred miles away! Is that clear?"

Pure fire sparked from his dark eyes and he reached for her, stopping just before he actually touched her. Then he whirled on his heel and stalked out of the house, his long legs eating up the distance at such a pace that she would have had to run to keep up with him.

After getting out of the chair, Cathryn went to the window and watched him climb into the truck, then head it across the pastures to the far side of the ranch where the fencing was needed. She said aloud, "The ground is wet after the rain yesterday. I hope he doesn't get stuck in the mud."

"If he does, there are enough hands to get him out," said Lorna. She chuckled quietly. "You know exactly how to get a rise out of him, don't you? There's been more life in his face in the few days you've been here than in all the years I've known him."

"People need to stand up to him more often," Cathryn muttered. "He's run roughshod over me since I was a child, but I won't stand for it now."

"He's going to have a hard time letting anyone else have a say in running the ranch," Lorna advised. "It's all been on his shoulders for so long now that he won't know how to let someone share the responsibility with him."

"Then he's going to have to learn," said Cathryn stubbornly, her eyes still on the far dot of the pickup as it drew out of sight. Suddenly it went into a dip and disappeared from view, and she turned away from the window.

"Do you know what you two remind me of?" Lorna asked suddenly, laughing again.

"Do I want to know?" Cathryn responded wryly.

"I don't think it'll come as any great surprise. You remind

me of a sleek little cat in heat, and he's the tomcat circling around you, knowing he's going to have the fight of his life if he tries to get what he wants."

Cathryn burst into laughter at the image and admitted that they did fight like two snarling, spitting cats. "You do have a way with words," she choked, and the two women stood in the kitchen laughing like maniacs at what was, after all, a very apt observation.

To Cathryn's disappointment, Rule didn't return for lunch. Lorna told her that she had already packed a basket of sandwiches and coffee and sent it out to the men, and as Ricky was also with the men, Cathryn ate a silent lunch with Monica, who had returned some time during the morning while Cathryn had been in town. The two women had no common interests. Monica was absorbed in her own thoughts and didn't even ask where Ricky was, though perhaps she already knew.

They had finished lunch when Monica leaned back and lit a cigarette, a sure sign that she was nervous, as she seldom smoked. Cathryn looked at her and Monica said abruptly, flatly, "I'm thinking of leaving."

At first Cathryn was surprised, but when she thought about it she was more surprised that Monica had stayed as long as she had. Ranch life had never suited the older woman. "Why now?" she asked. "And where would you go?"

Monica shrugged. "I'm not really certain. It doesn't matter, so long as it's a city and I never have to smell horses and cows again. It's no secret that I've never liked living on a ranch. As for the timing, why not? You're here now, and it's your ranch, after all, not mine. I stayed on after Ward died because you were a minor, but that's not true anymore. I just let time drift, and now I'm tired of all this."

"Have you told Ricky yet?"

Monica gave her a sharp glance from her slanted cat eyes.

"We're not a package deal. Ricky's a grown woman; she can do what she wants."

Cathryn didn't reply right away. At last she murmured, "I haven't made a definite decision about staying."

"That doesn't matter," Monica replied coolly. "The ranch is your responsibility now, not mine. You can do what you want, and I'll do the same. Let's not pretend that we've ever been close. The only thing we've ever had in common was your father, and he's been dead for twelve years. It's time I started to live my life for myself."

Cathryn realized that Monica's presence hadn't been required for years anyway, not since Rule had taken over. Even if she herself didn't stay, the ranch would continue to run as always. If Monica left it wouldn't affect her own situation at all; she still had to make the decision whether to stay or go. The thought of selling the ranch slipped into her mind but was quickly pushed away. This was her home and she never wanted to sell it. She might not feel that she could live here, but it would be impossible for her to turn her back on her heritage.

"You know you're welcome to stay here forever," she told Monica quietly, bringing her thoughts back to the subject at hand.

"Thanks, but it's time I dusted off my dancing shoes and make the most of the time I have left. I've mourned Ward for long enough," she said in an odd tone, looking down at her hands. "I felt closer to him here, so I stayed even when there was no reason to stay. I've never been suited to this kind of life, and we both know it. I haven't seriously looked for an apartment, or even decided what city I'll go to, but I think within a few months I'll have it all settled."

Hesitantly, not certain if Monica would like the idea, Cathryn offered, "There's my apartment in Chicago. The lease is paid up through the end of next year. If I stay here it's available, if you think you'd like Chicago."

Monica smiled wryly. "I was thinking more along the lines of New Orleans, but…Chicago. I'll have to think about that."

"There's no hurry. It isn't going anywhere," said Cathryn.

Having said what was on her mind Monica wasn't inclined to linger and chat; she stubbed out her half-smoked cigarette and excused herself, leaving Cathryn dawdling over her iced tea.

Later that afternoon, after hours of trying to pass the time by cleaning the downstairs—a process that didn't proceed as quickly as it should have because she kept going to the window to see if Rule had returned—Cathryn at last heard the pickup and ran to the window again to see him pulling up beside the supply shed. Her heart was beating so swiftly that she could feel her skin heating, and for a moment she forced herself to take slow, deep breaths before she walked down to where he was. She had forgotten the quarrel they'd had that morning. She only knew that he had been gone for hours and that she was hungry for the sight of him, a secret hunger that had to be fed immediately.

She was still out of earshot of the shed when she stopped abruptly, paling as she watched the two figures who had been unloading the remainder of the fencing. Ricky was helping Rule, and though Cathryn couldn't hear what they were saying, she could see Ricky's face, see how it glowed as the young woman laughed up at him. Suddenly Ricky dropped the box of tools she was carrying and hugged him, her pretty face turned up to him as she laughed unrestrainedly. She rose on tiptoe and quickly kissed him, then sank back as Rule's hands went to her shoulders and moved her back from him. He must not have scolded her, because Ricky laughed again; then the two returned to their task.

Cathryn turned away, moving at an angle so they wouldn't look up and see her. As she did so she caught sight of another figure and she halted, her head jerking around. Lewis Stovall was leaning against the corral, his hard face expressionless as he watched Rule and Ricky unloading the truck. There was a certain tautness about his stance that puzzled her, but she was too upset to worry about him right then.

Cathryn returned quickly to the house, so shaken that she went to her bedroom and sat on the bed, her eyes wide with shock. Ricky had hugged Rule, had kissed him! He hadn't returned the embrace and it certainly hadn't been what she would call a passionate encounter, yet she felt sick as she remembered how Ricky's slender arms had gone around his waist. Lorna had said that Ricky was in love with Rule, but Cathryn hadn't believed it then and still found it hard to swallow. Yet if it were true…no wonder Ricky was so bitter, trying wildly to hurt Cathryn even if she had to use Rule as her weapon. Had Rule ever made love to her? Had Mr. Franklin's accusation not been so wild, after all?

No, it wasn't true. She couldn't let herself think that it was, because she couldn't bear the thought of it. Moaning softly, she pressed her icy hands over her face. Ricky didn't have any right to touch him! That was the basis of it all. Recognizing her sick jealousy for what it was, Cathryn tried to chide herself out of it. After all, hadn't she herself given him permission to go to other women? He wasn't a monk—far from it. He was a healthy, hotly virile man. But she hadn't meant it! She couldn't stand the thought of any other woman melting under his demands.

It had been an innocent scene. She had to believe that, or she wouldn't be able to bear it. It had been only a quick hug and a kiss, and he hadn't returned either of them. She had no reason to be jealous, no reason at all.

Yet it was more than an hour before she felt sufficiently under control to go downstairs and sit through dinner, carefully keeping her face blank and trying not to look directly at either Rule or Ricky. She wanted to do something violent, and she was afraid that if she saw either of them smirk she would lose her temper. Rule would like that; he had a tendency to use her loss of control against her.

She toyed listlessly with her beef casserole, neatly separating it into four equal portions on her plate and taking a tiny bit from each section in turn. The day had been a total disaster. Like a fool she had let Rule bully her into quitting her job. Now she realized that she had given up one more piece of her personal independence, bringing her that much more firmly under Rule's domination. The fight with Mr. Franklin, the fight with Rule, the shock of seeing Ricky kiss him...all of it was just too much. She began to wish he'd say something nasty so she could throw her plate at him.

But the meal continued silently, until at length Rule excused himself and went into the study, shutting himself inside. Feeling like she could scream, Cathryn got ready for bed. What else was there to do? She vented some of her frustration on the pillow, then tried to read. At length she succeeded in making herself sleepy and she turned out the light, sliding down between the sheets. Moments after she had closed her eyes she heard a faint sound and her eyes flew open, her heartbeat quickening to double time as she wondered if Rule had decided to break their agreement and come to her anyway. But no one was there, and to her horror tears welled up in her eyes. Quickly she subdued the impulse to sob like a child.

Had he already reduced her to that? After one night of his lovemaking, was she so addicted to him that she craved him like a potent drug?

Damn him, didn't he realize how upsetting the day had been to her?

No, he didn't realize, and she was lucky that he didn't. If he had any inkling that she was feeling so weak and uncertain of herself, he would move in like the hungry panther he reminded her of, ready for the metaphorical kill.

If only David were still alive! He had been a warm, sheltering harbor, a quiet, strong man who had loved her and left her free to be herself, instead of demanding more than she had to give. Rule demanded more. He wanted all of her under his control, and the terrible thing about it was that she would glory in being his completely, if only she could be certain of him, secure in his love. But how could she be? He would take everything she had to give but keep himself guarded, locked away from her searching heart.

She wouldn't be able to stand it, every day spent worrying over the puzzle that was Rule's personality, becoming more and more frantic as she failed to solve it. Why had she agreed to stay? Was she trying to drive herself crazy?

The thought of Chicago was heaven. She could still go back; she still had to close up her apartment, and she definitely needed her clothing. She had been scratching by with the bare minimum that she had brought, since she had thought that she would be staying only a weekend. That would be an ironclad excuse to leave, and once she was in Chicago, out of his reach, she wouldn't come back. There were other jobs.

Clinging to the thought of her quiet apartment, she drifted to sleep. It must have been a sound sleep, because she didn't awaken when her door was opened the next morning. It wasn't until a hard hand slapped her bottom lightly that she shot up in bed, pushing her hair out of her eyes to glare up at the tall man standing beside the bed. "What are you doing in here?" she snarled.

"Waking you up," he replied in the same tone of voice. "Get up. You're going with me today."

"I am? When was this decided?"

"Last night, while I watched you sulk over your dinner."

"I wasn't sulking!"

"Weren't you? I've been watching you sulk on and off for quite a few years now, and I know all the signs. So haul your pretty self out of that bed and get your clothes on, honey, because I'm going to keep you so busy you won't have time to pout."

Cathryn debated giving him a fight, but she quickly realized that she was in a difficult position and gave in with poor grace. "All right. Get out so I can get dressed."

"Why should I? I've seen you naked before."

"Not today you haven't!" she shouted furiously. "Get out! Get...*out!*"

He leaned down and flipped the cover back, then locked his fingers around her wrist and dragged her off the bed. Standing her before him as if she were a naughty child, he pulled her nightgown over her head with one swift movement and tossed it aside. His dark eyes flashed down her body, finding every detail and touching her with heat. "Now I have," he snapped, and turned aside to pull open dresser drawers until he found her underwear. After throwing a pair of panties and a bra at her, he went to the closet and pulled out a shirt and a pair of soft, faded jeans. Thrusting those into her hands, too, he said, "Are you going to get dressed, or are we going to fight? I think I'd like the fight. I remember what happened the last time you tried nude wrestling."

Temper glowing hotly in her cheeks, Cathryn turned her back on him and hastily donned her underwear. Damn him, no matter what she did, he won. If she dressed, she was doing as she was told. If she didn't get dressed, she knew that they would be in bed in a matter of minutes. Having to admit to herself that she didn't have the willpower to resist him left a bitter taste in her mouth. Any abstinence was due entirely to *his* willpower, and Rule had plenty of that. He had been bending everyone to his will for years.

As she jabbed her arms into the sleeves of the shirt, his hands closed on her shoulders and gently turned her around to face him. Swiftly she looked up at him and wasn't surprised to find that his expression was closed, his face stony. He pushed her hands down and buttoned the shirt himself, his fingers lingering on the soft swells of her breasts. Cathryn drew a deep breath and tried to fight back the longing that surged through her, making her nipples ache and pucker tautly under the lace of her bra.

"Would I be breaking our deal if I kissed you?" he murmured harshly.

With a jolt Cathryn realized that he was fiercely angry at the limitations she had set for him. Rule was a man used to having a woman whenever he needed one, and celibacy was riling him. The knowledge that she was upsetting him made her smile. Looking up at him, she hedged, "Just one kiss?"

For a moment he looked as if he would explode with fury. The glare he gave her was so violent that she took a step backward, prepared to scream at the top of her lungs if he made a move toward her. Then he controlled himself, reining in his temper and visibly forcing himself to relax. "I'm going to have you again," he promised softly, holding her eyes with his. "And when I do, I'm going to make up for this, so prepare yourself."

"Written in stone?" she asked just as softly, her tone mocking.

"Written in stone," he assured her.

"That's odd; I'd never thought you'd be rough on a woman."

A smile suddenly lit his somber features. "I wasn't talking

about being rough, honey. I was talking about satisfying a lot of urges."

He was making love to her with words, seducing her with memories. Her body quickened as she thought of the night they had spent together. She swallowed and opened her mouth to grant him his kiss…as many kisses as he wanted…but he forestalled her by turning abruptly away. "Get dressed, Cat. Now. I'll be downstairs."

Shivering, she stood for a moment watching the door that he had left open in the wake of his departure. She ached for him, willing him to return. Then she shook herself out of her sensual fog and pulled on her jeans and boots, her hands trembling from both regret and relief. How unlike Rule to deny himself sexual gratification! He had to have known that she had been trembling on the brink of surrender, but he had pulled her back. Because she had threatened to leave? Did he want her to stay so badly?

After brushing her teeth and combing the tangles from her hair, she ran downstairs and burst into the kitchen, suddenly afraid that he hadn't waited for her. He was sprawled at the table, nursing a cup of coffee. Something flickered briefly in his eyes when she entered, then was quickly veiled before she could read it.

Her stomach jumped unpleasantly when she saw Ricky sitting close beside him. Murmuring a good-morning, she sat down and reached for the cup of coffee that Lorna had promptly placed before her.

Ricky arched an eyebrow at her. "Why are you awake so early?" she asked snidely.

"I woke her up," said Rule curtly. "She's going with me today."

Ricky's pretty face pulled into a scowl. "But *I* was planning on going with you again!"

"You can go where you want," Rule said without looking up from his coffee. "Cat's going with me."

Cathryn stared at him, troubled by the way he casually brushed Ricky aside, when only the day before they had been laughing together as they unloaded the truck. A quick glance at Ricky revealed a quivering bottom lip that had been bitten and conquered.

Lorna slid filled plates before them, drawing everyone's attention to their food, for which Cathryn was grateful. Rule ate with his usual hearty appetite, though Cathryn and Ricky did little more than pick at their food, at least until Rule looked up and frowned when he saw Cathryn's full plate. "You didn't eat last night," he said pointedly. "You'll eat that if I have to feed it to you myself."

Delightful visions of egg dripping down his face danced with wicked temptation in Cathryn's mind, but she reluctantly turned them away. Hurriedly she gulped her breakfast, drained her cup and jumped to her feet. Kicking his ankle, she snapped, "Hurry it up! What's taking you so long?"

Behind her she heard Lorna quickly stifle a chuckle. Rule rose to his feet and clamped his fingers around her wrist, dragging her in his wake. He paused at the back door to jam his battered black hat on his head, then grabbed up another one, which he pushed onto Cathryn's head. She knocked at it and said sulkily, "This isn't my hat."

"Tough," he muttered as he hauled her across the yard to the stable.

Cathryn dug her heels in every inch of the way, pulling back on her wrist and trying to twist her arm out of his grasp. When that failed she tried to trip him, managing once to send him stumbling, but she didn't accomplish much, since he retained his grip on her and she had to stumble after him. The thought came fleetingly that it was becoming commonplace for him to drag her across the yard, and she wondered what the ranch hands thought of it. The mental picture of grinning male faces gave her the strength to liberate her wrist with a violent twist. "Stop dragging me around!" she snapped when he whirled to face her, his expression thunderous. "I'm not a dog to be dragged around on the end of a chain!"

"Right now I think a chain would do you good," he snarled softly. "You damned little redheaded wildcat! You refuse to let me touch you, but everything you do is a dare to me. I never had you pegged for a tease, honey, but you could have changed while you were away."

Aghast, Cathryn stared at him. "I'm not teasing you!"

"Does that mean you're serious when you give me the come-on?"

"I'm not giving you any such thing!" she denied hotly. "Just look at the way you've acted this morning—and yesterday, too! Yet you expect everything to be roses. I'm angry with you… no, make that furious. Enraged. Am I getting through to you?"

He looked astounded. "Just what have I done now?"

Out of the corner of her eye Cathryn saw Lewis Stovall leaning negligently against the stable door and almost grinning, which probably meant that he found it all highly amusing. She sniffed and evaded Rule's question by saying, "It's time we got started," and walking around him to the stable.

Only the presence of Lewis and several of the other hands kept Rule under control, she was certain. She saddled her own horse, choosing the gray gelding she had ridden her first day home. When Rule was mounted on his big chestnut he led the way across the pastures, and looking at the set of his broad shoulders, Cathryn knew that he hadn't forgotten the subject of their earlier conversation. Just let him bring it up! she thought fiercely. She had a few things to tell Mr. Rule Jackson!

CHAPTER 6

He waited only until they were out of the others' hearing before he kneed his horse close beside hers and said with dangerous calm, "You'd better have a good explanation."

Cathryn gave him a fierce, narrow-eyed stare. "The same goes for you," she fired back. "For instance, why were you kissing and hugging with Ricky yesterday afternoon, but this morning you treated her like dirt? Was it an act for my benefit?"

Sudden amusement lit his dark eyes. "Ricky's never done anything for your benefit."

"Stop playing games with me, damn it!" she said furiously. "You know what I mean."

"You're jealous," he drawled, looking so pleased with himself that Cathryn almost exploded with anger.

"I am not!" she yelled. "You can run around with every woman in Texas for all I care! I want to know why you were so friendly with her yesterday but treated her like a stray hound this morning. The rumor in town is that you're sleeping with Ricky." She felt sick even saying the words, and her hand tightened on the reins, making the gray dance and shake his head.

"Oh, you care, all right," he replied. "Why else have you been throwing such a tantrum this morning?"

Cathryn ignored the provocation of that remark, no longer able to avoid asking him straight out. "Have you ever made love to Ricky?" she asked in a harsh voice; then she had to swallow a sudden surge of nausea. What would she do if he admitted it, when the very thought of him touching another woman made her feel sick? She wouldn't be able to bear it.

"No," he said easily, totally unaware that her very sanity hinged on his answer. "But not for lack of opportunity. Does that answer your question? Or do you have something else you want to accuse me of? Surely there's some woman left in the county who you've managed not to suspect me of messing around with."

She almost flinched from his sarcasm. Rule didn't usually argue, but when he did he had a deadly tongue. Her dark eyes were huge and miserable as she stared at him. "Ricky's in love with you," she said. She hadn't wanted to tell him, though on reflection she was certain that he knew it. Ricky wasn't a subtle woman.

He snorted. "Ricky doesn't love anyone but herself. She goes from man to man the way a butterfly tries all the flowers. But why should you care who warms my bed? You don't want to share it. You even told me to take myself elsewhere when I needed sex."

Cathryn's throat closed and she stared at him helplessly. Was he so blind? Couldn't he see that every inch of her ached for him? But thank God that he didn't see, because if he knew how she felt she would never be able to control him...or herself. She wanted to be sure of him; she wanted to trust him before she became so deeply involved with him that she had no self-protection left, yet she felt pressured from all sides to throw caution to the winds. If she didn't claim him, Ricky would; if she didn't satisfy him sexually, someone else would.

He reined in his horse and leaned across to grasp her reins, stopping the gray. "Look," he said directly, his dark eyes unreadable in the shadow of his black hat. "I need sex. I'm a normal, healthy man. But I control my needs, they don't control me. I don't want Ricky. I want you. I'll wait...for a while."

Sudden fury gave her back her voice and she pushed his hand away from her reins. "And then what?" she spat. "Will you go roaming like a tomcat?"

He moved swiftly, his gloved hand darting out and catching her by the back of the neck. "I won't have to roam," he crooned on a dangerously silky note. "I know exactly where your bedroom is." She opened her mouth to yell at him and he leaned over, catching the hot words with his mouth as he brought her closer to him, the steely hand on her neck holding her just where he wanted her.

Cathryn shuddered with hot, soft reaction, her lips shaping themselves to the movement of his, tasting the coffee flavor of his mouth, as she allowed his tongue entrance. His free hand squeezed gently on her breasts, then began to trace a wandering path down her stomach. She was helpless to stop him, not even thinking of stopping him, her body waiting pliantly for his intimate touch. But his horse took exception to the situation and danced away from the gelding, forcing Rule to release her and secure his seat again. He quieted the stallion with a murmur, but his eyes seared her with dark fire. "Don't take too long making up your mind," he advised softly. "We're wasting a lot of time."

She watched in helpless confusion as he rode away from her, his tall body moving in perfect rhythm with the powerful horse. She didn't know what to do anymore. She thought of going back to the house, but the memory of how lost and miserable she had been the day before sent her riding after Rule. At least when she was with him she was able to look at him, to secretly savor the thrill she got whenever she saw him. The need she felt for him was so strong that it was almost an obsession, an illness. It had kept him constantly in her thoughts even though they were separated by years and hundreds of miles, and now that he was so close she was driven by the compulsion to watch him.

For the remainder of the week she rode by his side, taking every step he took, riding endless miles until she ached in every muscle and every bone. Yet a combination of pride and stubbornness kept her from either complaining or giving up. She was well aware that he knew the discomfort she suffered. Too often she caught a gleam of amusement in his dark eyes. But Cathryn wasn't a complainer, so she bore it all silently and every night took comfort from the bottle of liniment that had become a fixture on her nightstand. She could have remained at the house, but that had no attraction at all for her. Riding with Rule had its rewards, despite the physical punishment she was taking, because she had the delight of secretly feasting her eyes on him all day long.

In any case, she became absorbed in the grinding routine that was part of every day on the ranch. After her one trip to pick up supplies, Rule didn't suggest again that Cathryn run any errands for him. He rolled her out of bed every morning before dawn, and by the time the first gray light had appeared they were in the saddle. If he rode fence, she rode fence; if he moved horses from one pasture to another, so did she. Rule turned his hand to every chore on the ranch, disdaining nothing, and she realized more fully than ever before why he had the respect and uncomplaining obedience of every man who worked there.

She was astounded at his stamina. She did none of the physical work that he did, merely followed in his tracks, and by the end of the day she was so tired that she could scarcely stay in the saddle on the ride back to the house. But Rule's shoulders were as straight at the end of the day as they had been at the beginning, and she often saw the admiring, respectful looks that the men gave him. He wasn't a straw boss. He did everything he asked the men to do, and in addition he oversaw the completion of everything else. Lewis Stovall was his right-hand man, almost sullenly quiet, but so capable that often Rule had only to nod his head in a certain direction and Lewis knew exactly what he wanted. Remembering her accusing words when she had discovered that Lewis was the foreman, she felt ashamed; even with Lewis's help, Rule still did the work of two men.

The horses were Rule's special concern, though in no way did he neglect any other aspect of the ranch. The horses were treated with intense care. No injury, regardless of how slight, was allowed to go untreated. No illness was ignored, and anything that concerned their comfort was done without question. He often exercised the stallions himself and the spirited animals were better behaved with him than with the other men entrusted with their exercise.

Cathryn would sit on the fence and watch him with the stallions, almost dying with envy because she wanted to ride one of the beautiful animals so much, but Rule adamantly refused to let her near them. Though she sulked, she accepted his edict because she knew how valuable they were, and she admitted that if one of them decided not to obey her, she wasn't strong enough to force her will on him. The stallions were always kept carefully separated from each other and never exercised at the same time, not only to prevent fights but to keep them calm. A rival in the vicinity upset the blooded stallions even if things didn't progress to a fight.

Rule reminded her of his stallions; but he behaved himself scrupulously during those days, not even stealing a kiss, though she sometimes caught his gaze lingering on her lips or the thrust of her breasts against the cotton shirts she wore. Though she knew that he was waiting to hear her decision, she didn't even try to make up her mind during those days; she was having fun, and in addition to that she was so tired at the end of the day that she didn't feel like indulging in any soul searching. She was doing exactly what she had wanted: being with him, learning him. But Rule was far too complicated for only a few days to give her any insight into him.

The breeding pens were also off limits to her, another edict she didn't argue with. Though Ricky was apparently completely at ease there, for once Cathryn wasn't jealous of her. Even if Rule didn't care to protect Ricky, he did extend that care to Cathryn, and she was glad. She was too sensitive, too attuned to Rule's sensuality, to be comfortable with the actual breeding. So one day while Rule was occupied in the pens she returned to the house for a rare hour of relaxation. But after sitting for a few minutes feeling her aching muscles slowly unknot, she began to feel guilty for doing nothing while Rule was still working. Then the happy thought that she could relieve him of some of the paperwork occurred to her and she made herself comfortable in the study. After a rapid look though the stacks of correspondence and bills that littered the desk, she realized that he was surprisingly well organized. All of the bills were current. But then, how else would it be? Rule was efficient in everything he did. Only the past couple of days' worth of mail hadn't been opened, but he had been working late and hadn't had a chance to catch up on the paperwork. Satisfied with her choice of occupations, Cathryn sorted the mail into a stack that was addressed to Rule personally, and another stack of bills, which was gratifyingly small, proof that the ranch was on solid ground.

Swiftly she opened the bills and studied them: bills for grain; bills for fencing; utility bills; bills for the mountain of supplies that were needed to keep the ranch running; veterinary bills that seemed astronomical to her. Apprehensive again, she opened the ledger and pulled it to her, wondering if there would be enough to pay these bills and still have enough for the ranch hands' salaries. Her finger moved to the balance column and ran down it to the last figure.

Stunned, she stared at it for a full minute, unable to believe her eyes. Was the ranch doing that well? She had somehow gotten the impression that the ranch was solid but not rich, able to provide a good living but not a luxurious one. How could she reconcile that idea with the figure that stared her in the face, that figure written in Rule's bold, slashing hand? If all the profits were turned back into the operation, what accounted for this?

A sudden chill raced down her spine and she flipped through the bills again. Why hadn't she noticed the first time? Why hadn't she picked up on the hint that she had received in town? Every one of those bills was in Rule Jackson's name. Knowing what she would find, she hunted for the checkbook and instead found a ledger of checks, all of them bearing the name Rule Jackson, and beneath that the legend: Bar D Ranch.

All of that proved nothing, she told herself sternly. Of course his name was on the checks. He signed them, didn't he? Yet she got up and went in search of Monica, who had been trustee until Cathryn reached her twenty-fifth birthday, and whose name should have been on those checks.

"Oh, that," said Monica in a bored tone, waving her hand. "I signed control of the ranch over to Rule years ago. Why not? As he pointed out, he was just wasting time by having to come to me for decisions."

"You should have told me!" Cathryn said sharply.

"For what reason?" Monica demanded just as sharply. "You were going away to college, so you weren't going to be here anyway. If you were all that concerned, why did you wait until now to come home?"

Cathryn couldn't tell her that; instead she returned to the study and sat down heavily, trying to get it straight in her mind. So Rule had had direct control of the ranch and her money for all of these years. Why did that alarm her? She knew he hadn't cheated her. Every cent would be accounted for. She simply felt betrayed in some way that she hadn't yet figured out.

If Monica had signed control over to Rule before Cathryn had gone away to college, it had to have been during that summer when she was seventeen. She had decided to attend college at the last minute, torn between the agony of leaving her home and the almost uncontrollable fear she'd had of Rule. Having always considered that sexual scene by the river to be her fault, she had been afraid of her own body and the way it responded to him. But now...had he made love to her deliberately? He had already had control of the ranch, but he would have known that it was only a temporary control and could come to an abrupt halt when she came of age. The next logical move was to bring her under his control, too, to dominate her so completely that she would never try to wrest the ranch away from him.

She didn't want to think that. She felt sick, distrusting him so much when he had worked so hard. But, damn it, it wasn't just the ranch that she was concerned with! She had herself to think of! Was she letting herself fall for a man who saw her only as a means to an end, a way of finally making the ranch really, completely his? He knew her better than any other person on earth knew her. He knew that he could control her with his sensual magic. No wonder her demand that he stay away from her had rattled him so badly! She had really thrown his plans off!

Taking a deep breath, Cathryn tried to halt the wild thoughts that were circling madly in her mind. She couldn't be certain of that. She had to give him the benefit of the doubt, at least for now. If only she knew what went on in his head! If only he would talk to her, tell her if the ranch was more important to him than anything else. She would understand. Rule had gone through hell, and she couldn't blame him if the ranch had become a sanctuary that he wanted to cling to. The idea was incongruous in a way. He was so strong. Why would he need a sanctuary? But he wouldn't talk about what he had experienced, wouldn't let anyone else share that burden with him, so she really had no idea what he felt about the ranch or anything else.

She wasn't prepared to face him when the door opened suddenly, nor was she prepared for the black rage that swept over his face when he saw the ledger open on the desk. "What are you doing?" he snarled softly.

A calmness born out of a numbing certainty that her worst fears had been correct enabled her to stay in her chair and face him, and give her voice its even tone when she said, "I'm looking at the books. Do you have any objections?"

"I might, especially when you act like you've been trying to catch me cheating you. Do you want to hire an accountant to go over things to make certain I'm not finagling? You'll find that every penny is right where it should be, but go ahead." He paced around the side of the desk and stood looking down at her, his dark eyes hard. Glancing sideways, she saw that he was gripping his hat so tightly that his knuckles were white.

Abruptly she slammed the ledger shut and jumped to her feet, pain blooming inside her so acutely that she couldn't sit still any longer. Lifting her chin, she met his gaze head on. "I'm not worried that you've taken any money; I know better than that. I was just…surprised to find that everything is in your name. Monica isn't even a figurehead any longer, and hasn't been for years. Why wasn't I told? You'd think I'd be aware of what goes on with *my* ranch, or at least I should be."

"You should have been," he agreed. "But you weren't."

"What about now?" she challenged. "I'm involved now. Shouldn't all of this be changed over into my name? Or have you begun to believe all of the talk in town about 'Rule Jackson's spread'?"

"So change it!" he said violently, and a sudden sweep of his hand sent the ledger crashing to the floor. "It's your damned ranch and your damned money; do whatever you want with it! Just don't whine to me because I kept the place running while you never bothered to even ask how it was doing!"

"I'm not whining!" Cathryn yelled, shoving at the stack of bills and sending them fluttering to the floor. "I want to know why you never told me that Monica had signed control of the ranch over to you!"

"Maybe I don't have a reason! Maybe I just never thought of it! I've been working like a slave for years. I haven't had time to chase you down every time some little something came up. Do I have your permission to pay the hands, Mrs. Ashe? Will it be all right if I write a check to pay for the fencing, Mrs. Ashe?"

"Oh, go to hell! But before you do, tell me why there's so much money in the balance column when you've gone out of your way to make me think that there was no extra, that all the profits had been turned back into the ranch?"

One of his hands shot out, and he clamped it on her upper arm, holding her in a grip that would leave the imprint of his hand on her flesh. "Do you have any idea how much money it takes to run a stud?" he ground out. "Do you know what a good stallion costs? We've been breeding quarter horses, but we're branching out into Thoroughbreds and we need two more stallions, more brood mares. You can't charge them on your credit card, baby! It takes a hell of a lot of money on hand to— Hell!" he suddenly snarled. "Why should I explain anything to you? You're the boss, so you can do what you damned well please with it!"

"Maybe I will!" she yelled, wrenching her arm away from his punishing fingers. Despite her best efforts, tears glistened in the darkness of her eyes as she stared up at him for a moment; then she whirled and ran from the room before she could disgrace herself by really crying.

"Cat!" she heard him call as she closed the door, but she didn't return. She went upstairs to her room and carefully locked the door, then settled in the rocking chair with a spy thriller that she held in her hands but didn't—couldn't—read. She refused to give way to tears, though occasionally a lump formed in her throat and she had to struggle with herself. It was a waste of time to cry. She just had to accept things as they were.

Rule's violent reaction at finding her going through the books meant only one thing to her: He didn't want her to know how the ranch operated because he didn't want her to take over any of his authority. Despite his accusation she knew that he was bone-deep honest and she sensed that he didn't really think she suspected otherwise. No, he had attacked her because Rule was a good warrior and he knew the most important rule of combat: Be the first to strike.

So he was something of a fanatic about the ranch, she tried to reason with herself. At least she could depend on him to do the best thing, rather than look for a way to line his own pockets. It was just that she wanted him to think as much of her as he did of the ranch.... Not more, she wouldn't ask that, but simply to care for her and the ranch equally.

She had thought that they had grown closer during these last days; even when they had snapped at each other she had been aware of a bond between them and had known that he felt it too. It had been more than a sexual bond, at least for her. Though she never looked at him without remembering in some small corner of her brain the intensity of his lovemaking, she had felt close to him in other ways. So much for daydreams, she thought, letting the book drop to her lap. Hadn't she learned yet that Rule was a difficult man to read?

Though she was awake early the next morning, she didn't go downstairs to have breakfast with him and spend the day by his side. Instead she remained in bed until she knew that he had gone, then spent the day giving the upstairs a good cleaning, more to keep herself busy than because the house was in dire need of it. She avoided Rule at lunch, too, though she heard Ricky's laughter wafting upward and knew that her stepsister was keeping him company. So what if she was?

After Cathryn's own hurried lunch, eaten while standing in the kitchen after Rule had returned to the range, she returned to her cleaning. She had left Rule's room for last, and she was stunned when she entered it to find herself so moved by his lingering presence. His warm male scent seemed to fill the room. The pillow was still dented where his head had rested. His bed looked like a war had been fought on it. The clothing he had worn the day before had been dropped to the floor and probably kicked out of the way. Nothing else could have produced such a tangle of shirt, shorts, jeans and socks.

She had restored the room to order and was polishing the oak furniture when Ricky came in and draped herself across the bed. "The housewifely bit won't impress him," she drawled.

Cathryn shrugged, holding on to her temper with difficulty. Everything about Ricky rubbed her the wrong way lately. "I'm not trying to impress him. I'm cleaning house."

"Oh, come on. You've spent every day with him, showing him how interested you are in the ranch. It won't make any difference. He'll take whatever you offer him and use it for as long as he wants it, but he doesn't offer anything of himself in return. That's the voice of experience speaking," she added dryly.

Cathryn dropped the polishing cloth, her fingers clenching into fists. Whirling on Ricky, she said heatedly, "I'm getting tired of that line. I think you're plain poison jealous. He's never been your lover and you can't convince me that he has. I think you've tried your best to get him to go to bed with you and he's always turned you down flat, but now you've finally faced the fact that he never will be your lover and you can't stand the truth."

Ricky sat up, her face turning pale. Cathryn tensed herself for an assault, knowing that Ricky always flared up at the least hint of opposition; but instead the other woman looked at Cathryn for a long time, her entire body taut. Then slow tears welled in her eyes. "I've loved him for so long," she whispered. "Do you have any idea how I feel? I've waited for years, certain that he'd decide one day that it's me he really wants; then you show up to claim your own and it's just like he's slammed a door in my face. Damn you, you were gone for years! You wouldn't give him the time of day, but because you own this godforsaken ranch he's dropped me flat so he can chase after you."

"Make up your mind," Cathryn snapped. "Is he using me, or am I using him?"

"He's using you!" Ricky spat. "You're not my rival; you never have been, not even when he was making love to you on riverbanks. It's this ranch, this piece of land, that he loves! You're nothing to him, none of us are. I've tried to get you to ask him about it, but you're too much of a coward, aren't you? You're afraid of what he might tell you!"

Cathryn's lip curled. "I don't ask for statements of commitment unless the relationship is serious."

"And you're using him to let off steam?" Ricky sniped. "Does he know that?"

"I haven't used him for anything," denied Cathryn, looking around for something to throw, a holdover from childhood that she stifled with difficulty.

"I'll just bet you haven't!"

Only Ricky's departure, as abrupt as her entrance had been, saved Cathryn from a temper tantrum in the end. She stood in the middle of the floor, her breasts heaving as she tried to control her temper. She shouldn't let Ricky upset her like that, but she had a hair-trigger temper and Ricky had always known just how to set it off. She had obtained some measure of serenity while married to David, but since returning to Texas it seemed that it had all fled. These days she was reacting simply to the signals that she received from her brain, whether to love or to fight; all her control seemed to be gone.

She still didn't want to see Rule, so the phone call she had that afternoon from Wanda Wallace was very welcome, especially when Wanda cheerfully reminded her of the long-standing Saturday night dances. It was Saturday, and suddenly Cathryn wanted to go. "I've told everyone that you're coming," Wanda laughed, indulging in a bit of gentle blackmail. "All the old gang will be there, in dancing shape or not, so you can't let us down. It'll be fun. It's still informal, nothing fancier than a sundress at the most. We older ones tend to stay away from jeans now that our fannies are so much wider," she said wryly.

"It seems forever since I've been in a dress," sighed Cathryn. "You've talked me into it. I'll see you there."

"We'll save a seat for you," Wanda promised.

The thought of seeing her old classmates filled Cathryn with anticipation as she showered and applied her makeup, then brushed her dark-fire hair into a loose cloud that swirled around her shoulders. The sundress she chose was simple, with wide straps that were comfortable on her shoulders, and the flaring skirt emphasized the slenderness of her waist. She clasped a gold serpentine belt around her waist and slid graceful matching bracelets onto each wrist. Dainty sandals with only a small heel completed the outfit. She made a face at herself in the mirror. In that innocent white dress she looked like a teenager again.

She popped into the kitchen to inform Lorna of her destination and the cook nodded. "Do you good to socialize some. Why don't you pick one of those gardenia blossoms off the bush in front and put it behind your ear? I'm partial to gardenias," she said dreamily.

Wondering what past romance had been associated with gardenias, Cathryn obediently plucked one of the creamy white blossoms and held it to her nose for a moment to inhale the incredibly sweet scent. She anchored it behind her ear and returned to the kitchen to show Lorna the result, and the older woman indicated her approval. With Lorna's admonition to drive carefully following her, she went out to the station wagon and slid behind the wheel, glad that she had avoided catching even a glimpse of Rule all day long.

The dance had been held at the community center for as long as she could remember. It was a fairly large building, able to accommodate a crowd of dancers, enough tables and chairs for those who wished to sit, a live band on a raised stage, and a small refreshment center that sold soft drinks to the younger dancers and beer to the older ones. The teenagers had little chance of getting a beer because everyone knew everyone else, so they had no hope of lying about their ages. There already was a respectable crowd when Cathryn arrived and she had to park the station wagon at the far end of the lot, but even before she was able to reach the building she was being hailed by former classmates, and she finally entered at the center of a noisy, laughing group.

"Over here!" she heard Wanda call, and looked around until she saw her friend stretched on tiptoe and waving frantically. Cathryn waved back and made her way through the milling crowd until she reached Wanda's table, where she dropped thankfully into the chair that had been saved for her.

"Whew!" she laughed. "I must be older than I thought! Just getting through the crowd has tired me out."

"You don't look tired," a dark-haired man said admiringly, leaning across the table to her. "You still look like the charmer who broke my heart back in junior high."

Cathryn looked at him with intense concentration, trying to place him among her classmates and utterly failing. Then his lopsided smile fell into place in her memory and she said warmly, "Glenn Lacey! When did you come back to Texas?" His family had left Texas when she was still in junior high, so she had never thought to see him again.

"When I finished law school. I decided that Texas needed the benefit of my wisdom," he teased.

"Don't pay any attention to him," advised Rick Wallace, Wanda's husband. "All that education has addled his wits. Do you recognize everyone else?" he asked Cathryn.

"I think so," she said, looking around the table. Her special friend Kyle Vernon was there with his wife, Hilary, and she hugged both of them. She remembered again that it had been the fond prediction of both Ward Donahue and Paul Vernon that their children would get married to each other when they grew up, but the childhood friendship had remained friendship and neither of them had ever been romantically interested in the other. Pamela Bowing, a tall brunette who concealed a genius for mischief behind a languorous demeanor, had been Cathryn's best friend in high school, and they had an enthusiastic reunion. Pamela was with a man Cathryn didn't recognize, and he was introduced as Stuart McLendon, from Australia. He was visiting the area while he studied Texas ranching. That left Glenn Lacey as the only unattached male, which automatically paired him with Cathryn. She was happy enough with that arrangement, because she had liked him when they were younger and saw no reason now to change her opinion.

They tried to catch up on old gossip for a time, but the band was in full swing and they gave up the effort. Wanda grimaced at the whirling crowd. "Since the Texas swing has become popular it's gotten harder and harder to get the band to play nice, slow, dreamy numbers," she complained. "And before that, it was disco!"

"You're showing your age," Rick teased her. "We didn't dance nice, slow, dreamy numbers when we were in school."

"I wasn't the mother of two monsters when we were in school, either!" she retorted. But regardless of what she thought of the current style of dancing, she took his hand and led him onto the dance floor. Within minutes the table was empty, and Cathryn was naturally still paired with Glenn Lacey. He was tall enough that she felt comfortable dancing with him. His technique was smooth and easy to follow and he didn't bother with any fancy steps. He simply held her firmly, but not so closely that she would have protested, and they moved in time with the music.

"Are you back to stay?" he asked.

She looked up into his friendly blue eyes and smiled. "I

don't know yet," she said, not wanting to go into the whole story.

"Any reason why you shouldn't stay? The ranch is yours, isn't it?"

He seemed to be the only one who realized that, and the smile she flashed him reflected her appreciation. "It's just that I've been away for such a long time. I have a life and friends in Chicago now."

"I was away for a long time, too, but Texas was always home."

She shrugged. "I haven't decided yet. But I don't have any immediate plans to return to Chicago."

"That's good," he said easily. "I'd like to give you a chance to break my heart again, if you don't mind."

She threw back her head and laughed up at him. "That's a good line! When did I break your heart, anyway? You moved away before I was old enough to begin dating."

He considered that and finally said, "I think it began when I was twelve and you were about ten. You were a shy little thing with huge dark eyes, and you aroused my protective instincts. By the time you were twelve I was hooked for good. I never was able to get away from those big eyes of yours."

His eyes were twinkling as he told her of his youthful infatuation and they were able to laugh together, remembering the painful and awkward loves that everyone developed in adolescence.

"Wanda told me that you're a widow," he said gently a moment later.

She never failed to feel a twinge of grief at the thought of David, and her dark lashes swept down to cover the sadness in her eyes. "Yes. My husband died over two years ago. Have you married?"

"Yes, while I was still in college. It didn't last through law school. Nothing very traumatic," he said with his charmingly crooked smile. "It couldn't have been a lasting love because we just drifted apart and divorced without any of the bitter fights that seem almost mandatory. We had no children or property to fight over, so we just signed the papers, collected our clothing, and that was it."

"And no special friends since then?"

"A couple," he admitted. "Again, nothing lasting. I'm in no hurry. I'd like to get my practice established before I begin seriously looking for a wife, so it'll be another few years."

"But you definitely want a wife?" she asked, a little amazed at such an attitude. Most single men she knew, especially those who had been through a divorce, had definite ideas about avoiding marriage again and living life in the fast lane instead.

"Sure. I want a wife, kids, the whole bit. I'm domesticated," he admitted. "I'd probably take the plunge now if I met the woman who gave me that special zing, but so far I haven't found her."

Cathryn was relieved to find out that he hadn't felt that special zing with her, and the knowledge left her totally relaxed in his presence. He looked on her as a friend, not a romantic interest, which was exactly what she wanted. Because of that she danced several dances with him and returned to the table in desperate need of something cold to drink.

"I'll do the honors," said Kyle Vernon. "Any of you ladies want a beer?"

None of the women did, opting instead for soft drinks, and he pushed his way into the crowd. Despite the number of people there he returned in five minutes with a tray on which were crowded long-necked bottles of beer and the requested cans of cola. The time passed pleasantly as they talked and occasionally traded dance partners. Glenn asked Cathryn out to dinner for the following weekend and she accepted, certain that by then she would go crazy without the prospect of some time away from Rule's territory.

It was growing late and she was dancing with Glenn again, the crowd having thinned out because some people had started to leave, when she found herself staring straight across the room into Rule's dark eyes. He was standing well back, not talking with anyone, and she felt the heat of his gaze on her. Startled, she got the feeling that he had been standing there for some time, watching her as she danced with Glenn. His face wore that hard, expressionless mask. Casually she looked away from him and continued dancing. So he was here. So what? She had done nothing to feel guilty about.

Within fifteen minutes everyone was making preparations to call it a night. As she was saying good-night to her friends, she felt long fingers wrap themselves around her arm and she knew that touch, knew who held her arm before she turned to look at him.

"I need to beg a ride back to the ranch," he said softly. "One of the men came with me and he's borrowed my truck."

"Certainly," Cathryn agreed. What else could she do? She didn't doubt that he had loaned his pickup out, though she did wonder how long he'd had to hunt to find someone to loan it to. None of that really mattered, though. Within seconds she was walking down the long expanse of the parking lot with him by her side, his hand still warm on her elbow.

"I'll drive," he said, taking the keys from her hand as she started to unlock the door. Without protest she got in and slid over to the passenger side of the car.

He drove in silence, his hard-planed features revealing nothing in the dim lights glowing from the dash. Cathryn looked up at the thin sliver of moon in its last quarter now, and she remembered the full silvery light that had bathed the bed when he had made love to her. The memory ignited a slow-burning flame in her body and she moved in involuntary response. If only she wasn't so aware of him sitting beside her! She could smell the warm, excitingly delicious male scent of him, and she recalled in frustrating detail just how it felt to be clasped against him in the timeless movements of lovemaking.

"Stay away from Glenn Lacey."

The low, raspy growl startled her, tore her from her sensual dreams, and she stared at him. "What?" she demanded, though she knew that she had understood him perfectly.

"I said I don't want you going out with Glenn Lacey," he obliged her by explaining more fully. "Or any other man, for that matter. Don't think that just because I agreed to stay out of your bed I'll stand by and watch you let someone else into it."

"If I want to go out with him, I will!" she said defiantly. "Who do you think you are, talking to me as if I'm in the habit of jumping into bed with any man who asks me? We're not engaged, Rule Jackson, and you have no right to tell me who I can see."

She saw his jaw tighten, and he snapped, "You may not have my ring on your finger, but you're a fool if you think I'll pretend there's nothing between us. You're mine, Cathryn Donahue, and I don't let anyone trespass on what's mine."

CHAPTER 7

Cathryn was almost paralyzed by a confusing surge of mingled pleasure and rage. She was delighted that he might be jealous, but then her inevitable response to his arrogant manner overwhelmed her sense of pleasure and she lashed back at him. "You don't own me, and you never will!"

"Do you feel secure in that little dream world you've built?" he asked with silky menace, and the tone of his voice was a warning. She fell silent, and nothing more was said during the drive to the ranch.

Despite, or perhaps because of, the silence, the atmosphere between them became heavy with hostility and a growing sensual awareness. Just that afternoon she had thought herself so angry and disillusioned with him that he couldn't tempt her any longer but already she was discovering how deeply in error that assumption had been. She couldn't even glance at him now without being reminded of the moonlight on his face as he had made love to her, without tasting his mouth in memory or reliving the strong rhythm of his movements.

When he pulled the car up by the steps to the house, she was out of the vehicle before the tires had stopped rolling. She hurried up the steps and through the kitchen almost at a run, hearing the thudding of his bootheels echoing behind her as he followed. The house was dark, but she knew her home and moved swiftly through the darkness, wanting to reach the safety of her room and shut him out. But it was his home, too, and she was only halfway up the stairs when the force of his body knocked her off-balance and she was swept entirely off her feet by a hard arm that passed around her waist and lifted her like a child.

"Put me down!" she whispered, kicking backward in an effort to trip him as she disregarded their precarious position on the stairs. He grunted as she made painful contact with his shin, just above his boot top. Shifting his hold on her, he slid his other arm under her knees and lifted her up against his chest. She could see only the shadowy form of his face as it came closer and she demanded once more, "Rule! Put me down!" There was no answer, and when she tried to protest again he cut her off by clamping his mouth on hers in a hot, rough kiss that bruised her lips and set drums to thundering in her veins.

The darkness and his movements confused her, left her feeling disoriented as he removed his arm from beneath her knees and let her body slide downward against his, all the while keeping his hungry, bruising mouth fused to hers. Cathryn shivered as she felt the burgeoning proof of his virility brush against her; then his hand cupped her bottom and pulled her firmly in to him, branding her through the layers of their clothing with the heat and power of his desire.

It took a supreme effort of will, but she pulled her mouth away from his and protested in a fierce whisper, "Stop it! You promised! Monica—"

"Damn Monica," he growled, the sound rumbling up from deep in his chest. His hard hand cupped her chin and lifted it. "Damn Ricky, and damn everyone else. I'm not some tame gelding you can prance in front of without expecting to be taken up on what you're offering, and I'll be damned if I'll watch you waltz off with some other man."

"There's nothing like that between Glenn and me!" she almost yelled at him.

"And I'm going to make damned sure there never is," he said roughly.

Abruptly he reached out and snapped on the light, and Cathryn saw with astonishment that she was in her own bedroom. She had been so confused by the darkness that she had thought they were still in the hallway. Swiftly she stepped back from him, wondering uneasily if she could talk him out of his dangerous mood. He looked more than dangerous; with his eyes narrowed, his nostrils flared, he reminded her for all the world of one of those blooded stallions in the paddocks. He began unbuttoning his shirt with silent intent and she rushed into speech. "All right," she gave in shakily. "I won't see Glenn if that's what you want—"

"It's too late for that," he cut in with that soft, almost soundless tone that told her he meant business.

She had never seen a man undress so fast. He shed his clothing with a few economical movements and tossed the garments aside. If anything, he was even more menacing naked than he was clothed, and the sight of his hard, muscle-corded body stifled any further arguments in her throat. She put out a slim, useless hand to hold him off and he caught it, turning it palm up and bringing it to his mouth. His lips seared her skin; his tongue danced an ancient message against her sensitive palm. Then he pressed her hand to his hair-roughened chest. Cathryn moaned at the heady sensations aroused by touching him, unaware that she had even made the sound. Already the rising heat of desire was making her forget that she hadn't wanted this to happen again. He was so beautiful, so dangerous. She wanted to stroke the panther just one more time, feel his sleek muscles flex under her fingertips. She moved closer and put her other hand on his chest, spreading her fingers out and flexing them against his hard, warm flesh. His chest was rising and falling with increasing speed as his breath began to race out of his lungs, and his heart was thudding wildly against her palm, slamming against the strong rib cage that protected it.

"Yes," he moaned. "Yes. Touch me."

It was a sensually loaded invitation that she would never be able to resist. She sought out his small, flat male nipples with her sensitive fingertips and teased the tiny points of flesh into rigidity. He made a sound deep in his throat that was half purr, half snarl, and reached behind her to find the zipper of her dress. In half a minute she stood before him wearing only the bracelets on her wrists and the blossom in her hair. The sight of her soft, womanly body broke his control and he snatched her hard against him, crushing the soft fullness of her breasts to the hard planes of his body. His lips were on hers and his tongue penetrated her mouth and conquered a foe that didn't resist. The panther was no longer lying down to be stroked.

"Gardenias are my favorite," he muttered, releasing her long enough to pluck the flower from her hair. Her breasts were still pressed against him by the hard circle of his right arm around her, and he tucked the creamy flower into her cleavage, trapping it between their bodies. Then he was moving her backward and the bed touched the back of her knees; she fell onto it and he fell with her, never letting their bodies separate.

"I want you so much," he said on a groan, sliding down to bury his face in the sweet valley of her breasts, laden with the rich perfume of the crushed gardenia. His lips and tongue roamed over the rich mounds, sucking the pink nipples into taut buds; and wild shivers began to race through her body. Why did it have to be like this with him? Not even David had been able to persuade her to make love with him before their marriage, but with Rule it seemed that she had no will, no morals. She was his for the taking, whenever he wanted. The bitter self-knowledge in no way diluted the strength of her response to him. Heavy need was throbbing in her loins, making her entire body ache with an intimate pain that only he could assuage. She arched against him and he left her breasts to come fully over her, his hairy legs rough and heavy on the graceful length of hers. "Say you want me," he demanded harshly.

There was no use in denying it when her own body would make her a liar. Cathryn ran her palms down his muscled sides and felt his entire body tense with desire. "I want you," she said freely. "But this doesn't solve anything!"

"On the contrary, it solves a major problem of mine," he said, nudging her thighs apart. He fit himself solidly against her and Cathryn closed her eyes on a spiral of delight. Instantly he was shaking her, making her open her eyes again. "Look at me," he directed from between clenched teeth. "Don't close your eyes when I'm making love to you! Look at me; watch my face while I enter you."

It was so erotic that she couldn't bear it. She slowly took him inside her while she watched his face mirror the same sensations that were swamping her. His eyes were dilated; waves almost of pain washed again and again over his features as he initiated the rhythm of lovemaking. Tears flooded her eyes as she felt herself arching helplessly closer to fulfillment. "Stop it!" she wept, begging, digging her nails into his side. "Rule, please!"

"I'm trying to please you. Cat—oh, *Cat!*"

She heard the cry that was wrenched out of him, then it was all too much. Dying had to be like that, the utter loss of self, the gathering intensity, then the explosion of senses, followed by a drifting, a growing weaker, a falling away from reality. It was the most frightening experience of her life, yet she embraced it completely and let herself be conquered by it. She was aware, on the fringes of perception, of the demands his powerful body was making on hers as he also reached completion, and for a moment that physical perception was her only link with consciousness. Her full range of senses returned gradually and she opened her eyes to find him above her, stroking her hair away from her face while he softly crooned to her and enticed her back to him. His entire body was glistening with perspiration, his dark hair plastered to his skull, his dark eyes gleaming. He was the quintessential male, primal and triumphant in his renewed victory over the mystery of woman.

But his first words were tenderly concerned. "Are you all right?" he asked, disentangling their bodies and cradling her close to his side.

She wanted to shout that she couldn't possibly be all right, but instead she nodded and turned her face into the damp hollow of his shoulder, still too stricken to attempt speech. What could she tell him, anyway? That she needed him with a need that went beyond rational thought, beyond the control of a will that had held her proudly upright even during her husband's death? She couldn't understand it herself, so how could she explain it to him?

His palm gently cupped her chin and tilted it up. She didn't open her eyes, but she felt the kiss that he placed on her soft, bruised lips with a touch as delicate as a whisper. Then he wrapped his arms around her and settled her more closely against him, his breath stirring the hair at her temple. "Go to sleep," he ordered in a soft growl.

She did, exhausted by the night of dancing, the late hour, and his steamy, demanding lovemaking. It felt so perfect to sleep in his arms, as if she belonged there.

Yet she woke with the certain knowledge that something was wrong. She was no longer in his arms, though her hand was lying on his chest, the fingers buried in the curly hair that decorated it. The room was dark, the moon no longer lending its meager light. There were no unusual sounds, nothing was stirring, yet something had awakened her. What?

Then, as she came more fully awake, Cathryn became aware of the unnatural rigidity of Rule's body beneath her hand, the fast and shallow breathing that made his chest rise and fall. She could feel the perspiration forming on his skin.

Alarmed, she started to shake him, wanting to make certain that he was all right, but before she could move he bolted upright in the bed, silently, not a sound coming from him. His right hand was clenched around the sheet. With obvious effort, every movement as slow as death, he opened his hand and released the sheet. A curiously soft sigh eased from his lungs; then he swung his long legs off the bed and got up, moving to the window, where he stood staring out at the night-darkened land.

Cathryn sat up in the bed. "Rule?" she asked in a puzzled voice.

He didn't answer, though she thought she saw the outline of his body stiffen at the sound of her voice. She remembered what Ricky had said, that he sometimes had nightmares and would spend the night walking around the ranch. Had this been a nightmare? What sort of dream was it, that he suffered it in such taut silence?

"Rule," she said again, getting out of bed and going to him. He was stiff and silent as she put her arms around him and rested her cheek on his broad back. "Did you have a dream?"

"Yes." His voice was guttural, wrenched out of him.

"What happened?" He didn't answer, and she prodded, "Was it about Vietnam?"

For a long moment he didn't answer; then another "Yes" was forced past his stiff lips.

She wanted him to tell her about it, but as the silence lengthened she realized that he wouldn't. He had never talked about

Vietnam, never told anyone what had happened that had sent him back to Texas as wild and dangerous as a wounded animal. Suddenly it was important to her that he tell her what had haunted him in his dreams; she wanted to be important to *him,* wanted him to trust her and let her share the burden that still rode his shoulders.

She moved around to face him, sliding her body between him and the window. Her hands moved in a soft caress on his hard form, giving him the comfort of her touch. "Tell me," she demanded in a whisper.

If anything, he went even stiffer. "No," he said harshly.

"Yes!" she insisted. "Rule, listen to me! You've never talked about it, never tried to put it in perspective. You've kept it all locked inside, and it can't be that way, don't you see? You're letting it eat you alive—"

"I don't need an amateur psychiatrist," he snapped, thrusting her away from him.

"Don't you? Look at how hostile—"

"God damn you," he snarled thickly. "What do you know about hostility? What do you know about perspective? I learned one thing pretty damned fast: there's no perspective about death. The dead don't care one way or the other. It's the ones who are left alive who have to worry about it. They want it clean. They don't want to be blown into a thousand bloody little pieces in somebody else's face. They don't want to be burned alive. They don't want to be tortured until they're not even human anymore. But do you know something, honey? You're just as dead from one neat bullet as you are if you're scattered over a solid acre. That's perspective."

His raw anger, the bitterness in his voice, slammed into her like a body blow. Involuntarily she reached out for him again, but he stepped back, evading her touch as if he couldn't bear the closeness of another human being. Her hands fell uselessly to her sides. "If you would talk about it…" she began.

"No. Never. Listen to me," he growled. "What I saw, what I heard, what I went though will never go any further. It stops with me. I'm handling it; maybe not the way the text-book reads, but I'm handling it my way. It took years before I could sleep an entire night without waking up with my guts in knots, my throat tight with other people's screams. I can do it now, the dreams only come every so often, but I'm not about to lay this on someone else."

"There are organizations of veterans—"

"I know, but I've always been a lone wolf, and I'm already over the worst. I can look at a tree now; I can let someone walk up to my back. It's finished, Cat. I don't wallow in it."

"It's not finished if it still bothers you," she said quietly.

He drew a ragged breath. "I got out of it alive. Don't ask for anything else." A soundless laugh moved his chest as he walked even farther away. "And I didn't even ask for that. At first…God, at first I prayed every night, every morning. Just get me out alive, let me get through this alive, don't let me be blown into obscene little red pieces of meat. Then, after about six months, the prayer changed. Every morning I prayed that I wouldn't make it out alive. I didn't want to come back. No human being should have to live through that and still face the sunrise every morning. I wanted to die. I tried to. I took chances that no sane person would take, but I made it anyway. One day I was in the jungle, and the next I was in Honolulu, and those damned fools were walking under trees, letting people walk up to them, smiling and laughing and staring at me, some of them, like I was some kind of freak. Oh, hell…" he finished, his voice sliding away.

Cathryn felt something on her face and brushed the back of her hand over her cheek, surprised to feel dampness. Tears?

She had been too young to understand the horror of Vietnam while it was happening; but she had read about it since, had seen pictures, and she could remember Rule's face the day her father had brought him to the ranch. Rule's battered, bitter face, the silence of him, was her picture of Vietnam.

But while she had only a picture, he had the reality of his memories and his dreams.

A low cry came from her as she rushed across the floor to him, wrapping her arms about him so tightly that he couldn't shove her away again. He didn't try to; he enclosed her in the tempered steel of his embrace, bending his head down to rest it on hers. He felt the liquid grief on her face as it touched his chest, and he dried her cheeks with the palm of his hand. "Don't cry for me," he muttered, kissing her hard, almost brutally. "Give me comfort, not pity."

"What do you want?" she whimpered.

"This." He lifted her high, kissing her again and again, stealing her breath until she was dizzy and clung to him with her arms and legs, afraid that she would fall if he relaxed his hold. But he didn't let her fall. He lowered her slowly, slithering her body along his torso, and she cried out as she felt his entry.

"I want this," he said harshly, his breath rasping in and out of his lungs. "I want to bury myself in you. I want you to go wild beneath me when I'm making love to you, and you do, don't you? Tell me, Cat. Tell me you go wild."

She buried her face in his neck, sobbing with the fire he had ignited with his powerful, driving loins. "Yes," she moaned, giving in to any demand he made.

The hot rush of delirium swept over them simultaneously. He went down with her to the floor and she didn't even notice the hardness or her discomfort as he surged against her. At last the sweet, hot pulsing of his body had stopped and he lifted her onto the bed, once again cradling her soft body to him until she slept.

When she awoke again it was a sunny morning and Rule still lay beside her, a faint smile gentling the hard contours of his face as he watched her as she stretched and realized that she wasn't alone. She looked at him and gave him a sleepy smile. Then he drew her to him with one hand on her waist and without a word made love to her again.

When it was over he lifted his head and dared her in a velvet rasp, "Marry me."

Cathryn was so stunned that she could only gape at him.

A rueful smile curved his hard, chiseled lips, but he repeated the words. "Marry me. Why do you look so surprised? I've planned to marry you since you were...oh, fifteen or so. Since the day you slapped my face and got your little fanny tanned for your effort, as a matter of fact."

Suddenly terrified of this new demand he was making on her, Cathryn sat up away from his arms and said in a shaking voice, "I can't even decide if I should stay here or not, and now you want me to marry you. How can I decide about that?"

"That part's simple," he assured her, drawing her down beside him again. "Don't think about it; don't worry about it. Just do it. We may fight every inch of the way to bed every night, but once we get there it will be worth every bruise and scratch. I can promise you that you'll never crawl into a cold bed at night."

Cathryn was shaken to the core. Oh, God, she wanted him so much! But despite the drugging intensity of his lovemaking, he would share nothing of himself with her except for the physical part of a relationship. She had all but begged him to trust her and he had shoved her away.

Shudders of reaction began racing through her. "No!" she cried wildly, afraid most of all of the powerful temptation to blindly do as he said and marry him despite everything. She wanted him so much that it was terrifying, but he hadn't said that he loved her, only that he had planned to marry her. He had planned everything. He made no secret of his devotion to the ranch. He was obsessed with it, perhaps to the point that he would marry simply to keep it under his domination. Last night she had seen part of what Vietnam had done to him and she understood more fully why he clung so fiercely to this ranch. Hot tears suddenly scalded her face and she almost screamed, "I can't! I can't even think when you're around! You promised you wouldn't touch me, but you broke your word! I'm going back to Chicago. I'm leaving today. I can't stand being pressured like this!"

She had never been more miserable, and she was made more so by his tight-lipped silence as he dressed and left her room. Cathryn lay rigidly, occasionally wiping at the tears that managed to escape despite her desperate efforts at control. She ached in both body and mind, battered by the fierce, untamed need for him that she could neither control nor understand. She had wanted him to leave her alone, but now she lay feeling as if part of her had been torn away. She had to grind her teeth together in concentration to prevent herself from creeping down the hall to his room and crawling into the strength of his embrace. She *had* to leave. If she didn't get away from his influence, he would use her weakness for him as a means of binding her to him permanently, and she would never know if he wanted her for herself or for the ranch.

It was obvious that Rule desired her physically. Why not? She wasn't a raving beauty, but she was passable in most areas and many people found her leggy grace and exotic coloring attractive. Rule was a normal male with all the normal male needs and responses, so there was no reason why he shouldn't want her. It was when she delved below the surface that she became overwhelmed by doubts and possibilities, none of them pleasant.

As well as she knew Rule, as intimate as she was with every line of his body and nuance of his expression and voice, she was violently aware that he kept a great deal of himself locked away. He was a man who had lived through hell and emerged from the fires with nothing of value left, no illusions or dreams to buffer him from the stark reality of what he had experienced; and he had returned "home" to find that in fact he had no home, that emotionally he had been cast adrift. The hand that Ward Donahue had extended to him had literally saved his life, and from that moment he had poured his devotion into the ranch that had sheltered him and allowed him to rebuild the blasted ruin of his life.

She could marry him, yes, but she would never know if he had married her for love of herself or for love of the ranch that came with her. She was a package deal, and for the first time in her life she wished that the ranch weren't hers. Leaving wouldn't solve the problem for her, but it would give her the opportunity to decide in a rational way whether she could marry Rule and live with him in any sort of serenity, able to accept that she would never know for certain. She couldn't be rational around Rule; he reduced her to the most basic responses.

It was an old problem, one that heiresses were traditionally troubled with: Did he want her or her possessions? In this case it wasn't a question of money but of security and dark emotions buried so deep in Rule's subconscious that perhaps even he wasn't aware of his motivation.

Cathryn finally got out of bed and listlessly began packing. She had barely begun when the door opened and Rule stood there.

He was dressed in fresh clothing, his expression blank, but

lines of weariness scored his face. He said evenly, "Come riding with me."

She looked away. "I have to pack—"

"Please," he interrupted, and she quivered at hearing that unaccustomed word from him. "Come riding with me this one last time," he coaxed. "If I can't convince you to stay, then I'll take you to wherever you want to go to catch a flight out of Texas."

She sighed, rubbing her forehead in an agitated gesture. Why couldn't she just make a clean break? She had to be the world's biggest glutton for punishment. "All right," she gave in. "Let me get dressed."

For a moment he looked disinclined to leave, his dark eyes telling her that that was a silly thing to say to a man who had made love to her as he had the night before. But then he nodded and closed the door. With her senses acutely aware of him, she felt his presence and knew that he was leaning against the wall outside her room. Quickly she dressed and brushed the worst of the tangles from her hair. When she opened the door, he straightened and extended his hand to her, then let it drop before she could decide whether to take it or not.

They walked in silence to the stables, where they saddled the horses. The early morning was pleasantly cool and the horses were full of energy, impatient with the slow walk that the firm hands on the reins held them to. After several minutes of silence Cathryn kneed her horse closer to Rule's and said abruptly, "What did you want to talk about?"

His eyes were shadowed by the battered black hat that he habitually wore low as protection against the fierce Texas sun, and she could read nothing in the portion of his face that was exposed to her gaze. "Not now," he refused. "Let's just ride and look at the land."

She was content enough to do that, loving the well-tended

look of the pastures, and aching inside at the thought of leaving all of this again. The fencing was sturdy and in good repair; all of the outbuildings were clean and freshly painted. Rule's stewardship had been nothing short of outstanding. Even when her resentment had been at its hottest she had never doubted his feelings for the land. She had acknowledged that even in the depths of adolescent confusion.

They were away from the paddocks and barns now, and crossing a pasture. Rule reined in his horse and nodded in the direction of the ranch buildings. "I've been holding this place for you," he said harshly. "Waiting for you to come back to it. I can't believe you don't want it."

She swallowed a flash of anger and cried indignantly, "Not want it! How can you think that? I love this place; it's my home."

"Then live here; make it your home."

"I've always wanted to do that," she said, bitterness lacing her tone. "It's just that…oh, damn you, Rule, you must know that you're the reason I've stayed away!"

His mouth twisted as her bitterness was reflected back at her. "Why? Do you believe everything that was said about me when I came back from Nam?"

"Of course not!" she denied hotly. "Nobody does!"

"Some did. I have a vivid recollection of several people trying their level best to make me pay in blood for every-thing they thought I'd done." His face was stony, cold, as he brought one of his black memories up into the fresh and sunny morning.

Cathryn shuddered and reached out to grasp his muscu-lar forearm, bared by the rolled-up sleeve of his denim work shirt. "It was never anything like that, believe me! I…at the time, I resented you so much that I couldn't think straight."

"Do you still resent me?" he demanded.

"No." The confession was made in a low voice; she looked at him with troubled, doubtful eyes. Somehow she couldn't just tell him that she was afraid that he wanted the ranch more than he wanted her. She knew that if she exposed her doubts to him, he would be able to talk her out of them using her weakness for him to railroad her into doing whatever he wanted. She didn't just want him physically. She wanted his emotional commitment, too.

"Will you reconsider?" he rasped. "Will you think about staying?"

She had to force herself to look away, to keep him from seeing the longing in her eyes. If only she *could* stay! If only she could be content with what he was offering her, what she suspected was all he was capable of offering to any woman. But she wanted so much more than that, and she was afraid that she would destroy herself if she tried to compromise on that. "No," she whispered.

He danced Redman around to face her and closed his gloved hand over her reins. His dark face was taut with frustration, his jaw set in a grim line. "Okay, so you leave. What if you're pregnant? What then? Are you going to insist on handling that on your own? Will you even tell me if I'm going to be a father, or will you just get rid of my baby and pretend that it never existed? When will you know?" he said fiercely.

The words, the idea, stunned her almost as deeply as his unexpected proposal of marriage had done a few hours before. Helplessly she stared at him.

One corner of his mouth curled upward in a smile that was a travesty of amusement. "Don't look so surprised," he taunted. "You're old enough to know how it happens, and neither of us did anything to prevent it."

Cathryn closed her eyes, shaken by the sweetness she felt at the thought of having his child. Against all common sense, for a moment she prayed with wild longing that it was so, that she was already harboring his child. A tiny, otherworldly smile touched her lips and he cursed between clenched teeth, his gloved hand moving up to grip the nape of her neck.

"Get that look off your face!" he growled. "Unless you want to be on the ground with me, because right now I want you—"

He broke off and Cathryn opened her eyes, devouring the sight of him, unable to control her expression. A muscle flexed in his cheek as he repeated, "When? When will you know?"

Silently she counted, then said, "In a week or so."

"And if you are? What will you do?"

Cathryn swallowed, facing the inevitable. She really had no option. She wasn't a woman who could force illegitimacy on a child when the father was more than willing to marry her. A pregnancy would settle everything except her own doubts. She whispered, "I won't keep it from you if...if I am."

He took his hat off and ran his hand through his thick dark hair. Jamming the hat back on his head, he said harshly, "I've sweated it out before, wondering if I had made you pregnant. I guess I can do it again. At least this time you're not just a kid yourself."

She swallowed again, inexplicably moved to learn that he hadn't been so unaffected by that day so long ago. She started to speak, though she had no idea what she was going to say, but Rule kneed his horse away from her. "I have work to do," he muttered. "Let me know when you decide what time you're leaving. I'll have the plane ready to go."

She watched as he rode away from her; then she turned her horse's head and walked it slowly back to the stables. Their talk had accomplished exactly nothing, except to make her aware of the possible consequences of their nights together.

After returning to the house and picking at her breakfast,

she called the airline in Houston and made reservations for the following day, then made a stab at packing. She hadn't much to pack, really. Most of her clothing was still in Chicago. She had been making do with the old clothes that she had left at the ranch.

The hours dragged; she could scarcely wait until lunch, when she would be able to see Rule again, even if she had forbidden herself the joy of having him. She went downstairs and puttered around, helping Lorna put the meal together, looking constantly out the window.

A horse was galloped into the yard and the rider flung himself off. Cathryn could hear muffled shouts and sensed his urgency, but she couldn't hear what he was saying. She and Lorna exchanged worried glances and both stepped to the back door. "What is it?" Cathryn called as Lewis's tall, lean form ran from the stables to the pickup. "What's wrong?"

He turned, his hard face drawn. "Rule's horse went down with him," he called tersely. "He's hurt."

The words punched her in the stomach and she reeled backward, then forced herself upright. On shaking legs she ran to the pickup, where a man had placed one of the mattresses from the bunkhouse in the bed of the truck, and she clambered into the cab beside Lewis. He shot a look at her utterly white face and said nothing, instead slamming the gearshift through its pattern as he raced the truck across the pastures. It seemed that they spent an eternity bouncing in the dust before they reached a small knot of men grouped anxiously around the prone figure on the ground.

Cathryn was out of the truck before it had stopped, sliding to her knees beside him and kicking a fine spray of dust over him. A sickening panic seized her as she saw his closed eyes and pale face. "Rule!" she cried, touching his cheek and not getting a response.

Lewis knelt beside her as her shaking fingers tore at the buttons of Rule's shirt. It wasn't until she slid her hand inside and felt the reassuring thud of his heartbeat that she let out the breath she had been holding and raised frantic eyes to Lewis. Lewis was running his hands over Rule's body, pausing when he reached a point about halfway between knee and ankle on his left leg. "His leg's broken," he muttered.

Rule drew in a shuddering breath and his dark lashes fluttered open. Quickly Cathryn bent over him. "Rule...darling, do you understand me?" she asked, seeing the unfocused look in his eyes.

"Yes," he muttered. "Redman?"

She swiveled her head around to look at the horse. He was standing on all four legs and she couldn't see any serious swelling. "I think he's okay. He's definitely in better shape than you are. Your left leg is broken."

"I know. I felt it snap." He gave her a weak smile. "I took quite a knock on the head, too."

Once again Cathryn raised her worried eyes to meet Lewis's. A knock on the head meant a possible concussion, and coupling that knowledge with the length of time Rule had been unconscious, the possibility became a probability. Despite his rational answers, the quicker he was taken to a hospital, the better. There was also the horrifying thought of neck or back injuries. She would have given anything to be able to take the pain herself if he would be spared, and in that moment she admitted beyond doubt that she loved him. It wasn't just desire that she felt for him; she loved him. Why else would she have been so upset that he might have made love to someone else? Why else be so jealous of his kisses? Why else feel so hopeful that he had made her pregnant? She had loved him for a long time, long before she had been mature enough to recognize it for what it was.

The men were moving quickly, efficiently, and she was gently crowded away from Rule. They lifted him gently onto a blanket that had been spread on the ground beside him. She heard a stifled cry of pain and bit down hard on her lower lip, bringing tiny dots of blood to the surface. Lewis said, "You must be getting clumsy, boss, falling off a horse like that," which brought a tight grin to Rule's face. The grin faded abruptly when he was lifted, the blanket serving as a stretcher. From between clenched teeth he spat words that Cathryn had heard separately, but never together and with such inventiveness as Rule was using. Sweat was beaded on his face by the time he was placed on the mattress in the back of the truck. Cathryn and Lewis climbed in back with him and Cathryn automatically wiped his face.

"Take it easy on the ride back," Lewis instructed the man who was doing the driving now, and the man nodded his understanding.

Even when taken at a slow pace, every bump in the ground made Rule's hands clench into fists, and his face took on a grayish tinge. He brought his hands up and clenched them around his head as if he could buffer it from the swaying of the pickup. Cathryn hovered over him anxiously, suffering for him with every lurch of the truck, but there was nothing she could do.

Lewis met her eyes across Rule's prone form. "San Antone is closer than Houston," he said quietly. "We'll take him there."

When they reached the ranch two seats were quickly removed from the plane and Rule was placed, mattress and all, in the vacated space. His eyelids were drooping and Cathryn cupped his face in her hands. "Darling, you can't go to sleep," she said softly. "Open your eyes and look at me. You can't go to sleep."

Obediently he looked at her, his eyes dazed as he concentrated on what she said with heart-wrenching intensity. A half smile touched his pale lips. "Look at me," he whispered, and she remembered his lovemaking. Was he remembering, too?

"I'll be all right," he assured her drowsily. "It's not that bad. I had a lot worse than this in Nam."

The doctor at the hospital in San Antonio agreed. Though Rule did have a concussion and would be kept under observation at least overnight, his condition was in no way severe enough to indicate a need for surgery. Except for the lump on his head and his broken leg, they could find no other injuries but various bruises. After the strain of crouching beside him during the flight and trying to keep him awake, finding out that he would be all right had the same effect on Cathryn that bad news would have had: she turned her head into Lewis's chest and burst into tears.

Instantly his arms went around her and he hugged her tightly. "Why cry now?" he sputtered with relieved laughter.

"Because I can't help it," she sniffled.

The doctor laughed and patted her shoulder. "Cry all you want," he said kindly. "He'll be fine, I promise. You can take him home in a day or so, and the headache from that concussion should keep him in bed long enough for that leg to get a good start on healing."

"May we see him now?" asked Cathryn, wiping her eyes. She wanted to see him for herself, to touch him and let him know that she and Lewis were still close by.

"Not yet. We've taken him downstairs to have his leg X-rayed and set. I'll let you know when we have him settled in a room."

She and Lewis waited in the visitors' lounge with cups of bitter coffee obtained from the vending machine in the corner. She was grateful for the presence of the man, stranger though he was. He had never once acted upset or out of control, though he had moved swiftly. If he had revealed any fear, Cathryn knew that she would have fallen apart.

Lewis sprawled back in the uncomfortable plastic chair, his long, booted legs outstretched and reminding her of Rule. Her stomach rumbled and she said, "Rule must be starving. He didn't have any breakfast this morning."

"No, he won't be hungry until after his system is over the shock," said Lewis. "But we're another matter. Let's find the cafeteria. We could both use a meal and a decent cup of coffee."

"But Rule—"

"Won't be going anywhere," insisted Lewis, taking her hand and urging her out of the chair. "We'll be back long before they're finished with him, anyway. I've had my share of broken bones, just like he has; I know how long it will take."

His prediction was correct. Though they lingered in the cafeteria it was almost an hour after they returned to the waiting room that a nurse approached them and gave them the welcome information that Rule was now in a room. They went to the proper floor and met the doctor in the corridor.

"It was a clean break. He'll be as good as new," he assured them. "I'm certain we don't have anything to worry about. He's too ill-tempered to be injured very badly." He looked at Lewis and shook his head in awe. "He's the toughest son of a—" With a quick glance at Cathryn he cut himself off short. "He refused any sort of anesthetic, even a local. Said he didn't like them."

"No," said Lewis blandly. "He doesn't."

Cathryn moved impatiently and the doctor smiled at her. "Do you want to see him now?" he asked in amusement.

"Yes, of course," said Cathryn quickly. She needed to get to Rule, to touch him and satisfy herself that he was really all right.

She wasn't certain what to expect. She was braced for bruises and bandages—something she didn't know if she could bear when Rule was the patient concerned. What she found when they opened the door was tousled dark hair, a face that managed to be both sleepy and annoyed, and a leg encased in a pristine cast that was supported by a sling rigged from a contraption stationed at the foot of the bed.

They had put him in a regulation hospital gown, but that state of affairs hadn't lasted long. The garment was in a tangled heap on the floor, and she knew that beneath the thin sheet there was only Rule. Despite herself, she began to laugh.

He began to turn his head with the utmost care, and behind her, Cathryn heard Lewis's stifled chuckle. Rule gave up trying to turn his head and instead only moved his eyes, which still caused him to wince noticeably. "Well, don't just stand there gloating," he growled at Cathryn. "Come hold my hand. I could use some sympathy."

Obediently she crossed to his bedside, and though she was still laughing she felt the hot sting of tears in her eyes. She took his hand in hers and lifted it to her lips for a quick kiss on the lean, powerful fingers. "You scared me half to death," she accused him, her voice both teasing and tearful. "And now you don't even look hurt, except for your leg. You just look grouchy!"

"It hasn't been a picnic," he told her feelingly. His hand tightened on hers, and he drew her even closer to the bed; but his glance shifted to Lewis. "Lew, how badly is Redman hurt?"

"Nothing serious," Lewis assured him. "He was walking okay. I'll keep an eye on him, watch for swelling."

Rule forgot himself and nodded, a lapse that he paid for immediately. He groaned aloud and put his hand on his head.

"Damn," he swore weakly. "I've got a hell of a headache. Didn't they leave an ice pack or something?"

Cathryn looked around and found the ice pack on the floor where it had evidently been flung along with the hospital gown. She picked it up and placed it on his forehead. He sighed with relief, then returned to Lewis.

"Go on back to the ranch," he instructed the foreman. "There's too much to be done before the sale for both of us to be gone, even for a day. The dun mare should come in tomorrow or the next day. Put her with Irish Gale."

Lewis listened attentively as Rule outlined what had to be done during the next two days. He asked a few brief questions; then he was gone before Cathryn could quite comprehend that she had been left behind. Rule hadn't released his grip on her hand in all that time. Now he turned his sleepy attention to her.

"You don't mind staying with me, do you?"

It hadn't occurred to her to leave, but asking her permission after she had already been stranded made her give him a wry look. "Would it have mattered if I did?"

His dark eyes grew even darker; then his jaw hardened. "No," he said flatly. "I need you here." He shifted on the bed and muttered a curse when his head throbbed. "This changes things. You can't leave the ranch now, Cat. With the sale coming up I need your help. There's too much for Lewis to handle on his own, and when it comes down to basics, it's your responsibility because it's your ranch. Besides, if you'll ever be safe from me, that time is now. I couldn't fight a kitten, let alone a full-grown Cat."

She couldn't even smile at his pun. He looked so unnaturally helpless that she wished she had never said anything. All thoughts of leaving the ranch had disappeared from her mind the minute she'd heard that Rule was hurt, but she didn't tell him that. She merely smoothed a damp strand of dark hair back from his forehead and said quietly, "Of course I'll stay. Did you really think I'd leave now?"

"I didn't know," he muttered. "I couldn't stop you if you wanted to go, but I hoped the ranch meant more to you than that."

It wasn't the ranch that held her, it was Rule; but his accident hadn't deprived her of her common sense, and she didn't tell him that, either. Instead she plucked the sheet a little higher on his torso and teased, "I have to stay, if only to protect your modesty."

He gave her a roguish look despite the pallor of his face and the not-quite-focused expression in his eyes. "You're too late to save my modesty. But if you'd like to protect my virtue, I could use some help in fighting off these fresh nurses."

"Does your virtue need protecting?" She felt almost giddy with the unusual pleasure of teasing him, of actually flirting. It was odd that he had to be flat on his back and unable to move before she felt easy enough with him to tease him, but then, she had always been wary of him. It just wasn't good sense to turn your back on a panther.

"Not at the moment," he admitted, his voice fading away. "Even the spirit isn't willing right now."

He slipped easily and swiftly into sleep and Cathryn tucked his hand under the sheet. The air-conditioner was on full blast and it felt cold in the room to her, so she lifted the sheet over his naked shoulders, then sat down in the chair by his bedside and drew her legs up under her.

"What now?" she wondered aloud, her eyes never leaving the hard profile, softened somewhat as he relaxed deeply into sleep. In one morning everything had changed. Instead of fleeing to safety she was sitting by his side, and she knew that nothing could induce her to leave. He was weak and injured and he hadn't been lying when he had said that he would need her at the ranch during the coming weeks. The horse sale alone involved a great deal of work, and regardless of how competent Lewis was, he wasn't a superman. He couldn't be everywhere at once. That took care of any logical arguments she had. On an emotional level she admitted that she wouldn't leave Rule now even if there were no need for her to stay at all.

Rather than suddenly falling in love with him, she had awakened to the realization that she had loved him for a long time. She had loved David, too, with a very real love, but it had been a shallow emotion compared to the intensity of her feelings for Rule. It was so intense that when she was younger it had frightened her and she had fled from it. It had destroyed her control and her self-confidence, prevented her from accepting its existence. She was still frightened of the furious strength of her emotions. She had been running yet again because she wasn't certain that he returned even a fraction of that emotion. Watching him now, Cathryn made a painful decision, wondering wryly if she had reached a new level of maturity or if she were merely being foolhardy. At whatever risk, she was going to stay at the ranch. She loved him. It didn't make sense. It was against all the rules of human behavior that she should have loved him so young and so fiercely; but she had, and the feeling had endured.

Her glance swept blindly around the small, dim room and settled on a black object so familiar that it took her breath. How had his hat gotten here? She couldn't remember its being on the plane, but it must have been, because here it was. Had Lewis brought it? Or had Rule unconsciously clutched it in his hand? It didn't really matter, though she gave a wobbly smile at the thought.

Rule's hats were disaster areas. He was rougher on his headgear than any man she had ever seen. She had no idea what he did to his hats to get them in such shape, though she had sometimes suspected him of stomping on them. Whenever he was forced to buy a new one—something he did only reluctantly—within a week the new hat had taken on a battered, defeated shape, as if it had been run over by a herd of stampeding cattle. Tears blurred her eyes as she reached out for the dusty, shabby hat and hugged it to her breast.

She could be risking her entire future if she were wrong in staying, but today she had been forced to realize that Rule was as human and as vulnerable as any other man. An accident could easily take him from her at any time, and she would be left with nothing but the bitter thought, what if? He had asked her to marry him. She didn't know about that. She was far too upset and confused to plan anything concrete, but she was finished with running. It hadn't solved anything before. She had been haunted by thoughts of him, memories that had continually surfaced until his face had been a mental veil through which she had viewed all other men. She loved him. She had to face it squarely and accept whatever that love brought her, whether pain or pleasure. If she had learned nothing else from the eight years she had spent away from him, she had learned that she could never forget him.

CHAPTER 8

Rule was an angel. He was a perfect patient—obedient, un-complaining, as docile as a lamb…as long as Cathryn was by his side. She had had no idea what she was letting herself in for when she had promised to stay with him, until the first time a nurse came in to wake him up and check his pulse rate and blood pressure. Rule's eyes flared open wildly and he tried to sit up before the pain in his head made him sink back with a groan. "Cathryn?" he demanded hoarsely.

"I'm here," she reassured him quickly, jumping up from her chair to take his hand and twine her fingers through his.

He glared at her with dazed intensity. "Don't leave me."

"I won't leave you. I promised, remember?"

He sighed and relaxed, closing his eyes again. The nurse frowned and leaned closer, asking, "Mr. Jackson, do you know where you are?"

"I'm in a damned hospital," he snarled without opening his eyes.

The nurse, a chubby brunette with sharp brown eyes, smiled up at Cathryn in sympathy. "We'll be waking him every hour to make certain it's a normal sleep and that he hasn't gone into a coma. It's just a precaution, but it's always better to be safe."

"Don't talk about me like I'm not here," he grumbled.

Again the nurse's eyes met Cathryn's and she rolled them expressively. Cathryn squeezed Rule's fingers and admonished, "Behave yourself. Being grouchy won't help."

Still without opening his eyes, Rule carried her hand to his face and cuddled it against his cheek. "For you," he sighed. "But it's hard to smile when your head is exploding."

He was as good as his word; for Cathryn, he was so docile that it was ludicrous. The nurses, however, quickly learned that if they asked Cathryn to step aside, he refused to cooperate with anything they wanted to do. He demanded her constant presence, and after a few abortive attempts to manage him, so did the nurses. Cathryn knew that he was shamelessly using his injuries to keep her by his side, but rather than being exasperated, she was filled with an aching tenderness for him and she fetched for him and waited on him tirelessly.

It was late afternoon before her rumbling stomach reminded her that she was stranded without benefit of money, makeup, a change of clothes, or so much as a comb. Lewis had paid for the sandwich she'd left half-eaten that morning, and now she was in danger of starving to death, or so her stomach warned her. She carefully spoon-fed Rule the few bites of gelatin that he would eat, but he refused the split pea soup and when she tasted it she understood why. Even as hungry as she was, she couldn't eat it. Split pea soup had never been on her personal menu, and Rule shared the same lack of interest in it.

He wasn't so ill that he didn't notice what went on around him. After watching through slitted eyes as she tasted the soup and grimaced, he said gently, "Go on to the cafeteria and get something to eat. You must be hungry by now. I'll be good while you're gone."

"I'm starving," she admitted, but added wryly, "However, I don't think they'll feed me on the basis of my looks. I don't even have a comb with me, let alone money or fresh clothes. I never thought to get my purse. We just loaded you up and took off."

"Call Lewis and tell him what you need. He can bring it down tonight," he instructed.

"I couldn't ask him—"

"You *can* ask him. It's your ranch, isn't it?" he demanded testily. "No, I'll call him myself. In the meantime, get my wallet out of the upper drawer in the nightstand and go feed yourself."

She hesitated. Then, as he tried to push himself into an upright position, his face blanching even whiter when he moved, she snapped, "Okay, okay!" as she quickly eased him back onto the pillows. When she opened the drawer the wallet was right on top and she lifted it out, then stood for a moment looking at it regretfully. She hated to spend his money, though why it should bother her, she couldn't say.

"Go on," he ordered, and because she was so hungry she did.

While she was sitting in the cafeteria, slowly chewing on stale crackers and eating potato soup, she succumbed to the temptation to go through his wallet. Looking around guiltily as she did so, she first examined the few snapshots he carried. One was obviously of his mother, whom Cathryn couldn't remember at all, because she had died when Rule was a small boy. The faint resemblance in the shape of the brows and mouth was all that proclaimed their family ties. Another was of Rule's father, tall and lean, with a thin ten-year-old boy standing stiffly beside him, scowling at the camera. Cathryn smiled mistily, having seen that scowl many times on the adult man's face.

When she flipped the plastic holders again her mouth dropped open. While she had half hoped to find a snapshot of herself, the one that she found wasn't what she had expected. She had thought that perhaps he would carry the class portrait made in her senior year in high school, or even one of her college snapshots, but the picture that Rule carried with him was the one that had been made when she started first grade. She had been the youngest in her class, still in possession of all of her teeth, and those little teeth had been clamped down on her lower lip in painful intensity as she stared at the camera with huge, somber dark eyes. How had he gotten that snapshot? She had been at least twelve, perhaps thirteen, when he came to the ranch. She couldn't remember exactly. He could only have gotten this particular picture by going through the family album.

There was one other picture…of Ward Donahue. Cathryn stared at her father with blurred eyes, then returned to her prying. Rule carried only the basic means of identification: his driver's license, pilot's license and social security card. Except for that and forty-three dollars, his wallet was empty.

Tears stung her eyes. Four pictures and three cards were the extent of his personal papers. There was nothing tucked in any of the slots, no notes, nothing to indicate the nature of the man who kept himself so tightly locked inside. She suddenly knew that in his whole lifetime Rule Jackson had said "I need you" to only one person, and she had almost walked out on him anyway.

She drew a deep, shaky breath. She had nearly made the worst mistake of her life, and she was almost grateful for Rule's accident, because it had kept her from leaving and perhaps causing an irreparable rift between them. She loved him, and she would fight for his love.

She had decided not to say anything to him, but late that night the words tumbled out anyway. "How did you get that picture of me that you have in your wallet?"

A wry smile tugged at one corner of his mouth. "I wondered if you'd be able to resist the temptation. Obviously you weren't."

Though she flushed, Cathryn ignored his teasing. "Where did you get it?" she persisted.

"Out of a shoebox crammed full of old snapshots. There are several stored in the attic. Why?"

"I don't understand. Why that particular picture?"

"It reminds me of something," he finally said reluctantly.

"Such as?"

He carefully turned his head to look at her, his eyes as dark as midnight. "Are you sure you want to know?"

"Yes. It seems such an unlikely choice."

"Not really. It was the eyes that got me," he muttered. "You had that same serious, frightened expression in your eyes when you opened them and looked up at me after we had made love that first time, by the river."

The memory was like a lightning bolt, stunning her, as vivid in her mind as if it had just happened. He had lifted himself to his elbows, taking his weight from her young, delicate breasts, and he had said, "Cat," in a quietly demanding voice. Until that moment she had been wrapped in unreality, but at the sound of his voice she had become aware of many things: the searing heat of the sun overhead; the prickle of the grass beneath her bare body; the lazy drone of a bee as it searched for a tempting little wildflower; the musical calls of the birds in the tree nearby. She had also become aware of the enormity of the thing she had just done and whom she had done it with, the identity of the man who still held her in intimate possession. She had become aware of the unfamiliar aches in her body, while the echoes of pleasure still lingered. Terrified as she was of the tumult that had shaken her emotionally and physically, the budding desire to do it all over again had almost been more than she could bear. Her frightened eyes had flown open to stare at him, reflecting in their soft dark depths the uncertainty she had felt at having taken the first and most important step into womanhood.

She was unable to say anything now, and after a moment he

sighed wearily and closed his eyes. Anxiously her eyes wandered over his pale face. She had stood vigil beside David's bed for the long weeks before he died, and she was painfully reminded of those endless days. Not that there was any real comparison—Rule would assuredly recover—but the surface resemblance was enough to twist her heart. It had been awful to lose David. If anything happened to Rule, she would never be able to bear it.

It was a bad night. Cathryn never even bothered to put on the nightgown Lewis had brought her. Though she rented one of the cots that were available to people who stayed the night with the patients, she might as well have sat in the chair for all the sleep either she or Rule had that night. Between the discomfort of his leg and the nauseating headache he was suffering, Rule was restless, and it seemed that every time he managed to settle down and drift off to sleep, a nurse came in to wake him. By dawn his stated opinion of that practice had long since passed out of the realm of politeness and Cathryn would have been in a nervous fit if she hadn't been so weary.

Perhaps it was the pain he was enduring that caused him to dream of Vietnam, but over and over again he would awake from light, fretful sleep with his hands clenched and sweat pouring from his body. Cathryn didn't ask him any questions, merely soothed him with her presence, talking gently to him until he relaxed. She was exhausted, but she was by his side every time his eyes flared open, her love evident in every tender touch of her fingers. He might not have been able to put a name to it, but he responded to her touch, calming down whenever she was near. He was a sick man that night, and all the next day he ran a low fever. Though the nurses assured her that it wasn't unusual, she hovered over him anyway, keeping an ice pack on his forehead and continually cooling his torso with a damp cloth.

He slept the entire night through the second night, which was fortunate, because Cathryn had collapsed onto the cot and didn't stir all night long. It was doubtful that she would have heard him if he had called her.

On Tuesday morning she was both relieved and alarmed when the doctor released him to go home. They would be more comfortable at the ranch, but she wasn't at all certain that Rule was well enough to do without constant medical supervision. The doctor assured her kindly that he was doing well, but gave her careful instructions to keep Rule quiet for at least the remainder of the week. He was to stay strictly in bed until his headache and dizziness were completely gone, as it would be too risky for him to attempt walking with crutches while his balance wasn't what it should be.

The flight back to the ranch left him exhausted, and his face was alarmingly pale when, not without some difficulty, several of the ranch hands carried him upstairs and placed him on the bed. Despite their careful handling he was clutching his head in pain, and Lorna, who had met them with expressions of relief and anxiety warring on her face, left the room with tears in her eyes. The men filed out and left Cathryn to get him settled.

Gently she removed his shirt and jeans, the left leg of which had been cut off to enable him to get them on over the cast. After propping his leg on pillows and bracing it on either side with rolled-up blankets, she tucked the sheet around him. "Are you hungry?" she asked, worried that his appetite was still almost nonexistent. "Thirsty? Anything?"

He opened his eyes and looked around the room. Without answering her questions he muttered, "This isn't my room."

Cathryn had done a great deal of thinking about the situation at the house and had instructed Lorna to have Rule's things moved into the front guest room. His own bedroom was at the back corner of the house, overlooking the stables, and Cathryn didn't think he would be able to rest with all the activity in the yard. Not only that, the guest room was next to her own bedroom, making it more convenient for her if he called her; and it had a connecting bath, the only bedroom in the house with that luxury. Considering Rule's relative immobility, the location of the bathroom was a major factor. She only hoped he would cooperate.

Calmly she said, "No, it's the room next to mine. I wanted you close to me during the night. It also has a bathroom," she added.

He considered that, his eyelashes drooping to shield his eyes. "All right," he finally conceded. "I'm not hungry, but ask Lorna for some soup, or something like that. It'll make her feel better."

So he had noticed that Lorna was upset, despite his own condition. Cathryn didn't question Lorna's devotion to him. Who knew what secrets were hidden behind the cook's stoic face? And she was glad that he cared for other people, because for too long she had thought him incapable of caring.

"Where's Lew?" Rule was fretting. "I need to talk to him."

Cathryn looked at him sternly. "Now you listen to me, Rule Jackson. You're under strict orders to stay quiet, and if you give me any trouble I'll have you loaded up and taken back to that hospital so fast that your head will spin even worse than it already is. No working, no worrying, no trying to get up by yourself. Agreed?"

He glared at her. "Damn it, I've got a sale coming up and—"

"And we'll handle it," she interrupted. "I'm not saying that you can't talk to Lewis at all, but I'm going to make certain that you do a lot more resting than you do talking."

He sighed. "You're mighty big for your britches now that I'm as helpless as a turtle on its back," he said with deceptive mildness. "But this cast won't be on forever, and you'd better remember that."

"You're frightening me to death," she teased, leaning down to kiss him swiftly on the mouth and straightening before his dulled reflexes could react. His sleepy dark eyes drifted down her form with a lazy threat; then his lashes refused to open again and just like that he dozed off.

Cathryn quietly raised the window to let in some fresh air, then tiptoed out and closed the door behind her.

Ricky was leaning against the wall outside the room, her slanted hazel eyes narrowed in fury. "You told Lewis not to take me to the hospital so I could see Rule, didn't you?" she charged. "You didn't want me to be with him. You wanted him all to yourself."

Afraid that the woman's angry voice would wake him, Cathryn grabbed Ricky's arm roughly and pulled her away from the door. "Be quiet!" she whispered angrily. "He's sleeping, and he needs all the rest he can get."

"I'll just bet he does!" Ricky sneered.

Cathryn had spent a horrible two days and her temper was frayed. She snapped. "Think what you like, but stay away from him. I've never meant anything as much as I mean that. I'm warning you, I'll do whatever I have to do to keep you from upsetting him while he's still so ill. This is my ranch, and if you want to stay here you'd better pay attention to what I'm saying!"

"Oh, God, you make me sick! *Your* ranch! *Your* house! You've always thought this stupid little ranch made you better than everyone else."

Cathryn's fist doubled. *She* was sick. Sick and tired of Ricky's jealousy and pure nastiness, even though she understood them. Perhaps Ricky saw the last bit of control vanish from Cathryn's expression, because she moved quickly away and went downstairs, leaving Cathryn standing in the hallway trying to control the rage that burned through her.

After several minutes she went down to the kitchen and passed along Rule's request for soup, knowing from previous experience that his nap would be a short one, and wanting to have something ready for him to eat when he awoke. Lorna's damp eyes lit up at the information that Rule wanted her to do something for him and she began rushing about the kitchen. Within half an hour the tray was prepared with a bowl brimming with the rich, thick vegetable soup that she made, and a glass of iced tea. As Cathryn carried the tray upstairs she reflected that if Rule were still asleep she could eat the soup herself, because suddenly she was starving.

But Rule stirred when she opened the door, moving restlessly on the bed. He tried to struggle into a sitting position and she hurriedly set the tray on the night table and rushed to help him, putting an arm behind his neck to provide support while she punched the pillows into position to brace him. Then she had to get his leg settled comfortably, a process that had him clenching his jaw before it was finished.

He ate the soup with more appetite than he had shown for anything in the hospital, but the bowl was still half-full when he pushed it away and said irritably, "It's hot in here."

Cathryn sighed, but he had a point. The windows faced southwest, and the room took the full blast of the hot afternoon sun. It wasn't so noticeable to someone who didn't have to spend the entire day in the room, but already perspiration was glistening on his face and torso. Central heating and air-conditioning had never been installed in the old house, so the only solution she could think of was to buy a window unit. In the meantime she remembered that they had an electric fan and searched it out. At least that would keep the air moving until she could buy an air-conditioner.

She plugged the fan into the outlet and turned the switch on, directing the flow of air onto his body. He sighed and threw his right arm up to cover his eyes. "I remember one day in Saigon," he murmured. "It was so ungodly hot that the air was almost syrupy. My boots were sticking to the pavement when I walked across the helicopter pad. *That* was hot, Cat—so miserably hot that if Nam wasn't hell, it came in second. For years the feel of sweat crawling down my back was as bad as a snake crawling on me, because it reminded me of that day in Saigon."

Cathryn stood as if she had been turned to stone, afraid to say anything. It was the first time he had shared any of his memories of the war, and she wasn't certain if he was slowly becoming accustomed to talking about it or if he wasn't quite rational. He resolved that question when he moved his arm and looked at her, his dark eyes steady. "Until one day in July, eight years ago," he whispered. "It was hot that day, blistering hot, and when I saw you swimming naked in the river I envied you, and I thought about jumping in with you. Then I thought that some other man could have seen you as easily as I had, and I wanted to shake you until your teeth rattled. You know what happened," he continued softly. "And while I was making love to you the sun was burning down on my back and sweat was running off me, but I didn't think of Vietnam that day. All I could think of was the way you had turned so sweet and wild in my arms, lying under me and burning me with a different kind of heat. I never minded being hot and sweaty after that day, because all I had to do was look up at that Texas sun and I thought of making love with you."

Cathryn swallowed, unable to speak or move. He held out his hand to her. "Come here."

She found herself on her knees beside the bed, his hand clenched in her hair as he pulled her forward. He didn't make the mistake of trying to meet her halfway; he forced her all the way to him, stretching her half across the bed. Their mouths met wildly and his tongue sent her a virile message that left her senses spinning. "I want you now," he murmured into her mouth, taking her hand and sliding it down his body. Cathryn moaned as her fingers confirmed his need.

"We can't," she protested, pulling her lips free, though she mindlessly continued to caress him gently, her hand straying upward to stroke his lean hard belly. "*You* can't. You shouldn't be moving...."

"I won't," he promised, cajoling in a husky murmur. "I'll be perfectly still."

"Liar." Her voice was vibrantly tender. "No, Rule. Not now."

"You're supposed to keep me satisfied."

"That's not what the doctor said," she sputtered. "I'm supposed to keep you quiet."

"I'll be quiet—if you keep me satisfied."

"Please be reasonable."

"Horny men have never been reasonable."

Despite herself she had to laugh, burying her face against the curly hair of his chest until she had her giggles under control. "You poor baby," she crooned.

He smiled and abandoned his attempt to talk her into bed, though she doubted that she could have resisted his sensual pleas if he had persisted for much longer.

He drew his fingers through her hair, watching the dark red strands sift downward. "Are you thinking of leaving, now that I can't do anything to stop you?" he asked, his manner deceptively casual.

Cathryn raised her head swiftly, pulling her hair as she did so. She winced and he dropped the strands that he still held. "Of course not!" she denied indignantly.

"You haven't thought about it at all?"

"Not at all." She smiled down at him and traced a finger around the tiny male nipple that she had found in the curls of hair. "I think I'll stay around after all. I couldn't possibly miss my chance to boss you around. I may never have another."

"So you're staying for revenge?" He was smiling, too, a crooked little smile that barely lifted the corners of his mouth, but for Rule that was something. Laughter didn't come easily to him.

"I certainly am," she assured him, teasing the little point of flesh into tautness. "I'm going to pay you back for every kiss and enjoy watching you squirm. I still owe you for that spanking you gave me, too. I may not be able to pay you back in kind, but I'm certain I'll think of something."

A shuddering breath lifted his chest. "I can hardly wait."

"I know," she said gleefully. "That's my revenge. Making you wait...and wait...and wait."

"You've made me wait for eight years. What do you do for an encore? Turn me into a monk?"

"You were far from that, Rule Jackson, so don't try to tell me different! Wanda told me about your reputation in town. 'Wild as a mink' was the way she described you, and we both know what that means."

"Gossiping women," he grumbled.

Despite his better mood he was tiring rapidly, and when she moved to help him lie down he didn't protest.

The air-conditioner was first on her list of things to get, but Lewis, having taken the time to fetch Rule home from the hospital, was far too busy now for her to ask him to fly back to San Antonio, which would probably be the nearest city where she could purchase a small air-conditioner that wouldn't require additional electrical work on the house. That meant she would have to drive, a trip that took almost two hours one way. And the weather report called for more of the same: hot, hot and hot. Rule needed that air-conditioner.

But she was exhausted now, and the thought of that long drive was more than she could face. She would get up early in the morning and be at the appliance store in San Antonio when it opened. That way she could be back on the ranch before midday and would miss the worst of the heat.

After a long shower she checked in on Rule again and found him still asleep. That was the longest he had slept at any one stretch and she was reassured that he was mending. Gazing pensively at the white cast that covered his leg from knee to toes, she wished that it was gone and Rule was once more where he belonged, out on the range. As much as she relished the thought of having him at her mercy for at least a few days, it still hurt her to see him weak and helpless.

Taking advantage of the quiet, she stretched out across her own bed and instantly fell asleep, only to be awakened by a deep, irritable voice calling her name. She sat up and pushed her hair out of her face, glancing at the clock as she did so. She had slept for almost two hours. No wonder Rule was calling her! He must have been awake for some time, wondering if he had been abandoned.

Hurrying to his room, she found that that wasn't the case at all. His flushed face and tousled hair testified that he had just woken up himself and had called for her in instant demand. After two days of having her constantly with him, he was used to having her at his beck and call.

"Where've you been?" he snapped fretfully.

"Asleep," she said, and yawned. "What did you want?"

For a moment he lay there looking grumpy; then he said, "I'm thirsty."

There was a pitcher of water and a glass on the table beside his bed, but Cathryn didn't protest as she poured the water for him. The doctor had told her that Rule's headaches would give him the very devil for several days, and that the least movement would be painful. She slipped her arm under his pillow to gently raise his head as she held the glass for him. He gulped the water. "It's so damned hot in here," he sighed when the glass was empty.

She had to agree with him on that point. "I'm driving into San Antone in the morning to buy a window air-conditioner," she said. "Stick it out for the rest of the day, and tomorrow you'll be comfortable."

"That's a lot of unnecessary expense—" he began, frowning.

"It's not unnecessary. You won't regain your strength as fast if you lie here sweating yourself half to death every day."

"I still don't like—"

"It's not up to you to like it," she informed him. "I said I'm buying an air-conditioner, and that's that."

His dark eyes settled on her sternly. "Enjoy yourself, because when I'm up and around again, you're in trouble."

"I'm not afraid of you," she laughed, though it was a little bit of a lie. He was so tough and hard and held such sensual power over her that she was, if not actually afraid of him, more than a little cautious.

After a long moment the expression in his eyes softened fractionally. "You still look like you're dead on your feet. Instead of running back and forth, why don't you sleep in here with me? We'd both probably sleep better."

His suggestion was so provocative that she almost climbed in beside him right then, but she remembered his half-serious attempt at seduction only a few hours before and she reluctantly decided against such a move. "No way. You'd never get any rest if you had a woman in bed with you."

"How about next week?" he murmured, stroking her bare arm with one finger.

Cathryn was torn between laughter and tears. Did he sense how drastically her feelings had changed? It was as if he knew that the only thing keeping her out of his bed was her concern for his injuries. He was acting as if everything were settled between them, as if there were no more doubts clouding her mind. Perhaps there weren't. She hadn't really had time to decide exactly what she would do in regard to his marriage proposal, but she knew that no matter what happened now she couldn't run from him again. Maybe her decision was already made and she had only to face it. So many maybes...

But she would be foolish to commit herself to anything right now. She was tired, exhausted from the trauma of the past two days. And she had a ranch to run, a horse sale to prepare for, Ricky's malice to contend with, Rule's demands on her time. She had too much on her mind right now to make such a serious decision. One of her basic rules was not to make any irrevocable decisions when she was under stress. Later, when Rule was back on his feet, there would be plenty of time for that.

She smiled at him and stroked his hair back from his forehead. "We'll talk about that next week," she said.

CHAPTER 9

"Cat!"

"Mrs. Ashe, what do you think about—"

"Cathryn, we need—"

"Cat, I need a shave—"

"For God's sake, Cathryn, can't you do something about—"

"Cathryn, I'm sorry, but Rule won't let me do anything for him—"

Never before had Cathryn had so many people calling her name and demanding her time and attention. It seemed that everywhere she turned, someone had a problem that needed her immediate attention. There were a thousand and one things to be done every day on the ranch and Lewis Stovall was indispensable, but there were decisions that he couldn't make and that Rule wasn't in any shape to be handling. Monica always seemed to want something, and Ricky had her share of complaints. Lorna tried to take some of the burden of nursing Rule from Cathryn's shoulders, but she was thwarted in that by Rule himself. No one but Cathryn could shave him, feed him, bathe him, see to his personal needs. No one but Cathryn could keep him entertained.

Of all the voices calling her every day, Rule's sounded by far the most often. She ran up and down the stairs countless times every day to answer his demands. It wasn't that he was a difficult patient, simply that he wanted her—and only her—to take care of him.

She had bought an air-conditioner the day after bringing

him home from the hospital, and he rested better when the room was a more comfortable temperature. The quiet hum of the motor also masked the noises that might have disturbed him otherwise. He slept a great deal, but when he was awake he wasn't very patient if Cathryn didn't come immediately.

She couldn't get angry with him, not when she could see for herself how pale he became if he tried to move very much at all. His leg still hurt him, and was beginning to itch under the cast, as well, and he couldn't do anything to ease either condition. She wasn't surprised that he was short-tempered; anyone would have been under the circumstances. For a man of his temperament, he was doing much better than she had expected.

However, understanding didn't stop her legs from aching after a hundred trips up the stairs. She wasn't getting enough sleep, or enough to eat, and the only time she was sitting down was when she was either on a horse or feeding Rule. After only two days she was ready to drop in her tracks.

That night she actually did fall asleep beside Rule. She could remember feeding him, and when he was finished she had set the plate back on the tray and leaned down for a moment to rest her head on his shoulder. The next thing she knew it was morning, and Rule was groaning from the cramp in his arm. He had held her all night long and spent the night propped up on his pillows, his right arm wrapped around her. He kissed her and smiled, but discomfort shadowed his face and she knew that he had slept badly, if at all.

The entire morning was hectic, with one problem after another cropping up. She had just ridden into the stables, having returned to feed Rule his lunch, when a pickup truck rolled into the yard and a familiar figure emerged.

"Mr. Vernon," Cathryn called warmly, going up to greet her old friend. Another man got out of the vehicle and she glanced at him curiously before she recognized him. He was the man who had been with Paul Vernon the day she had met him in front of the drugstore, but she couldn't recall his name.

Paul Vernon solved that problem by indicating the man with a sweep of his big hand and saying, "You remember Ira Morris, don't you? Met him a week or so back."

"Yes, of course," said Cathryn, extending her hand to the man.

He shook hands, but he wasn't looking at her. His eyes were sliding over the stables and barns, resting finally on the horses that were grazing peacefully in the pastures.

"I've heard a lot about this place," he said, "and none of it was bad. Good, solid, well-mannered horses, the best quarter horses to be found in the state. But you're breeding for speed now, too, I hear. Branching out into Thoroughbreds, aren't you? They doing well?"

A few days before Cathryn wouldn't have known if they were or not, but she had absorbed a lot of the business by necessity. "We sold a colt last year who's been winning big in California this season."

"I've heard of him," said Ira Morris. "Irish Venture, by Irish Gale, out of Wanderer. Word is out that the mare's dropped another foal by Irish Gale; I'd like to get in ahead of the sale."

"None of the horses listed in the catalog will be sold until the day of the sale," said Cathryn firmly.

"All right, I can understand that," he readily agreed. "Would it be all right if I saw the colt?"

She shrugged and smiled. "I don't mind, but the foal is a filly, not a colt. Her name is Little Irish, but Rule calls her Hooligan."

"She's headstrong?" Paul Vernon asked.

Cathryn's smile grew broader and she lifted her hand to point out a dainty filly prancing around in the pasture. "Hooligan is just different," she said. They watched the graceful movements in silence as the young horse danced lightly over the green grass. It was only when the filly came alongside another horse that you could get an idea of her size. Because she was so graceful, it wasn't at first apparent that she was a tall, strong horse. Her sleek hide effectively masked the strength of her muscles; an observer first noticed her burnished beauty, the spirited arch of her neck and the delicacy with which she placed each hoof as she ran. Later, like a slow dawn, would come the realization that the filly had speed to burn, that those slender legs were as strong as steel.

"She's not for sale," said Cathryn. "At least not this year. Rule wants to keep her."

"If you don't mind, I'd like to speak to him."

"I'm sorry," said Cathryn, stretching the truth a bit. She didn't quite like Ira Morris. He seemed to be a cold, calculating man. "Rule had an accident earlier this week and he's restricted to bed; he can't be disturbed."

"I'm sorry to hear that," Mr. Vernon said instantly. "What happened?"

"His horse stumbled and went down with him, then rolled on Rule's leg."

"Broken?"

"I'm afraid so. He also has a concussion, and we have to keep him quiet."

"That's a damned shame, with this sale coming up."

"Oh, he won't miss the sale," Cathryn assured him. "If I know Rule Jackson, he'll be hobbling around before then. I just hope I'll be able to keep him down for the rest of this week."

"Headstrong, ain't he?" Mr. Vernon laughed.

"As a mule," agreed Cathryn fervently.

Ira Morris shifted impatiently and she realized that he wasn't interested in Rule's health. He was interested only in the horses, and as far as she was concerned they had no horses to sell until the day of the sale. Rule would know instantly which horses he had listed in the catalog, but as the catalogs hadn't arrived yet from the printers, Cathryn had no way of knowing without running to ask him, which she refused to do.

Mr. Morris cast another look over the ranch. "Just one thing, Mrs. Ashe," he said brusquely. "I came here to talk business, but now I'm not sure who I should be talking to. Who runs this outfit, you or Jackson?"

Cathryn paused, considering that. "I own the ranch," she finally said in a neutral tone. "But Mr. Jackson runs it for me, and he knows more about the horses than I do."

"So his decisions are final?"

She was beginning to feel annoyed. "Just what are you asking, Mr. Morris? If you want to buy horses now, then my answer is, I'm sorry, but not until the sale. Or is there something else on your mind?"

He smiled a hard, wintry smile, his cold eyes flashing at her. "What if I want to buy it all? Everything—horses, land, buildings."

That shook her. Pushing a wayward strand of hair away from her eyes, she looked around. Sell the Bar D? That old house was where she had been born. She knew every inch of this land, every rise and dip, every scent and sound of it. This was where she had first begun to love Rule, where she had come to know herself as a woman. It would be impossible to sell it.... She opened her mouth to tell him so, but then came the unbidden thought that if she didn't own the Bar D she wouldn't have to worry whether Rule wanted her land more than he wanted her. She would know for certain....

If she wanted to know. A sharp pain went through her at

the thought that the answer might be more painful than the question. Rule would never forgive her if she sold the ranch.

To Mr. Morris, she gave a forced smile. "That's a big 'if,'" she said. "And it's one that I haven't considered before. I couldn't make a snap decision on that."

"But you will think about it?" he pressed.

"Oh, yes," she assured him wryly. "I'll think about it." It would be hard for her to think about anything else. In a twisted way Mr. Morris had just reversed the roles for her and Rule. Which did she want more, the ranch or Rule Jackson? If she kept the ranch she might never know how he really felt about her; on the other hand, if she sold it she might lose him forever, but she would know exactly where she stood.

It was an offer that she knew would have to be discussed with Rule, though she also knew in advance what his reaction would be. He would be violently opposed to selling the ranch. But he was the manager and he was entitled to know what was going on, even though she dreaded the idea of upsetting him.

She was later than usual in taking his lunch up. First she had been detained by Paul Vernon and Ira Morris; then she was so dusty that she took a quick shower before she did anything else. While Lorna prepared Rule's lunch tray, Cathryn leaned against the cabinets and wolfed down a sandwich, wondering why Rule wasn't already calling her. Perhaps he was napping....

He wasn't asleep. When she opened the door he carefully turned his head to look at her and she was struck by the flinty expression in his eyes. His gaze went slowly over her, taking in her freshly scrubbed appearance from the top of her head, where she had subdued her hair into one long braid, down over her cool sleeveless cotton blouse, faded jeans, and finally her bare feet. Carefully placing the tray on the nightstand, she asked, "What's wrong? Is your head hurting—"

"I hear you're considering selling the ranch," he said harshly, trying to lever himself up on his elbow. The abrupt movement dislodged his broken leg from the cushions where it was propped and he fell back against his pillows with a sharp cry, followed by some lurid cursing. Cathryn leaped around the end of the bed and gently lifted his leg back onto the pillows, bracing it more securely. Her mind was racing. How had he heard about that so fast? Who had told him? The yard and stables had been busy. Any one of twenty men could have overheard the offer to buy the ranch, but she didn't think that any of them had made a special trip to the house to tell Rule about it. Lewis was in the house a lot, but she knew that at the moment he was in the far south pastures.

"Ricky told me," Rule snapped, accurately reading her thoughts.

"She made the trip for nothing," Cathryn replied evenly, sitting down beside him and reaching for the tray. "I was going to tell you myself."

"When? After the papers were signed?"

"No, I was going to tell you about it while you were eating."

He angrily waved away the spoon that she lifted to his mouth. "Damn it, don't try to poke that in my mouth like I'm a baby. This would solve all your problems, wouldn't it? Get rid of the ranch, get rid of me, make a lot of money to live it up on in Chicago."

With difficulty Cathryn restrained her impulse to lash back at him. She set her jaw and replaced the tray on the nightstand. "Evidently Ricky also took it upon herself to add a few little details to the original conversation. First, I didn't agree to sell the ranch. Second, you will be involved in any decision I make concerning the ranch. And third, I'm damned tired of you jumping down my throat, and as far as I'm concerned you can feed yourself!" She got up and stomped out, closing the door sharply on his furious order that she come back.

Ricky stood at the head of the stairs, an openly delighted smile on her face, and Cathryn realized that the other woman had been listening to every word. Her eyes narrowing, she stopped in front of her stepsister and said from between clenched teeth, "If I see you in Rule's room again, or hear of you being in there, I'll throw you off this ranch so fast you'll have windburn."

Ricky arched a mocking brow. "You will, little sister? You and who else?"

"I think I can handle it, but if I can't, there are a lot of ranch hands to help me."

"And what makes you think they'll side with you? You're a stranger to them. I've ridden beside them, worked with them, been close…friends…with some of them."

"I'm sure you have," said Cathryn cuttingly. "Fidelity has never been one of your characteristics."

"And has it been yours? Do you think it's such a well-kept secret that you've been Rule's little plaything since you were only a kid?"

Horrified, Cathryn realized that Ricky had probably been spreading her malicious gossip for years. The Lord only knew what the woman had said about her. Then she straightened her shoulders and even smiled, thinking that she wasn't ashamed of loving Rule. He wasn't the easiest man in the world to love, but he was hers, and she didn't care if the whole world knew it.

"That's right, I have been," she admitted freely. "I love him, and I'll keep on loving him."

"You loved him so much that you ran away and married another man?"

"Yes, that's right. I don't have to explain myself to you, Ricky. Just make certain you stay away from Rule, because that was your last chance."

"Well, Ricky, you can't say you weren't warned," Monica drawled from behind them, her voice amused. "And unless you're prepared to find a job and start supporting yourself, I suggest that you listen to her."

Ricky tossed her head. "I've helped the ranch hands for years, but I've never seen you do anything more than make your own bed. What about you? You live off of this ranch, too."

"Not for long," said Monica breezily. "I'll never find another husband while I'm stuck out here in the sticks."

Oddly, Ricky turned pale. "You're leaving the Bar D?" she whispered.

"Well, surely you knew that I wouldn't stay here forever," said Monica, mildly puzzled. "The ranch belongs to Cathryn, and it looks as if she's come home to stay. It's time I made a home for myself, and I've never wanted it to be on a ranch. I tolerated ranch life, but only for Ward Donahue." She gave a graceful shrug. "Men like him don't come along too often. I'd have lived in an igloo if that was what he wanted."

"But...Mother...what about me?" Ricky sounded so distressed that suddenly Cathryn felt sorry for her, even if she was a spiteful witch.

Monica smiled. "Why, darling, you can find your own husband. You're a little too old to be living with Mommy, anyway, aren't you? Cathryn has offered me the use of her apartment in Chicago and I just might take her up on it. Who knows? I may find a Yankee who just loves my accent."

Magnificently unconcerned, Monica continued down the stairs, then stopped and turned back to look at her daughter. "My suggestion to you, Ricky, is to stop playing games with

that cowboy you've been teasing. You could do a lot worse
than to take him up on what he'd like to offer you." She continued on her way, leaving a thick silence behind her.

Cathryn looked at Ricky, who was slumped against the
railing as if she had been hit over the head. Perhaps she had,
because Monica could never be accused of subtlety. "What
was she talking about?" Cathryn asked. "Which cowboy?"

"Nobody important," Ricky mumbled, and walked slowly
down the hall to her room.

Feeling both battered and confused, Cathryn sought ref-
uge in the kitchen with Lorna. She collapsed into a chair and
propped her elbows on the table.

"Ricky told Rule that I was going to sell the ranch," she
said baldly. "Rule jumped to the conclusion that the tale was
true. We had an argument and I told him to feed himself; he's
probably thrown the tray against the wall. Then I had an argument with Ricky over Rule, and right in the middle of it
all Monica told Ricky that she's planning to leave the Bar D,
and Ricky looked like someone had slapped her. I don't know
what's going on anymore!" she wailed.

Lorna laughed. "Mostly what's going on is that you're so
tired you're functioning on willpower alone and nothing's
making a lot of sense to you right now. Monica and Ricky
have argued all their lives; it's nothing unusual. And Monica
has always said that if you came back she was leaving. Ricky...
well, what Ricky needs is a good, strong man who loves her
and makes her feel like she's worth something."

"I feel sorry for her," said Cathryn slowly. "Even when I
want to choke her, I feel sorry for her."

"Sorry enough for her to let her have Rule?" Lorna put
in slyly.

"No!" Cathryn's response was immediate and explosive,
and Lorna laughed.

"I didn't think so." She wiped her hands on her apron. "I suppose I'd better go upstairs and see to Rule, though if he hasn't thrown the tray at the wall he'll be sure to throw it at me when he sees I'm not you. Are you going to see him at all?"

"I suppose I'll have to," Cathryn sighed. "But not right now. Let him cool down, and maybe then we can talk without yelling at each other."

After Lorna had gone upstairs, Cathryn sat at the table for a long while, staring at the homey, comfortable kitchen. It wasn't only Rule who needed to cool down; her temper was at least as hot as his, and if she were being truthful with herself, she had to admit that he usually controlled his far better than she did hers.

The back door opened and Lewis Stovall leaned his tall frame against the doorway. "Come on, Cathryn," he cajoled. He'd dropped the "Mrs. Ashe" during the last few days and started calling her by her given name, which was only the logical thing to do considering how closely they had been working together. "There's work to be done."

"Did Rule tell you to keep me so busy that I wouldn't have the energy to do anything but work and sleep and look after him?" she asked suspiciously.

His hard eyes crinkled at the corners as a tiny smile touched his face. "Tired, aren't you?"

"Punch-drunk," she agreed.

"It won't be for much longer. Rule should be up and around next week, and he'll probably be back in the saddle the week after that. I've seen him do it before."

"With a cast on his leg?" she asked doubtfully.

"Or his arm, or with his ribs taped up, or his collarbone broken. Nothing's kept him down for long. This concussion has put him on his back longer than anything else."

She got up and went over to the door, sighing as she pulled

on clean socks and stamped her feet into her boots. Lewis stood watching her with an odd expression in his eyes, and she looked up in time to catch a fleeting glimpse of it. "Lewis?" she asked uncertainly.

"I was just thinking that underneath the big-city glamour you're really nothing but a country girl."

"Glamour?" she laughed, tickled by the idea. "Me?"

"You'd know what I'm talking about if you were a man," he drawled.

"If I were a man you wouldn't even be thinking it!"

His laughter acknowledged the truth of that. As they walked across the yard, Cathryn worked up enough nerve to ask him a question that had been in the back of her mind since she'd first met Lewis. "Were you in Vietnam with Rule?" she asked casually.

He looked down at her. "I was in Vietnam, but not with Rule. I didn't meet him until almost seven years ago."

She didn't say anything else, and when they were almost at the stables he asked, "Why?"

"You seem so much alike," she replied slowly, not certain why they seemed to be cut out of the same mold. They were both dangerous men, hard men who had seen too much death and pain.

"He's never mentioned Vietnam to me." A harsh note crept into Lewis's voice. "And I don't talk about it, either—not anymore. The only people who would know what I was talking about were there too, and they have their own troubles. My marriage broke up because my wife couldn't handle it, couldn't handle *me* when I first came back."

The look she gave him was painful with sympathy, and he grinned—actually grinned. "Don't drag out the violins," he teased. "I'm doing okay. Someday I'll probably even get married again. Most men moan and groan about marriage, but there's something about women that keeps them coming back for more."

Cathryn had to laugh. "I wonder what that is!"

Her new sense of closeness to Lewis carried her through the remainder of the day, which was as hectic and troubled as the morning had been. One of the stallions was colicky, and two mares showed signs that they would be foaling before the night was over. When she finally trudged back to the house it was after seven, and Lorna reported that she had already carried Rule's tray up to him.

"He's in an awful mood," she reported.

"Then he'll have to stay in one," Cathryn said tiredly. "I don't feel up to soothing him down tonight. I'm going to take a shower and fall into bed."

"You're not going to eat?"

She shook her head. "I'm too tired. I'll make up for it in the morning, I promise."

After showering she fell across her bed, too tired even to crawl under the sheet. She fell asleep immediately, which was fortunate, because in what seemed like only a few minutes she was being shaken awake.

"Cathryn, wake up." It was Ricky's voice, and Cathryn forced her eyes open.

"What's wrong?" she asked groggily, noticing that Ricky was still dressed. "What time is it?"

"It's eleven-thirty. Come on. Both mares are in labor, and Lewis needs help." Ricky's voice was totally lacking in hostility, but then she had always been interested in ranch work. It didn't seem strange that Lewis had sent for the two women instead of waking some ranch hands to help him; they had both aided foaling mares before, though it had been years since Cathryn had done so. But the ranch was hers, and it was her responsibility.

Quickly she dressed and they hurried to the foaling barn, where only a few dim lights burned in the stalls with the mares. They had to be quiet to keep from upsetting the expectant mothers, so they didn't talk except in low tones. Lewis and the foaling man, Floyd Stoddard, were waiting in an empty stall.

Lewis looked up as the two women entered the stall. "Shouldn't be too much longer with Sable," he said. "Andalusia will take a while more, I think."

But though they waited, Sable still didn't foal, and Floyd began to get worried. It was almost two in the morning when he checked on her again and came back to the stall where they had remained, his face strained. "Sable's down," he reported. "But the foal's turned sideways. We're going to have to help it. Everybody wash up."

The two men stripped to the waist and washed in warm soapy water, then ran to Sable's stall. Ricky and Cathryn rolled their sleeves up as far as they would go and washed too, though they wouldn't actually be helping to turn the foal. The lovely dark brown mare was lying down, her swollen sides bulging grotesquely. "Hold her head," Floyd directed Ricky, then knelt behind the mare.

At a loud, distressed whinny from the other stall, they jerked their heads around. Lewis swore. "Cathryn, see about Andalusia!"

Andalusia was down, too, but she wasn't in any undue stress. Cathryn reported back, then considered the situation. Ricky was using all her energy holding Sable's head down; Lewis was applying external pressure to help Floyd turn the foal.

"Andalusia's fine, but she's ready now, too. I'll stay with her."

Sweat was pouring down Lewis's face. "Do you know what to do?" he grunted.

"Yes, don't worry. I'll call if there's any trouble."

Andalusia raised her pearl gray head and gave a soft whinny when Cathryn entered her stall, then dropped her head into the hay again. Cathryn knelt beside her, her gentle touch telling the mare that she wasn't alone. The animal's large, dark eyes rested on Cathryn with touching, almost human serenity.

The mare's sides heaved with another contraction, and the sharp, tiny hooves appeared. Andalusia didn't need any help. Within minutes the foal was squirming on the hay, still encased in the shimmering sac. Quickly Cathryn slit the sac and freed the little animal, then took a soft, dry cloth and began rubbing it with long, rhythmic strokes. She crouched on the hay as the mare struggled to her feet and stood with her head down, her sides heaving. Cathryn tensed, ready to grab the foal and run if the mare didn't accept the baby. But Andalusia blew softly through her muzzle and came over to investigate the little creature trembling on the hay. Her loving, motherly licking took the place of Cathryn's cloth.

The little chestnut colt struggled to place his front legs, but as soon as he had them braced and tried to make his back legs obey, the front ones would betray him and he'd collapse. After several abortive tries he managed to stand, then looked around in infant confusion, not certain what he was supposed to do next. Andalusia, fortunately, was an old hand at this; she gently nudged the foal in the proper direction and instinct took over. Within seconds he was greedily nursing, his thin little legs braced wide apart as he balanced precariously on them.

When Cathryn returned to the other stall, Ricky was kneeling beside an unusually small foal, rubbing it and crooning to it. Lewis and Floyd were still working with the mare and Cathryn saw at once that this was a double birth. Her heart twisted a little, because so often with twin foals one or both of them failed to survive. From the looks of the frail little creature with Ricky, the odds were all against it.

Soon the other foal was on the hay and it was larger than the other one, though the markings were almost identical. It was an active little filly, who struggled to her feet almost immediately and raised her proud little head to survey the strange new world she was living in.

Floyd was taking care of Sable, so Lewis came over to examine the other foal. "I don't think she'll be strong enough to nurse," he said doubtfully, taking in the limp way the foal was lying. But no one on the Bar D just left a horse to die. They worked all night with the foal, keeping her warm, rubbing her to keep her circulation stimulated, dribbling a few drops of milk from her mother down her throat. But she was very weak, and soon after sunrise she died without ever having been on her feet.

Tears burned Cathryn's eyes, though she had known from the beginning what the outcome was likely to be. There was nothing to say. Everyone in the barn was silent, looking at the still little creature. But when they looked in the other direction they saw not death but glorious, beautiful life as the other two newborns pushed their delicate muzzles into every nook of their expanded territories.

Lewis shrugged his shoulders, shaking the kinks out of them. "It's been a long night," he sighed. "And we've got a long day in front of us. Let's go clean up and eat."

Cathryn had almost reached the house when she realized that Ricky wasn't with her. Looking around, she saw that Ricky was standing with Lewis. She opened her mouth to call out, when suddenly Lewis's hand shot out to grab Ricky's arm. Evidently they were quarreling, though they hadn't been just a moment earlier. Then Lewis slid his arm around Ricky's waist and forced her along as he strode to the small house that was his private quarters. Not that Ricky needed to be forced, thought Cathryn wryly, watching the door shut behind them.

Well, well. So Lewis was the cowboy Monica had mentioned. She hadn't even suspected, though if she'd been less preoccupied with Rule she might have noticed the way that Lewis looked at Ricky. He had been watching Ricky that day when Cathryn had seen her hug Rule. Maybe Ricky didn't know it yet, but Lewis Stoval was a man who knew what he wanted and how to get it. Ricky had better enjoy her last days of freedom, thought Cathryn, smiling. That should certainly take care of Ricky's chasing after Rule.

"How did things go?" Lorna asked as Cathryn moved slowly into the kitchen, groaning with every step.

"Sable had twins, but one died just a few minutes ago. But Andalusia's foal is a big colt, as red as fire, so that should please Rule. He likes red horses."

"Speaking of Rule…" said Lorna meaningfully.

Cathryn flinched. "Oh, Lord. Lorna, I can't. Not just yet. I'm dead on my feet and he'll make mincemeat out of me."

"Well, I'll try to explain." But Lorna looked doubtful, and Cathryn almost gave in. If her body hadn't been throbbing with weariness she might have surrendered to the urge to see him, but she was just too tired to face him now.

"Tell him about the foals," she directed, yawning. "And tell him that I've gone straight to bed for a few hours of sleep, and I'll see him when I get up."

"He won't like that. He wants to see you *now*."

Suddenly Cathryn chuckled. "Tell you what. Tell him that I've forgiven him. That'll make him so mad that if you're lucky he won't even speak."

"But you won't see him now?"

"No, not now. I'm really too tired."

Later, lying drowsily in her bed, she wished that she had

gone to talk to him. She could have told him about the foals and he would have understood if she had cried a little on his shoulder. She was teaching him a lesson, but she wished that she didn't have to learn it with him. She wanted to be with him, to touch him and take care of him. It was a good thing that she had promised to see him later, because a day without being with him was almost more than she could bear.

Lorna woke her that afternoon to take a phone call. Groggily she staggered to the phone. "Hi," said Glenn Lacey cheerfully. "I just wanted to remind you of our date tonight. Guess where we're going."

Cathryn was dumbfounded. She had forgotten all about having made a date with Glenn for that night. "Where?" she asked weakly.

"I've got tickets to the Astros' game in Houston tonight. I'll pick you up at four and we'll fly in to the city for an early dinner before the game. How does that sound?"

"That sounds great," Cathryn gulped, thinking bleakly of the man lying upstairs.

CHAPTER 10

If it hadn't been for Rule, Cathryn would have had fun. On the surface she was happy, smiling and talking, but underneath she was miserable. It was as if he were on the date with her, invisible to everyone but her. If she laughed at something, she thought of Rule lying in bed waiting for her to come to him because he was unable to get up and go to her, and she felt guilty for laughing. She felt guilty anyway, because Glenn was an amusing, undemanding companion and she just couldn't give him her complete attention.

Once they were at the ball game she was able to concentrate on what was happening and push thoughts of Rule aside. She had never been a great baseball fan, but she liked watching the crowd. There were people of every shape, size and description wearing every type of outfit imaginable. One couple, obviously in a mellow mood, paid no attention at all to the ball game and proceeded to conduct a romance in the midst of thousands of witnesses. A man sitting just below them, wearing only sneakers, cutoffs, and a tee shirt tied around his head, cheered loudly and equally for both teams. Glenn was of the opinion that he didn't know which team was which.

But even crowd watching had its painful moments. A man with thick dark hair caught her eye and her breath squeezed to a halt for a painful moment. What was Rule doing now? Had he eaten anything? Was he in pain?

She had upset him, and the doctor had told her to keep him quiet. What if he tried to get up by himself and fell?

She was aware, as if of a deep chill in her bones, that if he hadn't been furious before, he would be now. Yet she couldn't have backed out of the date with Glenn at the last minute; Glenn was too nice to be treated so shabbily. Perhaps he would have understood and been a good sport about it, but Cathryn felt that it would have been tacky to stand him up after he had already gotten the tickets to the ball game.

Sudden, bitter tears burned her eyes and she had to turn her head away from Glenn, pretending to look over the crowd. She ached to be home, just to be under the same roof with Rule, so she could look in on him and make certain he was all right, even if he were angry enough to eat nails. Love! Who ever said that love made the world go round? Love was a killing pain, an addiction that had to be fed; yet even in her pain she knew that she wouldn't have it any other way. Rule was a part of her, so much so that she would be only half-alive without him. Hadn't she already learned that?

She loved Rule and she loved the ranch, but between them they were driving her crazy. She didn't know which was more demanding, and the way she felt about both only complicated matters.

Glancing at Glenn, she realized that she couldn't imagine Rule sitting hunched over in a stadium, absently chewing on an already mangled hot dog and drinking warm, watery beer. She had never seen Rule relaxing at anything. He pushed himself until he was so tired that he had to sleep, then began the cycle again the next morning. He read a great deal, but she couldn't say that it was recreational reading. He read thick technical books on breeding and genetics; he studied lineages, kept abreast of new medicines and veterinary practices. His life was built around the ranch. He had gone to the dance, but he hadn't participated. He had gone merely to make sure that she didn't get involved with any other man. Did anything exist for him except that ranch?

Suddenly a wave of resentment washed over her. The ranch! Always the ranch! She would be better off if she *did* sell it. She might lose Rule, but at least then she would know one way or the other how he felt about her. She realized bitterly that she was far more jealous of the ranch than she had ever been of any woman. Ricky's attempts to attract Rule's attentions had been infuriating, but rather pitiable, because Cathryn had known that her stepsister had no chance of succeeding. Ricky didn't have what it took; she didn't have the ranch.

If she had any guts at all she'd ask Rule right out what he wanted from her. That was the hard part of loving someone, she thought bitterly; it left you so insecure and vulnerable. Love turned sane people into maniacs, bravery into coward-ice, morals into quivering need.

When Glenn stood and stretched, yawning, Cathryn real-ized with a start that the ball game was over, and she had to look quickly at the scoreboard to figure out who had won. The Astros had, but only by one run. It had been a low-scoring game, a duel of pitchers rather than hitters.

"Let's stop for some coffee before we start back," Glenn sug-gested. "I only had one beer, but I'd like to feel a little more alert before I get in a plane and start flying."

At least *he* was still sane, thought Cathryn. Aloud she agreed that coffee sounded like a good idea and they spent a lei-surely hour in the coffee shop at the airport. She was aware of the minutes ticking by, aware that if Rule was still awake he would be shaking with fury by now. The thought made her both eager and loath to return, wanting to put it off for as long as possible.

When they were strapped into their seats in the plane, it seemed that she would get her wish. Glenn abruptly killed the engine. "Fuel pressure isn't coming up," he muttered, crawling out of his seat.

The fuel pump had gone bad. The time it took to obtain and install a new one made it past midnight before they were finally in the air. Rather than wake everyone at the ranch by landing, Glenn took the plane back to its hangar and drove her home. After he had kissed her casually on the cheek and left her at the door, she took off her shoes like a kid sneaking in late from a date and tiptoed through the dark house, avoiding the places in the old floor that she knew would creak.

As she tiptoed past Rule's door she noticed the thin line of light beneath it and hesitated. He couldn't reach the lamp to turn it off. If everyone had gone to bed without turning the lamp off for him it would burn all night. Not that there was much left of the night, she thought in wry amusement. Why not just admit that she wanted to look at him? It had been roughly thirty-six hours since she had seen him, and suddenly that was far too long. Like any drug addict, she needed her fix.

Moving slowly, cautiously, she opened his door and peeped in. At least he was lying down, so someone had remembered to help him from his propped-up position. His eyes were closed and his broad, heavily muscled chest rose and fell evenly.

A hot little quiver ran through her and rattled her composure. God, he looked so good! His silky dark hair was tousled, his jaw darkened with stubble; one powerful arm was thrown up beside his head, his long-fingered hand relaxed. Her gaze wandered down the sheen of his bronzed shoulders, stopped at the virile growth of dark hair that covered his chest and ran down his abdomen, then fought free to linger on the naked expanse of muscled thigh that was visible. He had the sheet pulled up to just below his navel, but his left leg was completely uncovered, the heavy cast propped on the pile of pillows for support.

Trembling in appreciation of his male beauty, she walked silently to the bed and leaned down to feel for the switch on the lamp. She made no noise at all, she was certain of it, yet abruptly his right arm snapped out and his fingers clamped around her wrist. His dark eyes flared open and he stared at her for several seconds before the feral gleam in the dark depths faded. "Cat," he muttered.

He had been sound asleep. She would have sworn to it. But his instincts were still honed to battle pitch, aware of any change in his surroundings, any other presence, and his body had acted even before he was awake. She watched him as the jungle faded from his mind and he recalled his present location. His look of hard savagery changed to one of narrow-eyed anger. The pressure of his fingers lessened, but not enough to allow her to pull away. Instead he drew her to him, bending her over the bed in an awkward position, holding her by the strength of his arm.

"I told you to stay away from Glenn Lacey," he snarled softly, holding her so closely that his breath heated her cheek.

Who had told him? she wondered bleakly. Anyone could have. The entire ranch must have seen Glenn arrive to pick her up. "I'd forgotten that I'd made a date with him," she confessed, keeping her voice low. "When he called, he already had tickets to the ball game in Houston and I just couldn't turn him down after he'd gone to so much trouble. He's a nice man."

"I don't care if he's the next American saint," Rule replied, still in the same tone of soft, silky menace. "I told you that I won't have you going out with other men and I meant it."

"It was just this once, and besides, you don't own me!"

"You think so? You're mine, and I'll do whatever it takes to keep you."

She gave him a guarded, painful look. "Would you?" she murmured, afraid that she knew all too well what his reaction would be if she sold the ranch. He would hate her. He'd drop her so fast that she'd never recover from the devastation of it.

"Push me and find out," he invited. "That's what you've been doing anyway. Pushing me, trying to find the limits of the invisible chain that's around your pretty little neck. Well, honey, you've reached it!"

The pressure on her arm resumed and he pulled her closer. Cathryn braced her left arm on the bed and tried to pull away, but even flat on his back he was still far stronger than she was. She gave a soft cry as her arm gave way and she sprawled across him, trying frantically to keep from jarring him or knocking against his broken leg.

He released her arm and thrust his hand into her hair, tangling his fingers in the long silky length of it and forcing her head down. "Rule! Stop it!" she wailed, an instant before his mouth clung to hers.

She tried to refuse his kiss, tried to keep her teeth clenched and her lips firmly together. She failed in both. Without hurting her, he caught her jaw and applied just enough pressure to open her mouth to him, and his tongue moved past the barrier of her teeth, licking little fires into life everywhere it touched. Dazed, she felt the strength leave her body and she sank limply against him.

He kissed her so long and so hard that she knew her lips would be swollen and bruised the next day, but at the time all she was aware of was the intoxicating taste of him, the sensual thrust of his tongue, the stinging little bites that he used as both punishment and reward, stringing them from her mouth down her throat and over her sensitive collarbone to the soft curve of her shoulder. It was only then that she realized he had unbuttoned the front of her dress and pulled it open, and she moaned in her throat. "Rule...stop it! You can't...."

Carefully he let his head fall back on the pillow but he

didn't release her. His hand shoved under the cup of her bra and he nestled her breast in his hot palm. "No, I can't, but you can," he murmured.

"No...your head...your leg," she protested incoherently, closing her eyes against the heated delight that coursed through her veins as he continued to fondle her.

"My head and my leg aren't bothering me right now." He pulled her closer and began kissing her again, insisting on the response that he knew she was capable of. The thrusting depth of his kisses made her head spin, and she sank against him once more.

He tugged at the straps of the bra until they came free; then he reached behind her and deftly unsnapped the back strap, freeing her breasts completely. Cathryn whispered a choked, "Please," not even knowing herself if she was begging him to stop or continue. She shuddered wildly when his hand swept up under her skirt and caressed her with bold aggression, and though she kept mindlessly whispering her mingled protests and pleas, she was clinging to him with all the strength in her arms.

He groaned harshly and tugged her leg over his hips, pulling her into position. Sudden tears dampened her cheeks, though she hadn't been aware that she was crying. "I don't want to hurt you," she sobbed.

"You won't," he crooned. "Please, honey, make love to me. I need you so much! Can't you feel how I ache for you?"

At some point during those bold, intimate caresses he had removed her panties, impatiently tossing away the silken barrier that kept him from the secrets of her body. His hands guided her slowly, easing her down until they were fully joined.

It was so sweet and wild that she almost cried out, stifling the sound in her throat at the last moment. With every fiber of her body she was aware of the particular sexiness of a man who lay back and let a woman enjoy his body, let her set the tempo of their loving. It was all the more enticing because Rule was so compellingly masculine, his power undiminished by his injuries. She loved him, loved him with her heart and soul and the undulating magic of her body. With exquisite tenderness she took what he offered and returned it to him tenfold, presenting him with the gift of her soaring pleasure and returning to earth to savor his writhing response as he too was pleasured.

She was lying on his chest in drowsy completion, her half-closed eyes moving idly over the room, when she saw the open door and stiffened. "Rule," she moaned in mortification. "I didn't close the door!"

"Then close it now," he instructed softly. "From the inside. I'm not finished with you, honey."

"You need to sleep...."

"It's almost dawn," he pointed out. "We seem to do all our loving in the early morning hours. And I've done nothing but sleep for a week. We need to talk, and now's as good a time as any."

That was true, and she was loath to leave him anyway. She eased out of the bed, careful not to jostle him any more than she already had, and closed the door, locking it for good measure. It would be just like Ricky to come bursting in in the morning, knowing that Cathryn was with him. Then she slipped out of her dress, poor covering that it was, considering that he had dropped the top of it to her waist and lifted the skirt to the same level. Naked, she climbed under the sheet with him and pressed against his side, almost drunk with the pleasure of lying beside him once more. She nuzzled her face into the hollow of his shoulder and inhaled the heady male scent of him. She was so relaxed, so replete...

"Cat," he murmured into her hair, feeling the way she lay against him. She didn't answer. A sigh of raw frustration escaped him as he realized that she was asleep; then he curved her slender body more tightly against him and pressed a kiss into the tumble of dark red hair that streamed across his shoulder.

When Cathryn woke several hours later, roused by a pain in her arm caused by the fact that she had been resting all her weight on it, Rule was asleep. Cautiously she raised her head and studied him, seeing how pale and tired he looked, even in sleep. Their lovemaking had been sweet and urgent, but he hadn't really been well enough. She eased away from him and stood up, massaging her arm to restore circulation to it. A thousand tiny pins pricked her skin and she hugged the arm to her until the worst of it had passed; then she silently pulled on her dress and picked up the remainder of her clothing, slipping out before he woke.

She was tired. Those few hours of sleep hadn't been nearly enough, but she showered and dressed for the day's chores. Lorna smiled at her when she entered the kitchen. "I thought you'd give it a rest today," she clucked.

"Did Rule ever give it a rest?" asked Cathryn wryly.

"Rule's a lot stronger than you are. We'll get by; the ranch is too well run to fall apart in a couple of weeks. How about waffles for breakfast? I've already got the batter mixed."

"That'll be fine," Cathryn replied, pouring a cup of coffee for herself. She leaned against the cabinet and sipped it, feeling the weariness weighing her limbs down like lead weights.

"Mr. Morris has called twice already," Lorna said casually, and Cathryn's head jerked up. She had almost spilled her coffee and she set the cup down.

"I don't like that man!" she said fretfully. "Why doesn't he leave me alone?"

"Does that mean you're not going to sell the ranch to him?"

Nothing was private, Cathryn realized, rubbing her forehead absently. No doubt everyone on the ranch knew that Mr. Morris had offered to buy the ranch. And no doubt everyone also knew whose bed she had woken up in that morning! It was like living in a fishbowl.

"In a way I'm tempted," she sighed. "But then again..."

Lorna deftly poured the batter into the waffle iron. "I don't know what Rule would do if you sold the ranch. He couldn't work for Mr. Morris, I don't think. So much of his life is tied up with this place."

Cathryn felt every muscle in her body tense at Lorna's words. She knew that. She had always known it. She might own the Bar D, but she was only a figurehead. It belonged to Rule, and he belonged to it, and that was far more important than what was recorded on any deed. He had paid for it in his own way, with his time and sweat and blood. If she sold it he would hate her.

"I can't think," she said tensely. "There are so many things pulling me in different directions."

"Then don't do anything," Lorna advised. "At least until things have settled down some. You're under a lot of pressure right now. Just wait a while; in three weeks your outlook could be completely different."

Lorna's common-sense advice was only what Cathryn had told herself many times, and she realized all over again that it really was sensible. She sat down and ate her waffle, and surprisingly the few minutes of quiet made her feel better.

"Cat!"

The low, compelling call wafted down from upstairs and immediately she was tense again. Lord, she was almost terrified at the thought of talking to him! It doesn't make sense, she told herself sternly. She had just slept in his arms; why should she dread talking to him so much?

Because she was afraid that she wouldn't be able to prevent herself from throwing herself in his arms and promising to do anything he asked, that was why! If he asked her to marry him again she'd probably melt against him like an idiot and agree without thinking, completely disregarding the fact that he had never said anything about *love,* only about his plans.

"Cat!" This time she thought she could discern a tautness in his voice and she found herself on her feet, automatically responding to it.

When she opened his door he was lying with his eyes closed, his lips pale. "I knew it was too soon!" she cried softly, placing a cool hand on his forehead. His dark eyes opened and he gave her a tight smile.

"It seems you're right," he grunted. "God, my head feels like it's going to explode! Fill up the icepack, okay?"

"I'll bring it right up," she promised, smoothing his hair with her fingertips. "Do you feel like eating anything?"

"Not just yet. Something cool to drink will do fine, and turn on the air-conditioner." As she turned away to do his bidding, he said evenly, "Cat…"

She turned back to him and raised her eyebrows inquiringly. He said, "About Glenn Lacey…"

She flushed. "I told you, he's just a friend. There's nothing between us, and I won't be going out with him again."

"I know. I realized that last night when I saw that you were wearing a bra."

He was looking at her from beneath half-closed lids, stripping her, and the flush on her cheeks grew hotter. She didn't need him to finish the thought, but he did anyway. "If you had been with me, you wouldn't have been wearing a bra, would you?" he asked huskily.

Her voice was weak as she admitted huskily, "No."

Again the corners of his mouth moved in a little smile. "I didn't think so. Go get that drink for me, honey. I'm not in any shape for provocative conversation right now."

She couldn't stop the chuckle that escaped her lips as she left the room. How like him to put her on the defensive, then reveal that he had attacked with nothing more dangerous in his armory than a smile and a sensual remark. He was more than she could handle, and abruptly she realized that she didn't *want* to handle him. He was his own man, not something to be controlled. Nor did he really try to handle her. Sometimes she felt, oddly, that he was a little wary of her, but he didn't usually tell her if she could or couldn't do something. Except in the case of Glenn Lacey, she thought, smiling. And even then she had done as she had wanted. In her case, her red hair was a signal of stubbornness as well as temper.

Rule didn't feel well enough to start any deep conversations, for which she was grateful. She tended to him and got him settled after he had downed a glass of iced tea; with an icepack easing his headache, he lay quietly and watched her as she straightened the room. "Lewis told me about the other night," he murmured. "He said that you helped Andalusia by yourself. Did you have any trouble?"

"No, the mare knew just what to do."

"She's a good little mother," he said sleepily. "It was too bad about the other foal. We had a set of twins survive a few years ago, but it was a chancy thing. The smaller foal never did catch up to its twin in size or strength, but she was a sweet little horse. She was so small that I was afraid it would kill her if I tried breeding her to any of the other horses, so I sold her to a family who wanted a gentle horse for their kids."

Cathryn felt guilty for not checking on the other mare's

well-being, and she said hesitantly, "Did…has Lewis said anything about Sable? How she's doing?"

"She's fine. Have you seen the foal?"

"Not since she was born. She's a strong little thing, tall and frisky. She was on her feet almost right away."

"Her sire is Irish Gale. Looks like he's turning out fast fillies instead of colts. Too bad about that; most fillies can't run with the boys, even when they're fast."

"What about Ruffian?" demanded Cathryn, indignant on behalf of the fillies. "And a filly won the Derby not so many years ago, smarty."

"Sweetheart, even in the Olympics the women don't run with the men, and the same goes for horses…except in special, isolated cases," he conceded. His eyes slowly closed, and he muttered, "I need to get up. There's a lot to be done."

She started to assure him that everything was under control but realized that he had slipped into a light doze, and she didn't want to disturb him. She had noticed that sleep was the best remedy for his headaches. Let him rest while he still would. Soon, probably too soon, he would be forcing his body to do his bidding. That was the first time in days that he had mentioned getting up, but she knew it wouldn't be the last.

When she stepped outside, the heat slammed into her like a blow to the body. It probably wasn't any hotter than it had been before, but in her fatigue she felt it more intensely. It wasn't just the scorching rays of the sun. It was the heat that rose in shimmering waves from the earth and slapped her in the face. It had been this hot that July when Rule had— Forget about that, she told herself sternly. She had work to do. She had shirked her duty yesterday, and today she was determined to make up for it.

She stopped in at the foaling barn to check on the two new mothers and their foals. Floyd assured her that Sable was in good condition after her ordeal, then invited her to help him anytime he had a mare in foal. Cathryn looked at him doubtfully and he laughed.

"You did just fine with Andalusia, Miss Cathryn," he assured her.

"Andalusia did just fine," she corrected, laughing. "By the way, do you know what direction Lewis went in this morning?"

Floyd frowned, thinking. "I'm not sure, but I think it was Lewis I saw with Ricky this morning, tearing across the pasture in the truck." He pointed due east to where she knew the small herd of cattle was grazing.

If Ricky was in the truck, it probably was Lewis in there with her, Cathryn thought shrewdly with her new knowledge of their relationship. She was torn between relief that Ricky had evidently transferred her attentions away from Rule and sympathy for Lewis. Didn't he realize that Ricky was nothing but trouble?

Suddenly she was riveted by a shout that curdled the blood in her veins. She stood frozen, staring at Floyd, and on his face she saw mirrored the same horror.

"Fire! In the stables!"

"Oh, God," she moaned, suddenly released from her spell, whirling on the spot and starting for the door at a dead run. Floyd was right beside her, his face pale. Fire in the stables! It was one of the worst things that could happen on a ranch. The animals panicked and often resisted any efforts to rescue them, resulting in tragedy. And as she ran the agonized thought surfaced that if Rule heard the commotion he would force himself out of bed and do any amount of damage to his health by trying to assist them.

"Fire!"

"Oh, God, be quiet!" she yelled. The ranch hand looked

startled; then he saw her glance at the house and he appeared to understand. Heavy black smoke was drifting almost lazily out the open doors, and she could hear the frightened whinnies of the horses, but she couldn't see any flames.

"Here!" Someone slapped a wet towel across her face and she dashed into the murky interior, coughing even through the towel as the acrid smoke sifted into her lungs. She couldn't feel any heat, though, but now wasn't the time to look for any flames; the horses came first.

The frightened animals were rearing in their stalls and kicking at the wood that held them. Cathryn fumbled for a door and opened it, squinting through the smoke at the horse and recognizing it as Redman, Rule's favorite. "Easy, easy," she crooned, taking a deep breath and whipping the towel away from her face to drape it over the horse's eyes. He calmed down enough to let her lead him swiftly out of the stable into the fresh air. Behind her, other horses were being led out in a quick, remarkably quiet operation. Willing hands helped settle the animals down.

The fire was caught while it was still smoldering. Luckily it hadn't gotten into the hay or the entire stable would have gone up in minutes. A young man whom Rule had hired only two months before discovered the source of the smoke in the tack room, where a fire had started in a trash can and spread to the saddle blankets and leather. The tack was ruined, the room blackened and scorched, but everyone breathed a sigh of relief that it hadn't been any worse than it was.

Astonishingly, Rule seemed to have been undisturbed by the commotion. Probably the whirr of the air-conditioner had masked the noise. Cathryn sighed, knowing that she would have to tell him, and knowing that he would be enraged. A fire in the stables was something that wouldn't have happened if he had been in charge. Knowing that the boss was out of commission, someone had gotten careless with a match or a cigarette, and only luck had prevented things from being much worse. As it was, a great deal of tack would have to be replaced. She had tried so hard to take up the slack, and then something like this had to happen.

Lorna's comforting arm slipped around her drooping shoulders. "Come on back to the house, Cathryn. You could use a good hot bath. You're black from head to foot."

Looking down, Cathryn saw that her crisp clothing, donned only a short time earlier, was now grimy with soot. She could feel the ash on her face and in her hair.

The feeling that she had let Rule down grew stronger as she stood under the shower. She couldn't even begin to imagine what he would say when she told him.

He had turned on the small radio by his bed, and that had kept him from being disturbed. He looked at her when she opened the door and his eyes narrowed at the strained expression on her face. He took in her wet hair and different clothing and set his jaw.

"What happened?" he ground out.

"There was a…a fire in the tack room," she stammered, coming a hesitant step closer. "It didn't spread," she assured him quickly, seeing the black horror that spread across his face. "The horses are all fine. It's just the…the tack room. We lost just about everything in there."

"Why wasn't I told?" he asked through clenched teeth.

"I—it was my decision. There was nothing you could do. We got the horses out first and—"

"You went into the stable?" he barked, heaving himself up on his elbow and wincing at the pain the movement caused him. Red fires were beginning to burn in the dark depths of his eyes, and suddenly she felt chills running down her back. He was more than angry; he was maddened, his fists clenching.

"Yes," she admitted, feeling tears form in her eyes. Hastily she blinked them away. She wasn't a child to burst into tears whenever she was yelled at. "The flames hadn't spread beyond the tack room, thank God, but the horses were frightened and—"

"My God, woman, are you stupid?" he roared. "Of all the reckless, half-witted things to do…!"

She *was* stupid, because the tears rolled down her cheeks anyway. "I'm sorry," she choked. "I didn't mean to let it happen!"

"Then what did you mean? Can't I let you out of my sight for a minute?"

"I said I'm sorry!" she gasped at him, and suddenly she couldn't stand there and listen to the rest of it. "I'll be back later," she sobbed. "I have to send someone to town for more tack."

"Damn it, come back here!" he was roaring, but she scooted out the door and slammed it behind her. She slapped at the wetness on her cheeks, then went into the bathroom and splashed cold water on her face until most of the redness had faded. She wanted nothing more than to hide in her room, but pride stiffened her back. There was work to be done, and she wasn't about to let someone else shoulder the burden for her.

CHAPTER 11

Someone had notified Lewis, and the pickup came tearing across the pasture and slid to a stop in the yard. Lewis was out of it in a flash, taking Cathryn's arm in a hold that was painfully tight. "What happened?" he asked, tight-lipped.

"The tack room caught on fire," she said wearily. "We got it before it spread, but the tack is ruined. All the horses are okay."

"Hell," he swore. "Rule will be fit to be tied."

"He already is." She tried to smile. "I told him a little while ago. Fit to be tied is putting it mildly."

He swore again. "Have you found out how it started?"

"The trash can caught on fire somehow; it looks as if the fire started there."

"Who's been in the tack room this morning? More importantly, who was in there last?"

She looked at him blankly. "I don't know. I hadn't thought to ask."

"When I find out who's responsible he can start looking for another job. No one, but no one, is supposed to smoke around a stable."

It seemed to Cathryn that no one would ever admit to smoking and causing the fire, but from the determined expression on Lewis's face, someone had better confess or everyone was in trouble. She found that she couldn't summon enough energy to care. She looked around vaguely, noticing that Ricky hadn't cared, either; she was walking to the house, twisting her hair up and pinning it carelessly on top of her head.

The stench of smoke still lingered on the hot, breezeless air, keeping the horses restless. Dull thuds reverberated through the stable as the nervy animals kicked at the stalls that held them. Everyone was kept busy trying to calm them and keep them from injuring themselves. Cathryn gave up trying to keep Redman settled down and led the big horse out of his stall, walking him around and around the yard. Part of his trouble was that he wasn't used to being cooped up, but with Rule out of commission no one had been giving him the exercise he thought was rightfully his.

Suddenly a ride seemed like just the thing. Cathryn was on the point of calling for a saddle when she remembered that there were no saddles left. She leaned her face into the horse's muscular neck and sighed. A day that had begun so delightfully had turned into a nightmare, and it seemed that there would be no escape from it.

Lewis was systematically questioning everyone who worked on the ranch, but Cathryn realized that the fire in the trash can could have smoldered for some time before actually blazing, and there were a lot of hands who were still out on the range, having left early that morning and not planning to return until dusk. She beckoned Lewis over to her. "Please, let it wait until later," she requested, then explained her reasoning to him. "We've got a lot of work to do right now. We have to notify the insurance company and I'm sure they'll want to do an on-site inspection."

Lewis was too sharp-eyed for anything to be hidden from him for long. He took a long, hard look at her and his stony expression softened slightly. "You've been crying, haven't you? Don't let it get to you. The fact that there was a fire at all is serious, but the damage could have been a lot worse."

"I know," she said tightly. "But I should have checked everything and I didn't. It was my fault that it got as out of hand as it did."

Lewis took Redman's lead rope from her hand. "Your fault, hell! You can't be expected to poke your nose into every corner—"

"Rule would have spotted it."

He opened his mouth to say something, then shut it because she was right. Rule *would* have spotted it. Nothing about the ranch escaped his notice. Lewis scowled as a thought struck him. "What did Rule say?"

"He had quite a lot to say," Cathryn replied cryptically, giving him a painful smile.

"Such as?"

In spite of herself those stupid tears began burning in her eyes again. "Do you want to start with the insults, or go on to the central theme?"

"He was just mad," said Lewis uncomfortably.

"I'll say!"

"He didn't mean it. It's just that a stable fire is so serious...."

"I know. I don't blame him." She really didn't. His reaction was understandable. He could have seen a lot of what he had worked so hard for over the years go up in smoke, and his beloved horses would have died a horrible death.

"He'll cool down and apologize to you. You'll see," Lewis promised.

Cathryn turned her eyes up to him in a doubtful gaze and he began to look sheepish. The idea of Rule Jackson apologizing was almost more than she could imagine, and evidently Lewis realized that, too.

"If it's anyone's fault, it's mine," Lewis sighed. "I should have been here, but instead I was—" He stopped abruptly.

"I know." Cathryn studied the tips of her boots, not certain if she should say anything else, but the words bubbled out. "Don't hurt her, Lewis. Ricky's stubbed her toes on a lot of rocks, and she's just not able to handle any more hurts right now."

He narrowed his eyes. "I could only hurt her if she was serious; she's not. She's playing with me, using me as entertainment. I know that, and I'm playing along with her. *If* I decide to put my foot down, she'll be the first to know. But for now I'm just not ready."

"Are men ever ready?" she asked a little bitterly.

"Sometimes. Like I told you before, women are a habit that's hard to break. It's the little things that get in a man's blood, like the smell of a hot meal when he comes dragging in, or the back rub, the laughter, even the fights. It's really special when you can have a roaring argument with someone and know that they still love you."

Yes, that would be special. And what was really painful was to have a roaring argument with a man you loved but whom you suspected of not loving you in return. Every angry word from Rule tore into her like a knife.

"Take Ricky," Lewis drawled. "She's been married twice, but all she's ever been is a decoration. Nobody has ever needed her; she's never felt useful. Why do you think she hangs around and works with the horses? It's the only time she's actually doing something productive. What that woman needs is a man who'll let her take care of him."

"Are you that man?"

He shrugged his big shoulders. "I've been taking care of myself for a long time now, and that's another habit that's hard to break. Who knows? Would you mind if I was?"

Cathryn looked up at him, startled. "Why should I mind?"

"I've got a lot of rough edges, and I've seen a lot of trouble."

She had to smile. "And started your share of it, too, I'll bet."

He started to smile too; then the sound of a car caught their attention and they turned to look at the vehicle coming up the road. "Who's that?" she asked, raising her hand to shade her eyes as she stared at it.

After a moment Lewis growled, "I think it's that Morris fellow."

She muttered an uncomplimentary word under her breath. "He's certainly pushy enough, isn't he? He doesn't like to take no for an answer."

"I wasn't sure that no was going to be the answer," said Lewis laconically, looking down at her.

"Well, it is," she said forcefully. She couldn't say just when she had decided. Perhaps she had always known that she wouldn't be able to sell the ranch. Too much of herself was bound up there to contemplate selling it to some stranger. She was tied by both the past and the future to this piece of Texas.

"Redman's settled down," Lewis observed as Ira Morris got out of his car. "I'll take him back to his stall."

She stood waiting for her unwelcome visitor, keeping her expression carefully blank. "Mr. Morris," she said in a neutral tone.

"Mrs. Ashe. I heard in town that you'd had some trouble out here this morning." His cold eyes darted over the stable, and Cathryn was amazed at how quickly the news had spread.

"Did you come out to see if you might want to withdraw your offer?" she asked sweetly. "As you can see, the damage is minor and none of the horses were hurt; however, I'll save you any additional time and trouble by telling you straight out that I won't be selling the ranch."

He didn't look surprised; he merely looked determined. "Don't be so hasty with that decision. You haven't heard my offer yet. When people start talking actual dollars and cents, a lot of them change their minds."

"I won't. I was born in that house, and I plan on dying there."

Totally ignoring her, he named a sum of money that would have staggered her if she had been wavering in her decision. As it was, she wasn't even tempted. She shook her head. "Not interested, Mr. Morris."

"You could live in comfort for the rest of your life with that much money."

"I live in comfort now. I'm where I want to be, doing what I want to do. Why should I throw that away for money?"

He sighed and thrust his hands into his pockets. "Think about it. A house is just a house. A piece of land is just a piece of land. There are other houses, more land. This kind of life isn't really suited to you. Look at you. You've got big city written all over you."

"What I have all over me, Mr. Morris, is dust. Texas dust. *My* dust. I lived in Chicago for several years, yes, but there wasn't a day that I didn't think about this ranch and wish that I was here."

Without a single change in his expression he raised his offer.

Cathryn was beginning to feel harried. "No. No. I'm not interested—at any price," she said firmly.

"You could travel all over the world—"

"No!"

"Buy jewelry and furs—"

Goaded almost beyond control, Cathryn clenched her jaw. "I don't intend to sell," she said stonily. "Why can't you believe that?"

"Mrs. Ashe," he warned, "if you're trying to force me to raise my offer again, it just won't work. I've talked with your Mr. Jackson and he gave me a fair idea of what this stud is worth. I'm in the market for horses and I like the idea of owning my own stud; not only that, but I was given to understand that you'll be returning to Chicago soon."

Cathryn was so stunned that she almost lost her breath. She grasped his arm. "What?" she gasped.

"I said I talked to your manager. You told me yourself that he knows more about the horses here than anyone else, so he was the logical person to ask. He also told me that you'd probably be leaving."

"Just when did you talk to him?"

"Last night. On the telephone."

The guest room had a telephone jack in it, so she could only suppose that someone had carried the phone into the room for Rule to use. But why would Rule tell this man anything? He was dead set against selling the ranch...or was he? What was going on?

"Just what did Mr. Jackson tell you?" she demanded.

"We didn't talk long. He merely indicated to me that he thought you were returning to Chicago and would sell if the price was right, and we discussed what that price should be. Going on the information he gave me, I think my last offer is more than fair."

Cathryn drew a shaking breath. "Well, he was wrong in his thinking, and so are you!" She was so upset that she was trembling, and she wavered between fury and tears. Just what was going on? She didn't know what game Rule Jackson was playing, but she was going to find out before another minute had passed. "The answer is no, Mr. Morris, and that's my final answer. I'm sorry you've wasted your time."

"So am I," he said tightly. "So am I."

She didn't wait to see him leave. She turned away and almost ran to the house, her entire being concentrated on reaching Rule and finding out what he had meant by telling Mr. Morris that she would sell. Was he trying to make her leave?

No, he couldn't be! Only last night he had made love to her as if he couldn't get enough of her. But...*why?*

She brushed past Lorna, not even seeing her, and flew up the stairs, her feet barely touching the steps. Without warning she threw open the door to Rule's bedroom.

At first the tangled bodies on the bed didn't make any sense to her and she stared at them blankly; then realization sank in and she had to lean against the doorframe to keep from collapsing to the floor. Of all the shocks she had sustained that day, this one was the worst. This one hit her in the stomach and drove all the breath from her body. This one tore at her insides, draining the blood from her face. Ricky was on the bed with Rule, her arm under his neck, her mouth glued to his while she writhed on top of him and her hands stroked his hard-muscled body. Her blouse was open, hanging half out of her jeans. Rule's hand was tangled in her hair.

Then the horror faded from Cathryn's mind and she saw the scene clearly. Rule wasn't holding Ricky's head to him; he was pulling back on her hair in an effort to free his mouth from her determined assault. Finally he managed to force her away, and he muttered, "Damn it, Ricky, would you stop? Leave me alone!"

Rage exploded through Cathryn's veins. She wasn't aware of crossing to the bed. A red mist swam before her eyes, blurring her vision as she grabbed the collar of Ricky's shirt and hauled her bodily off Rule. Fury gave her strength that she had never before known she possessed. "This is it," she ground out, the words rough as sand as she tore them from her constricted throat. "This finishes it."

"Hey!" Ricky squealed as Cathryn slung her around to the door. "What do you think you're doing? Have you gone crazy?"

Without a word, so angry that she couldn't say anything

else, Cathryn dragged the other woman through the door and slammed it shut behind them, not hearing Rule's hoarse cry for her to come back.

The banisters of the staircase beckoned madly and the temptation was sugar sweet, but at the last moment a small piece of sanity returned and Cathryn refrained from simply dumping Ricky down the stairs. Ladies didn't do things like that, or that was what she told herself as she forced Ricky along the hall at a trot, handling the young woman with as much ease as if she were only a child. Ricky was yelling and wailing loudly enough to wake the dead, but Cathryn drowned her out with a roared, "Shut up!" as she rushed her into Ricky's own room.

"Sit down!" she bellowed, and Ricky sat. "I warned you! I told you to stay away from him. He's mine, and I won't tolerate you crawling all over him for another minute, do you hear? Get packed and get out!"

"Get out?" Ricky looked dazed, her mouth falling open. "Where to?"

"That's your problem!" Cathryn opened the closet and began hauling suitcases out. She threw them on the bed and opened them, then began pulling open drawers and dumping the contents into the bags, helter-skelter.

Ricky sprang to her feet. "Hey, don't blame it all on me! I wasn't exactly raping him, you know! One woman has never been enough for Rule—"

"It will be from now on! And don't try to make me believe that he invited you, because I don't believe it!"

Ricky glared at the tangle of clothing. "Damn it, quit throwing my clothes around like that!"

"Then pack them yourself!"

Abruptly Ricky bit her lip and tears slid down her cheeks. Cathryn stared at her in mingled disgust and amazement, wondering how anyone could cry and still look so lovely. No red and streaming nose, no blotched face, just diamond-bright tears sliding gracefully down.

"But I really don't have any place to go," Ricky whispered. "And I don't have any money."

The door opened and Monica came in, frowning her annoyance. "Must you two brawl through the house like wrestlers? What's going on?"

"She's trying to make me leave!" Ricky charged hotly, her tears drying up as if by magic. Cathryn stood silently, her hands on her hips and her expression implacable.

Monica glanced quickly at her stepdaughter and said in exasperation, "It's her house; I imagine she has the right to say who lives here."

"That's right, it's always been *her* house!"

"Stop that!" Monica said sharply. "Feeling sorry for yourself won't help anything. You must have known that eventually Cathryn would be coming back, and if you lacked the foresight to prepare yourself for the future, don't blame anyone else. Besides, do you really want to spend the rest of your life listening to the pitter-patter of someone else's kids?"

Evidently Monica observed a lot, even though she always seemed disinterested in anyone's concerns except her own. Cathryn pulled in a deep, calming breath. Of course! Life wasn't so complicated after all. It was really very simple. She loved Rule, she loved the ranch, and she wasn't about to give up either of them. Why tear herself up worrying about the depth of Rule's feelings? Whatever they were, they were there, and that was all that mattered.

With that thought full sanity returned. She sighed. "You don't have to leave right now," she told Ricky, rubbing her forehead to ease the tension that had begun to throb there. "I lost my temper when I saw... Anyway, you can take your time and make some plans. But you can't take forever," she warned. "I don't think you want to stay around for the wedding, anyway, do you?"

"Wedding?" Ricky turned pale; then two spots of color appeared on her cheeks. "You're awfully sure of yourself, aren't you?"

"I have reason to be," Cathryn replied evenly. "Rule asked me to marry him before he broke his leg. I'm accepting."

"Congratulations," Monica inserted with smooth precision. "I can see that we'll really be in the way, won't we? Ricky, dear, I've decided to take Cathryn up on her offer to use her apartment in Chicago. I suppose we can get along well enough for you to share the apartment with me, if you'd like. It *does* have two bedrooms, doesn't it?" she asked Cathryn hastily.

"Yes." It seemed a good idea to Cathryn. She looked at Ricky.

Ricky chewed her lip. "I don't know. I'll think about it."

"Don't think too long," advised Monica. "I'm making arrangements to leave by the end of the week."

"You said I was too old to live with Mommy," Ricky mimicked with a flash of resentment.

"Neither the arrangement nor the offer is a permanent one," snapped Monica. "For God's sake, make up your mind."

"All right." Ricky could look as sulky as a child when she tried, and she was really trying now, but Cathryn didn't care. She heaved a sigh of relief. When her temper cooled she would have felt guilty if she had thrown Ricky out of the house without giving her a chance to make some sort of arrangements. Now that she knew the time limit on Ricky's presence she felt better able to cope with it—so long as she didn't catch the woman touching Rule again.

Rule. Cathryn took another deep breath and prepared for the last battle. Rule Jackson's days as a bachelor were limited. It didn't matter if he didn't love her. She loved him enough for two, and she wasn't going to run away ever again. She was going to stay right there, and if he wanted the ranch he had to take her, too. One thing was certain: She couldn't bear the thought of any other woman thinking that he was unattached and jumping into his bed! She planned to attach him as soon as possible, and do it up right.

With the determination of a charging cavalry brigade, her dark eyes intent, she went down the hall to his room and thrust the door open.

She looked automatically at the bed and was stunned to find it empty. A chill ran down her back. She stepped into the room and at a movement to her right she turned her head. Aghast, she stared at him, a terrified cry of "Rule!" bursting from her throat.

He was out of the bed, struggling with the cast on his leg as he pulled on a pair of jeans. Somehow he had managed to tear open the seam of the left leg of the jeans so he could get them on over the cast. He was wavering precariously as he battled to dress himself, cursing between clenched teeth with every breath he drew, damning his own weakness, the cast on his leg, the throbbing of his head. He swung around clumsily at her cry and she nearly choked when she saw the raw despair that twisted his face, the tortured tears that streaked down his hard cheeks.

"Rule," she moaned, as he turned a look of such agony on her that she wanted to hide her eyes from it. He took a step toward her and lurched suddenly to one side when his broken leg was unable to take his weight. Wildly, Cathryn leapt across the room and caught him as he started to fall, holding him up with desperate strength.

"Oh, God," he groaned, wrapping his arms around her in a death grip, crushing her against his hard body. He bent his head to hers and harsh sobs shook him. "Don't go. God, baby, please don't go. I can explain. Just don't leave me again."

Cathryn tried to stiffen her legs, but she was slowly collapsing under the burden of his weight. "I can't hold you," she gasped. "You've got to get back in bed!"

"No," he refused thickly, his shoulders heaving. "I won't let you go. I couldn't get out of that damned bed, couldn't get my clothes on fast enough...I was so afraid you'd be gone before I could get to you, that I'd never see you again," he muttered brokenly.

Her throat closed at the thought of him battling his pain and injuries to reach her before she left. He couldn't walk, so how was he going to get to her? Crawl? Yes, she realized, he would have crawled if he had had to. The determination of this man was an awesome thing.

"I won't leave," she assured him through her tears. "I promise. I'll never leave you again. Please, darling, get back in bed. I can't hold you up much longer."

He sagged in her arms as some of the tension left him, and she felt her knees begin to buckle. "Please," she begged again. "You've got to get back in bed before you fall and break something else."

She was fortunate that the bed was only a few steps away, or she would never have made it. He was leaning heavily on her, sweat running down his face and mingling with the tears that wet it. He was almost at the end of his rope, and when she supported his head and shoulders as he lay back on the pillows he closed his eyes, his breath heaving in and out of his chest. He gripped her arm tightly, holding her beside the bed. "Don't leave," he said again, this time in little more than a whisper.

"I'm not leaving," she crooned. "Let me lift your leg up on the pillows. Oh, Rule, you shouldn't have tried to get up like that!"

"I had to stop you. You wouldn't have come back again."
But he released her arm and she moved to the foot of the bed
to lift his leg up. For a moment she stared at the gaping seam of
his jeans, wondering how he had managed to tear the heavy-
duty pants like that. She decided to get him out of the jeans
while he was weak and unable to put up much of a fight, so
she eased them down his hips and carefully drew them off.
He lay limply, his eyes closed.

She wet a washcloth in cold water and wiped the sweat from
his forehead, then the moisture from his cheeks. He opened
his eyes and stared at her in fierce concentration, strength already returning to his magnificent body.

"I didn't invite Ricky in here," he said harshly. "I know
what it looked like, but I was trying to make her stop. Maybe
I wasn't pushing her away too hard, but I didn't want to hurt
her—"

"I know," she assured him tenderly, placing her finger on
his lips. "I'm not an idiot, at least not completely. I'd already
warned her once before to stay away from you, and when I
saw her crawling all over you like that I blew sky-high. She
and Monica are leaving at the end of the week to take my
apartment in Chicago. They can save me a trip," she added
whimsically. "I left most of my clothes up there, and I need
them. They can ship them to me."

He sucked in a deep breath, his dark eyes as bottomless as
eternity. "You believe me?"

"Of course I believe you." She gave him an exquisite smile.
"I trust you."

For a moment he looked stunned by her unquestioning
faith; then a tiny scowl began to form between his brows.
"You had no intention of leaving?"

"None."

"Then, damn it all," he said from between clenched teeth,

"why did you go storming out of here and leave me lying in this bed screaming my guts out for you?"

Cathryn went very still, staring down at him. She hadn't realized it until this very moment, but his reaction said a lot. If he cared that much…was it possible? Did she dare dream…? She said carefully, "I never thought it would matter that much to you if I left or not, as long as the ranch stayed under your control."

He uttered a very explicit comment, then attacked fiercely. "Not matter! Do you think a man waits for a woman as long as I've waited for you if it doesn't matter to him whether she leaves or stays?"

"I didn't know you'd been waiting for me," she said simply. "I've always thought it was the ranch that meant the most to you."

His jaw tightened to granite. "The ranch does mean a lot to me. I can't deny that. I was almost at the bottom of a long downhill slide when Ward brought me here and saved my life, put me back together. I've worked myself half to death for years because this place meant salvation to me."

"Then why did you talk to Ira Morris?" she blurted, her dark eyes shadowed with the pain and shock she had felt at that betrayal. "Why did you tell him that I'd probably sell if the price was right? Why did you tell him how much the ranch is worth?" She couldn't understand that, but then, there was so much about Rule that she didn't understand. He was so deep, hiding so much of himself. He'd have to learn to talk about himself, to share his thoughts with her. And he *was* learning, she thought hopefully.

He caught her hand, curling her fingers under his, and held it against his chest. A desperate look tightened his features before he looked away and deliberately wiped his face clear of expression. "I was scared," he finally said in a strained voice.

"More scared than I ever was in Nam. At first I was furious at the thought that you might sell; then it really hit me and I was scared. But I was scared for myself, and what I might lose. Finally I realized that the ranch is yours, not mine, just like you've been telling me all along, and if you weren't happy here then the best thing for you would be to sell it and go somewhere where you could be happy. When Morris called I agreed to talk to him. I want you to be happy, honey. Whatever it takes, I want that for you."

"I *am* happy," she assured him softly, turning her hand under his so she could feel the hard warmth of his body beneath her fingertips. She stroked the dark curls with absorbed delight. "I'll never sell the Bar D. You belong here, and if this is where you are, then I'll be here, too." She caught her breath as soon as the words were out, unable to look at him as she waited in agony for his response. The seconds ticked by and still he was silent. She swallowed and forced herself to lift her gaze to him.

She hadn't expected him to shout hosannas, but neither was she expecting the way his eyes had narrowed, or the guarded expression that masked his face. "What are you saying?" he rumbled slowly.

It was now or never. She had to commit herself, had to take the first step, because if she backed off now she knew that Rule would, too. He had gone as far as he could go, this proud man of hers. She assured herself that it really wasn't that much of a gamble. She couldn't live without him—it was that simple. Cut and dried. She'd take him on any terms. "You asked me to marry you," she said carefully, choosing her words and watching the effect of each one on his expression. "I accept."

"Why?" he rapped out.

"Why?" she echoed, looking at him as if he had gone mad. Didn't he know? Did he really not understand? The horrible thought arose that he might have changed his mind. "Is...is the offer still open?" she stumbled, painful uncertainty evident in both her voice and her face. He reached up with his other hand and caught a handful of her hair, forcing her inexorably down to him. When their noses were almost bumping he stopped and regarded her with such intensity that she felt as if he were walking inside her mind.

"The offer is still open," he growled softly, the words whispering against her lips. "Just tell me why you're accepting it. Are you pregnant? Is that it?"

"No!" she denied, startled. "It isn't that. I mean, I don't know. How could I know yet? There hasn't been time."

"Then why are you agreeing to marry me?" he persisted. "Tell me, Cat."

He was pinning her down, refusing to let her hide behind anything, and suddenly she didn't want to hide. Serenity and inner strength flooded her. Let him have his confession. She could give it to him out of the richness of her love. She freed her hand from under his and cupped his face in both palms, her fingers lovingly molding the hard contours of his jaw. "Because I love you, Rule Jackson," she said with aching tenderness. "I've loved you for years…for what seems like forever. And it doesn't matter if you don't love me, if the ranch is all you care about. If you want the ranch, you have to take me. It's a package deal. So, Mr. Jackson, you'd better start learning how to be a husband."

He looked thunderstruck and his grip on her hair tightened. "Are you crazy?" he shouted. "What the hell are you talking about?"

"The ranch," she said steadily. "If you want it, you have to marry me to get it."

Raw fury began to form visibly on his face, in his eyes. He said something that didn't bear repeating, but it illustrated his feelings. His entire body shuddered as what little control he had left exploded, and he roared at her, "To hell with the ranch! Sell it! If that's what's been standing between us for all of these years, then get rid of it! If you want to live in Chicago, or Hong Kong, or Bangkok, then I'll live there with you, because *you're* what I've always wanted, not this damned ranch! My God, Cat, I've got a ranch of my own if that was what I wanted! Dad left everything to me when he died, you know." His hand swept over her body. "Did you think *this* was because I wanted the ranch? Sweet hell, woman, can't you tell that you make me crazy?"

Her blank expression told him that she had never even thought of it from that angle. He pulled her down on the bed beside him and clamped her to his side. "Listen to me," he said slowly, deliberately, every word separate and distinct. "I don't want the ranch. It's a good life and it saved me, and I'd miss it if we lived somewhere else, but I can live without it. What I can't live without anymore is you. I've tried. For eight years I got through life day by day, feeding myself on the memory of the one time I'd had you, hating myself for driving you away. When you finally came back I knew I'd never be able to let you go again. I'll do whatever it takes to keep you, honey, because if you walk out on me again I might as well stop living."

Cathryn felt as if her heart had stopped beating. He hadn't actually said the words yet, but he was telling her that he loved her as desperately, as powerfully as she loved him. It was almost more than she could take in, more than she could allow herself to believe. "I didn't know," she whispered dazedly. "You never said...you never told me."

"How could I tell you?" he asked roughly. "You were so young, too young for everything I wanted from you. I never meant for that day by the river to happen, but when it did I couldn't regret it. I wanted to do it again, over and over, until that terrified look in your eyes was gone and you looked at me with the same need I felt for you. But I didn't, and you ran. I regret that, because you met David Ashe and married him. It's a good thing you didn't come around for quite a while after that, Cat, because I've never wanted to take a man apart as badly as I did him."

"You were jealous?" She still couldn't make herself comprehend everything he was telling her, and she pinched herself surreptitiously; the small pain was real, and so was the man who lay beside her.

The look he gave her spoke volumes. "Jealous isn't the word for it. I was insane with it."

"You love me," she whispered in wonder. "You really love me. If only you'd told me! I had no idea!"

"Of course I love you! I *need* you, and I've never needed anyone before in my life. You were as wild and innocent as a foal, and I couldn't keep my eyes away from you. You made me feel alive again, made me forget the nightmares that jerked me up in bed. When I made love to you, we fit together perfectly. Everything was right, all the moves and reactions. You nearly burned me alive every time I touched you. I had to be with you, had to see you and talk to you, and you had no idea how I felt?"

He looked outraged, and Cathryn managed a small laugh as she snuggled closer to him. "It's that stone face of yours," she teased. "But I was so afraid of letting you know how I felt, afraid you didn't feel the same way."

"I feel the same," he said gruffly, then demanded, "Tell me again." He slid his palm up her side and cupped a breast. "Let me hear it again."

"I love you." She complied gladly, joyously with his demand. Saying the words aloud was a celebration, a benediction.

"Will you tell me that when we're making love?"

"As often as you want," she promised.

"I want. Now." His voice had roughened with desire and he pulled her to him, his mouth clinging to hers. The old familiar magic seared through her veins again and she melted against him, not noticing when he unbuttoned her shirt, only aware of the intense pleasure she felt when his hand touched her bare skin.

A dying glimmer of caution prompted her words. "Rule… we shouldn't. You need to rest."

"That's not what I need," he murmured in her ear. "Now, Cathryn. *Now.*"

"The door is open," she protested weakly.

"Then close it and come back to me. Don't make me chase you down."

He probably would, she thought, broken leg and all. She got up and closed the door, then came back to him. She couldn't touch him enough, couldn't satisfy her need to feel his hard, warm flesh beneath her fingers. She made love to him, lavishing him with her love, trailing kisses all over him and whispering "I love you" against his skin, imprinting him with the words. Now that she could say the words aloud, she found that she couldn't say them enough, and she made a litany of them as she loved him, lingering so long in her caresses that suddenly he couldn't take any more, lifting her bodily above him and fusing his flesh with hers in a quick, strong movement.

She danced the dance of passion with him, attacking and retreating, but always pleasuring. She was aware of nothing but him, the hot desire in his dark eyes, and something else, the glow of love returned.

"Don't stop saying it," he commanded, and she obeyed until the words wouldn't come, until all she could do was gasp his name and writhe against him. His powerful hands on her hips took over the motion, driving her higher and higher, until with an almost silent wail she collapsed, shuddering, on his chest.

In the quiet, sleepy aftermath he smoothed her tousled hair and held her tightly to him. "I'll need to hire more hands," he said drowsily.

"Mmmm," said Cathryn. "Why?"

"To take up the slack. I can tell right now that I won't be spending as much time on the range. I'll have a major problem just getting out of bed in the mornings. Taking care of a woman like you will be time-consuming, and I intend to do my best."

"I'll drink to that," she toasted, lifting an imaginary glass.

"We'll get married next week," he said, nuzzling his face into her hair.

"Next week?" She made a startled move away from him. "But you're still—"

"I'll be up by then," he soothed. "Trust me. And ask Monica if she and Ricky will stay for the wedding. Always mend your fences, honey."

She smiled. "I know. I don't want any bad feelings between us. And who knows? Lewis may keep Ricky here."

"Don't put any money on it. They both have too many hurts bottled up inside. He may want her, but I don't think he could live with her. Things don't always work out the way you want them to."

Silence fell again, and she felt herself slipping into sleep. A thought nagged at the edges of her consciousness, and she muttered, "I'm sorry about the tack room."

"It wasn't your fault," he comforted, his arms tightening about her.

"You called me stupid."

"I apologize. I panicked at the thought of you going into

a burning stable, fighting with those horses to get them out. What if something had happened to you? I'd have gone mad."

"You don't blame me?" she whispered.

"I love you," he corrected. "I couldn't stand it if you were hurt."

She felt as if her heart would burst with happiness. So that tantrum had been purely because he didn't want her taking risks! She opened her eyes and looked up at him from where she lay with her head cradled on his powerful shoulder, and softly, as tenderly as a dream, she said, "I love you."

Rule's arms tightened around her even more, and he murmured, "I love you."

A moment later his deep voice drifted into the silence. "Welcome home, honey."

And at last she *was* home, in Rule's arms, where she belonged.

★ ★ ★ ★ ★

FATAL AFFAIR
MARIE FORCE

Acknowledgments

When I first began work on the book that became *Fatal Affair,* I quickly realized that I couldn't begin to replicate the District of Columbia's complex Metropolitan Police Department. So the department portrayed in *Fatal Affair* is my version of the MPD and is in no way intended to mirror the real thing.

I want to thank my husband, Dan, who loves a good excuse to surf the internet. He did tons of research for me, and I appreciate his help. My children, Emily and Jake, put up with me when I'm writing and have learned not to ask me any important questions when I'm lost in thought.

To the rest of my home team: Christina Camara, Paula DelBonis-Platt and Lisa Ridder, thank you for reading, critiquing, editing and proofreading. To Julie Cupp, thank you for braving the cold to take me to Eastern Market, for answering my many questions about Washington and for your help, as always, in naming characters. The shed is set for you to move in whenever you're ready to become my full-time assistant.

Thank you to Newport, Rhode Island, police lieutenant Russell Hayes for reading the book, providing critical input and taking me on a memorable ride-along. To my friend Newport police sergeant Rita Barker, thank you for reading and introducing me to Russ. Thanks to my WIP buddy Theresa Ragan for coming up with the perfect name for the book.

Special thanks to my agent, Kevan Lyon, and my Carina editor, Jessica Schulte. Both of you helped to make this a much better book than it would have been otherwise, and I'm grateful for your contributions. To Angela James and everyone on the Carina team, your energy astounds me, and I'm delighted to be a part of this grand new adventure.

For Sam and Nick, who've taken me on an unforgettable journey—
in more ways than one.

CHAPTER 1

The smell hit him first.

"Ugh, what the hell is that?" Nick Cappuano dropped his keys into his coat pocket and stepped into the spacious, well-appointed Watergate apartment that his boss, Senator John O'Connor, had inherited from his father.

"Senator!" Nick tried to identify the foul metallic odor.

Making his way through the living room, he noticed parts and pieces of the suit John wore yesterday strewn over sofas and chairs, laying a path to the bedroom. He had called the night before to check in with Nick after a dinner meeting with Virginia's Democratic Party leadership, and said he was on his way home. Nick had reminded his thirty-six-year-old boss to set his alarm.

"Senator?" John hated when Nick called him that when they were alone, but Nick insisted the people in John's life afford him the respect of his title.

The odd stench permeating the apartment caused a tingle of anxiety to register on the back of Nick's neck. "John?"

He stepped into the bedroom and gasped. Drenched in blood, John sat up in bed, his eyes open but vacant. A knife spiked through his neck held him in place against the headboard. His hands rested in a pool of blood in his lap.

Gagging, the last thing Nick noticed before he bolted to the bathroom to vomit was that something was hanging out of John's mouth.

Once the violent retching finally stopped, Nick stood up

on shaky legs, wiped his mouth with the back of his hand, and rested against the vanity, waiting to see if there would be more. His cell phone rang. When he didn't take the call, his pager vibrated. Nick couldn't find the wherewithal to answer, to say the words that would change everything. *The senator is dead. John's been murdered.* He wanted to go back to when he was still in his car, fuming and under the assumption that his biggest problem that day would be what to do about the man-child he worked for who had once again slept through his alarm.

Thoughts of John, dating back to their first meeting in a history class at Harvard freshman year, flashed through Nick's mind, hundreds of snippets spanning a nearly twenty-year friendship. As if to convince himself that his eyes had not deceived him, he leaned forward to glance into the bedroom, wincing at the sight of his best friend—the brother of his heart—stabbed through the neck and covered with blood.

Nick's eyes burned with tears, but he refused to give in to them. Not now. Later maybe, but not now. His phone rang again. This time he reached for it and saw it was Christina, his deputy chief of staff, but didn't take the call. Instead, he dialed 911.

Taking a deep breath to calm his racing heart and making a supreme effort to keep the hysteria out of his voice, he said, "I need to report a murder." He gave the address and stumbled into the living room to wait for the police, all the while trying to get his head around the image of his dead friend, a visual he already knew would haunt him forever.

Twenty long minutes later, two officers arrived, took a quick look in the bedroom and radioed for backup. Nick was certain neither of them recognized the victim.

He felt as if he was being sucked into a riptide, pulled further and further from the safety of shore, until drawing a breath became a laborious effort. He told the cops exactly what hap-

pened—his boss failed to show up for work, he came looking
for him and found him dead.

"Your boss's name?"

"United States Senator John O'Connor." Nick watched the
two young officers go pale in the instant before they made a
second more urgent call for backup.

"Another scandal at the Watergate," Nick heard one of them
mutter.

His cell phone rang yet again. This time he reached for it.

"Yeah," he said softly.

"Nick!" Christina cried. "Where the *hell* are you guys? Trev-
or's having a heart attack!" She referred to their communications director who had back-to-back interviews scheduled for
the senator that morning.

"He's dead, Chris."

"Who's dead? What're you talking about?"

"John."

Her soft cry broke his heart. *"No."* That she was desperately
in love with John was no secret to Nick. That she was also a
consummate professional who would never act on those feelings was one of the many reasons Nick respected her.

"I'm sorry to just blurt it out like that."

"How?" she asked in a small voice.

"Stabbed in his bed."

Her ravaged moan echoed through the phone. "But who...I
mean, *why?"*

"The cops are here, but I don't know anything yet. I need
you to request a postponement on the vote."

"I can't," she said, adding in a whisper, "I can't think about
that right now."

"You have to, Chris. That bill is his legacy. We can't let all
his hard work be for nothing. Can you do it? For him?"

"Yes...okay."

"You have to pull yourself together for the staff, but don't tell them yet. Not until his parents are notified."

"Oh, God, his poor parents. You should go, Nick. It'd be better coming from you than cops they don't know."

"I don't know if I can. How do I tell people I love that their son's been murdered?"

"He'd want it to come from you."

"I suppose you're right. I'll see if the cops will let me."

"What're we going to do without him, Nick?" She posed a question he'd been grappling with himself. "I just can't imagine this world, this *life,* without him."

"I can't either," Nick said, knowing it would be a much different life without John O'Connor at the center of it.

"He's really dead?" she asked as if to convince herself it wasn't a cruel joke. "Someone killed him?"

"Yes."

Outside the chief's office suite, Detective Sergeant Sam Holland smoothed her hands over the toffee-colored hair she corralled into a clip for work, pinched some color into cheeks that hadn't seen the light of day in weeks, and adjusted her gray suit jacket over a red scoop-neck top.

Taking a deep breath to calm her nerves and settle her chronically upset stomach, she pushed open the door and stepped inside. Chief Farnsworth's receptionist greeted her with a smile. "Go right in, Sergeant Holland. He's waiting for you."

Great, Sam thought as she left the receptionist with a weak smile. Before she could give in to the urge to turn tail and run, she erased the grimace from her face and went in.

"Sergeant." The chief, a man she'd once called Uncle Joe, stood up and came around the big desk to greet her with a firm handshake. His gray eyes skirted over her with concern

and sympathy, both of which were new since "the incident."
She despised being the reason for either. "You look well."

"I feel well."

"Glad to hear it." He gestured for her to have a seat. "Coffee?"

"No, thanks."

Pouring himself a cup, he glanced over his shoulder. "I've
been worried about you, Sam."

"I'm sorry for causing you worry and for disgracing the
department." This was the first chance she'd had to speak directly to him since she returned from a month of administrative leave, during which she'd practiced the sentence over and
over. She thought she'd delivered it with convincing sincerity.

"Sam," he sighed as he sat across from her, cradling his mug
between big hands. "You've done nothing to disgrace yourself
or the department. Everyone makes mistakes."

"Not everyone makes mistakes that result in a dead child,
Chief."

He studied her for a long, intense moment as if he was making some sort of decision. "Senator John O'Connor was found
murdered in his apartment this morning."

"*Jesus*," she gasped. "How?"

"I don't have all the details, but from what I've been told so
far, it appears he was dismembered and stabbed through the
neck. Apparently, his chief of staff found him."

"Nick," she said softly.

"Excuse me?"

"Nick Cappuano is O'Connor's chief of staff."

"You know him?"

"*Knew* him. Years ago," she added, surprised and unsettled
to discover the memory of him still had power over her, that
just the sound of his name rolling off her lips could make her
heart race.

"I'm assigning the case to you."

Surprised at being thrust so forcefully back into the real work she had craved since her return to duty, she couldn't help but ask, "Why me?"

"Because you need this, and so do I. We both need a win."

The press had been relentless in its criticism of him, of her, of the department, but to hear him acknowledge it made her ache. Her father had come up through the ranks with Farnsworth, which was probably the number one reason why she still had a job. "Is this a test? Find out who killed the senator and my previous sins are forgiven?"

He put down his coffee cup and leaned forward, elbows resting on knees. "The only person who needs to forgive you, Sam, is you."

Infuriated by the surge of emotion brought on by his softly spoken words, Sam cleared her throat and stood up. "Where does O'Connor live?"

"The Watergate. Two uniforms are already there. Crime scene is on its way." He handed her a slip of paper with the address. "I don't have to tell you that this needs to be handled with the utmost discretion."

He also didn't have to tell her that this was the only chance she'd get at redemption.

"Won't the Feds want in on this?"

"They might, but they don't have jurisdiction, and they know it. They'll be breathing down my neck, though, so report directly to me. I want to know everything ten minutes after you do. I'll smooth it with Stahl," he added, referring to the lieutenant she usually answered to.

Heading for the door, she said, "I won't let you down."

"You never have before."

With her hand resting on the door handle, she turned back

to him. "Are you saying that as the chief of police or as my Uncle Joe?"

His face lifted into a small but sincere smile. "Both."

CHAPTER 2

Sitting on John's sofa under the watchful eyes of the two policemen, Nick's mind raced with the staggering number of things that needed to be done, details to be seen to, people to call. His cell phone rang relentlessly, but he ignored it after deciding he would talk to no one until he had seen John's parents. Almost twenty years ago they took an instant shine to the hard-luck scholarship student their son brought home from Harvard for a weekend visit and made him part of their family. Nick owed them so much, not the least of which was hearing the news of their son's death from him if possible.

He ran his hand through his hair. "How much longer?"

"Detectives are on their way."

Ten minutes later, Nick heard her before he saw her. A flurry of activity and a burst of energy preceded the detectives' entrance into the apartment. He suppressed a groan. *Wasn't it enough that his friend and boss had been murdered? He had to face her, too? Weren't there thousands of District cops? Was she really the only one available?*

Sam came into the apartment, oozing authority and competence. In light of her recent troubles, Nick couldn't believe she had any of either left. "Get some tape across that door," she ordered one of the officers. "Start a log with a timeline of who got here when. No one comes in or goes out without my okay, got it?"

"Yes, ma'am. The patrol sergeant is on his way along with Deputy Chief Conklin and Detective Captain Malone."

"Let me know when they get here." Without so much as a glance in his direction, Nick watched her stalk through the apartment and disappear into the bedroom. Following her, a handsome young detective with bed head nodded to Nick.

He heard the murmur of voices from the bedroom and saw a camera flash. They emerged fifteen minutes later, both noticeably paler. For some reason, Nick was gratified to know the detectives working the case weren't so jaded as to be unaffected by what they'd just seen.

"Start a canvass of the building," Sam ordered her partner. "Where the hell is crime scene?"

"Hung up at another homicide," one of the other officers replied.

She finally turned to Nick, nothing in her pale blue eyes indicating that she recognized or remembered him. But the fact that she didn't introduce herself or ask for his name told him she knew exactly who he was. "We'll need your prints."

"They're on file," he mumbled. "Congressional background check."

She wrote something in the small notebook she tugged from the back pocket of gray, form-fitting pants. There were years on her gorgeous face that hadn't been there the last time he'd had the opportunity to look closely, and he couldn't tell if her hair was as long as it used to be since it was twisted into a clip. The curvy body and endless legs hadn't changed at all.

"No forced entry," she noted. "Who has a key?"

"Who *doesn't* have a key?"

"I'll need a list. You have a key, I assume."

Nick nodded. "That's how I got in."

"Was he seeing anyone?"

"No one serious, but he had no trouble attracting female companionship." Nick didn't add that John's casual approach to women and sex had been a source of tension between the two men, with Nick fearful that John's social life would one day lead to political trouble. He hadn't imagined it might also lead to murder.

"When was the last time you saw him?"

"When he left the office for a dinner meeting with the Virginia Democrats last night. Around six-thirty or so."

"Spoke to him?"

"Around ten when he said he was on his way home."

"Alone?"

"He didn't say, and I didn't ask."

"Take me through what happened this morning."

He told her about Christina trying to reach John, beginning at seven, and of coming to the apartment expecting to find the senator once again sleeping through his alarm.

"So this has happened before?"

"No, he's never been murdered before."

Her expression was anything but amused. "Do you think this is funny, Mr. Cappuano?"

"Hardly. My best friend is dead, Sergeant. A United States senator has been murdered. There's nothing funny about that."

"Which is why you need to answer the questions and save the droll humor for a more appropriate time."

Chastened, Nick said, "He slept through his alarm and ringing telephones at least once, if not twice, a month."

"Did he drink?"

"Socially, but I rarely saw him drunk."

"Prescription drugs? Sleeping pills?"

Nick shook his head. "He was just a very heavy sleeper."

"And it fell to his chief of staff to wake him up? There wasn't anyone else you could send?"

"The senator valued his privacy. There've been occasions when he wasn't alone, and neither of us felt his love life should be the business of his staff."

"But he didn't care if you knew who he was sleeping with?"

"He knew he could count on my discretion." He looked up, unprepared for the punch to the gut that occurred when his eyes met hers. Her unsettled expression made him wonder if she felt it, too. "His parents need to be notified. I'd like to be the one to tell them."

Sam studied him for a long moment. "I'll arrange it. Where are they?"

"At their farm in Leesburg. It needs to be soon. We're postponing a vote we worked for months to get to. It'll be all over the news that something's up."

"What's the vote for?"

He told her about the landmark immigration bill and John's role as the co-sponsor.

With a curt nod, she walked away.

An hour later, Nick was a passenger in an unmarked Metropolitan Police SUV, headed west to Leesburg with Sam at the wheel. She'd left her partner with a staggering list of instructions and insisted on accompanying Nick to tell John's parents.

"Do you need something to eat?"

He shook his head. No way could he even think about eating—not with the horrific task he had ahead of him. Besides, his stomach hadn't recovered from the earlier bout of vomiting.

"You know, we could still call the Loudoun County Police or the Virginia State Police to handle this," she said for the second time.

"No."

After an awkward silence, she said, "I'm sorry this happened to your friend and that you had to see him that way."

"Thank you."

"Are you going to answer that?" she asked of his relentless cell phone.

"No."

"How about you turn it off then? I can't stand listening to a ringing phone."

Reaching for his belt, he grabbed his BlackBerry, his emotions still raw after watching John being taken from his apartment in a body bag. Before he shut the BlackBerry off, he called Christina.

"Hey," she said, her voice heavy with relief and emotion. "I've been trying to reach you."

"Sorry." Pulling his tie loose and releasing his top button, he cast a sideways glance at Sam, whose warm, feminine fragrance had overtaken the small space inside the car. "I was dealing with cops."

"Where are you now?"

"On my way to Leesburg."

"God," Christina sighed. "I don't envy you that. Are you okay?"

"Never better."

"I'm sorry. Dumb question."

"It's okay. Who knows what we're supposed to say or do in this situation. Did you postpone the vote?"

"Yes, but Martin and McDougal are having an apoplexy," she said, meaning John's co-sponsor on the bill and the Democratic majority leader. "They're demanding to know what's going on."

"Hold them off. Another hour. Maybe two. Same thing with the staff. I'll give you the green light as soon as I've told his parents."

"I will. Everyone knows something's up because the Capitol Police posted an officer outside John's office and won't let anyone in there."

"It's because the cops are waiting for a search warrant," Nick told her.

"Why do they need a warrant to search the victim's office?"

"Something about chain of custody with evidence and pacifying the Capitol Police."

"Oh, I see. I was thinking we should have Trevor draft a statement so we're ready."

"That's why I called."

"We'll get on it." She sounded relieved to have something to do.

"Are you okay with telling Trevor? Want me to do it?"

"I think I can do it, but thanks for asking."

"How're you holding up?" he asked.

"I'm in total shock…all that promise and potential just gone…" She began to weep again. "It's going to hurt like hell when the shock wears off."

"Yeah," he said softly. "No doubt."

"I'm here if you need anything."

"Me, too, but I'm going to shut the phone off for a while. It's been ringing nonstop."

"I'll email the statement to you when we have it done."

"Thanks, Christina. I'll call you later." Nick ended the call and took a look at his recent e-mail messages, hardly surprised by the outpouring of dismay and concern over the postponement of the vote. One was from Senator Martin himself—"What the fuck is going on, Cappuano?"

Sighing, he turned off the BlackBerry and dropped it into his coat pocket.

"Was that your girlfriend?" Sam asked, startling him.

"No, my deputy."

"Oh."

Wondering what she was getting at, he added, "We work closely together. We're good friends."

"Why are you being so defensive?"

"What's your *problem?*" he asked.

"I don't have a problem. You're the one with problems."

"So all that great press you've been getting lately hasn't been a problem for you?"

"Why, Nick, I didn't realize you cared."

"I don't."

"Yes, you made that very clear."

He spun halfway around in the seat to stare at her. "*Are you for real?* You're the one who didn't return any of my calls."

She glanced over at him, her face flat with surprise. "What calls?"

After staring at her in disbelief for a long moment, he settled back in his seat and fixed his eyes on the cars sharing the Interstate with them.

A few minutes passed in uneasy silence.

"What calls, Nick?"

"I called you," he said softly. "For days after that night, I tried to reach you."

"I didn't know," she stammered. "No one told me."

"It doesn't matter now. It was a long time ago." But if his reaction to seeing her again after six years of thinking about her was any indication, it *did* matter. It mattered a lot.

CHAPTER 3

The Loudoun County seat of Leesburg, Virginia, in the midst of the Old Dominion's horse capital, is located thirty-five miles west of Washington. Marked by rolling hills and green pastures, Loudoun is defined by its horse culture. Upon his retirement after forty years in the Senate, Graham O'Connor and his wife moved to the family's estate outside Leesburg where they could indulge in their love of all things horses. Their social life revolved around steeplechases, hounds, hunting and the Belmont Country Club.

The closer they got to Leesburg, the tenser Nick became. He kept his head back and his eyes closed as he prepared himself to deliver the gruesome news to John's parents.

"Who were his enemies?" Sam asked after a prolonged period of silence.

Keeping his eyes closed, Nick said, "He didn't have an enemy in the world."

"I'd say today's events prove otherwise. Come on. Everyone in politics has enemies."

He opened his eyes and directed them at her. "John O'Connor didn't."

"A politician without a single enemy? A man who looks like a Greek god with no spurned lovers?"

"A Greek god, huh?" he asked with a small smile. "Is that so?"

"There has to be *someone* who didn't like him. You can't

live a life as high profile as his without someone being jealous or envious."

"John didn't inspire those emotions in people." Nick's heart ached as he thought of his friend. "He was inclusive. He found common ground with everyone he met."

"So the privileged son of a multi-millionaire senator could relate to the common man?" she asked, her tone ripe with cynicism.

"Well, yeah," Nick said softly, letting his mind wander back in time. "He related to me. From the moment we met in a history class at Harvard, he treated me like a long-lost brother. I came from nothing. I was there on a scholarship and felt like an imposter until John O'Connor took me under his wing and made me feel like I had as much reason as anyone to be there."

"What about in the Senate? Rivals? Anyone envious of his success? Anyone put out by this bill you were about to pass?"

"John hasn't had enough success in the Senate to inspire envy. His only real success was in consensus building. That was his value to the party. He could get people to listen to him. Even when they disagreed with him, they listened." Nick glanced over at her. "Where are you going with this?"

She mulled it over for a moment. "This was a crime of passion. When someone cuts off a man's dick and stuffs it in his mouth, they're sending a pretty strong message."

Nick's heart staggered in his chest. "Is *that* what was in his mouth?"

Sam winced. "I'm sorry. I figured you'd seen it..."

"Jesus." He opened the window to let the cold air in, hoping it would keep him from puking again.

"Nick? Are you all right?"

His deep sigh answered for him.

"Do you have any idea who would have reason to do such a thing to him?"

"I can't think of anyone who disliked him, let alone hated him that much."

"Clearly, someone did."

Nick directed her to the O'Connors's country home. They drove up a long, winding driveway to the brick-front house at the top of a hill. When he reached for the door handle, she stopped him with a hand on his arm.

He glanced down at the hand and then up to find her eyes trained on him.

"I have to ask you one more thing before we go in."

"What?"

"Where were you between the hours of ten p.m. and seven a.m.?"

Staring at her, incredulous, he said, "*I'm* a suspect?"

"Everyone's a suspect until they aren't."

"I was in my office all night getting ready for the vote until five-thirty this morning when I went to the gym for an hour," he said, his teeth gritted with anger, frustration and grief over what he was about to do to people he loved.

"Can anyone confirm this?"

"Several of my staff were with me."

"And you were seen at the gym?"

"There were a few other people there. I signed in and out."

"Good," she said, seeming relieved to know he had an alibi. "That's good."

Nick took a quick glance at the cars gathered in the drive-way and swore softly under his breath. Terry's Porsche was parked next to a Volvo wagon belonging to John's sister Lizbeth, who was probably visiting for the day with her two young children.

"What?"

"The whole gang's here." He pinched the bridge of his nose, hoping to find some relief from the headache forming behind his right eye. "They'll know the minute they see me that something's wrong, so don't go flashing the badge at them, okay?"

"I had no plans to," she snapped.

Nonplussed by her tone, he said, "Let's get this over with." He went up the stairs and rang the bell.

An older woman wearing a gray sweat suit with Nikes answered the door and greeted him with a warm hug.

"Nick! What a nice surprise! Come in."

"Hi, Carrie," he said, kissing her cheek. "This is Sergeant Sam Holland. Carrie is like a member of the family and keeps everyone in line."

"Which is no easy task." Carrie shook Sam's outstretched hand and sized up the younger woman before turning back to Nick, her approval apparent. "I've been telling Nick for years that he needs to settle down—"

"Don't go there, Carrie." He made an effort to keep his tone light even though his heart was heavy and burdened by what he had to tell her and the others. How he wished he were here to introduce his "family" to his new girlfriend. "Are they home?"

"Down at the stables with the kids. I'll give them a call."

Nick rested his hand on her arm. "Tell them to leave the kids there, okay?"

Her wise old eyes narrowed, this time seeing the sorrow and grief that were no doubt etched into his face. "Nick?"

"Call them, Carrie."

Watching her walk away, Nick sagged under the weight of what he was about to do to her, to all of them, and was surprised to feel Sam's hand on his back. He turned to her and was once again caught off guard by the punch of emotion that ripped through him when he found her pale blue eyes watching him with concern.

They stared at each other for a long, breathless moment

until they heard Carrie coming back. Nick tore his eyes off Sam and turned to Carrie.

"They'll be here in a minute," she said, clearly trying to maintain her composure and brace herself for what she was about to hear. "Can I get you anything?"

"No," Nick said. "Thank you."

"Come into the living room," she said, leading the way.

The house was elegant but comfortable, not a showplace but a home—a place where Nick had always been made to feel right at home.

"Something's wrong," Carrie whispered.

Nick reached for her hand and held it between both of his. He sat that way, with Carrie on one side of him and Sam on the other, until they heard the others come in through the kitchen.

Hand-in-hand, John's parents, Graham and Laine O'Connor, entered the room with their son Terry and daughter Lizbeth trailing behind them. Graham and Laine, both nearly eighty, were as fit and trim as people half their age. They had snow-white hair and year-round tans from spending most of their time riding horses. When they saw Nick, they lit up with delight.

He released Carrie's hand and got up to greet them both with hugs. Terry shook his hand and Lizbeth went up on tip-toes to kiss his cheek. He introduced them to Sam.

"What're you doing here?" Graham asked. "Isn't the vote today?"

Nick glanced down at the floor, took a second to summon the fortitude to say what needed to be said, and then looked back at them. "Come sit down."

"What's going on, Nick?" Laine asked in her lilting Southern accent, refusing to be led to a seat. "You don't look right. Is something wrong with John?"

Her mother's intuition had beaten him to the punch.

"I'm afraid so."

Laine gasped. Her husband reached for her hand, and right before Nick's eyes, the formidable Graham O'Connor wilted.

"He was late for work today."

"That's nothing new," Lizbeth said with a sisterly snicker. "He'll be late for his own funeral."

Nick winced at her choice of words. "We couldn't reach him, so I went over there to wake him up."

"Damned foolish of him to be sleeping late on a day like this," Graham huffed.

"We thought so, too," Nick conceded, his stomach clutching with nausea and despair. "When I got there…"

"What?" Laine whispered, reaching out to grip Nick's arm. *"What?"*

Nick couldn't speak over the huge lump that lodged in his throat.

Sam stood up. "Senator, Mrs. O'Connor, I'm so very sorry to have to tell you that your son's been murdered."

Nick knew if he lived forever, he would never forget the keening wail that came from John's mother as Sam's words registered. He reached for Laine when it seemed like she might faint. Instead, she folded like a house of cards into his arms.

Carrie kept saying, "No, no, no," over and over again.

With Lizbeth crying softly behind him and Terry's eyes glassy with tears and shock, Graham turned to Sam. "How?"

"He was stabbed in his bed."

Nick, who continued to hold the sobbing Laine, was grateful that Sam didn't tell them the rest. He eased Laine down to the sofa.

"Who would want to kill my John? My beautiful, sweet John?"

"We're going to find out," Sam said.

"Sam is the lead detective on the case," Nick told them.

"Excuse me," Graham mumbled as he turned and rushed from the room.

"Go with him, Terry," Laine said. "Please go with him." Terry followed his father.

Lizbeth sat down on the arm of the sofa next to her mother. "Oh, God," she whispered. "What will I tell the kids?"

Painfully aware of how close John was to his niece and nephew, Nick looked up at her with sympathy.

"That he had an accident," Laine said, wiping her face. "Not that he was killed. You can't tell them that."

"No," Lizbeth agreed. "I can't."

Laine raised her head off Nick's shoulder. "Where is he now?" she asked Sam.

"With the medical examiner."

"I want to see him." Laine wiped furiously at the tears that continued to spill down her unlined cheeks. "I want to see my child."

"I'll arrange it tomorrow," Sam said.

Laine turned to Nick. "There'll be a funeral befitting a United States senator."

"Of course."

"You'll see to it personally."

"Anything you want or need, Laine. You only have to ask."

She clasped his hand and looked at him with shattered eyes. "Who would do this, Nick? Who would do this to our John?"

"I've been asking myself that question for hours and can't think of anyone."

"Whoever it is, Mrs. O'Connor, we'll find them," Sam assured her.

"See that you do." As if she couldn't bear to sit there another second, Laine got up and made for the door with Lizbeth and Carrie following her. At the doorway, Laine turned back to

Nick. "You know you're welcome to stay. You're a part of this family, and you belong here. You always will."

Touched, Nick said, "Thank you, but I'm going to head back to the city. I need to spend some time with the staff."

"Please tell them how much we appreciate their hard work for John."

"I will. I'll see you tomorrow."

"Mrs. O'Connor," Sam said, rising to face Laine. "I'm so sorry to have to do this now, but in this kind of investigation, the first twenty-four hours are critical…"

"We'll do whatever we can do to find the person who did this to John," Laine said, her tear-stained face sagging with grief.

"I need to know the whereabouts of you and the other members of your family between the hours of ten p.m. last night and nine o'clock this morning."

"You aren't serious," Laine said stiffly.

"If I'm going to rule out any family involvement—"

"Fine," Laine snapped. "The senator and I entertained friends until about eleven." She glanced at Carrie, who nodded in agreement.

"I'll need the name and number of your friends." She handed Laine her card. "You can leave the information on my voicemail. And after eleven?"

"We went to bed."

"You, too, ma'am?" Sam asked Carrie.

"I watched television in my room until about two. I couldn't sleep."

"And you?" Sam asked Lizbeth.

Her expression rife with indignation, Lizbeth said, "I was at home in McLean with my husband and children."

"I'll need a phone number for your husband."

Lizbeth met Sam's even gaze with a steely stare before she

stalked from the room and returned a minute later with a
business card.

"Thank you," Sam said.

The three women left the room.

"You really had to do that today?" Nick asked Sam when
they were alone. "Right now?"

"Yes, I really did," she said, looking pained. "I have to play
by the book on something this high profile. Surely you can
understand that."

"Of course I do, but they just found out their son and
brother was murdered. You could've given them fifteen minutes to absorb that before you went into attack cop mode."

"I have a job to do, Nick. When I make an arrest, I'm sure
they'll be relieved that his killer is off the streets."

"What the hell difference will that make to them? Will it
bring John back?"

"I need to get back to the city. Are you coming?"

Taking a long last look around the room, remembering so
many happy times there with John, Nick followed her out
the front door.

CHAPTER 4

Feeling as if the world had quite simply come to an end, Graham O'Connor leaned against a white split-rail fence to look out over the acres that made up his estate but saw nothing through a haze of tears and grief. *John is dead. John is dead. John is dead.*

From the moment Carrie called them to say Nick was waiting at the house, Graham had known. With the most important vote of John's career scheduled for that day, there was only one reason Nick would have come. Graham had known, just as he had always known there was something shameful about a father loving one of his children more than the others. But John had been extraordinary. From the very earliest hours of his youngest child's life, Graham had seen in him the special something that inspired so many others to love him, too.

His face wet with tears, Graham wondered how this could have happened.

"Dad?"

The sound of his older son's voice filled Graham with disappointment and despair. God help him for thinking such a thing, but if he'd had to lose one of his sons why couldn't it have been Terry instead of John?

Terry's hand landed on Graham's shoulder, squeezed. "What can I do for you?"

"Nothing." Graham wiped his face.

"Senator?"

Graham turned to find Nick and the pretty detective approaching them.

"We're going back to Washington," she said, "but before we do I need to confirm your whereabouts last night. After ten."

He somehow managed to contain the hot blast of rage that cut through him at the implication that he could have had something to do with the death of the one he loved above all others—except for Laine, of course. "I was right here with my wife. We had friends over, played some bridge and went to bed around eleven or so."

She seemed satisfied with his answer and turned next to Terry. "Mr. O'Connor?"

"I was…ah…with a friend."

Terry's womanizing had gotten completely out of hand since a DUI derailed his political aspirations weeks before he was supposed to declare his candidacy for the Senate. It made Graham sick that Terry was no closer to settling down and having a family at forty-two than he had been at twenty-two.

"I'll need a name and number," the detective said.

Terry's cheeks turned bright red, and Graham knew what was coming next. "I…ah…"

"He doesn't know her name," Graham said, casting a disgusted look at his son.

"I can find out," Terry said quickly.

"That'd be a good idea," the detective said.

"It's not a coincidence, is it, that this happened on the eve of the vote?" Graham said.

"We're not ruling anything out," the detective said.

"Check Minority Leader Stenhouse," Graham said. "He hates my guts and would begrudge my son any kind of success."

"Why does he hate you?" she asked.

"They were bitter rivals for decades," Nick told her. "Stenhouse has done everything he could to block the immigration bill, but it was going to pass anyway."

"Take a good look at him," Graham said, his chest tight with rage and his voice breaking. "He's capable of anything. Taking my son from me would give him great joy."

"Can you think of anyone else?" she asked. "Anyone who might've tangled with your son, either on a personal or professional level?"

Graham shook his head. "Everyone loved John, but I'll think about it and let you know if anyone comes to mind."

Nick stepped forward to embrace him.

Graham wrapped his arms around the young man he loved like a son. "Find out who did this, Nick. Find out."

"I will. I promise."

As Nick and Sam walked away, Graham noted the hunched shoulders of his son's closest friend and trusted aide. To Terry he said, "Get the name of your bimbo, and get it now. Don't show your face around here again until you do."

"Yes, sir."

On the way back to Washington, Nick checked his Black-Berry and read through the statement his office had drafted.

With tremendous sorrow we announce that our colleague and friend, Senator John Thomas O'Connor, Democrat of Virginia, was found murdered in his Washington home this morning. After Senator O'Connor failed to arrive for work, his chief of staff, Nicholas Cappuano, went to the senator's home to check on him. Mr. Cappuano found the senator dead. At the request of the Metropolitan Police, we'll have no further statement on the details of the senator's death other than to say we will do everything within our power to assist in the investigation. Subsequent information on the investigation will come from the police.

We will make it our mission to ensure passage of the landmark immigration legislation Senator O'Connor worked so hard to bring to the Senate floor and to continue his work on behalf of children, families and the aged.

Our hearts and prayers are with the senator's parents, Senator and Mrs. Graham O'Connor, his brother Terry, sister Lizbeth, brother-in-law Royce, niece Emma and nephew Adam. Funeral arrangements are incomplete but will be announced in the next few days. We ask that you respect the privacy of the O'Connor family at this difficult time.

Nick nodded with approval and read it again before he turned to Sam. "Can I run this by you?"

"Sure." She listened intently as he read the statement to her. "Sounds like they covered every base."

"The part about the investigation was okay?"

"Yes, it's fine."

Nick placed a call to Christina. "Hey, green light on the statement. Go ahead and get it out."

Christina replied with a deep, pained sigh. "This'll make it official."

"Tell Trevor to just read it and get out of there. No questions."

"Got it."

"You guys did a great job. Thank you."

"It was the hardest thing I've ever had to do," she said, her voice hoarse.

"I'm sure."

"So, um, how'd it go with his parents?"

"Horrible."

"Same thing with the staff. People are taking it really hard."

"I'm on my way back. I'll be in soon."

"We'll be here."

Nick ended the call.

"Are you all right?" Sam asked.

"I'm fine," he said stiffly, still pissed that she had talked alibis with the O'Connors so soon.

"I was just doing my job."

"Your job sucks."

"Yes, a lot of times it does."

"Do you ever get used to telling people their loved ones have been murdered?"

"No, and I hope I never do."

As bone-deep exhaustion began to set in, he put his head back against the seat. "I appreciated you saying the words for me back there. I just couldn't bring myself to do it."

She glanced over at him. "You were very good with them."

Surprised by the unexpected compliment, Nick forced a weak smile. "I was in uncharted waters, that's for sure."

"You're close to them."

"They're family to me."

"What does your own family think of that?"

They hadn't taken the time to compare life stories the first time they met. They'd been too busy tearing each other's clothes off. "I don't have much of a family. I was born to parents who were still in high school and was raised by my grandmother. She passed away a few years ago."

"What about your parents?"

"They breezed in and out of my life when I was a kid."

"And now?"

"Let's see, my mother is married for the third time and was living in Cleveland the last time I heard from her, which was a couple of years ago. My father is married to a woman who's younger than me, and they have three-year-old twins. He lives in Baltimore. I see them once in a while, but he's hardly a father to me. He's only fifteen years older than me."

Her silence made him realize she was waiting for him to say more.

"I remember the first weekend I spent with the O'Connors. I thought families like theirs only existed on TV."

"They always seemed almost too good to be true."

"They're not, though. They're real people with real faults and problems, but they have such a strong belief in giving back and in public service that it's impossible to be around them for any length of time and not be sucked in. They changed my whole career plan."

"What were you going to do?"

"I'd considered accounting or finance, but after a few meals at Graham O'Connor's table, I was bitten by the political bug."

"What's he like? Graham?"

"He's complicated and thoughtful and demanding. He loves his family and his country. He's fiercely patriotic and loyal."

"You love him."

"More than any man I've ever known—except his son."

"Tell me about John."

Nick thought for a moment before he answered. "If his father is complicated, thoughtful and demanding, John was simple, forgetful and lackadaisical. But like his father, he loved his family and his country and was proud to serve the people of Virginia. He took those responsibilities seriously but didn't take himself too seriously."

"Did you like working for him?"

"I liked being around him and helping him to succeed. But from a political staff perspective, he could be a bit of a handful."

"How so?"

Nick paused, considered and decided. "Right now, my chief goal is to protect his legacy and ensure he's afforded the dignity and stature he deserves as a deceased United States senator."

"And *my* goal is to figure out who killed him. If I'm going to do that, I'll need you and the rest of your staff to be forthcoming. I can do it faster and more efficiently with your help than without it. I need to know who he was."

Nick wished he couldn't smell her, wished he wasn't so aware of her. And more than anything, he wished he didn't so vividly remember the night he'd spent lost in her. "I was furious," he said in a soft tone.

"When?" she asked, confused.

"On my way to his place this morning. If he hadn't been dead when I got there, I might've killed him myself."

"Nick…" Her tone was full of warning, reminding him not to forget who he was talking to.

"If you want to know who John O'Connor was, the fact that his chief of staff was on his way to haul him out of bed— *again*—should tell you everything you need to know."

"It doesn't tell me everything, but it's a start."

CHAPTER 5

Sam's memories of Nick Cappuano should have faded over the years, but they hadn't. He remained a larger-than-life character from a single night that shouldn't have meant as much as it had. But she *had* forgotten the reality of him—his height, easily six-three or -four, broad shoulders, chocolate brown hair that curled at the ends, hazel eyes that missed nothing, olive-toned skin, strong, efficient hands that changed forever what she expected from a lover, crackling intelligence, and the cool aura of reserved control she'd found so fascinating the first time she met him.

Cracking that control had been one of the best memories from her night with him. When he didn't call, she'd wondered if their intense connection had scared him off. But now that she knew he *had* called, that he *had* wanted to see her again… that changed everything.

"Can I ask you something that has nothing to do with the case?" she said as they cut across the District on the way to the Watergate where he'd left his car. Along the way, they noticed a few American flags already lowered to half-mast in John's honor. The word was out, and the official mourning had begun.

"Sure."

Her heart raced as she picked at a scab she'd mistakenly thought healed long ago. "When you called me…after…that night…do you remember who you talked to at my house?"

He shrugged. "Some guy. One of your roommates maybe."

Knowing the answer before she even asked, she said, "You didn't get his name? I lived with three guys."

"Shit, I don't know. Paul maybe."

"Peter?"

"Yes. Peter. That was it. I talked to him a couple of times."

Gripping the steering wheel so tightly her knuckles turned white, Sam wanted to scream.

"Was he your boyfriend?"

"Not then," she said through gritted teeth.

"Later?"

"He's my ex-husband."

"Ah! Well, now it all makes sense," he said but there was a bitter edge to his voice that she understood all too well. She was feeling rather bitter herself at the moment.

"Too bad you didn't give me your cell number instead of your home number."

"I only had a department cell then, and I never used it for personal business." They were quiet until she pulled into the Watergate. "I'd like to interview your staff in the morning," she said as the car idled.

"I'll make sure they're available." He rattled off the Hart Senate Office Building address where she could find them.

"In the meantime, here's my card in case you think of anything that might be relevant. No matter how big or how small, you never know what'll crack a case wide open."

He took the card and reached for the door handle.

"Nick," she said, her hand on his arm to stop him from getting out.

Looking down at her hand and then up to meet her eyes, he raised an eyebrow.

"I would've liked to have gotten those messages," she said, her heart racing. "I would've liked that very much."

He sighed. "I can't process this on top of everything else that's happened today. It's just too much."

"I know." She raised her hand to let him go. "I'm sorry I brought it up."

He surprised her when he reached for her hand and brought it to his lips. "Don't be sorry. I really want to talk about it. Later, though, okay?"

Sam swallowed hard at the intense expression on his handsome face. "Okay."

He released her hand and opened the car door. "I'll see you in the morning."

"Yes," she said softly to herself when he was gone. "See you then."

Frederico Cruz was a junk food addict. However, despite his passion for donuts, his ongoing love affair with the golden arches, and his obsession with soda of all kinds except diet, he managed to maintain a wiry, one-hundred-seventy-pound frame that was usually draped by one of the many trench coats he claimed were necessary to staying in character.

In some sort of cosmic joke, Sam had drawn the dietary disaster area known as Freddie for a partner. In the midst of the HQ detective pit chaos, Sam watched fascinated and envious as he chased a cream-filled donut with a cola. She swore that spending most of every day with him for the last year had put ten unneeded pounds on her. "Where are we?" she asked when he put down the soda can and wiped his mouth.

"Still at square one. The neighbors didn't hear anything or see anyone in the elevator or hallways. I sent a couple of uniforms to pick up the security tape—not an easy task, I might add. You'd think we were planning to send G. Gordon Liddy back in there or something. I had to threaten them with warrants."

"What was the hang-up?" Sam asked, eyeing his second donut with lust in her heart.

"Resident privacy, the usual bull. I had to remind them—twice—that a United States senator had been murdered in his apartment and did they really want any *more* unfavorable publicity than they're already going to get?"

"Good job, Freddie. That's the way to be aggressive." She was forever after him to get in there and get his hands dirty. In turn, he nagged her about getting a life away from the job.

"I learned from the best."

She made a face at him.

"We also seized everything from the senator's home and work offices—computers, files, etc. The lab is going through the computers now. We can hit the files tomorrow."

"Good."

"What's your take on the O'Connors?"

"The parents were devastated. There was nothing fake about it. Same with his sister."

"What about the brother?"

"He seemed shocked, but he says he was with a woman whose name he doesn't remember."

"He'll have to produce her if he's going to rely on her for an alibi."

"He's painfully aware of that," Sam said, smirking at her recollection of Terry O'Connor's discomfort and Graham's obvious disapproval.

"That's what he gets for sleeping with a stranger. Imagine going up to someone you slept with to ask for her name."

Sam's face heated as memories of her one-night stand with Nick chose that moment to resurface. "Easy, Freddie. Don't get all proper on me."

"It's just another sign of the moral decline of our country."

Groaning at the familiar argument, she said, "Any word from the M.E.?"

"Not yet. Apparently, they had a backlog to get through."

"Who comes before a murdered U.S. senator?"

He shrugged. "Don't kill the messenger."

"My favorite sport."

"Don't I know it? The guy who found him checked out? Cappuano?"

"Yeah." Sam decided right in that moment not to tell Freddie about her history with Nick. Some things were personal, and she didn't want or need Freddie's disapproval. She was still dealing with her own disapproval for bringing up their former personal relationship in the midst of a murder investigation. "He was at work all night with other people from the staff, which I'll confirm tomorrow."

"So what's next?"

"In the morning, we'll interview O'Connor's staff and pay a visit to the senate minority leader," she said, filling him in on Graham O'Connor's long-running feud with Stenhouse.

Freddie rubbed his chiseled cheek. On top of his many other faults, he was GQ handsome, too. Life wasn't fair. "Interesting," he said.

"Senator O'Connor questioned the timing—on the eve of the biggest vote of his son's career as a senator."

"Someone didn't want that vote to happen?"

"It's the closest thing to a motive I've seen yet. When we talk to his staff tomorrow, we need to cover both sides—the political and the personal. Who was he dating? Who might've had an axe to grind? You know the drill."

"What's your gut telling you, boss?"

He knew she hated when he called her that. "I'm not loving the political angle."

"The timing works."

"Yeah, but would a political rival cut off his dick and stuff it in his mouth?"

Freddie cringed and covered his own package.

"We're going to keep that detail close to the vest and see where it takes us. But my money's on a woman."

"You know what's bugging me?" Freddie asked.

"What's that?"

"No sign of a struggle. How does someone get a hold of your dick and do the Lorena Bobbitt without you putting up a fight?"

"Maybe he was asleep? Didn't see it coming?"

"Someone grabs my junk, I'm *wide* awake."

"Spare me the visual, will you, please?"

"I'm just saying…"

"That it was someone he knew, someone he wasn't surprised to see."

"Exactly." He picked up the second donut and took a bite. With a dollop of white cream on his lower lip, he added, "He had one of those butcher block knife things in his kitchen. The butcher knife was the one holding him to the headboard."

"So the killer didn't arrive armed."

"It doesn't seem so. No."

Standing up, Sam said, "I want to see those tapes. What the hell is taking them so long?"

Driving from the Watergate to the office, Nick should have been thinking about what he was going to say to his staff. They'd be looking to him for leadership, for answers to questions that had no answers. But rather than prepare himself for what would no doubt be an emotional ordeal, he kept hearing Sam's voice: "I would've liked to have gotten those messages."

Pounding his hand on the steering wheel, he let loose with an uncharacteristic string of swears. Like it wasn't enough that

John had been murdered. To also have to face off with the one woman from his past who he'd never worked out of his system was…well, calling it unfair wouldn't do it justice.

He knew she wanted to talk about what happened all those years ago and why they never saw each other again. It made him so mad to think about her malicious ex not giving her the messages. But he couldn't process the implications of this discovery in the midst of the mayhem caused by John's murder. Dealing with Sam Holland solely on a professional level would take all the fortitude he could muster, never mind getting personal.

Years ago, when she failed to return his calls, he'd been angry and hurt—so much so that he hadn't pursued it any further, which he now knew had been stupid. He couldn't help but wonder what might have been different for him—for both of them—if she had gotten his messages and returned his calls. Would they still be together? Or would it have burned out the way all his relationships inevitably did?

He realized, with a clarity he couldn't explain or understand, that they would probably still be together. He'd never had that kind of connection with anyone else, which was why he'd been so acutely aware of her all day today.

CHAPTER 6

After spending an excruciating hour with his grieving staff, Nick sent them home with orders to be back to work at nine in the morning to meet with the detectives and to plan the senator's funeral. He instructed them not to discuss the case or the senator with anyone and to avoid the press in particular.

He lowered himself into his desk chair, every muscle in his body aching with fatigue as the sleepless night and agonizing day caught up to him.

"Have you eaten?" Christina asked from the doorway.

Nick had to think about that. "Not since the bagel I puked up this morning."

"There's pizza left from before. Want me to get you some?"

Not at all sure he'd be able to get it down, he said, "Sure, thanks."

"Coming right up."

She returned a few minutes later with two slices that she had warmed in the microwave.

"Thank you," he said when she handed him the plate and a can of cola. Her blue eyes were rimmed with red, her face puffy from crying. "How're you doing?"

With a shrug, she collapsed into a chair on the other side of his desk. "I feel like all the air has been sucked out of my lungs, and I can't seem to breathe."

"I know you cared for him a great deal," Nick said haltingly. They'd never discussed Christina's feelings for John.

"For all the good it did me."

"He loved you, Chris. You know he did."

"As a friend and colleague. Big whoop."

"I'm sorry."

"So am I because now I have to live the whole rest of my life wondering what might've happened if I'd had the courage to tell him how I felt."

"I'm kind of glad you didn't."

"I'm sure you are," she said with a laugh.

"Not because of work. I loved him like a brother. You know that. But he wasn't good enough for you. He would've broken your heart."

"Probably," she said. "No, definitely."

"If it makes you feel any better, I was confronted with a blast from my romantic past today. We spent a memorable night together six years ago, and I haven't seen her since—until she walked into John's apartment this morning as the detective in charge of the case."

Christina winced. "Awkward."

"To say the least."

"Do you trust her to handle the case?"

"Sam's a damned good detective."

"I thought you hadn't seen her in six years."

"Doesn't mean I haven't read about her."

"Hmm," she said, studying him.

"What?"

"Oh, nothing." Her eyes widened all of a sudden. "What's her last name?"

"Holland."

"Oh my God! She's the one who ordered the shoot-out at that crack house where the kid was killed!"

"Yes."

"But, Nick, do we really want *her* investigating John's murder? Couldn't we get someone else?"

"I trust her," Nick said. "She has one blemish on an otherwise stellar career. And think of it this way, she's got something to prove right now."

"I guess you're right," she said, still wary. The phone on Nick's desk rang, and Christina reached for it. "Nick Cappuano's office." Once again her eyes widened, and she stammered as she said, "Of course. One moment please."

"Who is it?" Nick asked.

"The president," she whispered.

Nick quickly swallowed a mouthful of pizza and reached for a napkin and the phone at the same time. "Good evening, Mr. President." He had met President Nelson on several occasions—mostly in receiving lines at Democratic Party fundraisers—but a phone call from him was unprecedented.

"Hello, Nick. Gloria and I just wanted to tell you all how sorry we are."

"Thank you, sir. I'll pass that along to the staff. And thank you for the statement you issued to the press."

"I've known John since he was a little boy. I'm heartbroken."

"We all are."

"I can only imagine. I also wanted to make myself available for anything you might need over the next few days."

"I appreciate that. I know Senator and Mrs. O'Connor would be honored if you could speak at the funeral."

"*I'd* be honored."

"I'll work with your staff on the details."

"Let me give you my direct number in the residence. Feel free to use it."

Nick took down the number with a sense of disbelief. "Thank you."

"I spoke earlier with Chief Farnsworth and made the full resources of the federal government available to the Metropolitan Police. I'm sure you'll be close to the investigation. If there's anything you feel they could be doing that they're not, don't hesitate to contact me."

"I won't, sir."

The president released a deep sigh. "I just can't imagine who would do such a thing to John of all people."

"Neither can I."

"Do you think Graham and Laine would be up for a phone call?"

"I'm sure they'd love to hear from you."

"Well, I won't keep you any longer. God bless you and your staff, Nick. Our thoughts and prayers are with you all."

"Thank you so much for calling, Mr. President." Nick put down the phone and looked over at Christina.

"Unreal," she said.

"Surreal," he added, filling her in on what the president had said.

She began to cry again. "I keep waiting for John to come bounding in here asking why we're all sitting around."

"I know. Me, too."

"I actually had a few people ask me today how this affects their jobs," she said with disgust.

"Well, you can't blame them. They have families to support."

"Couldn't they have waited a day or two to bring that up?"

"Apparently not. I'll talk to them about it tomorrow and tell them we'll do our best to get them placed somewhere in government."

"What'll you do?" she asked.

"Shit, I don't know. I can't think about that until after we get through the funeral. The two of us, maybe a couple of others, will be needed for a while until the governor appoints someone to take John's place. Whoever it is will want to bring in their own people, so we'll help with the transition and then figure out what's next, I guess."

Christina looked so sad, so despondent that Nick felt his heart go out to her. "Why don't you go home, Chris? There's nothing more we can do here tonight."

"What about you?"

"I'll be going soon, too."

"All right," she said as she got up. "I'll see you in the morning."

"Try to get some sleep."

"As if."

He walked her to the door and sent her off with a hug before he wandered into John's office. The desk had been swept clean and the computer removed. If it hadn't been for the photo of John with his niece and nephew on the windowsill, there would've been no sign of him or the five years he'd spent working in this room. Nick wasn't sure what he hoped to find when he sat in John's chair. Swiveling to look out the window, he could see the Washington Monument lit up in the distance.

Resting his head back, he stared at the monument and finally gave himself permission to do what he'd needed to do all day. He wept.

Sam arrived home exhausted after a sixteen-hour day and smiled when she heard the whir of her father's chair as he came out to greet her.

"Hi, Dad."

"Late tonight."

"I'm on O'Connor."

The side of his face that wasn't paralyzed lifted into a smile. "Are you now? Farnsworth's got you right back on the horse."

She kicked off her boots and bent to kiss his cheek. "So it seems."

Celia, one of the nurses who cared for him, came out from the kitchen to greet Sam. "How about we get ready for bed, Skip?"

Sam hated the indignation that darted across the expressive side of his face. "Go ahead, Dad. I'll be in when you're done. I've got a couple of things I want to run by you."

"I suppose I can make some time for you," he teased, turning the chair with his one working finger and following Celia to his bedroom in what used to be the dining room.

Sam went into the kitchen and served herself a bowl of the beef stew Celia had left on the stove for her. She ate standing up without tasting anything as the events of the day ran through her mind like a movie. Under normal circumstances, she'd be obsessed with the case. She'd be thinking it through from every angle, searching out motives, making a list of suspects. But instead, she thought of Nick and the sadness that had radiated from him all day. More than once she had wanted to throw her arms around him and offer comfort, which was hardly a professional impulse.

Deciding it was pointless to try to eat, she poured the rest of the soup into the garbage disposal and stood at the sink, her shoulders stooped. She was still there twenty minutes later when Celia came into the kitchen.

"He's ready for you."

"Thanks, Celia."

"He's been kind of..."

"What?" Sam asked, immediately on alert.

"Off. He hasn't been himself the last few days."

"The two-year anniversary is coming up next week."

"That could be it."

"Let's keep an eye on him."

Celia nodded in agreement. "What do you know about Senator O'Connor?"

"Not as much as I'd like to."

"What a tragedy," Celia said, shaking her head. "We've been glued to the news all day. Such an awful waste."

"Seemed like a guy who had it all."

"But there was something sort of sad about him, too."

"Why do you say that?"

"No reason in particular. Just a vibe he put out."

"I never noticed," Sam said, intrigued by the observation. She made a mental note to find some video of O'Connor's speeches from the Senate floor and TV interviews.

"Go on in and see your dad. He so looks forward to his time with you."

"The stew was great. Thank you."

"Glad you liked it."

Sam went into her father's bedroom where he was propped up in bed, a respirator hose snaking from his throat to the machine on the floor that breathed for him at night.

"You look beat," he said, his speech an awkward staccato around the respirator.

"Long-ass day." Sam sat in the chair next to the hospital bed and propped her feet on the frame under the pressurized mattress that minimized bedsores. "But it feels good to be doing more than pushing paper again."

"What've you got?" he asked, reverting to his former role as the department's detective captain.

She ran through the whole thing, from the meeting with Chief Farnsworth to reviewing the tapes the Watergate had finally produced. "We only got traffic in the lobby. Nothing jumped out at us, but I'm going to show them to his chief of staff in the morning to see if he can ID anyone."

"That's a good idea. Why do you get a funny look in those blue eyes of yours when you mention the chief of staff? Nick, right?"

"I went out with him once." She spared her father a deeper explanation of what "going out" had meant in this case. "A long time ago."

"But it was hard to see him?"

"Yeah," she said softly. "I found out he *did* call me after that night. Guess who took the messages and never gave them to me?"

"Oh, let's see, could it be our good friend Peter?"

"One and the same, the prick."

Skip's laugh was strained. "You able to be objective on this one with your Nick from the past part of the mix?"

Surprised by the question, she glanced up at him and found him studying her with sharp, blue eyes that were just like hers. "Of course. It was six years ago. No biggie."

"Uh-huh."

She should have known he would see right through her. He always did.

"You need to get some sleep," he said.

"Whenever I close my eyes, I'm back in that crack house with Marquis Johnson screaming. And then I break out in a cold sweat."

"You did everything right, followed every instinct." He gasped for air. "I wouldn't have done it any differently."

"Do you ever think about the night you got shot?" She had never thought to ask that until she'd been haunted by her own demons.

"Not so much. It's all a blur."

Her cell phone rang. Sam reached for it on her belt and checked the caller ID. She didn't recognize the 703 number. "I need to take this."

"Go on."

She kissed her father's forehead and left the room. "Holland."

"Sam, it's Nick. Someone's been in my house."

Her heart fluttered at the sound of his deep voice. This was *not* good. "Has it been ransacked?" she asked, making an effort to sound cool and professional.

"No."

"Then how do you know someone's been there?"

"I *know*. Stuff's been moved."

"Where do you live?"

He rattled off an address in Arlington, Virginia.

Even though it was out of her jurisdiction, she grabbed her coat. "I'm on my way."

CHAPTER 7

Thirty minutes later, Sam stormed up the stairs to Nick's brick-front townhouse.

He waited just inside the door and held it open for her. "Thanks for coming."

"Sure." She stole a quick glance around a combined living room/dining room where it appeared nothing was out of place. In fact, the space seemed better suited to a furniture showroom rather than someone's home. "How can you—"

He grabbed her hand. "Come."

Startled, she let him lead her into his office, which was as neat as the other rooms but more lived in than what she had seen so far.

"See that?"

Following the direction of his pointed finger, she studied a small stack of books on the desk. "What about it?"

"It's at an angle."

"So?"

"It's not supposed to be."

"*Seriously?* You called me over here at eleven o'clock at night because your stack of books isn't anally aligned?"

With a furious scowl, he grabbed her hand again and all but dragged her upstairs to his bedroom. *Now we're talking! Relax, Sam, he's not dragging you off to bed, as much as you wish he were.* Reminding herself that she was investigating a break-in at the home of a player in a homicide investigation, she pushed aside her salacious thoughts and tuned in to what he was showing her.

Pointing to the dresser, he said, "I didn't leave it like that."

A tiny scrap of white fabric poked out through the closed drawers. Deciding to humor him, Sam leaned in to inspect the cloth. "It's not possible your tighty whities got caught in the drawer and you didn't notice?"

"No, it's not possible," he said through gritted teeth.

She stood up and studied him like she had never seen him before, as if she hadn't once seen him naked. "Have you always been so anal?"

"Yes."

"Hmm."

"What does that mean? Hmm? Aren't you going to call someone?"

"To do what?"

"To figure out who's been in my house!"

"Nick, come on."

"Forget it. Go home. I'm sorry I bothered you."

His eyes, she noticed, were rimmed with red. She ached at the thought of him alone and heartbroken over his murdered friend. "Fine. If you really think someone's been in here—"

"I do."

"I left my phone in the car. May I use yours?"

He handed her his cell phone.

"This is Detective Sergeant Sam Holland, MPD. I need a crime scene unit," she said, giving the address.

When she hung up, she turned to find him watching her intently.

"Thank you."

She nodded, unsettled by the heat coming from his hazel eyes. Had she caused that or was it the fault of the person who had supposedly invaded his private space?

★ ★ ★

An hour later, Sam sat with Nick on the sofa, out of the way of the Arlington cops who were dusting for prints.

"How do you think they got in?" Desperate to maintain some semblance of distance from him, she spoke in the clipped, professional tone she used to interview witnesses.

"I have no idea."

"Does anyone have a key?"

"John had the only other one."

"Where did he keep it?"

"I'm not sure. I gave it to him in case I ever locked my-self out."

"Which probably never happens."

"It hasn't yet."

"You don't use the security system?" she asked.

"It came with the place. I've never had it turned on."

"You might want to think about that."

"Really? Gee, thanks for that advice, Sergeant."

She shot him a warning look.

"I'm sorry," he said, dropping his head to run his fingers through thick dark hair.

Sam licked her lips, wishing she could do that for him.

"I don't mean to snap at you. It's just the idea of some-one in my *home*, going through my stuff...It has me kind of skeeved out."

"Any idea what they might be looking for?"

His shoulders sagged with fatigue. "None."

Sam's heart went out to him. He'd had a horrible, painful day, and she wished she could find an appropriate excuse to hug him. She made an effort to soften her tone. "Is it possible someone is trying to find something here they couldn't find at the senator's place?"

"I can't imagine what. Neither of us ever took anything sensitive out of the office. There're all kinds of rules about that."

"What kind of sensitive stuff was he involved with?"

"After the midterm election, he was appointed to the Senate Homeland Security Committee, but most of his work was in the areas of commerce, finance, children, families and the aged. None of that was overly sensitive."

Watching his tired face with much more than professional interest, she was dying to address the elephant in the room—the six years' worth of unfinished business and the tension that zipped through her every time she connected with those hot hazel eyes of his. "Is it possible he was involved in something you didn't know about?"

Nick scoffed. "Highly doubtful."

"But possible?"

"Sure it is, but John didn't operate that way. He relied on us for everything."

"You alluded earlier to him being high maintenance for the staff. Other than having to wake him up in the morning, how did you mean?"

Nick was quiet for a long moment before he glanced at her. "This is all for background, right? I won't read about it in tomorrow's paper?"

"I think we've missed the deadline for the morning edition."

"I'm serious, Sam. I don't want to say or do anything to cause his parents any more grief than they're already dealing with."

"It's for my information now, but I can't guarantee it'll stay that way. If something you tell me helps to make this case, it's apt to come out in court. As much as we might wish otherwise, murder victims are often put on trial right along with their killers."

"That's so wrong."

"Unfortunately, it's just the way it is."

Nick made an A-frame out of his hands and rested his chin on the point. "John was a reluctant senator. He used to joke that he was Prince Harry to Terry's Prince William. Terry was the anointed one, groomed all his life to follow his father into politics. While Terry always lived in the public eye, John had a relatively normal life. For some reason, the press took an unusual interest in Terry's comings and goings. His name was mentioned on the political and gossip pages almost as often as his father's, and this was long before his father announced his retirement."

"It must've been tough to deal with all that attention."

Nick laughed, which chased the tension from his face. "Terry loved it. He ate it up. He was Washington's most eligible bachelor, and he took full advantage, let me tell you."

"That doesn't sound like a smart political strategy."

"Oh, it wasn't. He and the senator—his father, I mean— had huge, knock-down brawls over his lifestyle. I witnessed a few of them. But somehow Terry managed to stay one step ahead of the scandalmongers—that is until he got arrested for drunk driving three weeks before he was supposed to announce his candidacy for his father's seat. No amount of spin can get you out of that."

"Ouch. I remember this. It's all coming back to me now."

"Graham was devastated. Before today, I've never seen him so crushed. That this son he'd placed all these hopes and dreams on had so totally let him down…"

"How did Terry take it?"

"Like a wounded puppy, like it was someone else's fault. He was full of excuses. John was totally disgusted by him. At one point, he said, 'Why doesn't he just be a man and admit he made a mistake?'"

"Did he say this to Terry?"

"I doubt it. They were never really close. Terry loved all the attention, and John did his best to stay well below the radar."

"Until Terry forced him into the spotlight," Sam said, starting to get a clearer picture of the O'Connor family.

"Yes, and forced is the right word. John wanted nothing to do with running for the Senate. In fact, I remember him grousing about how 'lucky' he was that he'd just turned thirty, which is the minimum age to run for the Senate. He was sitting atop a nice little technology firm that made a chip for one of the DoD's weapons systems. He and his partner were very successful."

"What happened to the company when John ran for Senate?"

"His partner bought him out and later sold the company."

"Would he have any reason to want John dead?"

"Hardly. He made hundreds of millions when he sold the company. The last I knew, he was living large in the Caribbean."

"What about Terry? Is he still harboring resentment that his younger brother got the life he was supposed to have?"

"Maybe, but Terry wouldn't have the stones to kill him. At the end of the day, Terry's a wimp."

Regardless of that, Sam made a note to look more closely at Terry O'Connor.

"Sergeant?" The lieutenant in charge of the crime scene unit approached them. "We're just about done here. We didn't find any sign of forced entry at either door or any of the ground-floor windows."

"Prints?"

"Just one set." He glanced at Nick. "We assume they're yours, but we'll have to confirm that."

Nick swore softly under his breath.

"Thanks, Lieutenant." Sam handed the other officer her

card. "I'll write up what I have if you'll shoot me your report as a courtesy. There may be a connection to Senator
O'Connor's murder."

"Of course."

After a perfunctory clean up of the dust left over from the
fingerprint powder, the other cops left a short time later.

"Do you want some help cleaning up?" she asked Nick
when they were alone.

"That's all right. I can do it."

He stood and extended a hand to help her up.

Sam took his hand, but when she tried to let go, he tightened his grip. Startled, she looked up at him.

"I'm sorry I dragged you over here for nothing."

"It wasn't nothing—" Her words got stuck in her throat
when he ran a finger over her cheek. His touch was so light
she would have missed it if she hadn't been staring at him.

"You're tired."

She shrugged, her heart slamming around in her chest. "I
haven't been sleeping too well lately."

"I read all the coverage of what happened. It wasn't your
fault, Sam."

"Tell that to Quentin Johnson. It wasn't his fault, either."

"His father should've put his son's safety ahead of saving
his crack stash."

"I was counting on the fact that he would. I should've
known better. How someone could put their child in that kind
of danger…I'll just never understand it."

"I'm sorry it happened to you. It broke my heart to read
about it."

Sam found it hard to look away. "I, um…I should go."

"Before you do, there's just one thing I really need to know."

"What?" she whispered.

He released her hand, cupped her face and tilted it to receive his kiss.

As his lips moved softly over hers, Sam summoned every ounce of fortitude she possessed and broke the kiss. "I can't, Nick. Not during the investigation." *But oh how she wanted to keep kissing him!*

"I was dying to know if it would be like I remembered."

Her eyes closed against the onslaught of emotions. "And was it?"

"Even better," he said, going back for more.

"Wait. Nick. *Wait.*" She kept her hand on his chest to stop him from getting any closer. "We can't do this. Not now. Not when I'm in the middle of a homicide investigation that involves you."

"I didn't do it." He reached up to release the clip that held her hair and combed his fingers through the length as it tumbled free.

Unnerved by the intimate gesture, she stepped back from him. "I know you didn't, but you're still involved. I've got enough problems right now without adding an inappropriate fling with a witness to the list."

"Is that what it would be?" His eyes were hot, intense and possibly furious as he stared at her. "An inappropriate fling?"

"No," she said softly. "Which is another reason why it's not a good idea to start something now."

He moved closer to her. "It's already started, Sam. It started six years ago, and we never got to finish it. This time, I intend to finish it. Maybe not right now, but eventually. I was a fool to let you slip through my fingers the first time. I won't make that mistake again."

Startled by his intensity, Sam took another step back. "I appreciate the warning, but it might be one of those things that's better left unfinished. We both have a lot going on—"

"I'll see you tomorrow," he said, handing her the hair clip.

Sam felt his eyes on her back as she went to the door and let herself out. All the way home, her lips burned from the heat of his kiss.

CHAPTER 8

Early the next morning, as she stood over the lifeless, waxy remains of Senator John Thomas O'Connor, age thirty-six, it struck Sam that death was the great equalizer. We arrive with nothing, we leave with nothing, and in death what we've accomplished—or not accomplished—doesn't much matter. Senator or bricklayer, millionaire or welfare mother, they all looked more or less the same laid out on the medical examiner's table.

"I'd place time of death at around eleven p.m.," Dr. Lindsey McNamara, the District's chief medical examiner, said as she released her long red hair from the high ponytail she'd worn for the autopsy.

"That's shortly after he got home. The killer might've been waiting for him."

"Dinner consisted of filet mignon, potatoes, mixed greens and what looked like two beers."

"Drugs?"

"I'm waiting on the tox report."

"Cause of death?"

"Stab wound to the neck. The jugular was severed. He bled out very quickly."

"Which came first? The cut to the neck or the privates?"

"The privates."

Sam winced. "Tough way to go."

"For a man, probably the toughest."

"He was alert and aware that someone he knew had dismembered him," Sam said, more to herself than to Lindsey.

"You're sure it was someone he knew?"

"Nothing's definite, but I'm leaning in that direction because there was no struggle and no forced entry."

"There was also no skin under his nails or any defensive injuries to his hands."

"He didn't put up a fight."

"It happened fast." Lindsey gestured to O'Connor's penis floating in some sort of liquid.

Sam fought back an unusual surge of nausea. This stuff didn't usually bother her, but she had never seen a severed penis before.

"A clean, fast cut," Lindsey said.

"Which is why the killer was able to get the knife through his neck while he was still sitting up in bed."

"Right. He would've been reacting to the dismemberment. He might've even blacked out from the pain."

"So he never saw the death blow coming."

"Probably not."

"Thanks, Doc. Send me your report when it's ready?"

"You got it," Lindsey said. "Sam?"

Sam, who had reached for her cell to check for messages, looked over at the other woman.

"I wanted you to know how terrible I felt about what happened with that kid," Lindsey said, her green eyes soft with compassion. "What the press did to you...well, anyone who knows you knows the truth."

"Thank you," Sam said in a hushed tone. "I appreciate that."

By seven o'clock, Sam was in her office wading through four sets of phone records drawn from the senator's home, office and two cell phones. Her eyes blurry from the lack of sleep that she blamed on Nick's kiss and the memories it had resurrected, she searched for patterns and nursed her second diet cola of the day. Most of the calls were to numbers in the District and Virginia, but she noticed several calls per week to Chicago that usually lasted an hour or more. She made a note to check the number.

A few other numbers popped up with enough regularity to warrant a follow-up. Sam made a list and turned it over to one of the other detectives who had been assigned to assist her.

Grabbing another soda and a stale bagel left over from yesterday, she stopped to brief Chief Farnsworth before heading out to meet Freddie on Capitol Hill. A crush of reporters waited for her outside the public safety building. When she saw how many there were, she briefly considered going back to ask a couple of uniforms to help her get through the crowd. Then she dismissed the idea as cowardly and stepped into the scrum.

"Sergeant, how close are you to naming a suspect?"

"How was the senator killed?"

"Who found him?"

"What do you think of the headlines in today's paper?"

That last one made her stomach roil as she could only imagine what the papers were saying about the detective the department had chosen to lead the city's highest profile murder investigation in years. She held up a hand to stop the barrage of questions.

"All I'll say at this time is the investigation is proceeding, and as soon as we know anything more, we'll hold a press conference. I'll have no further comment until that time. Now, would you mind letting me through? I have work to do."

They didn't move but also didn't stop her from pushing her way through.

Rattled and annoyed, Sam got into her unmarked department car and locked the doors. "Fucking vultures," she muttered.

Outside the Hart Senate Office Building, she dropped two quarters into the *Washington Post* box and tugged out the morning's issue where a banner headline announced the senator's murder. In a smaller story below the fold, a headline read, Disgraced Detective Tapped to Lead Murder Investigation. Sam released a frustrated growl when the words appeared jumbled on the page as they often did during times of stress or exhaustion. *Goddamned dyslexia.* Taking a deep calming breath, she tried again, taking the words one at a time the way she'd trained herself to do.

The story contained a recap of the raid that had led to the death of Quentin Johnson and stopped just short of questioning her competence—and the chief's.

"Great," she muttered. "That's just *great*." Tossing the paper into the trash, she took the elevator to the second floor where Freddie enjoyed a glazed donut while he waited for her.

"Did you see the paper?" he asked, wiping the sticky frosting from his mouth with the back of his hand.

She nodded brusquely, and before he could get into a further discussion about the article, she brought him up to speed on the possible break-in at Nick's, the autopsy and the phone records. Gesturing to the door to Senator O'Connor's suite of offices, she said, "Let's get to it."

After a thorough look through the remaining items in John's office where they found nothing useful to the case, Sam and Freddie worked their way up from administrative assistants through legislative affairs people to the staff from the senator's Richmond office to the communications director. They asked each of Senator O'Connor's employees the same questions—where were you on the night of the murder, did you have a key to his apartment, what do you know about his personal life, and can you think of anyone who might've had a beef with him?

The answers were the same with few variations—I was here working (or at home in Richmond with my husband/wife/girlfriend), I didn't have a key, he guarded his privacy, and everyone liked him, even political rivals who had good reason not to.

"Who's next?" Sam asked, feeling like they were spinning their wheels.

"Christina Billings, deputy chief of staff," Freddie said.

"Bring her in."

"Ms. Billings," Sam said, gesturing the pretty, petite blonde to a seat across the conference room table. Sam always felt like an Amazon next to tiny women like her. "Let me begin by saying how sorry we are for your loss."

The sympathy brought tears to Christina's blue eyes. "Thank you," she whispered.

"Can you tell us where you were the night of the senator's murder?"

"I was here. With the vote the next day we had so much to do to get ready for the aftermath—press conferences, appearances on talk shows, interviews...We were doing everything we could to ensure the senator got the attention he deserved." Her shoulders sagged, almost as if life had lost its purpose. "He'd worked so hard."

Intrigued by the gamut of emotions emanating from Christina, Sam said, "You were here in the office the entire night?"

"Except for when I left to get food for everyone."

"What time?" Freddie asked.

"I don't know. Maybe around eleven or eleven-thirty?"

Freddie and Sam exchanged glances.

"Where did you get the food?"

She named a Chinese restaurant on Capitol Hill, and Sam made a note to check it out later. "Did you go anywhere else?"

"No. I picked up the food and came right back. Everyone was hungry."

"Do you have a key to the senator's apartment?" Freddie asked.

Nodding, she said, "He gave it to me some time ago so I could pick up his mail and water the plants when he was in Richmond or Leesburg."

"When was the last time you used it?"

Christina thought about that. "Maybe three months ago. He's been in town for most of the session working on gathering the votes needed for the immigration bill."

"What do you know about his personal life?" Freddie asked. "Was he dating anyone?"

Her expression immediately changed from grief-stricken to hostile. "I have no idea. I didn't discuss his love life with him. He was my boss."

Something in the tone, in the flash of the blue eyes, set off Sam's radar. "Ms. Billings, were you romantically involved with the senator?"

Christina pushed back the chair and stood up. "I'm done."

"The hell you are," Sam snapped. "Sit down."

Trembling with rage, her lips tight, Christina turned and met Sam's steely stare with one of her own. "Or what?"

"Or we'll do this downtown. Your choice."

With great reluctance, Christina returned to her seat, her body rigid, and her hands clasped together.

"Before we continue, I'll advise you of your right to have counsel present during this interview."

Christina gasped. "Am I under arrest?"

"Not at this time, but you may request an attorney at any point. Do you wish to continue without counsel?"

Christina's nod was small and uncertain. Her posture had lost some of its rigidity at the mention of lawyers.

"I'll ask you again," Sam said. "Were you romantically involved with the senator?"

"No," Christina said softly.

"Did you have feelings of a romantic nature for him?"

Christina's eyes flooded. "Yes."

"And these feelings were unrequited?"

"I have no idea. We never discussed it."

"How did you feel about him dating other women?" Freddie asked.

"How do you think I felt?" Christina shot back at him. "I loved him, but he didn't see me that way. To him I was a trusted aide and a friend he could count on to pick up his mail."

"What were your specific duties as his deputy chief of staff?" Sam asked.

"I oversaw his daily schedule, kept his appointment calendar, supervised the administrative assistants, and basically managed his time."

"So you worked closely with him?" Freddie asked.

"Yes."

"More closely than Mr. Cappuano?"

"On many days. Yes."

"And in all this time you spent with him, he had no idea how you felt about him?" Sam asked.

"I went to great lengths to hide it from him and everyone else. He was my boss. I felt like a bad cliché."

"So no one else knew?"

"Nick had figured it out, but I didn't know that until after the senator was…killed," she said, her voice trailing off.

"Why didn't you leave?" Sam asked, working hard to contain her fury at Nick for keeping this from her.

"Because he needed me. He said he'd be lost without me."
Christina shrugged. "I know that sounds so pathetic, but it
was better than nothing."

"Was it?" Sam asked.

"If you're implying I killed him because he didn't notice
me as a woman, you're way off."

"People have killed for less."

"I didn't. I loved him. Receiving that phone call from Nick
was the single most devastating moment of my life." After a
long moment of silence, Christina started to push back her
chair. "May I go?"

"Before you do," Freddie said, "let me ask you this—you
say you kept his schedule and managed his life. Did I get that
right?"

"Yes."

"So wouldn't you know who he was seeing outside the office?"

Christina's jaw clenched with tension.

"Is that a yes?" Freddie asked.

"There were several," Christina finally said.

"We'll need a list," Sam said. "I'd also like a list of anyone
else you know of who had a key to his apartment and his appointment calendar for the last six months—by the end of the
day, please."

With a curt nod, Christina got up.

"Stay available," Sam said before the other woman could
leave the room.

"What does that mean?"

"Exactly what you think it means."

The moment the door slammed shut behind Christina, Sam
turned to Freddie.

"I know what you're going to say." He counted off on his

fingers. "A break in the alibi at the same time as the murder, a key to the apartment, unrequited love…"

"It's almost enough to arrest her," Sam said.

"Except?"

Sam sighed. "I believed her when she said his death was the most devastating thing that's ever happened to her."

"Doesn't mean she wasn't responsible for it."

"No, it doesn't."

"I'll do some digging around in Ms. Billings's background."

"Freddie, you read my mind. We also need to look into who would stand to gain financially from the senator's death."

"Would the chief of staff know that?"

"He might. He's next. Do you want to go grab some lunch before we get to him?"

"I thought you'd never ask." Freddie stretched, rubbing his belly with glee. "Something for you?"

"A salad." She slapped a ten-dollar bill into his hand. "Low-fat dressing."

He made a disgusted face. "Coming right up."

The moment he was gone, Sam marched into Nick's office and slammed the door.

"Well, good afternoon to you, too, Sergeant," he said with a small, private smile that let her know he'd been thinking of her since they'd kissed the night before.

"Save the charm for someone who's interested."

He raised a swarthy eyebrow in amusement. "Oh, you're interested. But if you want to play hard to get, don't let me stop you."

"What happened last night can't happen again."

"It can, and it will."

"Not until this case is closed, Nick. I mean that." Deciding it was time to move past their personal debate, she planted her hands on her hips. "Were you planning to mention that your deputy was in love with the senator?"

Nick looked stricken. "She *told* you that?"

"I got it out of her. One of my special talents."

"I'll bet," he said dryly.

"Why didn't you think it was important enough to share with me?"

"It was personal, and I didn't see how it was relevant."

"*Everything* is relevant, Nick! This is a *homicide* investigation!"

"I'm sorry. It never occurred to me that it would matter."

"She left here to get food at the exact time the M.E. has placed the time of death. She had a key to his place. She was in love with him."

Nick's handsome face went pale. "You can't possibly be suggesting—"

"I can, and I am."

"There's no way, Sam. She adored him. She was devoted to him. She could never have harmed him."

"How well do you know her?"

"I've worked with her for five years. She's a great colleague and friend."

"What do you know about her background?"

"She grew up in Oregon, came here for college, and has been working for the legislative branch since she graduated. She's worked her way up from the admin level."

"You trust her?"

"Implicitly."

"What level clearance does she have?"

"Secret."

Sam tugged the notebook from her back pocket and made a note to get a hold of the background check Christina Billings would've been required to undergo for a government security clearance. "What about you?"

"Top secret."

"As of when?"

"As of the senator's appointment to the Committee on Homeland Security and Governmental Affairs. Before that it was secret."

"Who else has top secret?"

"Only the senator."

"Who're his heirs?"

Nick considered that. "Well, I suppose it would be his niece and nephew, Emma and Adam."

"But you don't know for sure?"

He shook his head.

"Who would?"

"Probably his father and their attorney, Lucien Haverfield." Sam wrote down Haverfield's name.

Freddie came into the room carrying two bags of take-out. "Start without me, boss?"

"We're talking heirs," Sam told him. "Mr. Cappuano believes it's most likely the senator's niece and nephew."

"Makes sense," Freddie said. "Are we doing this here or in the conference room?"

Nick gestured to a small table. "Here is fine with me."

"Let me grab the recorder," Freddie said.

"Do you mind if we eat in here?" Sam asked Nick. "Detective Cruz gets cranky if he doesn't get his mid-day influx of grease on time."

Nick smiled but Sam noticed his eyes were tired and sad. "No problem. I eat at that table more often than I do at home."

"Speaking of home, did you notice anything else out of place or missing?"

He shook his head.

"Let me know if you do."

"So you believe me? That someone broke in."

She replied with a small nod and had trouble meeting his intense gaze, startled to realize she was afraid of what she might find in those incredible hazel eyes.

"Am I interrupting something?" Freddie said when he returned with the recorder.

Sam cleared her throat. "No. Let's get this done. We've got a lot of ground to cover today."

CHAPTER 9

After a quick stop at the Chinese restaurant on Capitol Hill where they confirmed that Christina Billings had in fact picked up take-out around eleven the night before last, Sam drove Freddie back to the office.

"So," he said. "Do you want to tell me what that was all about before?"

"What?"

"You and Cappuano. I felt like a third wheel on a hot date."

Sam shot him a glance. "What the hell are you talking about?"

"Well, gee, let's see." Counting on his fingers, he said, "Pregnant pauses, simmering gazes, and of course the entertaining innuendo. Need I continue?"

Unnerved that Freddie had noticed the sparks flying between her and Nick, she realized she should have known her savvy partner would have tuned in to what she had tried so hard not to encourage during their hour-long interview with Nick. The effort to keep things professional and focused had left her drained. "You're imagining things."

"No, I'm not. What gives, Sam?"

"Nothing. I barely know the man." That much was true—sort of. "Whatever you *think* you saw was the result of your overactive and undersexed imagination."

"Wow," Freddie said on a long exhale. "Who said anything about sex?"

Simmering with retorts she didn't dare pursue, Sam pulled into the parking lot at the public safety complex.

Before she could get out, Freddie stopped her. "What happened on that trip to Loudoun County yesterday?"

"Nothing." Now, *that* was true.

"I'm your partner, Sam." He gripped her jacket to keep her from escaping. "Talk to me."

She tugged her arm free of him. "There's nothing to say! We've got a million things to do, and you've got time to grill me about something you're *imagining?*"

"I'm a trained observer—trained in large part by you. I don't care what you say, there was enough heat in that room to burn down the capitol."

Sam fumed in silence. This was *exactly* why she told Nick that what happened the night before couldn't happen again. She didn't need any more aggravation right now.

In a softer tone Freddie said, "Whatever's going on, I hope you're being careful. You've got a lot at stake right now."

"Thanks, Freddie. I'm glad you reminded me of that. Otherwise I might've forgotten about the child who died on my watch."

"Sam—"

"We have work to do."

"I'm on your side. I hope you know that. If you want to talk—"

"Thank you. Can we get to work now?"

With a deep sigh, he reached for the door handle.

Sam stalked inside, again pushing her way through the gaggle of reporters gathered in the foyer. Leaving them wanting and frustrated gave her tremendous joy.

She felt bad about being so testy to Freddie who'd been a pillar of support in the wake of the Johnson case, but she didn't want to hear what he'd have to say about her past relationship with a witness—a relationship she hadn't disclosed, knowing that if she did, she'd be taken off the case. That couldn't happen. She desperately needed a big win on a high-profile case like this one to get her career back on track.

That was why she planned to work around the clock, if that's what it took, to break this case as fast as she could—long before anyone found out that she had once spent a night with the man who'd found the senator dead. If she was unsuccessful and her superiors discovered that she'd had yet another lapse in judgment, she could kiss her hard-won career goodbye. And then what would she do? What was she without this job? *Who* was she? No one.

Shaking off that unpleasant thought, Sam told Freddie she'd be back after the press conference and headed for Chief Farnsworth's office. On the way, she stopped in the restroom to splash cold water on her face. Looking up at her reflection, she was startled by the bruised-looking circles under her eyes, the pale, almost translucent skin made more so by weeks of sleepless nights, and eyes that couldn't hide the torment.

She had told them she was ready to come back, had assured the department psychologist she could handle anything the job threw her way. But could she handle seeing Nick Cappuano again? Could she handle how it had felt—even six years later— to be engulfed once again by those strong arms, to be kissed by those soft lips, to be on the receiving end of those heated eyes? *God!* Those eyes of his were flat-out amazing.

"Stop, Sam," she whispered to the face in the mirror, a face she barely recognized. "Please stop. Do your job and stop thinking about him. Think about the senator."

Reaching for a paper towel, she blotted the excess water from her face and took a deep breath. "The senator," she said once more as she prepared to stand next to the chief at the press conference.

★ ★ ★

The questions were brutal.

"How can you trust someone with Sergeant Holland's poor judgment to oversee such an important investigation?"

Chief Farnsworth, bless his heart, made it clear that she was the detective best suited to lead the investigation, and she had his full confidence and trust.

As Sam imagined what he'd have to say about her relationship with a material witness, she swallowed hard. *Enough of that*, she thought. *You've made your decision where he's concerned. It was one night, so stop thinking about it. Yeah, right. Okay.*

Once the reporters were done attacking her, they moved on to more specific questions about the investigation.

"Do you have any suspects?"

The chief nodded at Sam to take the question. "We're considering a number of possible suspects but haven't narrowed it down to one yet."

"What's taking so long?"

"The senator led a complex, complicated life. It's going to take some time to put all the pieces together, but I'm confident that we'll bring the investigation to a satisfactory conclusion."

"Any word on funeral plans?"

"You'll have to ask his office about that."

"Can you tell us how the senator was murdered?"

"No."

"Was his apartment broken into?"

"No comment."

"Was there a struggle?"

"No comment."

The chief stepped in. "That's it for now, folks. As soon as we have more to tell you, we'll let you know." He ushered Sam off the stage and into his office. "You did a good job out there. I know that wasn't easy." Studying her for a long moment, he said, "You're not sleeping well."

She shrugged. "Got a lot on my mind."

"Maybe you should talk to Dr. Trulo about a prescription—"

Sam held up a hand to stop him. "I haven't reached that point yet."

"I need you at the top of your game right now."

"Don't worry. I am."

"I like this Christina Billings for a person of interest."

"I don't know," Sam said, shaking her head. "The people in the office said the food was hot when she returned with it, so it seems like she went straight back. The records at the parking garage show she returned twenty-eight minutes after she left."

"Could she have gone to his place before the restaurant?"

"She'd have had to drive across the District to the Watergate, kill him and get back with Chinese in half an hour. Not enough time. Plus, the knife severed his jugular. The blow would've sprayed blood all over her. Cappuano, the chief of staff, said she had on the same suit the next morning that she'd worn the day before because they pulled an all-nighter at the office to get ready for the vote the next day. Based on that, I'm on the verge of ruling her out."

The chief rubbed at his chin as he thought it over. "Do some digging into her. She had motive, opportunity and a key. Don't rule her out too quickly."

"Yes, sir."

"Same thing with his brother. Again, we have motive, opportunity and no alibi if he can't produce the woman he says he was with."

"Right. We're going to talk to him more formally. Another thought that's been running around in my head is the sister and brother-in-law, Lizbeth and Royce Hamilton."

"Why?"

"Their kids are most likely the senator's heirs. The O'Connor parents will be here at six to view the body. I'll ask Graham O'Connor about his son's will, and I've got Cruz digging into their finances. Then there's Stenhouse, the O'Connors' bitter political rival. He went home to Missouri for a long-planned fund-raiser today, but we've got an appointment with him in the morning."

"What do you think of that angle?"

"Not much, which is why I didn't stop him from going to Missouri. There's no way he had a key to the place, and I'm convinced that whoever did this was someone John O'Connor was close to."

"Girlfriends?"

"Billings is getting us a list of women he's seen socially in the last six months and anyone who had a key. I'm also going to ask the senior Senator O'Connor if there might be keys still floating around from when he lived there."

"The surveillance videos were no help?"

"We couldn't I.D. anyone and neither could Cappuano. The video captures activity in the lobby and elevator areas but not at individual doors, so that didn't help much. It was a cold night, and everyone was bundled up pretty tight with hats and scarves. We had trouble making out faces."

Startled, the chief looked up at her.

"What?"

"People were bundled up..."

"What about it?"

"Is it possible Christina Billings had a coat she ditched after the killing?"

Intrigued, Sam puzzled that over. "That would explain why the suit wasn't ruined."

"Exactly. Might be time to get a warrant to search her car."

"Jesus," Sam said. "Why didn't I think of this?"

"You would have. I think you've got a timing problem where she's concerned, but it seems to me like you've got every base covered, Sergeant."

"I'm trying."

They were interrupted by a knock on the door.

"Come in," the chief called.

The door opened and Freddie stepped into the room, looking nervous and uncertain.

"Detective Cruz."

"Hello, sir," Freddie stammered. "I'm sorry to interrupt, but the officers going through the documents taken from the senator's apartment have uncovered a life insurance policy that I think you need to see, Sergeant Holland." He handed it to her.

Sam scanned the document, her eyes widening at the two-million-dollar amount. An involuntary gasp escaped when she saw the beneficiary's name: Nicholas Cappuano.

Twenty minutes later, Sam stormed past Nick's startled staff straight into his office and slammed the door behind her.

He never looked up from what he was doing when he said, "Back so soon, Sergeant?"

"You son of a bitch!"

He finally glanced at her, but there was steel in his normally amiable eyes. "Care to explain yourself?"

"How about *you* explain *yourself.*" She slapped the insurance policy down in front of him.

Without breaking the intense gaze, he reached for the document. "What's this?"

"You tell me."

He finally looked away from her. "It's an insurance policy."

"To me it looks like a *two-million-dollar* insurance policy," Sam clarified. "Flip to the last page."

He did as she asked. *"I'm* the beneficiary?" he asked with what appeared to be genuine shock.

"As if you didn't know."

"I didn't! I had no idea he'd done this!" An odd expression settled on his face. "So…that's what he meant." His voice faded to a whisper.

She wanted to demand he say more but waited for him to collect his thoughts.

"I once told John, back when I first met him and figured out who his father was, that I couldn't imagine in my wildest dreams ever being a millionaire. He said, 'You never know.'" Nick ran his hand reverently over the pages of the policy. "Then about a month ago, the subject came up again because I made a joke about how rich I'm getting running his office. He said I still had plenty of time to be a millionaire and that what I was doing—what we're all doing—was more important than money." Nick looked over at Sam. "That was the first time it seemed to me that he really embraced the significance of the office he held. Then he said I could be a millionaire sooner than I thought and walked away."

"You didn't ask him what he meant by that?"

He shook his head. "It seemed like a throwaway line at the time, but now it takes on more significance."

"Do you think he knew he was going to die soon?"

"No, but he had a sense that he was going to die young. He'd get into these maudlin discussions when we'd been drinking. We called them his philosophical moods."

"Did he have these moods often?"

Nick considered that. "More often lately, now that you mention it. Christina asked me last week if I thought he might be depressed."

"Did you?"

"Distracted might be a better word than depressed. He definitely had something on his mind."

"And you have no idea what?"

"I tried to talk to him about it a couple of times, but he brushed it off. Said he was focused on the bill and getting it passed. I chalked it up to stress."

"You really didn't know about the insurance?"

"I swear to God. Give me a polygraph."

Sam studied him for a long moment. "That won't be necessary. Congratulations, looks like you're finally going to be a millionaire."

"Hell of a way to get there," he said softly.

The last of the steam she'd come in with dissipated. "Nick…" She resisted the powerful urge to walk around the desk and embrace him. Clearing the emotion from her throat, she said, "His parents are coming in at six. They want to see him. Do you think maybe you could come, too? It might help them to have a familiar face there."

"Of course."

"I could take you and bring you back later so you don't have to deal with the parking situation over there."

"Sure." He stood up and reached for the suit coat that was draped over the back of his chair.

Sam's mouth went dry as she watched the play of his muscles under the pale blue dress shirt he had worn without a tie. His hands were graceful as he adjusted his collar. She remembered the way those hands had felt moving over her fevered skin so many years ago. The memory shouldn't have been so vivid, but there it was, as bright and as real as if it had happened only yesterday.

He caught her watching him. "What?"

Her face heated. "Nothing."

Without looking away from her, he came around the desk

and stopped right in front of her. He reached out and ran a finger over her cheek. "I think about it, too. I never stopped thinking about it."

"Don't." She wondered how it was possible that he had read her mind so easily. "Please."

"Even in the midst of everything else that's going on, even as I plan my best friend's funeral, even as I deal with a traumatized staff and John's parents, I want you. I think about you, and I want you."

"I *can't*, Nick. My job is on the line. My whole career is riding on this investigation. I can't let you do this to me right now."

"What about later? After it's over?"

"Maybe. We'll have to see."

"Then that'll have to do." He gestured for her to lead the way out of his office. "For now."

CHAPTER 10

"What's the plan for the funeral?" Sam asked Nick as they sat in heavy traffic on Constitution Avenue.

"He'll lie in state at the capitol in Richmond for forty-eight hours, beginning on Friday. The funeral will be held at the National Cathedral on Monday with burial at Arlington a week or two later. It takes a while to get that arranged."

"I didn't realize he was a veteran."

"Four years in the Navy after college."

"If possible, I'd like to attend the funeral with you in case I need you to identify anyone for me."

"Sure. I'll do what I can."

"Thank you." She wanted to say more but found her tongue to be uncharacteristically tied in knots. After a long, awkward pause, she glanced over at him. "I, um, I appreciate the help you're giving me with background and insight into the senator's relationships."

"Have you spoken to Natalie yet?"

Sam's brain raced through the various lists of friends, family, coworkers, and acquaintances. "I haven't heard of a Natalie. Who is she?"

"Natalie Jordan. She was John's girlfriend for a couple of years."

"When?"

Nick thought about that. "I'd say for about two years before he ran for the Senate and maybe a year after he was sworn in."

"Did it end badly?"

"It ended. I was never sure why. He wouldn't talk about it."

"Yet you saw fit to toss her name into a homicide investigation."

He shrugged. "You were mad I didn't tell you Chris was in love with him. Natalie was important to him for a long time. In fact, she was the only woman I ever knew of who was truly important to him. I just thought you should know about her."

"Where is she now?"

"Married to the number-two guy at Justice. I think they live in Alexandria."

"Did he ever see her?"

"Sometimes they'd run into each other at Democratic Party events in Virginia."

"Would she still have a key to his apartment?"

"Possibly. They lived together there for the last year or so that they were together."

"Did you like her?"

Nick rested his head against the back of the seat. "She wasn't my type, but he seemed happy with her."

"But did you *like* her?"

"Not really."

"Why not?"

"She always struck me as a social climber. We rubbed each other the wrong way—probably because I couldn't do anything to advance her agenda so she didn't have much use for me."

"Knowing he dated someone like that seems contrary to the picture you and others have painted of him. To me, he wouldn't have had the patience for it."

"He was dazzled by her. She's quite…well, if you talk to her, you'll see what I mean."

"What do you think of his sister and brother-in-law?"

Nick appeared startled by the question. "Salt of the earth. Both of them."

"What's his story? Royce Hamilton?"

"He's a horse trainer. One of the best there is from what I've heard. Lizbeth has been crazy about horses all her life. John always said she and Royce were a match made in heaven."

"Any financial problems?"

"None that I ever heard of—not that I heard much about them. I saw them at holidays, occasional dinners in Leesburg, fund-raisers here and there, but we don't travel in the same circles."

"What circle do they travel in?"

"The Loudoun County horse circle. John adored their kids. He talked about them all the time, had pictures of them everywhere."

"What did Senator O'Connor think of his only daughter marrying a horse trainer?"

"Royce is an intelligent guy. And more important, he's a gentleman. The senator could appreciate those qualities in a potential son-in-law, even if he wasn't a doctor or a lawyer or a politician. Besides, Lizbeth was wild about him. Her father was smart enough to know there'd be no point in getting in the way of that."

"What about her? Could she have had some sort of dispute with John?"

Nick shook his head. "She was completely and utterly devoted to him. She was one of our best campaigners and fund-raisers." He chuckled. "John called her The Force. No one could say no to her when she went out on the stump for her 'baby brother.' There's no way she had anything to do with this." More emphatically, he added, "No way."

"Did she have a key to the Watergate apartment?"

"Most likely. Everyone in the family used the place when they were in town."

"That place has more keys out than a no-tell motel."

"It was just like John to give keys to everyone he knew and think nothing of it."

"Yet he was the only other person in the world who had a key to your place. Can you see the irony in that?"

"He led a bigger life than I do."

"Tell me about your life," she said on an impulse.

He raised that swarthy eyebrow. "Who's asking? The woman or the detective?"

Sam took a moment to appreciate his quick intelligence, remembering how attractive she had found that the first time she met him. "Both," she confessed.

He glanced at her, and even though her eyes were on the road, she felt the heat of his gaze. "I work. A lot."

"And when you're not working?"

"I sleep."

"No one—not even me—is that boring."

He flashed her a funny, crooked grin that she caught out of the corner of her eye. "I try to get to the gym a couple of times a week."

Judging from the ripped physique she had been pressed against the night before, he put those gym visits to good use. "And? No wives, girlfriends, social life?"

"No wife, no girlfriend. I play basketball with some guys on Sundays whenever I can. Sometimes we go out for beers afterward. Last summer, I played in the congressional softball league, but I missed more games than I made. Oh, and every other month or so, I have dinner with my father's family in Baltimore. That's about it."

"Why haven't you ever gotten married?"

"I don't know. Just never happened."

"Surely there had to have been *someone* you might've married."

"There was this one girl…"

"What happened?"

"She never returned my calls."

Shocked and speechless, Sam stared at him.

"You asked."

Tearing her eyes off him, she accelerated through the last intersection before the turn for the public safety parking lot. "Don't say that to me," she snapped. "You don't mean that."

"Yes, I do."

She pulled into a space and slammed the car into park.

He grabbed her arm to stop her from getting out. "Calm down, Sam."

"Don't tell me what to do." She tugged her arm free of his grasp. "And save your cheesy lines for someone who's buying. I don't believe you anyway."

"If you didn't, you wouldn't be so pissed right now."

"Do you want to know what happened to your friend?"

With one blink, his hazel eyes shifted from amused to furious. "Of course I do."

"Then you have to stop doing this to me, Nick. You're winding me up in knots and pulling my eye off the ball. I need to be focused, one hundred percent *focused* on this case, and *not* on you!"

"What about when you're off duty?" The teasing smile was back, but it didn't steal the sadness from his eyes. "Can I wind you up in knots then?"

"Nick..."

Fixated on the drab-looking public safety building, he sighed. "We're about to go in there and take John's parents to see him laid out on a cold slab, and yet, all I can think about right now is how badly I want to kiss you. What kind of a friend does that make me? To him or to you?"

His tone was so full of sadness and grief that Sam softened a bit. "You were a great friend to him, and in the last twenty-four hours, except for the whole kissing thing, you've been helpful to me, too. Can we keep it that way? Please?"

"I'm trying, Sam. Really I am, but I can't help that I feel this incredible pull to you. I know you feel it, too. You felt it six years ago—as strongly as I did—and you still do, even if you don't want to. If we had met again under different circumstances, can you tell me the same thing wouldn't be happening between us?"

"I have to go in now." Her firm tone hid her seesawing emotions. "His parents are probably waiting for me, and I don't want to drag this out for them. Are you coming?"

"Yeah." He opened the door. "I'm coming."

Freddie met them inside. "We've got the O'Connors in there." He pointed to a closed conference room door. "And the Dems from Virginia the senator had dinner with the night he was killed are in there."

Sam glanced back and forth between the two closed doors. "Will you take Mr. Cappuano and the O'Connors to see the senator, please?" she asked Freddie.

"No problem."

She rested a hand on Freddie's arm and looked up at him. "Utmost sensitivity," she whispered.

"Absolutely, boss. Don't worry."

To Nick, she said, "I'll catch up to you."

He nodded and followed Freddie into the room where Graham and Laine O'Connor waited with their daughter and another man who Sam assumed was Royce Hamilton. With a brief glance, Sam noticed that both O'Connors had aged significantly overnight.

"Senator and Mrs. O'Connor, my partner, Detective Cruz, will take you to see your son. I'll join you in a few minutes."

"Thank you," Graham said.

With a deep breath to change gears and force her mind off the intense conversation she'd just had with Nick, Sam entered the room where two portly men sat waiting for her. She judged them both to be in their late sixties or early seventies.

Upon her entrance, they leapt to their feet.

"Gentlemen," she said, reaching out to shake their hands. "Detective Sergeant Sam Holland. I appreciate you coming in."

"We're just *devastated*," drawled Judson Knott, who had introduced himself as the chairman of the Virginia Democratic Party. "Senator O'Connor was a dear friend of ours and the people of the Commonwealth."

"I'm not looking for a sound bite, Mr. Knott, just an idea of how the senator spent his last few hours."

"We met him for dinner at the Old Ebbitt Grill," said Richard Manning, the vice chairman.

"How often did you all have dinner together?"

The two men exchanged glances. "Every other month or so. We offered to reschedule that night because he had the vote the next day, but he said his staff had everything under control, and he had time for dinner."

"How did he seem to you?"

"Tired," Manning said without hesitation.

Knott nodded in agreement. "He said he'd been working twelve- and fourteen-hour days for the last two weeks."

"What did you talk about over dinner?"

"The plans for the campaign," Knott said. "He was up for re-election next year, and although he was a shoo-in, we take nothing for granted. We've been gearing up for the campaign for months, but now…" His blue eyes clouded as his voice trailed off. "It's just such a tragedy."

"What time did you part company after dinner?"

"I'd say around ten or so," Knott said.

"And where was he headed from there?"

"He said he was going straight home to bed," Knott said.

"Who will take his place in the Senate?"

"That's up to the governor," Manning said.

"No front-runners?"

Knott shook his head. "We haven't even talked about it, to be honest. We're all just in a total state of shock right now. Senator O'Connor was a lovely person. We can't imagine how anyone would want to harm him."

"No one in the party was jealous of his success or bucking for his job?"

"Only his brother," Manning said with disdain. "What a disappointment *he* turned out to be."

"Was he jealous enough to kill the senator?"

"Terry?" Knott said with a nervous glance toward the door, as if he was afraid the O'Connors might hear him. "I doubt it. It would require he get his head out of his ass for more than five minutes."

"The O'Connors had their problems, like any family," Manning added. "But they were tight. Terry might've been jealous of John, but he wouldn't have done this to his mother." Shaking his head with dismay, he said, "Poor Laine."

"We saw them outside," Knott said. "Our hearts are broken for them."

"Thank you for coming in." Sam handed each of them her card. "If you think of anything else, even the smallest thing, let me know."

"We will," Manning said. "We'll do anything we can to help find the monster who did this."

"Thank you." Sam saw them out and headed for the morgue.

CHAPTER 11

Following the O'Connors into the cold, antiseptic-smelling room, Nick thought he had properly prepared himself. After what he had seen yesterday, he should have been able to handle anything.

However, nothing could have prepared him for the sight of John lifeless, waxy, and so utterly *gone*. Nor could he have prepared for Laine's reaction.

With one look at her son's face, John's mother fainted into a boneless pile. It happened so fast that no one was able to reach her in time to keep her head from smacking the cement floor.

"Jesus, God!" Graham cried as he dropped to his knees. "Laine! Honey, are you all right?"

"Mom," Lizbeth said as tears rolled down her face. "Mom, open your eyes."

Several tense minutes passed before Laine's eyes fluttered open. "What happened?"

"You fainted," Lizbeth said. "Do you think you could sit up?"

"I need to get out of here. Take me out of here, Lizzie."

Lizbeth and Royce helped her mother up. Without another glance at the body on the table, they escorted her from the room.

"Are you all right, Senator?" Nick asked when they were alone.

His complexion gray, his hands trembling, Graham O'Connor fixated on the white bandage covering the neck wound that ended his son's life. "It's all so wrong, you know?" the older man said in a hoarse whisper.

"Sir?"

"Standing over the body of your child. It's wrong."

Nick's throat tightened with emotion. "I'm sorry. I wish there was something I could say…" He kept his voice down so Detective Cruz, who was minding the door, wouldn't hear them.

Graham reached out haltingly to caress John's thick blond hair. "Who could've done this? How's it possible someone hated my John this much?"

"I just don't know." Nick looked down at John, wishing he had the answers they so desperately needed.

"Do you think it could be Terry?"

Shocked, Nick whispered, "Senator…"

"He never got over what happened. He resented John—maybe even hated him—for taking his place in a job he felt was his."

"He wouldn't have killed him over it."

"I wish I could be so certain." Graham looked up at Nick with shattered eyes. "If it *was* Terry…If he did this, it'll kill Laine."

Nick could only imagine what it would do to Graham.

"Um, excuse me," Sam said from behind them. "I'm sorry to interrupt."

Nick wondered if she had heard them speculating about Terry.

"Can I get you anything, Senator? Would you like to sit for a minute? I could get you a stool—"

Graham's expression hardened as he turned to Sam. "You can tell me you've found the person who did this to my son."

"I wish I could," she said. "I *can* tell you we're working very hard on the case. If you want to come with me to the conference room, I can update you and your wife on what we have so far."

The senator turned back to his son and stroked John's hair. Tears pooled in Graham's already-bloodshot eyes. "I love you, Johnny," he whispered, leaning over to press a kiss to John's forehead. Graham's shoulders shook as he clutched the sheet covering John's chest.

Nick had never seen such a raw display of grief. After a moment, he rested a hand on Graham's shoulder. The older man remained hunched over his son until Nick gently guided him up.

"Oh God, Nick," he sobbed, pressing his face to Nick's chest. "What're we going to do without him? *What'll we do?*"

Nick wrapped his arms around Graham. "I don't know, but we're going to figure it out. We're going to get through this." He glanced up to find Sam watching them with an expression of exquisite discomfort. Embarrassed by his own tears, he returned his attention to the senator. "Why don't we let Sergeant Holland fill us in on the investigation?"

Graham nodded and stepped out of Nick's embrace. With a long last heartbroken look at John, Graham headed for the door.

Swiping at his face, Nick followed him.

Sam directed them to the conference room where Lizbeth and Royce sat on either side of a pale and drawn Laine. Someone had gotten her a glass of water and an ice pack for her head.

Graham went to his wife, reached for her hands and drew her up into his arms.

Nick couldn't look. He simply couldn't bear to witness their overwhelming agony. Turning from where he stood in the doorway, he stepped out of the room.

"I'll…ah…give you a moment," he heard Sam say as she followed him.

In the hallway, she joined Nick in resting her head against the cinderblock wall. "Are you all right?"

"I was," he said with a sigh. "I was doing a really good job of convincing myself, despite what I saw yesterday, that he was in Richmond or at the farm. But after that, after seeing him like that..."

"Denial's not an option any more."

"No."

Soft words and sounds of weeping drifted from the conference room.

"I've never before felt like I didn't belong with them. Not once in all the years I've known them, have I ever felt I didn't belong...until in there...just now..." His voice caught, and he was surprised when her hand landed on his arm.

"They love you, Nick. Anyone can see that."

"John was my link to them. That's gone now." His head ached, his eyes burned. Hating the uncharacteristic bout of self-pity but needing her more than he'd needed anyone in a long time, he sighed. "He's gone...my job...everything."

Sam squeezed his arm and then removed her hand abruptly when Freddie came around the corner.

Seeming to sense he was interrupting something, Freddie paused and looked to her for guidance.

"They needed a minute after seeing him," she said. "Could you do me a favor and find Mr. Cappuano some water?"

"That's not necessary," Nick protested.

A nod from Sam sent Freddie off.

"You didn't have to—"

"It's water, Nick."

"Thank you." He glanced over at her. "How're you holding up?"

"I'm tired."

"And?"

"And what?"

"Something else."

She cast her eyes down at the floor and kicked at the tile with the pointed toe of her fashionable black boot. "I'm pissed. Seeing those people," she nodded toward the conference room. "Others like them. Something like this happens to them and their lives are permanently altered. That bothers me. A lot."

"You care. That's what makes you such a good cop."

"I don't know too many who'd call me a good cop lately."

Taking her hand, he saw that he'd startled her with his public display of affection. "There's no one else I'd rather have on John's case. No one." He surprised her further when he kissed the back of her hand and released it.

Before Sam could chew him out for the risky PDA, Freddie returned with a cold bottle of water for Nick.

"Thank you."

"May I have a word, Sergeant?" Freddie said.

"Of course," Sam said. To Nick, she added, "Tell them we'll be right in."

Sam followed Freddie into the conference room across the hall and closed the door. "I know what you're going to say, and it's not what you think."

"Guilty conscience, Sergeant?"

Since his question was accompanied by a teasing smile she didn't remind him that she outranked him by a mile and an insubordination complaint wouldn't look good on his record. "Not at all."

"The financials came back on all the principal players."

"And?"

"Royce Hamilton is up to his eyeballs in debt."

Sam's heart reacted to the burst of adrenaline by skipping in her chest. "Is he now?"

"There's a lien on their house, which is mortgaged to the hilt."

"And his kids were O'Connor's likely heirs. Very interesting, indeed."

"We also found a regular monthly payment of three thousand dollars from the senator's personal account to a woman named Patricia Donaldson. I ran the name and came up with hundreds of hits, which I've got some people checking into."

"We can ask his parents who she is."

"Third thing, the tox screen on the senator was clean, except for the small amount of alcohol we already knew about. No drugs, prescription or otherwise."

"Okay, that's good," she said, starting for the door. "One less thing to figure out."

"Wait," he said. "I wasn't done."

She waved an impatient hand to encourage him to proceed.

"They found porn on his home computer. A lot of it."

"Kids?"

"None so far, but what's there is hard core."

She smoothed her hands over her hair. "Christ, can you believe a United States senator would take such chances?"

Freddie frowned at her use of the Lord's name. "What do you suppose it means for the case?"

"I don't know. Let me think about it. Any word on the warrant to search Christina Billings's car and apartment?"

"I just checked when I went back to get the water and nothing yet."

"What the hell is taking so long?" she fumed. "If we don't have it by the time we finish with the parents, I'll get the chief involved."

"What about Hamilton?"

"After we get the wife and in-laws out of there, we'll go at him."

Freddie's eyes lit up with anticipation. "Good cop, bad cop?"

"If necessary."

"Can I be bad cop this time? *Please?*"

She shot him a withering look that said "as if."

"I *never* get to be bad cop," he said with a pout. "It's so not fair."

"Grow up, Freddie," she shot over her shoulder as she crossed the hall to where the O'Connors waited. Before she opened the door, she took a moment to collect herself, to take her emotions out of the equation. She appreciated that Freddie knew her moods well enough by then not to question what she was doing or why. "Ready?"

He nodded.

Sam opened the door. "I'm sorry to keep you waiting." She did her best to avoid looking directly at the four faces ravaged by grief as she took them through what the police knew so far, leaving out anything that would compromise the integrity of the investigation.

"So you're telling me that after two days, you've got absolutely nothing?" Graham said.

"We have several persons of interest we're taking a hard look at," Sam said as the chief slipped into the room. She nodded at him and returned her attention to the O'Connors. "I wish I could tell you more, but we're working as hard and as fast as we can."

Graham turned to the chief. "I've known you a lot of years, Joe. I need the very best you've got."

Chief Farnsworth glanced at Sam. "You're getting it. I have full faith in Sergeant Holland and Detective Cruz as well as the team backing them up."

"So do I," Nick said quietly from where he stood against the back wall.

Senator and Mrs. O'Connor turned to him.

With his eyes trained on Sam, Nick said, "I've known Sergeant Holland for six years. There's no one more dedicated or thorough."

As Sam fought to keep her mouth from dropping open in shock at the unexpected endorsement, Senator O'Connor held Nick's intent gaze for a long moment before he stood and held out his hand to his wife. "In that case, we should let you get back to work. We'll count on you to keep us informed."

"You have my word, Senator," Chief Farnsworth said. "I'll show you out."

"Before you go," Sam said, "can you tell us who Patricia Donaldson was to your son?"

Graham and Laine exchanged glances but their expressions remained neutral.

"She was a friend of John's," he said.

"From high school," Laine added.

"A friend he paid three thousand dollars a month to?"

"John was an adult, Sergeant," Graham said, appearing nonplussed to hear about the payments. "What he did with his money was his business. He didn't have to explain it to us."

"Where does she live?" Sam asked.

"Chicago, I believe," Graham said.

Interesting, Sam thought, that the senator knew, without a moment's hesitation, the exact whereabouts of his son's friend from eighteen years earlier. She debated pushing him harder and might have had the chief not been in the room. In the end, she decided to pursue it from other angles.

"If there's nothing else, I'd like to take my wife home," Graham said with a pointed look at Sam.

"We realize this is an extremely difficult time for you, but we may have other questions," she said.

"Our door's always open," Graham said, helping his wife from her chair.

Lizbeth and Royce got up to go with them.

"Mr. Hamilton," Sam said. "A minute of your time, please?"

Royce's eyes darted to his wife.

"Go ahead, Daddy." Lizbeth kissed her parents. "Take Mom home. We'll be by after a while."

After Graham and Laine left the room with Chief Farnsworth and Nick following them, Sam turned to Lizbeth. "We'd like to speak to your husband alone, Mrs. Hamilton."

Tall, blond, blue-eyed and handsome in a rugged, hard-working way, Royce slipped an arm around Lizbeth's shoulders. "Anything you have to say to me can be said in front of my wife."

Sam glanced at Freddie, who handed her the printout detailing the Hamilton's financial situation. "Very well. In that case, perhaps you can explain how you've come to be almost a million dollars in debt." Only because she was watching so closely did she see Royce tighten the grip he had on his wife's shoulder.

"A series of bad investments," Hamilton said through gritted teeth.

"What kind of investments?"

"Two horses that didn't live up to their potential, and a land deal that's tied up in litigation."

"We're handling it," Lizbeth said.

"By mortgaging your house?"

"Among other things," Lizbeth said, her tone icy.

"What other things?"

"We're considering a number of options," Royce said, adding reluctantly, "including bankruptcy."

"You expect us to believe the daughter of a multi-millionaire is on the verge of bankruptcy?"

"This has nothing to do with my father, Sergeant," Lizbeth snarled. "It's our problem, and we're handling it."

"Are your children the heirs to your brother's estate?"

Lizbeth gasped. "You think…" Her face flushed, and her eyes filled. "You're insinuating that we had something to do with what happened to John?"

"What I'm asking," Sam said, "is if your children are his heirs."

"I have no idea," Lizbeth said. "We weren't privy to the terms of his will."

"But he was close to your children?"

"He adored them, and they him. They're heartbroken by his death. And you think we would've done that to them— to *him*—over *money?*"

Sam shrugged. "He had it, you needed it."

Shaking with rage, Lizbeth moved out of her husband's embrace and stepped toward Sam. Speaking in a low, fury-driven tone, she said, "I had only to ask, and he'd have given me anything. *Anything.* There would've been no need for me— or Royce—to kill him for it."

"So why didn't you? Why didn't you ask him for help?"

"Because it was *our* problem, our business. Other than my husband and children, there was no one in this world I loved more than John. If you think my husband or I killed him, I encourage you to prove it. Now, if there isn't anything else, I need to take care of my parents."

"Stay available," she said to their retreating backs.

After they were gone, Sam turned to Freddie. "Impressions?"

"Pride goeth before the fall."

"My thoughts exactly. They'd rather declare bankruptcy than let her family know they're in trouble."

The door opened, and the chief stepped into the room. "What was that about with the son-in-law?"

"Nothing," Sam said, deciding it was just that. "Tying up a loose end."

"You know Nick Cappuano?" the chief asked.

Sam cleared her throat. "Technically, yes. I met him once, six years ago. I hadn't seen him since until yesterday. He's been a tremendous asset to the investigation."

"That was quite a show of support from someone you hardly know."

She shrugged. "It seemed to be what the senator needed to hear."

"Indeed." The chief's shrewd eyes narrowed as he studied her. "Is there anything else you want to tell me, Sergeant?"

He was handing her the opportunity to come clean. But if she told him she'd slept with Nick, had feelings for him—then and now—she'd be off the case and maybe off the force. It was too much to risk. "No, sir," she said without blinking an eye.

"Anything I can do to help?"

"We're waiting on a warrant to search Billings's car and apartment. If you could exert some muscle to speed that up, we'd appreciate it."

"Consider it done." He started to leave, but turned back. "Get me an arrest, Sergeant. Soon."

"I'm doing my best, sir."

CHAPTER 12

Sam spent two hours with Freddie and the other detectives assigned to the case going over everything they had so far. While she was with the O'Connors, the lab came back with the report from John's apartment—nothing was found in the sheets, the drain, or elsewhere in the apartment that didn't belong to the victim.

Beginning to feel frustrated, Sam doled out assignments, told Freddie to meet her at Senator Stenhouse's office at nine the next morning, and sent him home. Fifteen hours after she'd started her day, she returned to her office to find Nick in her chair with his feet on the desk.

"Comfortable?" she asked, leaning against the doorframe.

He dropped his BlackBerry into his suit coat pocket. "You were my ride."

"Oh shit. Sorry. You waited all this time? You could've grabbed a cab."

"I was hoping to talk you into dinner."

"I can't. I've still got a million things I need to do." She paused, looked closer. "Did you *clean* my desk?"

"I just straightened it up a bit. How can you work in such a messy space?"

"I have a system. Now I won't be able to find anything!"

"You need to eat, and you need to sleep. What good will you be to anyone if you make yourself sick?"

"So in addition to bringing your anal retentiveness to my

workplace, you've put yourself in charge of making sure I eat and sleep?"

His face lifted into a cocky, sexy grin. "Happy to oblige on both fronts."

"Food, yes. Sleep? No way in hell."

He shrugged, apparently pleased with the half victory. "Who's this?" he asked, picking up a photo from her desk.

"My dad." In the picture, Sam stood to the side of her father's chair, her arm around his shoulders. "He was injured on the job almost two years ago."

"I'm sorry. What happened?"

Stepping into the cramped office, she bumped his feet off the desk and sat. "He was on his way home in his department vehicle and saw a car weaving through traffic. He followed it for a mile or two before he pulled it over."

"He was a traffic cop?"

She shook her head. "He was deputy chief and three months shy of retirement. Anyway, he approached the vehicle, knocked on the window, and the driver responded with gunfire. He doesn't remember anything after stopping the car. The bullet lodged between the C3 and C4 vertebrae. He's a quadriplegic, but through some miracle, he can breathe on his own when sitting up. We've learned to be grateful for the small things."

"I remember reading about it, but I didn't realize he was your father. Happened on G Street?"

"Yes."

"Did they ever get the guy?"

"Nope. It's an open investigation. I work on it whenever I can, and so does every other detective in this place. It's personal to me, to all of us."

"I can imagine. I'm sorry."

She shrugged. "Life's a bitch."

He stood up, stepped around her, pushed the door closed, reached for her and held her tight against him.

Appalled by the lump that settled in her throat, she wrestled free of him. "What was that for?"

He kept his arms around her. "You seemed to need it."

"I don't." She placed her hands on his chest to put some distance between them and to calm her racing heart. "I can't be alone in here with you. People will talk, and I don't need that."

He reached for the door and opened it. "Sorry."

Sam was relieved to find no prying eyes on the other side of the door and annoyed to realize she *had* needed the comfort Nick offered, that it somehow helped. The discovery left her unsettled.

"What?" he asked, studying her with those intense hazel eyes that made her melt from the inside out. "You're staring."

"I was just thinking…"

He tipped his head inquisitively. "About?"

"You've aged well. Really well."

"Gee, thanks. I think."

"That was a *compliment*," she said, rolling her eyes.

"Thanks for clarifying. Of course, I could say the same to you. You're even sexier than I remembered—and I remembered *everything*." He took a step to close the distance between them.

Her heart tripping into overdrive, she held up a hand to stop him. "Stay out of my personal space."

"You're the one who started handing out the *compliments*," he said with a grin that she much preferred to the grief she'd witnessed earlier.

"Temporary lapse in judgment brought on by fatigue and hunger."

"Then how about that dinner?"

"Pizza and you're buying."

"That could be arranged."

"Speaking of arranged, the M.E. is set to release the senator's body to the funeral home in the morning."

Nick immediately sobered, and Sam was sorry she'd dropped it on him that way. "Okay. Once the funeral home is done, the Virginia State Police will accompany him to the state capitol in Richmond," he said. "I was going to ask you if I could get into his place to get some clothes. The funeral director needs them."

"After dinner. I'd like to go back there anyway. Poke around some more."

"It's a date."

She turned off her computer and the lamp on her desk. "It's not a date."

"Semantics," he said as he followed her from the office.

"It's *not* a date."

Over thick-crust veggie pizza and beer at a place where everyone seemed to know Nick, Sam asked him about Patricia Donaldson.

"Who?"

"According to his parents, she was a high school friend of John's who lives in Chicago."

His eyebrows knit with confusion. "I've never heard of her."

"He sent her three thousand dollars a month, has for years, called her several times a week and talked for as much as an hour."

Nick shook his head. "I don't know anything about her." He seemed puzzled, distressed even. "How's that possible?"

"Did you know he was into porn? Big time into it?"

Pausing mid-bite, he returned the pizza to his plate and wiped his mouth. "No. How do you know?"

"It was on his home computer."

His expression shifted from startled to disgusted. His breathing slowed as he fixated on a spot behind her. He was quiet for a long time. "I wish I could say I'm totally surprised, but I'm not. He took such chances with his reputation and his career."

"What else besides this?"

"Women. Lots of them. It was like he was looking for something he just couldn't seem to find. He'd be all hot over someone and a week later she'd be history."

"Did they have anything in common?"

"They were all blonde and well endowed. Every one of them. One Barbie doll after another. It got so I didn't even bother to make the effort to remember their names."

Sam swallowed the last of her beer in one long sip and had to admit she felt recharged after the meal. "Christina Billings sent over a list of the women he'd dated during the last six months. We're working through it now. I bet we'll find his killer among the Barbies."

"I doubt it."

"Why do you say that?"

"You said it was a crime of passion, right?"

She nodded.

"None of them were around long enough to feel the kind of passion you'd have to feel to do what was done to him—except Natalie, but that was over and done with years ago. If she were going to kill him, she probably would've done it a long time ago."

"We're going to talk to her tomorrow."

"How do you do it?" he asked.

"Do what?"

"Keep up this pace. It's relentless."

"You spent a night in your office this week. You do what it takes to get your job done. That's all I'm doing. Usually it's worse than this. I often have multiple cases going, but thanks to the forced vacation my load has been light lately."

"But dealing with murderers and victims and medical examiners…It's got to be so draining."

"It can be. Other times it's exhilarating. There's nothing quite like putting all the pieces together and coming out with a picture that leads to conviction."

"Did you always want to be a cop?" He hadn't asked that question the first time they met, when she had just made detective.

"That subject is kind of complicated."

"How so?"

She fiddled with the handle on her mug. "I'm the youngest of three girls. I think I was about twelve when it dawned on me that the only reason I'd been born was because my father wanted a son so desperately."

"You can't know that for sure."

"Oh, yes I can. My mother all but told me."

"Sam…"

She hated the sympathy that radiated from him. "So, knowing I'd disappointed him just by being born, I set out to win his approval every way I could think of. Name a high school sport—I played it. I went with him to Redskins games, Orioles games. He even branded me with a boyish nickname."

"You'll be Samantha to me," Nick declared. "From this moment on."

She sneered at him. "I don't let *anyone* call me that."

"You're going to have to make an exception because to me there's nothing boyish about you. You're *all* woman. Every beautiful, sexy inch of you."

Her face heated under the intensity of his gaze. "I'll allow an occasional Samantha, but don't overdo it. And not in front of anyone else."

"I'll save it for only the most important, *private* moments," he said with a grin that melted her bones. "So, you became a cop to please him, too."

"Huh?" she asked, captivated by his hazel eyes.

"Your father."

"Oh. Right. At first that's what it was about. I won't deny that. But I discovered I have a knack for it—or I thought I did until recently."

"You do. You can't let one incident shake your confidence or your faith in yourself."

"You sound like the department shrink," she said with a chuckle. "And while I know you're both right, there's something about a dead kid that shakes you to the core even when you know you did everything right." Sam fixated on a spot on the wall as the horror of it all came back to haunt her once again. She'd never forget the sound of Marquis Johnson's agonized shrieks after his son was hit by gunfire.

"What happened that night?"

The sick weight of it settled over her and turned a stomach so recently satisfied by food. She'd had a hard time choking down anything for weeks after the incident. "I'm not supposed to talk about it. I have to testify at the probable cause hearing next week."

Under the table, he took her hand, linked his fingers through hers and resisted her efforts to break free. "Stop," he said softly. "Just stop, will you?"

"Someone might see," she hissed.

"No one's looking at us, and the tablecloth hides a world of sin. There's nothing quite like a good tablecloth."

Sam gently extricated her hand and folded her arms while pretending not to notice the wounded look that crossed his face. "I'll bet you've done your share of public sinning."

"I'll never tell," he said, his lips quirking with amusement. "Is it so difficult for you?"

"What?"

"Sharing the burden."

"It's impossible," she confessed. "My inadequacy in that regard has caused me some major problems in my life."

"What kind of problems?"

"The marriage kind for one." She wished for something else to drink since her mouth was suddenly as dry as the desert. Glancing at Nick, she found him watching her with the patience of a man who had nothing but time. She reached for his half-empty glass of beer and took a long drink.

"Why'd you get divorced?"

Sam mulled it over, wondering if she should have this conversation with a man she was wildly attracted to but who was off limits to her. After a long pause, she decided what the hell? Why not? "My ex-husband claimed I didn't need him."

"And did you?"

"No," she snorted. "He turned out to be a total loser."

"Since he failed to deliver a couple of critically important messages, I'd have to agree with you there."

"I made such a big mistake with him," she sighed. "I didn't see him for what he really was until it was too late. I didn't listen to people who tried to warn me."

Nick straightened out of the slouch he'd slipped into. "Was he...I mean...He didn't *hit* you, did he?"

"No, but it almost would've been easier if he had. At least I could've fought back against that. His thing was passive aggression. He wanted total control over me. I let it go on for far longer than I should have because I didn't want to admit I'd been so incredibly wrong. Damned foolish Irish pride."

Despite her resistance, Nick moved closer. "I want to wrap my arms around you right now," he said gruffly against her ear, his warm breath sending goose bumps darting through her. "I hate the idea of someone making you feel inadequate."

"I let him," Sam said, the pillars of her resistance toppling like Dominoes. She wanted Nick's arms around her, wanted to lean her head on that strong, capable shoulder. For the first time in longer than she could remember, she wanted the comfort he offered. No, she *needed* it. What should have been terrifying was actually rather exhilarating. "Can we go?"

"Sure." He put some bills on the table, got up and offered her his hand.

"We've left the safety of the tablecloth," she reminded him as she stepped around his outstretched arm on her way to the door.

Grinning, he followed her out.

Heads bent against the blustery cold, they walked a block to where they'd parked her department vehicle. An odd chill that had nothing to do with the cold ran up her spine as she unlocked the door on the dark street. Glancing around, she expected to find someone watching her, but saw no one. Just her overactive imagination, she thought, as she reached over to unlock the passenger door for Nick.

He slid in next to her. "Before we go to John's place, I need to get my car."

"Okay." Sam started the car to get the heat going, but sat with her hands propped on the wheel.

"What's wrong?"

She gripped the wheel. "I'm sorry I can't give you more right now, Nick." Glancing over, she found him watching her intently. "It's not because I don't want to."

He reached over to caress her face. "I know that."

His touch sent a burst of longing sizzling through her, but she tamped it down. "Can you be patient with me?"

"I spent years wishing for another chance with you, Sam. I'm not about to bail just because it isn't going to be easy."

She released a deep sigh of relief. "Good."

"But after this case is closed…"

"I'll be right there with you."

"What we had six years ago is still there," he said, gazing into her eyes.

"So it seems."

"Whatever it is, I've never had it with anyone else."

"I haven't either. I was so sad when you didn't call. I couldn't believe I'd been so wrong about you."

"*Ugh.* That makes me furious. When I think about what we might've had, all these years…"

"Let me close this case," she said, her voice hoarse and tense. "The minute I close this case…"

Nick seemed to be resisting the urge to haul her into his arms. "Samantha?"

Surprisingly, the dreaded name didn't sound so bad coming from him. "Hmm?"

"We steamed up the windows."

"And we didn't even do anything!"

"Yet," he said, his voice full of promise.

Finding him harder to resist with every passing second, she shifted the car into drive and forced herself to focus on the road.

CHAPTER 13

Sam left Nick at the congressional parking lot, and timed her drive across the city to the Watergate. At that hour of the night, traffic was light but an accident on Independence Avenue screwed up her timing. She'd have to try again tomorrow night to determine whether Christina Billings would've had enough time to drive across the city, commit murder, and drive back with a stop to pick up Chinese food in twenty-eight minutes.

Reaching for her cell phone, she called to check on the search of Billings's car.

"I was just going to call you," Detective Tommy "Gonzo" Gonzales said. "We got a hit for blood on the front seat."

"I knew it!" Sam cried. "I'll bet she wrapped up her coat and left it on the seat. The blood soaked through!"

"Wait," Gonzo said. "Before you get too excited, she said she cut her hand scraping ice off her car two weeks ago and had to get three stitches. She has a raw-looking pink scar on her right hand and produced the form from the E.R. with wound care instructions. We're checking the blood anyway, but I'll bet a month's pay it's going to be hers. She willingly gave us a sample."

"*Son of a bitch*. We can't catch a single break in this one."

"We've narrowed down Billings's list of the senator's recent girlfriends from six to two. The other four could prove they weren't in the city that night."

Sam added visits to the two remaining Barbies to her ever-

MARIE FORCE

growing to-do list for the morning. "Do me a favor and set up some plain-clothes coverage for the senator's wake. Make sure you coordinate with Virginia State Police and Richmond."

"Sure thing. Do you want observation and video or just observation?"

"Let's tape it. Make sure the officers you send have the photos of the senator's family and girlfriends, so they'll know who to watch for."

"I'm on it."

"Thanks for the good work, Gonzo."

"You got it. Try to get some sleep tonight, Sam."

"Yeah, sure."

As she sat in the tangle of cars held up by the wreck, Sam banged her fist on the wheel in frustration that came from multiple sources. She couldn't stop thinking about Nick and how understanding he'd been when she put their fledgling relationship on hold. How often did she allow herself to lean on someone? Never. However, she couldn't lean on someone who was a material witness in the homicide case she was investigating. As much as she wanted to, she just couldn't.

She edged the car forward and finally cleared the accident. When she arrived at the Watergate, Nick was waiting for her in his black BMW.

"What took so long?" he asked as he stepped out of the car.

"Accident on Independence."

"You should've taken Constitution."

"Well, I know that *now*. Nice ride," she said, admiring the gleaming Beamer. "The taxpayers take good care of you."

"I have few vices," he said with a grin as he slid an arm around her. "Cars are one of them."

She scooted out from under his arm before they entered the lobby. "No PDA," she growled. Flashing her shield to the

officer at the security desk, she gestured to the bank of eleva-
tors. "We're taking another look at the senator's apartment."

The officer nodded and waved them through.

They rode to the sixth floor where the door to John's apartment was blocked by yellow crime-scene tape. Sam plugged in
the code to the police lock and pushed open the door. Lifting
the yellow tape, she encouraged Nick to go in ahead of her.

She heard his deep inhale and watched his broad shoulders
stoop as the memories came flooding back to him. Placing
her hand on his arm, she stopped him. "You don't have to be
here. I can get the clothes for you."

"No," he said softly. "I can do it."

"Take a minute. I'm going to wander."

Sam walked through the luxurious apartment where a light
sheen of fingerprint dust remained. Picking up knickknacks,
opening drawers and checking behind the television, she
looked for anything that might have been missed the first time
through. She had no doubt the place had been put together
by a decorator—probably when the senior Senator O'Connor
lived there. It was odd, really, how little of John O'Connor
could be found in the apartment.

In the senator's bedroom, the bed linens had been stripped
and sent off for DNA analysis. A single hair could have blown
the case wide open, but all the fingerprints, fibers and DNA
were John's. Since the apartment had not yet been cleaned,
blood stained the wall behind the bed as well as the beige car-
peting, and coagulated on the bedside table. The blow to the
jugular would've been messy. Blood would have burst like a
geyser from the wound, soaking the killer.

Sam stood at the foot of the bed and let her mind wander.
Had he fallen asleep sitting up? Or had he sat up in surprise
when the killer appeared? Obviously, he'd been naked in bed.
Had he thought he was going to have sex with the woman who

appeared in his bedroom? Is that how she gained easy access to his privates? Sam was absolutely convinced it was someone he knew well, which is why he hadn't had much of a reaction to finding her in his apartment.

"What's going on in that head of yours, Sergeant?" Nick asked from behind her.

"He was asleep," Sam said, her eyes fixed on the headboard where the gaping hole in the beige silk upholstery was a glaring reminder of what had happened there almost forty-eight hours ago. "Dozing. The TV was probably on."

"It wasn't on when I got here."

"She could've shut it off. Whoever it was, she was someone he wasn't surprised to see."

"She?"

"They were lovers." Sam spoke in a monotone as the scene played itself out in her imagination.

"Did he let her in?"

Sam shook her head. "She was waiting for him and took him by surprise. She had the knife behind her back. Maybe she was naked, too, which is why there's no one on the security tapes leaving with blood on their clothes. He thought he was going to get lucky, and that's how she managed to get a hold of his penis. By the time he became aware of the knife, she had already severed it. The pain would've been monstrous. He probably lost consciousness. If he came to before she killed him, he would have asked why. Maybe she told him, maybe she let him wonder."

"Would she have been strong enough to get a knife through his neck with one shot?"

"Good question. And you're right—it would've taken a tremendous blow to go all the way through his neck and lodge in the headboard. She would've been enraged by something he did or failed to do. Rage and adrenaline breeds strength.

It could've been a promise he made and didn't deliver on or maybe she caught him with another woman. People have killed over less. When she was done, she took a shower to get rid of the blood that would've been all over her. Then she cleaned the bathroom and scrubbed it so well there wasn't so much as a hair on the floor. The water in the tub had dried by the time he was found, so we can only speculate that she showered. But none of the towels had been used. If she used one, she took it with her. Before she left, she might've taken a long last look at him. She was filled with regret that he couldn't be what she needed him to be, but at the same time she was angry with him for making her do this."

"You're good, Sam," Nick said, his tone reverent.

As if she had been in a trance, Sam looked up at him. "What?"

"The way you describe it…If I were a juror, I'd convict."

"All I have to do now is prove it and figure out who did it."

"You will." He moved to the closet, opened the doors and contemplated the row of dark suits, dress shirts in white, various shades of blue and some with pinstripes. There were easily a hundred ties to choose from.

Peeking into dresser drawers, Sam asked, "Did he ever wear anything besides suits? Where're the jeans? The sweats?"

"He didn't keep a lot of that stuff here."

"Where else would it be?"

"At his place in Leesburg."

"He has a second home?"

Nick nodded. "A cabin near his parents' property. We both use it as a retreat from the insanity of Washington."

"Why didn't you say anything about it the other day?"

"To be honest, it never occurred to me. I'm sorry. I wasn't thinking clearly then. I'm still not. Between what happened to John and seeing you again…"

"Take me there."

"*Now?*"

She nodded.

"It's almost midnight. You've been at it for eighteen hours. I can take you tomorrow."

Shaking her head, she said, "I won't have time tomorrow. If you drive, I'll nap in the car—if you can stay awake that is."

"I'm fine. I do my best work from midnight to three a.m."

His comment was rife with double meaning that Sam refused to acknowledge. Her face, however, heated with embarrassment as she helped him decide on a dark navy suit, pale blue silk dress shirt and a tie decorated with small American flags. They unearthed a garment bag, and Sam zipped it over the suit.

"Underwear?" she asked.

"He didn't wear it in life."

"How in the hell do you know that?"

Nick laughed. "We were at a luncheon with the Daughters of the American Revolution a year or so ago, and everyone was starting to leave when one of the blue hairs came to tell me the senator needed me at the head table. I went into the room, and he was sitting all by himself."

"How come?"

"Apparently, he'd managed to split his pants and was in need of an exit strategy."

Sam laughed at the picture he painted. "Let me guess—he was in commando mode?"

"You got it. So I found him an overcoat—not an easy feat in July, I might add—and got him out of there with his pride intact."

"Where did that fall in your job description?"

"Under 'other duties as assigned,'" he said with a sad smile that tugged at her heart.

"All right then. No underwear. Shoes?"

"Would you want to spend eternity with your feet encased in wingtips? The tie will be bad enough. I'm sure I'll hear plenty about that when we meet up again in the afterlife." He reached for her hand and linked their fingers. "Thank you for helping me with this."

Flustered, she extracted her hand and jammed it in her pocket. "It's no problem."

"Is choosing clothes for the deceased part of *your* job description?"

"This is definitely a first."

On their way out of John's bedroom, Nick looked at her in a way that reminded Sam of what he wanted from her. A burst of yearning took her by surprise. Sam wasn't a woman who yearned, especially for a man. She was focused, efficient, dedicated to her work and her family, hard nosed when she needed to be, and independent—fiercely and completely independent. So it should have been unsettling to want a man as much as she wanted Nick.

Truth be told, she had fantasized about him for years after the night they spent together. She had followed Senator O'Connor's career and watched hours of congressional coverage in the hopes of catching a glimpse of the senator's trusted aide. But only rarely had she seen Nick. He apparently kept a much lower profile than his illustrious boss.

In the parking lot, he held the passenger door of his car for her.

She slid into the buttery soft leather seat and sighed with contentment. When he turned the car on, she quickly discovered the seats were heated and felt like she'd gone straight to heaven. "This car suits you."

"You think so?"

"Uh huh. It's classy but not showy."

"Is that a compliment, Samantha?"

She shrugged.

He reached for her hand as they headed out of the city. When she tried to resist, he held on tighter. "No one but us, babe."

"There's no tablecloth to hide under."

He flashed that irresistible grin and laced his fingers through hers. "Give me just this much, will you?"

Since he'd asked so nicely and it really wasn't much, she didn't argue with him even if the simple feel of his hand wrapped around hers set her heart to galloping and put her hormones on full alert. Guilt was mixed in there, too. She had no business spending this much time with him or wanting him so fiercely. But since it was dark and she was tired and no one was looking, rather than push him away, she tightened her grip on his hand.

CHAPTER 14

Sam hadn't expected to sleep. But the combined lull of the moving car, the heated seats, Nick's hand wrapped companionably around hers...

"Wake up, Sleeping Beauty. We're here."

Coming to, Sam looked out at the vast darkness and was able to make out the shape of a cabin in front of the car. "Let's get to it."

The rush of frigid air slapped at Sam's face. She followed Nick up the gravel path to the door and stood back while he used his key in the lock.

Inside, he flipped on lights.

Sam blinked a comfortable living area into focus. Big, welcoming sofas, a flat-screen TV mounted on the wall, overflowing bookshelves on either side of the stone fireplace, framed family photos and a couple of trophies. Here, at last, was Senator John Thomas O'Connor.

She shrugged off her coat, pushed up the sleeves of her sweater, tugged the clip from her hair and got to work. Two hours later, she had discovered that John loved Hemingway, Shakespeare, Patterson and Grisham. His musical taste ran the gamut from Melencamp to Springsteen, Vivaldi to Bach. She had sifted through photo albums, yearbooks and a file cabinet that seemed to have no rhyme or reason to anyone other than its owner.

She perused a series of essays John wrote for his senior project at Harvard, detailing the roles of government and the governed. The essays were bound into a small navy blue volume with smart gold embossing.

"He was proud of that," Nick said from the doorway to the office.

Startled, she glanced up at him. She had *almost* forgotten he was there.

"His father had the book made and gave it to everyone who was anyone." Nick stepped into the room and handed her a steaming mug.

"*Oh*, is that hot chocolate?" she asked, soaking in the mouthwatering aroma.

"I figured it was too late for coffee." He had removed his suit coat and released the top buttons on his dress shirt. Her eyes fixated on a dark tuft of chest hair.

"You figured right. Fat free, calorie free, I hope." Swirling her tongue over the dollop of whipped cream on top, she took a moment to appreciate the taste. Looking up at him again, she found his hazel eyes locked on her. "What?" she asked, her voice shakier than she intended it to be.

"It's just…you…and whipped cream. It's giving me ideas."

She swallowed, hard.

"I like your hair down like that," he added.

Choosing to ignore the comments and the flush of heat that went rippling through her body, she returned her attention to the book John had dedicated to his father. A photo slid out from between the pages and fell to the floor. Sam put her mug on the desk and leaned over to retrieve the picture of a strapping blond boy of about sixteen in a football uniform.

"What've you got there?" Nick asked.

"Looks like a photo of John when he was in high school." She turned it over to find the initials "TJO" and a date from four years earlier. "Oh. It's not him. Who's TJO?"

Nick took the photo from her, studied the likeness, and then turned it over. "I have no idea, but he could *be* John when I first met him."

"Did he have a son, Nick?" She thought of Patricia Donaldson and the three-thousand-dollar-a-month payments.

"Of course not."

"You're sure of that?"

"I'm positive," he said hotly. "I've known him since he was eighteen. If he had a son, I'd know it."

"Well, if that's not his son, whoever he is, he bears a striking resemblance to John." Sam tucked the photo into her bag with plans to ask the senator's parents about it in the morning. "He had quite a thing for Spider-Man, huh?" She gestured to the shelves in the corner that housed John's extensive stash of Spiderman collectibles.

Nick smiled. "He was obsessed."

She picked up a carved placard from the desk that bore Spider-Man's signature saying, With Great Power Comes Great Responsibility. Studying it for a long moment, she glanced at Nick. "Did he believe this?"

"Very much so. Despite his sometimes lackadaisical approach to his job, he took his responsibilities as seriously as he was able to."

"But not as seriously as you would have."

"Let's just say if our roles had been reversed, I would've done a lot of things differently."

"Have you ever wanted to be the one in the corner office?"

"God no," he said with a guffaw. "I work much better as the guy behind the guy." He seemed to sober when he remembered he had lost his guy when John died.

"With his parents' okay, I'd like to have a team go through here more methodically tomorrow." She stretched and got up. "I'm running out of gas after twenty hours."

"I'm guessing you'll want to talk to his parents about that

photo," Nick said, "so why don't we crash here and go see them in the morning?"

Her eyes darted up to meet his. "I'm not sleeping with you."

"I'm not asking you to," he said with a sexy smile. "There's a guestroom I use when I'm here. I'll take John's room."

Sam ran it around in her mind as she finished her hot chocolate. Technically, the cabin wasn't a crime scene, so she didn't have an issue there. She was exhausted, he didn't look much better, and she *could* knock a few things off her to-do list in the morning if she stayed in Leesburg, including another discussion with Terry O'Connor if he was available.

"All right," she said, even though she would've preferred separate hotel rooms, but hotels were in short supply in that corner of the county. She got up to follow Nick down the hallway to the bedrooms.

"Bathroom's in there," he pointed. In the guestroom, he rooted through an antique chest of drawers and pulled out a large T-shirt. "One of mine if you want something to sleep in. There're extra toothbrushes and anything else you might need in the bathroom closet."

"Thanks," she said, embarrassed and shy all of a sudden— two emotions she rarely experienced.

He slid a hand around her neck to draw her in close to him. For a long, breathless moment he just looked at her before he kissed her forehead. "I'll see you in the morning. Holler if you need anything."

Devastated by the simple kiss, she watched him cross the hall, her heart pounding and her hands damp. She hated being off balance and out of kilter, which of course was why he had done it. Feeling defiant, she used the bathroom and then left the shirt he had given her on the bed as she stripped out of her clothes and slid naked between the cool sheets.

Less than a minute later, she was out cold.

★ ★ ★

"Sam. Honey, wake up. You're dreaming."

Sam could hear him but couldn't seem to force her eyes open.

"Babe."

Her eyes fluttered open to find Nick sitting on the bed.

When he brushed the hair back from her face, she realized she was sweating and her heart was racing.

"Are you okay?" he asked.

"Mmm, sorry." It occurred to her that she must've been loud if she had woken him. She glanced at him, noticing he wore only a pair of sweats, and let her eyes take a slow journey over his muscular chest.

"It was a doozy, huh? The dream?"

"I don't know. I never remember the details, just the fear." She rubbed a weary hand over her cheek and wished for a glass of water. "Did I…um…say anything?"

He replaced the hand she had on her face with his own. "You kept saying, 'Cease fire, hold your fire.'"

"Shit," she said with a deep sigh.

He stretched out next to her on top of the comforter and settled her head on his shoulder. "It was a traumatic thing, Sam, but it wasn't your fault."

Steeped in the masculine scent of citrus and spice, she closed her eyes against the rush of emotion and absorbed the comfort he offered. Just for a minute. His chest hair brushed against her face, making her want him so fiercely. "If only I could forgive myself as easily as you've forgiven me."

He brought her closer to him.

"Um, Nick?"

"Hmm?"

"I'm kind of naked under here."

"Yeah, I noticed."

As all the reasons this was a bad idea came crashing down on her, she attempted to struggle out of his embrace. "I can't," she whispered. "I can't have this. I can't have you."

"Yes, you can."

Her face still pressed to his chest, Sam gave herself another second to wallow in the scent that she'd never forgotten. "Not here. Not now."

He released a deep, ragged breath. "I missed you, Sam. I thought about you, about that night, so often."

"I did, too," she said, her eyes closed tight against the onslaught of emotions she'd only felt this acutely once before.

"I've never wanted anyone the way I want you. If you're in the room, I want you."

"I seem to have the same problem."

"We've got a few hours until daybreak. Would it be okay if I just held you until then?"

"I'd love nothing more, but it's too tempting. *You're* too tempting."

Sighing again, he released her and sat up. He leaned down to press a soft kiss to her lips. "See you in the morning."

Sam watched him go, knowing she'd never get back to sleep with every cell in her body on fire for him.

CHAPTER 15

Sam corralled her hair into a ponytail, strapped on her shoulder holster, clipped the badge to her belt, and adjusted her suit jacket over the same scoop-necked top she'd worn yesterday. When she was ready, she took a long look around to make sure she wasn't leaving behind any sign that she had spent the night for the team she planned to send in there later that day. Satisfied by the quick sweep of the room, she emerged to find Nick waiting for her in the living room. Somehow he managed to appear pressed and polished in yesterday's clothes. His face was smooth and his hair still damp from the shower.

"Ready?" he asked.

She nodded.

Wrapping her coat and his arms around her, he hugged her from behind and pressed kisses to her neck and cheek before he finally let go.

The spontaneous demonstration of affection caught her off guard. Unless it was leading to sex, Peter had never bothered with the random acts of affection that Nick doled out so effortlessly. Nick seemed to *need* to touch her if she was near him. That she liked it so much was just another reason to keep her distance.

The O'Connors's home was located two miles up the main road from John's cabin. Once again, Carrie met them at the door and was surprised to see them out so early.

"Are they up?" Nick asked.

"They're having breakfast. Come on in." She led them into

the cozy country kitchen where Graham and Laine sat at the table lost in their own thoughts. Neither of them seemed to be eating much of anything.

Both had dark circles under their eyes. Weariness and grief clung to them.

"Nick?" Graham said. "You're out early. Sergeant."

Carrie handed mugs of coffee to Sam and Nick.

"Thank you," Nick said.

"I'm sorry to barge in on you so early." Sam stirred cream into her coffee and wished it was a diet cola. "But I have something I need to ask you."

"Of course," Laine said. "Whatever we can do to help."

Sam retrieved the photo from her bag. "Who is this?" She placed the photo on the table between them.

They looked at the photo and then at each other.

"Where'd you get this?" Graham asked.

"At the cabin," Nick said. "The photo was tucked into the essay book you had made for him."

"It's John's cousin, Thomas," Laine said, glancing up at Sam with cool patrician eyes. "His father is Graham's brother Robert."

"I don't remember John mentioning a cousin that young," Nick said.

Laine shrugged. "There were almost twenty years between them. They were hardly close."

"He looks an awful lot like your son," Sam said, testing for reactions.

"Yes, he does," Graham said, his expression neutral. "Is there anything else?"

"Do you know where I can find Terry?" Sam said.

The question seemed to startle both O'Connors.

"I believe he's working in the city this morning," Graham said.

"The address?"

He rattled off the name and K Street address of a prominent lobbying firm, which Sam wrote down in the small notebook she pulled from her back pocket. "If you have no objection, I'd like to send a team into the cabin today to make sure we're not missing something that could help with the case."

"Strange people in John's home?" Laine asked, visibly disturbed by the notion.

"Police," Sam clarified. "They'll be as respectful as possible."

"That's fine," Graham said with a pointed look at his wife. "If it'll help the investigation, do it."

"Can you tell me, Senator, who might still have keys to the apartment at the Watergate from when you lived there?"

Graham pondered that for a moment. "Only my family."

"No staffers or aides?"

"My chief of staff had one, but I distinctly recall him giving it back to me when we left office."

"Any chance he might've had others made, given them to other people?"

"No. He was a guard dog about my privacy. He didn't even like having the key himself."

"Are you aware, either of you, that John spoke with Patricia Donaldson in Chicago several times a week for an hour or more each time?"

Again the O'Connors exchanged glances.

"No, but I'm not surprised," Graham said. "They were close friends as children."

"Just friends?"

"Yes," Laine said pointedly, so pointedly in fact that it raised Sam's hackles and her radar. There was more to this story. Of that she had no doubt. She'd be speaking to Patricia Donaldson as soon as she could arrange a trip to Chicago.

"John is still due to be moved today to Richmond?" Laine asked Nick.

He nodded. "The motorcade is leaving Washington at noon."

"We'll be going down to Richmond this afternoon," Graham said. "The state police are escorting us and clearing the way for us to get in and out before they open it to the public."

"The staff will have a private viewing in the morning," Nick said.

"You got the clothes they needed?" Laine asked.

"Yes. I'm heading to the funeral home from here. Um, about the funeral...Have you decided who you want to have speak on behalf of the family?"

"You do it," Laine said with a weary sigh.

"Are you sure? You wouldn't rather have a family member?"

"You *are* family to us, Nick," Graham said. "You'll do him proud. We know that."

"I'll do my best," he said softly. "We should let you get back to your breakfast."

"We'll see you Monday, if not before," Laine said.

Nick leaned over to kiss her cheek. "I'll be in touch."

She squeezed the hand he rested on her shoulder. "Thank you for all you're doing. I know it can't be easy for you."

"It's an honor and a privilege."

Patting his hand once more, she released him.

Nick hugged Graham and kissed Carrie on his way out of the kitchen. With his hand on the small of her back, he steered Sam to the front door. Once they were outside, he took a deep, rattling breath of cold air.

Since there was little else she could do to comfort him, she held his hand between both of hers all the way back to Washington.

★ ★ ★

After fighting their way through rush-hour traffic, Nick pulled up to the Watergate with fifteen minutes to spare before Sam's appointment with Senator Stenhouse.

"So much for going home to change first," she grumbled. "Freddie will have a field day with this."

"Tell him you worked all night. Won't be a total lie."

"It'll be a good excuse to remind him that I outrank him and can order him to shut up. He likes that."

Nick smiled and reached for the inside pocket of his suit jacket. He withdrew a small leather case and handed her his business card. "Call me? My cell number is on there."

She took the card, stuffed it in her pocket and reached for the door.

He stopped her before she could get out. "Talk to me before Monday so we can arrange to go to the funeral together if you still want me to help you ID people."

"I do. I'll be in touch."

"Remember to eat and sleep, will you?"

"Yeah, right," she said on her way out the door.

Nick waited, probably to make sure her car started because he was polite that way, and then pulled into traffic just ahead of her.

On the way to Capitol Hill, Sam called Gonzo and asked him to oversee the sift through John O'Connor's cabin.

"It's not a crime scene, so I'm not interested in fingerprints or DNA. I'm just looking for anything we don't already know about him."

"Gotcha. So we got confirmation that the blood in Christina Billings's car was her own."

"Well, I guess that closes that loop," Sam said. "There's no way she made it across town, killed him, showered, cleaned up the bathroom and got back with Chinese food in twenty-eight minutes. Not in this town with this traffic, even at midnight."

"No way is right," Gonzo agreed. "I'll get a team together and get out to Leesburg this morning."

"You'd better notify Loudoun County, too, so we don't have jurisdictional trouble." She paused before she added, "Full disclosure—I crashed in the guestroom there last night. I needed to see his parents in the morning, and it saved me some time. Cappuano slept in the senator's room."

"Okay."

"If you could keep that tidbit to yourself, I'd owe you one."

He laughed. "I like having you indebted to me. Just let me know if there's anything else I can do."

"There is one thing," she said, playing the hunch. "Do a run on Graham O'Connor's brother, Robert. I need the deal on his family, offspring in particular. If you can get photos, even better."

"Will do," Gonzo said. "I'll call you with what I find out. So, um, you saw the papers this morning I assume…"

Sam's stomach took a queasy dip that reminded her she hadn't eaten or had either of the two diet colas she usually relied upon to jumpstart her day. "No, why?"

"Destiny Johnson is calling you a baby killer."

"Is that so?" Sam growled, the dip in her stomach descending into the ache that dogged her in times of stress. Two doctors had been unable to determine the cause. One had suggested she give up soda, which simply wasn't an option, so she lived with her stomach's annoying ability to predict her stress level.

"Don't take it to heart, Sam. Everyone knows that if she'd been any kind of mother, her kid wouldn't have been hanging out in a crack house in the first place."

"But she has the nerve to call *me* the baby killer." Of all the things she could've said, that hurt more than anything.

"I know. She made some pretty serious threats about what she'd do if you testify against her deadbeat husband next week. I'm sure you'll be hearing from the brass about it."

"That's great." She rubbed her belly in an effort to find some relief. "Just what I need right now."

"Sorry. You know we're all standing behind you. It was a clean shoot."

"Thanks, Gonzo." Her throat tightened with emotion she couldn't afford to let in just then. Clearing it away, she said, "Call me if you find anything useful at the cabin. I did a surface run last night, but I was operating on fumes. I could've missed something."

"Leave it to me. I'll let you know when we finish."

She gave him the O'Connors's phone number so he could get a key to the cabin from them and signed off. Weaving her way through traffic, she made it to Capitol Hill with minutes to spare and took off running for the Hart Senate Office Building.

Freddie was pacing in the hallway outside Senator Stenhouse's office suite. "There you are! I was just about to call you." His astute eyes took in her day-old suit and landed on her face.

"I worked all night, I haven't been home to change yet, and yes, I've heard about Destiny Johnson," she snapped. "So whatever you're going to say, don't bother."

"As usual, a night without sleep has done wonders for your disposition."

"Buzz off, Freddie. I'm truly not in the mood to go ten rounds with you."

"What were you doing working all night? And why didn't you call me? I would've come back in."

MARIE FORCE

"I went through O'Connor's place again and then his home in Leesburg."

Freddie raised an eyebrow. "By yourself?"

"Nick Cappuano was with me. He told me about the place in Leesburg and took me there. Otherwise I never would've found it. Do you have a problem with that?"

"Me?" Freddie raised his hands defensively. "I've got no problems, boss."

"Good. Can we get to work then?"

"I'm following you."

"Nice digs," she muttered under her breath as Stenhouse's assistant showed them into a massive corner office that was triple the size of that assigned to the junior senator from Virginia.

Stenhouse, tall and lean with silver hair and sharp, frosty blue eyes, stood up when they came in. He dismissed the assistant with orders to close the door behind her. "I'm on a tight schedule, Detectives. What can I do for you?"

Wants to play it that way? Sam thought. *Well, so can I.* "Detective Cruz, please record this interview with Senate Minority Leader William Stenhouse." She rattled off the time, date, place and players present.

"You need my permission to record this," Stenhouse snapped.

"Here or downtown. Your choice."

He glowered at her for a long moment before he gestured for her to proceed.

"Where were you on Tuesday evening between ten p.m. and seven a.m.?"

"You can't be serious."

Turning to Freddie, she said, "Am I serious, Detective Cruz?"

"Yes, ma'am. I believe you're dead serious."

"Answer the question, Senator."

Teeth gritted, Stenhouse glared at her. "I was here until ten, ten thirty, and then I went home."

"Which is where?"

"Old Town Alexandria."

"Did you see or speak to anyone after you left here?"

"My wife is at home in Missouri preparing for the holidays."

"So that's a 'no'?"

"That's a 'no,'" he growled.

"How did you feel about the immigration bill Senator O'Connor sponsored?"

"Useless piece of drivel," Stenhouse muttered. "The bill has no bones to it, and everyone knows that."

"Funny, that's not what we've been told, is it Detective Cruz?"

"No, ma'am." Freddie flipped open his notebook and rattled off the statement the president had issued days earlier, calling the immigration reform bill the most important piece of legislation proposed during his first term.

Stenhouse's glare could've bored a hole through a lesser cop, but Sam barely felt the heat. "Were you irritated to see Graham O'Connor's son succeeding in the Senate?"

"Hardly," he said. "He was nothing to me."

"And his father? Was he nothing to you as well?"

"He was a prick who overstayed his welcome."

"How did you feel when you heard his son had been murdered?"

"It's a tragedy," he said in a pathetic attempt at sincerity. "He was a United States senator."

"And the son of your longtime rival."

Awareness dawned all at once. "Did he tell you I did this? That bastard!" He stalked to the window and stared out for a moment before he turned to them. "I hate his fucking guts. But do I hate him enough to kill his son? No, I don't. I haven't given Graham O'Connor a thought in the five years since we saw the last of his sorry ass around here."

"I'm sure you've had cause to give his son more than a passing thought in the same five years."

"His son was in the Senate for one reason and one reason only—his pedigree. The O'Connors have the people of Virginia snowed. John O'Connor was even more useless than his father, and that's not just my opinion. Ask around."

"I'll do that," Sam said. "In the meantime, stay available."

"What does that mean? Congress will be in holiday recess after tomorrow. I'm heading home to Missouri the day after."

"No, you're not. You're staying right here until we close this case."

"But it's Christmas! You can't keep me here against my will."

"Detective Cruz, can I keep the senator here against his will?"

"I believe you can, ma'am."

"And do we have a jail cell with his name on it if we hear he leaves the capital region?"

"Yes, ma'am. We absolutely do."

Stenhouse breathed fire as the detectives had their exchange.

Sam took three steps to close the distance between them. Looking up at the senator, she kept her expression passive and calm. "Neither your rank nor your standing mean a thing to me. This is a homicide investigation, and I won't hesitate to toss you in a cage if you fail to cooperate. Stay available."

With that, she turned, nodded at Freddie to follow her, and left the room.

She was gratified to hear Stenhouse yell to his assistant, "Get Joe Farnsworth on the line. Right now!"

Terry O'Connor spent the days he was sober in a closet-sized office on Independence Avenue. Judging from the lack of anything much on his desk, Sam deduced the job was bogus and most likely a favor to his illustrious father.

Terry's already pasty complexion paled when the detectives appeared at his door.

"Good morning, Mr. O'Connor," Sam said. "We're sorry to interrupt your work, but we have a few follow-up questions for you."

"Um, sure," he said, gesturing to a chair.

Sam took the chair while Freddie hovered in the doorway.

"I have to leave soon," Terry said. "We're going to Richmond."

"Yes, I know. We won't keep you long. Have you made any headway in producing the woman you were with on the night of the murder?"

Terry seemed to shrink further into his chair. "No."

"Did you kill your brother, Terry?"

Misery turned to shock in an instant. "No!"

"You had good reason to want him dead. I mean, after all, he was living the life that should've been yours and was about to know real success as a senator when the immigration bill passed. Maybe that was just too much for you."

"I loved my brother, Sergeant. Was I jealous of him? You bet I was. I wanted that job. I *wanted* it. Down here, you know?" He gestured to his gut. "I'd prepared for it my whole life, so yeah, it bothered me that he had it when he didn't even want it. But killing him wouldn't change anything for me. You don't see the Virginia Democrats lined up outside my office wanting me to take his place, do you?"

"No."

"So what was my motive in killing him?"

"Pleasure? Revenge?"

"Do I look like I've got the energy to care that much about anything?" he asked, his tone heavy with utter defeat.

Sam stood up. "I'd still like the name of the woman you say you were with that night."

Terry sighed. "So would I, Sergeant. Believe me. So would I."

Outside, Sam turned to Freddie. "What do you think?"

"I don't want it to be him. I mean, think of those poor parents if it *was* him…"

Freddie's endless compassion could be alternatively comforting and aggravating. "He's a lot more than jealous of his brother. Check out that hole-in-the-wall office. You think it didn't bug the shit out of him that baby brother was snuggled into that suite in the Hart Building?"

"Enough to kill him?"

"I don't know. I still see a woman for this, but I'm not ruling out the brother angle. Not yet. I'm giving him until the funeral is over to produce his alibi and then he and I are going to have a more formal chat." She paused before she added, "I need to go home and get changed. Do you mind if we make a quick stop?"

"Nope. You know I like seeing the deputy chief."

"He likes you, too, for some unknown reason."

"My wit and charm are hard to resist."

"Funny, I seem to have no problem resisting."

"You are a rare and unique woman, Sergeant."

"And you'd do well to remember that."

Freddie laughed and followed her to the car.

CHAPTER 16

Sam wasn't surprised to receive a call from Chief Farnsworth as she drove home.

"Good morning, Chief. I assume you've heard from Senator Stenhouse."

"You assume correctly. Is it really necessary to retain him, Sergeant?"

"I believe it is, sir. He had a number of political reasons to want to see John O'Connor dead, not the least of which was his hatred for the senator's father."

"Hate is a strong word."

"It's his word." Glancing at Freddie she said, "Correct me if I'm wrong, Detective Cruz, but I believe the senator's exact words in reference to Graham O'Connor were, 'I hate his fucking guts.'"

Freddie nodded his approval.

"Detective Cruz has confirmed my account, sir."

"Tread carefully on this front, Sergeant. Stenhouse can make my life difficult, and if my life is difficult, so is yours."

"Yes, sir."

"The media is burning a hole in the back of my neck clamoring for information. How close are we to closing this one?"

"Not as close as I'd like to be. I don't have a clear-cut suspect at the moment—a few who had motive and opportunity—but no one's popping for me just yet."

"I'd like to see you when you get back to HQ."

"About what was in the paper this morning?"

"Yes."

"I can handle that, sir. There's no need—"

"My office, four o'clock," the chief said and ended the call.

"Shit," she muttered as she returned the cell phone to her coat pocket.

"They have to take those kinds of threats against an officer seriously, Sam," Freddie said. "They have no choice."

"She's a grieving mother who's looking for someone to blame. I'm convenient."

"Too bad she can't see that her crack-head husband is the one to blame, not you."

Sam parked on Ninth Street, rested her hands on the wheel, and looked over at Freddie. "Listen, in the event that she's not blowing smoke, there could be some trouble in the form of stray bullets flying at me. I'd understand if you wanted to partner up with someone else until this blows over."

"Nice try, Sergeant, but you're stuck with me."

"I could have you reassigned."

"You could," he conceded. "But let me ask you this—if someone was taking pot shots at me, would you bail?"

"No."

"Then why do you think I would?"

Under his junk food-loving, cover-boy exterior, Freddie Cruz was made of stuff Sam respected. "All right then," Sam said, attempting to return things to normal. "When you get your pretty head blown off, don't come crying to me."

He stuck out his jaw. "You really think my head is pretty? You've never told me that before."

"Shut *up*," she groaned, reaching for the door handle. "Jesus."

"I've asked you to refrain from using the Lord's name in vain."

"And I've asked *you* to refrain from preaching your Holy Roller crap to me." There. Back to normal.

The ramp that led to Skip Holland's front door was a stark reminder of the changes wrought by an assailant's bullet. Inside, Sam called for him and smiled when she heard the whir of his chair.

"There's my daughter who blows her curfew and stays out all night."

"I left a message that I know you got." She bent down to kiss his forehead. "So don't give me any grief."

"Morning, Detective Cruz. Have you eaten?"

"Earlier." Freddie squeezed Skip's right hand in greeting. "But you know me, there's always room for more."

"Celia made eggs. I think there's some left."

"Don't mind if I do." Freddie flashed Sam a grin as he headed for the kitchen.

She rolled her eyes. "Why do you have to encourage him?" she asked her father.

"He's a growing boy. Needs his protein."

"I hope I'm around when his metabolism slows to a crawl the way mine has." She reached for the mail stacked on a table. "You look tired."

"I could say the same for you, Sergeant. What kept you out all night?"

"Working the case. You know." She glanced at him, caught a hint of something in his wise eyes. "What?"

"I can still read."

"Oh." She released her hair from the ponytail and combed her fingers through it in an attempt to bring some order to it. "You saw the thing in the paper. She's looking for someone to blame."

"What's being done?"

She knew he meant by the department and wanting to quell his fears she told him of the meeting Farnsworth had called.

"He'll take you off the streets. Off O'Connor until you've testified."

"He'll take me off kicking and screaming. I can't let a useless excuse for a mother like Destiny Johnson get in the way of the job."

"She has a lot of friends—angry friends with guns. Farnsworth won't have any choice but to put you under protection after the threats she's made."

"If I go under, the case goes with me. I'll be surprised if they haven't already picked her up for threatening the life of a police officer."

"No doubt, but just because she's locked up doesn't mean the threat's been neutralized."

Sam leaned over to press another kiss to his forehead. "Don't worry."

A look of fury crossed the expressive side of his face. "You can say that to me? When I'm sitting in this chair incapable of doing a goddamned *thing* when the life of my daughter, *my child*, has been threatened by someone who has not only the will but the means to follow through? Worry is all I've got. Don't take that away from me, Sam, and don't patronize me. I expect better from you."

"I'm sorry. You're right." She expelled a long deep breath as her stomachache returned with a vengeance. Navigating his new reality was a slippery slope, even almost two years later. "Of course you're right."

"You're to take this seriously and do whatever you're told by your superior officers. I'm trusting Joe to do his part, so I need your word that you'll do yours."

She reached for his hand and squeezed the one finger that could still feel it. "You have it."

"Go get changed and then come down to have some breakfast."

Because he was her dad and needed to feel like he still had control over something, she did what she was told without reminding him that she was thirty-four and didn't have to.

Over eggs and toast, she and Freddie hashed out the case with Skip while Celia helped him with a cup of coffee.

"I agree with you about the female angle, the act of passion," Skip said.

"We haven't encountered a woman yet with the emotional baggage toward O'Connor that this would've required," Freddie said.

"We're talking to some ex-girlfriends when we leave here, so we're hoping to get lucky," Sam said.

"You're looking for a cool customer," Skip said, slipping into the zone. "Someone who keeps tremendous anger bottled up under a refined exterior. You'll find she's been abused or had complicated relationships with the significant men in her life—father, ex-husband, ex-lover. Men have disappointed her in some way and whatever the senator did was the final straw. The breaking point."

"Damn," Freddie said reverently. "You two are something else. She sees these things as clearly as you do."

Celia smiled at him. "It's in their genes. I wonder sometimes if I should be afraid, spending as much time as I do with people who can slide inside a criminal's mind as easily as these two can."

"Enough about our genes." Sam stood as she downed a last swallow of soda. "Thanks, Celia, for the chow, and you for the consult." She kissed her father's cheek. "See you tonight."

"I won't hold my breath," he said with a dry chuckle. To Freddie he added, "She uses me for a place to keep her considerable wardrobe."

"Seems to me she uses you for a lot more than that. Always a pleasure, Chief."

"All mine, Detective. The Skins are playing at home Sunday night if you want to stop by to watch the game. Celia tells me there'll be snacks. Maybe even a beer or two if I'm good."

"Snacks, beer *and* football?" Freddie reached out to squeeze Skip's hand. "Hard to resist an offer like that. I'll do my best to come by. Thanks for breakfast, Celia. It was fabulous as usual."

"Anytime, Detective," Celia said, blushing a little as even the strongest of women tended to do when on the receiving end of Freddie's formidable charm.

Outside, Sam paused before she got into the car. "I, ah, I just wanted to say thanks for that in there."

Freddie's eyebrows knitted with confusion as he studied her over the top of the car. "For what? Eating your food like I just got rescued from a deserted island?"

"No." She struggled to find the words. "For treating him like he's still a normal guy, a normal person."

"He is." Freddie maintained the puzzled air of innocent befuddlement. "Why would I treat him any other way?"

"You'd be surprised the way people treat him sometimes." They got into the car. "I'm only going to say this once, and if I hear you repeated it I'll deny it with everything I've got. Understand?"

"Gee, I can't wait to hear this. You leave me breathless with anticipation."

"Your sarcasm and significant dietary failings aside, you're a special guy, Freddie Cruz. A one-in-a-million good guy." She glanced over to find him staring at her with his mouth hanging open. "Now that we've got that bullshit out of the way, what do you say we get back to figuring out who killed the senator?" When Freddie failed to reply, she said, "For

Christ's sake, will you quit looking at me like I just hit you with the Taser?"

"Might as well have," he muttered. "Might as well have."

That he didn't mention her disrespectful use of the Lord's name told her she'd truly shocked him with the compliment, which made for a satisfying start to what promised to be a shitty day.

They found Natalie Jordan at home alone in Belle Haven, an upscale development of stately colonial homes in Alexandria. Red brick, white columns and black wrought iron fronted hers. The home reeked of old money and Virginia aristocracy.

"Nice crib," Freddie said, gazing around at the well-kept grounds.

"Looks like Natalie landed herself a sugar daddy after all," Sam said as she rang the doorbell. Chimes pealed inside.

Natalie answered the door dressed in a salmon-colored silk blouse, winter white wool pants and two-inch heels. A gold chain bearing a diamond the size of Sam's thumb encircled her slender neck, and her blond hair was cut into a sleek bob that perfectly offset her thin, angular face. Sharp blue eyes were rimmed with red and dark circles marred her otherwise flawless complexion. Sam could see what Nick had meant when he'd described Natalie as "quite something."

No slouch in the fashion department herself, Sam was immediately intimidated. Her stomach twisted. Willing the pain away with a quick deep breath, Sam flashed her badge. "Detective Sergeant Holland and Detective Cruz, Metro Police."

"Come in," Natalie said in a honeyed Southern accent. "I've been expecting you."

"Is that so?" Sam said as they followed her to a living room ripped from the pages of the *Town & Country* holiday issue.

"Senator O'Connor and I were involved for a number of

years. I assumed you'd want to speak to me at some point. May I offer you something? Coffee or a cold drink?"

Before Freddie could accept, Sam said, "No, thank you. Do you mind if we record this conversation?"

Natalie shook her head, and Sam gestured for Freddie to turn on the recorder.

Sam began by noting the people present and the location of their interview. "Can you tell me where you were on Tuesday between the hours of ten p.m. and seven a.m.?"

While Natalie might have been expecting them, she clearly hadn't been expecting that. "I'm a *suspect?*"

"Until we determine otherwise, everyone is. Your whereabouts?"

"I was here," she stammered. "With my husband."

"His name?"

"Noel Jordan."

"And where might we find him to confirm this?"

"He's the special assistant attorney general at Justice." She rattled off an address in the city. "He's at work right now."

With the wave of her hand to encompass the room, Sam said, "Swanky digs for a guy on a government salary."

"His family has...they're wealthy."

"Can you tell me the nature of your relationship with Senator O'Connor?"

Hands twisting in her lap, Natalie said, "We were involved, romantically, for just over three years."

"And it ended when?"

"About four years ago," she sighed. "A year or so after he was elected."

"Were you in love with him?"

"Very much so," she said with a wistful expression that had Sam speculating that Natalie's feelings for the senator remained intact.

"Why did the relationship end?"

"I wanted to get married. He didn't." She shrugged. "We argued about it. Several times. After one particularly nasty disagreement, he said our relationship had run its course and we should think about seeing other people."

"And how did you feel about that?"

"Devastated and shocked. I loved him. I wanted to spend my life with him. I had no idea he was that unhappy."

"Did he love you?"

"He said he did, but there was always something…off, I guess you could say. I was never entirely convinced he loved me the same way I loved him."

"Must've pissed you off to get dumped by the guy you'd planned to marry."

Raw blue eyes flashed with emotion. "I was too crushed to be pissed, Sergeant. And if you're wondering if I killed him, I can assure you I didn't. In fact, I was quite certain I was over him until I heard he was dead." Tears suddenly spilled down her porcelain cheeks. She wiped at them with a practiced gesture that indicated she'd done a lot of crying in the last few days. "Since then, I can't seem to turn off the waterworks." Pausing for a moment, she added, "I have a nice life now with a man I adore, a man who's good to me. I'd have nothing to gain by harming John."

"Do you still have a key to the senator's apartment at the Watergate?"

"I, um, I don't know." She appeared genuinely perplexed. "I might."

"So you had one when you were dating?"

"I lived with him there for the last year or so of our relationship." Red blotches formed on her cheeks. "I don't recall giving the key back to him when I moved out."

"I need to ask you something of a personal nature, and I apologize in advance if it offends you."

"Everything about this offends me, Sergeant. A good man, a man I loved, has been murdered. It offends me on a very deep level."

"I understand. However, my job is to find out who killed him, and to do that I have to ask you about his sexual preferences."

Taken aback, Natalie said, "What do you mean?"

"Was he into anything kinky?"

Her cheeks went from blotchy to flaming. "We enjoyed a satisfying sex life if that's what you're asking."

"Did he tie you up?" Sam asked, playing a hunch based on the type of porn they'd found on his computer. "Did he get rough? Want more than the usual deal?"

"I don't have to answer that," Natalie stuttered. "It's my personal business, *his* personal business."

"Yes, it is, but aspects of his murder were intensely personal, so if you'd answer the questions, I'd appreciate it."

Natalie took a long deep breath and exhaled it as she spun a huge diamond engagement ring around on her finger. "He was a creative lover."

Sam used her trademark steely stare to let Natalie know she'd have to do better than that.

"*Yes,*" she cried. "He tied me up, he could be rough, he asked for more than the usual deal." Descending into sobs, she added, "Are you satisfied?"

"Were *you?* Did you go along with it because you wanted to or because you felt you had to?"

"I loved him," she said in a defeated whisper that set Sam's already frazzled nerves further on edge. "I loved him."

"Did he ever bring other people into the relationship? Male or female?"

"Of course not," Natalie sputtered. "No!"

"Mrs. Jordan, I'm going to need you to stay available until we close this case."

"My husband and I are due to leave for Arizona in a few days to visit his parents for Christmas."

"You're going to have to change those plans."

Wiping her face, she said, "Do I need an attorney, Sergeant?"

"Not at this time. We'll be in touch."

CHAPTER 17

"Go ahead and say it," she muttered to Freddie when they were back in the car.

"Say what?"

"I was too hard on her. I'm a mean, insensitive bitch. Whatever's on your mind."

"I feel sorry for her."

She hadn't expected that. "Other than the obvious, why?"

"Did you notice the one thing she *didn't* say?"

"How about we skip the Q&A, and you tell me what you observed, Detective."

"She said she 'adored' her husband. She never said she loved him. How many times did she say she loved O'Connor? Four? Five?"

Startled, Sam could only stare at him.

"What?" he asked, squirming.

"We might just be making a detective out of you yet."

Freddie flashed that *GQ* smile, and damn it if her heart didn't skip a beat. He was so goddamned cute.

She started the car. "You know, you can feel free to jump in when we're interviewing people."

"And interrupt your groove? I wouldn't dream of it. Quite a pleasure to watch you work, Sergeant Holland. Shame on me if I spend a day with you and don't learn something."

"Are you sucking up?" She shot him a suspicious glance as she drove through Belle Haven. "What do you want?"

"Other than lunch, I couldn't ask for anything more than I already have. Where are we heading now?"

"We've got two more ex-girlfriends to knock off the list, and then I'd like to have a word with Noel Jordan."

"Are we going to ask the exes about their sex lives?"

"Damn straight."

He sighed. "I was afraid of that."

Tara Davenport, age twenty-four, worked the lunch shift at a high-end restaurant that catered to the Capitol Hill crowd. Sam presented her badge to the maître d'. "We need a few minutes with Tara Davenport."

"She's working. Can you come back at end of shift? Around five?"

"This isn't a social call. I can speak with her in a private space you'll provide or I can haul her out of here in cuffs and take you with us for interfering with a police investigation. What's it going to be?"

Looking down his snooty nose at her, the stiff said, "Wait here and keep your voice down, will you?"

"Mean and scary," Freddie murmured, drawing a laugh from Sam.

"Thank you."

"You would see that as a compliment."

"How else should I see it?"

They watched the stiff tap a slender but well-endowed young blonde on the shoulder and point to Sam and Freddie. He signaled to them, and they followed Tara to the back of the busy restaurant. On the way, more than a few patrons took notice of them. For some reason, that pleased Sam, so much so she hitched her hands into her pockets and put her weapon and badge on full display.

"Class act, Sergeant," the maître d' seethed.

"The next time myself or any of my colleagues appear at your door, perhaps you'll consider cooperating."

"You have fifteen minutes. After that you'll need a warrant to set foot in here again."

"Will I need a warrant if I wish to return for a follow-up visit, Detective Cruz?"

"No, ma'am, in most cases an informal interview of a potential suspect in a homicide investigation doesn't require a warrant."

The stiff paled. "Homicide?"

"Step aside and let me do my job," Sam said in a low growl. "So much as knock on that door and I'll haul your skinny ass downtown and put you in a cage with some guys who'd love nothing more than to make you their bitch."

He swallowed hard and moved to let them by.

"Mean *and* scary," Freddie said again.

Choking back a laugh, Sam opened the door to the break room where Tara Davenport waited, pale and trembling. As she introduced herself and Freddie to Tara, Sam questioned whether the woman had the physical strength to put a butcher knife through John O'Connor's neck.

"Is this about John?" she asked softly after agreeing to allow them to record the conversation.

"It is. Can you provide your whereabouts on the night of the murder? Tuesday, from ten p.m. to seven a.m.?"

Rattled but firm, Tara said, "I was out with some friends, early in the evening, but home by ten."

"I'll need you to give Detective Cruz a list of the people you were with. Do you live alone?"

She nodded.

"So no one can verify your whereabouts after ten?"

"No."

"No one saw you arriving home? Neighbors?"

"Not that I can recall."

"How and when did you meet Senator O'Connor?"

"I met him about six months ago. He was a regular here. He and his chief of staff, Nick, came in for lunch a couple of times a week when the Senate was in session."

Sam's belly twisted at the mention of Nick, whom she'd studiously tried to block from her mind all day. Remembering his muscular chest and the tender way he'd cared for her after the dream infused her with heat. She shrugged off her coat and slung it over a chair.

"John always asked to be seated in my section. He liked to tease and flirt. After a few months of that, he asked me out to dinner."

"Did that surprise you?"

"It did. I mean, he's a United States senator. What does he want with a waitress?"

"What *did* he want?"

"At first, I thought he was lonely," she said, her green eyes filling. "The first few times we went out, we talked for hours. He took me to nice places."

"You must've felt like Cinderella," Freddie said.

"In some ways, I did. He was a perfect gentleman, and so very handsome."

"Did you fall for him?" Sam asked.

"Yes," she whispered. "If you knew John at all, you'd know it would be hard not to."

"So what happened?"

Playing with her fingers, Tara said, "We had dated for a few weeks when he asked me to spend the night with him."

"And did you?"

Looking down at her lap, she nodded. "It was lovely. *He* was lovely." She swiped at tears. "We couldn't get enough of each other."

"Did you have a key to his place?"

"He gave me his once when I was meeting him there, but I gave it back to him that same night."

"Why did it end?" Freddie asked.

"He, ah...he was looking for more than I was willing to give."

"In the relationship?" Sam knew the answer before she asked.

Tara shook her head, her cheeks blazing with color. "In bed."

"What happened to lovely?"

"I wish I knew. After a few times, it changed. He became rough, almost aggressive. And he wanted...things...that I'm not into."

"What kind of things?"

"Is this really necessary?"

"I'm sorry, but it is."

"He..."

"I know this is terribly difficult for you, Ms. Davenport, but we're looking for a killer. Anything you can tell us that will aid in our investigation is relevant."

Tara took another moment to collect herself. "He wanted bondage and...anal."

"Did you have anal sex with the senator, Ms. Davenport?"

"No! I said no! I don't do that. I'm not into that."

"And how did he take it when you refused him?"

"He was mad, but he didn't try to force me."

"Honorable," Freddie muttered. "Did you see him again after you refused?"

She shook her head. "I never heard from him again."

"How did you feel about that?" Sam asked.

"I was sad, devastated. I thought we had something special,

and then it was just...over. Like you said. For a few weeks, I felt like Cinderella. It was right out of a fairy tale."

"But he wasn't your Prince Charming," Freddie said.

"No."

"Did he ever ask you about bringing other people into your sexual relationship?" Sam asked.

Tara's face lit up, her cheeks flaming. Bingo.

"Ms. Davenport?"

"Once," she said softly. "He said it would be amazing for me to have two guys at the same time." A shudder rippled through Tara's petite frame.

"Did it seem to you that he'd done that before?"

"Yes."

"And you said what to this request?"

"I told him that I was perfectly satisfied with just him. He seemed annoyed that I said no."

"That must've been disappointing," Sam said.

"It was."

"Were you disappointed enough to kill him, Ms. Davenport?"

She blanched. "*Kill him?* You think I *killed* him?"

Her shock was so genuine that it all but knocked her off the list of suspects. "If you could just answer the question."

"No, I wasn't disappointed enough to kill him. I didn't kill him."

"Have you told anyone else about why your relationship with the senator ended?"

"No. It's not something I'd ever talk about with even my closest friends. It's mortifying, to be honest."

"How did you feel when you heard he was dead?"

"Sad. I was overwhelmed with sadness. But to be honest, I wasn't entirely surprised that someone killed him. If you treat people the way he treated me, it's going to catch up to you eventually."

"I need you to stay available and in town for the time being."

"I'm working through the holidays," she said, her voice flat, devoid of hope or animation. "I'll be here."

"I have trouble understanding his type," Freddie said when they left the restaurant.

"You would. Do you think he was gay?"

"And in the closet? Working it out on women?"

"He certainly went for a type. The porcelain blonde. No way Tara is strong enough to get a knife through him on one stroke."

"I was thinking that very same thing." He paused and seemed to be pondering something. "So you know how we always joke that we spend more time together than we do with our own families?"

"*You're* the joker. I'm the serious law enforcement professional."

"Yeah, whatever."

"Your point?"

"I've known you a long time. Partnered with you over a year."

"Do you have a point? 'Cause if you could get to it in this decade, I'd like to get back to work."

"I have a point," he huffed. "It's just when she mentioned Cappuano in there, your face got all red and you had to take your coat off."

"I was hot! So what?"

"You were *flustered*. And you're *never* flustered."

Her stomach picked that moment to make its presence known. *Never flustered? Ha!* She spent half her life flustered but apparently did a good job of hiding it.

Freddie stopped on the sidewalk and turned to her. "Tell me the truth, Sam. Are you into him?"

She chose her words carefully. "The job, it takes almost everything I have. I work, I take care of my father, I help my sisters with their kids whenever I can. That's my life."

"Do you think I'd begrudge you wanting more?" His warm brown eyes flashed with emotion. "You think that?"

"He's off limits. There's no point talking about something I can't have."

"Why can't you have him?"

"He's a witness! He found O'Connor. He'll be wrapped up in this until sentencing."

"He didn't kill anyone. He's on our side."

She shook her head. "It's a murky ethical pit, and you know it."

"You're right. It's not clean. Few things in life ever are. But he wants this closed as much as we do, if not more. He *flusters* you, Sam. That's an amazing thing, if you ask me."

"I'd say unsettling is a better word." Glancing up at him, she added, "You won't say anything about this at HQ, will you?"

"Give me some credit, and while you're at it, ask your friend Cappuano if there's any chance the senator was gay."

"He'll say no."

"Humor me, and before you drag me into another interview that includes questions about peculiar sexual appetites, you're going to have to do something about mine."

She turned up her nose. "Your sexual appetite?"

"Nope." He chuckled and rubbed his belly. "The other one."

Sam pulled rank, insisted they have lunch at a vegetarian sandwich shop and was treated to Freddie's vociferous complaints about the lack of grease.

"Can't even get a stinking French fry in this place," he muttered as Sam downed her small veggie sub and wondered if it really had fewer than six grams of fat. No doubt every gram would find its way to her ass.

"If you're done sulking, we need to hit Total Fitness on Sixteenth."

He raised an eyebrow. "Are you taking up working out to go with this diet you're on?"

"Just because I choose to eat healthily doesn't mean I'm on a diet. Another of the senator's ladies works at the gym as a personal trainer." She consulted her notebook. "Elin Svendsen."

Freddie perked right up. "Swedish?"

"Sounds like it."

"Blonde, buff *and* Swedish? This day is suddenly on the upswing."

"Why, Freddie, I thought you were above such base human emotions as lust."

"Just because I'm choosy doesn't mean I don't enjoy a little eye candy as much as the next guy."

"This insight into the male psyche is fascinating. Truly."

"I'm here to serve."

Elin Svendsen was not only buff, she looked like she'd be capable of kicking some serious ass when provoked. Easily five-ten or -eleven, with white blonde hair, icy blue eyes and a figure that could stop a train dead on its tracks, Sam decided she wouldn't want to meet up with Elin in a dark alley.

They caught her between clients and followed her into the club's juice bar, which wasn't due to open for another hour. They declined her offer of fruit smoothies.

"Do you mind if I make one for myself? My energy is starting to flag. Been a long morning."

"Not at all," Sam said. "Do *you* mind if we record this?"

"Nope."

Noticing Freddie had his eyes glued to Elin's every movement, Sam nudged him to get his head back in the game.

He replied with a chagrinned smile.

Elin joined them at the table with a strawberry smoothie. "If you're here to ask if I killed John O'Connor, I didn't."

"Where were you the night of the murder, between ten p.m. and seven a.m.?"

"I had a date and was home by two or so."

"Alone?"

She nodded.

"Your date's name?"

"Jimmy Chen. He's a member here. We go out once in a while. No biggie."

"You never left your house after you got home?"

"Not until I left for work the next morning."

"Where did you meet the senator?"

"Here. He hired me to train him, we hit it off, one thing led to another..."

"And how long ago was this?"

"Three or four months ago." Sam did some quick math and realized he was seeing Elin and Tara at the same time.

"Do you have a key to his apartment?"

"I set him up with some home workout equipment, and he gave me a key so I could get in when he was at work to put it together."

"Did you give the key back to him?"

She thought about that for a moment. "You know, I don't think I ever did. Hmmm."

With a glance, Sam handed the ball to Freddie.

"Oh, um, what was the nature of your relationship with the senator, Ms. Svendsen?" he asked.

Sam had never seen him so tongue-tied around a woman and planned to poke at him about it the moment they left.

"Mostly we had sex."

Freddie's face flushed with embarrassment.

Sam sat back to enjoy the show. Folding her arms, she sent the message that she had no plans to bail him out.

"Could you, or I mean, would you mind if I asked you to be more specific about the, ah, sex you had with the senator?" Using Sam's words, he added, "Was it, um, the usual deal or more?"

Seeming to cue in to Freddie's exquisite discomfort, Elin smiled as she leaned toward him. "It was more, Detective. Much more. We were very well matched sexually."

Freddie cleared his throat.

"Were you still tearing up the sheets with the senator when he was killed?" Sam asked, realizing they were going to be there all day if she waited for Freddie to get on with it.

"No, we called it off a month or so ago."

"Who's doing?"

"Mine." She shrugged. "I was getting bored. It was time to move on."

"How did he take it when you ended it?"

"He was fine with it. This wasn't a love match, Sergeant. It was purely physical."

"Did he ever try to bring other people into the relationship."

"He did more than try." Elin seemed to be enjoying the effect she was having on Freddie. "We had a couple of memorable threesomes."

Sam glanced at Freddie to find his mouth hanging halfway open. She wanted to smack it shut.

"Male or female?" Sam asked.

"One of each on two separate occasions."

"Who sought out the extra parties?" Sam asked.

"I did. I know a lot of people from working here, and it was easier for me in light of who he was."

"What was his interaction with the other guy?"

"Hardly any. He was for me, not John."

"So John didn't have any kind of sex with him?"

Elin thought about that for a minute. "I think the guy sucked John's dick, but John didn't do anything to him."

"Did these 'extras' know who he was?"

"Nope. We just introduced him as 'John.' We didn't get into our life stories."

Sam left her with the standard line about staying available.

"Detectives?" Elin said as they headed for the door.

They turned back to her.

"He wasn't 'the one' for me, but he was a good guy. He didn't deserve to be murdered."

Sam nodded and pushed open the door, thinking the definition of "good guy" was all a matter of perspective.

"Did you enjoy that?" Freddie snapped the moment they were back in the cold air.

"Enjoy what?"

"Making me ask her those questions."

Sam stopped and turned to face him. "If you can't ask the questions, *any* question, *any* time, you shouldn't be carrying a gold shield, Detective."

"You're right." He sagged a bit as the anger seemed to leave him all at once. "I know you are, but it's just so freaking embarrassing asking a woman I've never met about what kind of sex she had with a dead senator."

"You think I like it any more than you do? It's part of the job. The best way to figure out who killed him is to figure out who and what he was."

"You're right, and I apologize for going queasy on you. It won't happen again."

"Yes, it will," she said with a sigh. "The day it doesn't bother you to ask those kind of questions is the day you're no longer

Freddie Cruz. It's supposed to bother you. Just don't let it stop you from doing what needs to be done."

"I won't," he vowed. "See what I mean about learning from you? That's what I meant. Right there."

"Kiss my ass, Cruz."

"While that's a lovely offer and one I take very seriously, I don't think it would be appropriate in light of our professional relationship. You know, with you being my superior officer and all."

She used her best withering look to shut him up. "If you're quite through, can we go see what Noel Jordan has to say about his wife's ex?"

"One thing we can say for Svendsen is that she certainly would've had the strength to get that knife through him in one shot."

"No doubt. And she had a key."

"The part about her breaking up with him threw me, though. I can see her being pissed if he dumped her, like he did with Davenport, but if she's the one who pulled the plug, what's her motive in offing him?"

"That's only her side of the story. Who knows how it really went down? She can tell us she dumped him because he's not here to refute it."

"Here again, I find myself learning from you."

"Keep that up and you're going to piss me off. I like her for the murder. So far, more than anyone else, I like her."

"I liked her, too," he joked.

"I could tell by the tongue hanging out of your face, but she's too scary and experienced for an innocent boy like you. She'd chew you up and spit you out."

"And that would be bad how exactly?"

"Pardon me while I get busy poking out my mind's eye."

CHAPTER 18

Gonzo called as they made their way toward the Justice Department on Pennsylvania Avenue.

"What've you got?" Sam asked.

"Nothing so far at the cabin, but I did that run you asked for on Robert O'Connor. Sixty-five years old, lives in Mechanicsville with his wife Sally, age sixty-three. They have three grown children—Sarah, forty, Thomas, thirty-six and Michael, thirty-four. Five grandchildren."

"Son of a bitch," Sam muttered. "They lied to me."

"Do you want me to do some more digging?"

"No, that's okay. Were you able to get pictures of the kids?"

"Yeah, I shot them to your e-mail."

"Thanks, Gonzo. Let me know if you turn up anything at the cabin."

"It's slow going. I'll call you when we're done."

"Who lied to you?" Freddie asked when she had ended the call.

"O'Connor's parents." She explained about the photo she had found at the cabin. "I think John had a son they swept under the rug. I'm going to Chicago tomorrow to find out."

"Want me to tag along?"

"No, I can take this one alone. I need you to confirm the info we got from Davenport and Svendsen about the people they were with the night of the murder. I'd also like you to check security at both their buildings. See if you can catch them coming home that night—or more importantly, going back out."

"Got it," he said, making notes. "I would've done that run you had Gonzo do."

"Don't pout, Freddie. An investigation of this magnitude requires we make use of all available resources."

After navigating building security and handing over their weapons—something that always left Sam feeling twitchy—she and Freddie were escorted to Jordan's office. As special assistant attorney general, he sat right next door to the attorney general himself. Jordan was tall with an athletic build, short blond hair that looked like it would be wildly curly if left to grow and sharp blue eyes. He wore a dark pinstriped suit that had clearly been cut just for him. *Nothing off-the-rack for this guy,* Sam thought, as she noted his almost startling resemblance to John O'Connor. Apparently, the late senator wasn't the only one who went for a "type."

"Detectives," he said, standing to shake their hands. He gestured for them to make use of the chairs in front of his desk. "What can I do for you?"

"You're aware that your wife had a long-term relationship with Senator O'Connor?"

"I am."

"Did she ever talk to you about him?"

"Occasionally, but nothing more than an off-hand comment or two. She respects me too much to throw him in my face. My wife and I are happily married, and none of our former relationships factor into our marriage."

"Did you ever meet the senator?"

"A few times. I'm active in the Virginia Democratic Party, and obviously he was as well."

"Did you like him?"

"I didn't dislike him, but neither would I say we were anything more than casual acquaintances. So he dated my wife? Big deal. She's a beautiful woman who had several relationships before me. I don't expect that her life—or mine—began the day we met. Although," he said, softening, "in many ways, mine did begin with her."

"Can you confirm your whereabouts on the night of the murder? Tuesday between ten p.m. and seven a.m.?"

He consulted a brown leather book. "On Tuesday evening we attended the annual Christmas fund-raiser/silent auction for the Capital Region Big Brothers and Big Sisters here in the city. We were home by ten, in bed by ten-thirty. We made love and went to sleep. Is that enough information?"

"Has your wife ever mentioned anything about her relationship with the senator that made her uncomfortable?"

For the first time, Jordan's cool composure wavered. "Uncomfortable in what way?"

"Any way."

"No, but like I said, we've never felt the need to share the intimate details of our past relationships."

When Sam stood up, Freddie followed her lead. "I know you had plans to be out of town for the holidays," she said, "but you'll need to remain in the area."

"I'm due to leave for Europe on the third of January. Work-related travel."

"Hopefully by then we'll have cleared this up. Until we do, you and your wife are required to stay local."

"Thoughts?" she asked Freddie after they had reclaimed their weapons. Relieved to have her gun back, Sam slid hers into her hip harness.

"First, he knew we were coming. Had that appointment book nice and handy."

"No doubt the wife tipped him. But guess what? He lied about one thing."

"What's that?"

"The Big Brothers/Big Sisters thing?"

Freddie nodded.

"That was *last* Tuesday. I know because I was there."

Freddie released a low whistle.

"It doesn't mean one of them killed the senator, though. It only means there's something he doesn't want us to know or his date book is messed up. We still can't place either of them at the Watergate."

"So we file this tidbit away and continue to work the case?"

"Exactly. The thing between the senator and Natalie was over years ago. Where's the motive?"

"True," Freddie said.

"My take is that he's crazy in love with her, still wonders how he ever managed to snag her and he's glad O'Connor's dead. He didn't kill him, but he sees it as a favor that someone else did."

"So you think he was threatened by the senator?"

"Big time," Freddie said. "He knows he wasn't the love of Natalie's life."

"Good. That's good. Crazy how much he looks like O'Connor, huh?"

"I'd say creepy would be a better word."

"Agreed. I want you to look into those 'other relationships' of hers that he referred to. Find out if any of the other men in her life met with an untimely demise, and while you're at it, do a search for unsolved cases involving dismemberment. The senator might not have been the first."

"Local or national?"

"Start local and see what pops. I'll be authorizing overtime for both of us, so while you're at it, get me everything you can find on the three women we met today. No detail is too big or too small. If they have a tattoo, I want to know what it is and where."

"Tramp stamps," he wrote as she snickered at the term. "Got it. You're really sure it was a woman, aren't you?"

"Every fiber of my being tells me this was a love affair gone very wrong."

"Or someone wants us to *think* that."

"We can't rule that out," she conceded.

"In light of what we've learned today, we also can't rule out that it might've been a love affair with a *man* that went very wrong."

"Right again," she said. "Nothing is ever as cut and dried as we'd like it to be, is it?"

"Nope."

"You've had a few girlfriends."

"So?" he said warily.

"Don't you compare notes on past relationships?"

His face flooded with color. "Depends on how serious it is with the new one and whether or not she asks."

"Is it weird that Natalie Jordan never told her husband that things got kinky with the senator?"

"I don't know, Sam. That falls into a serious gray area. What guy would want to know that his woman did it *all* with the ex?"

"Hmm. It just seems strange to me that she's never even alluded to it. I mean, they're *married*. And you saw his face. He had no idea what I was talking about."

"Did you share that kind of stuff with Peter?"

"Bad example. We weren't your typical married couple."

"Sorry to dredge up the past, but I think you'd be in a better position to answer your own questions than I would be, having never been married myself."

"Yeah, I guess, but I hardly had the kind of marriage where major sharing factored in."

"So what's next?" he asked, seeming anxious to change the subject.

"I need to go back to HQ, write up what we have so far, and deal with the brass on this thing with the Johnson case."

"What'll you do if they put you under?"

"*If* they do, it'll only be for a couple of days at most—one of those days I'll be in Chicago, another one we're taking off because we'll need to recharge, and then Monday is the senator's funeral. With all the local police and Secret Service who'll be there, I can't imagine they'll stop me from going. I can pull the strings from the sidelines, but I'm not letting it go."

"Even if they order you to?"

"Especially then."

"Righteous."

Back at her desk, Sam downed a soda, opened the e-mail Gonzo had sent, and discovered the real Thomas O'Connor was a thirty-six-year-old man with dark hair and eyes. She made a note to ask Nick whether John had ever mentioned having a cousin of the same age. Regardless, the man on her screen was not the boy in the picture, and she now had positive confirmation that Graham and Laine O'Connor had lied to her about the boy. But why? Why would they deny their own grandchild? Sam had no idea, but she intended to find out.

Her stomach clenched with pain as she read—and then re-read—an e-mail from the chief's admin, confirming her four o'clock appointment. Checking her watch, she realized she had just a few minutes to get there on time. She stood up, but the pain had other ideas. Collapsing back into her chair, she put her head down and tried to breathe her way through it. A bead of sweat slid down her back.

This was a bad one, but it had been getting progressively worse over the last few months despite her best efforts to ignore it. Sooner or later, she was going to have to do something about this "nervous stomach" situation, possibly even give up diet cola as she'd been told to do. But not now. No time for that now. When the worst of the pain had passed, she tested her shaky legs, took another long deep breath and set out for the chief's office.

She was waved right in but stopped short just inside the door. When Farnsworth called in the brass, he called in the brass. Seated in a wide half-circle in front of Farnsworth's desk were Deputy Chief Conklin, Detective Captain Malone, Lieutenant Stahl and Assistant U.S. Attorney Miller. Sam glanced at Miller's shoes, saw the stiletto heel, and confirmed it was Charity, one of the identical triplets who worked for the U.S. Attorney. Neither Faith nor Hope would be caught dead in stilettos.

"Well," Sam said, as the pain resurfaced with an ugly vengeance. Determined to stay cool, she took shallow breaths and slipped into the remaining chair. "You didn't tell me we were having a party, Chief. I would've brought snacks."

"Sergeant," Farnsworth said, his handsome face tight with stress that only added to Sam's. "Before we get into the Johnson matter, go ahead and brief us on the status of the O'Connor investigation."

Folding her hands tightly in her lap, she brought them up to speed, holding back the details about the senator's peculiar sexual appetites. She had decided to do her best to keep that out of the official record in deference to his parents and family.

"So almost seventy-two hours out, we don't have so much as a suspect?" Stahl said.

Sam made an effort not to show him what a jackass she thought him to be. "We have several individuals of interest we're actively pursuing. In addition, I believe the senator had a son who was kept hidden from the public. I request permission to travel tomorrow to Chicago to further investigate this thread."

"How's it relevant?" Stahl snapped.

Repulsed by the roll of fat around his belly and the huge double chin that wiggled when he talked, Sam said, "If it's true, the senator's relationship with the mother could be very relevant."

"I'll authorize the travel," Malone said, pulling rank on Stahl who fumed in silence.

"Thank you, Captain," Sam said.

"The Feds are sniffing around," Farnsworth said. "I've managed to hold them off thus far, but with every passing day, it's getting harder."

"Understood. We're moving as fast as we can."

"All available resources are at your disposal, Sergeant," Farnsworth added. "Use whatever you need."

"Yes, sir. Thank you."

"Now, on the other matter, we've got Mrs. Johnson on a seventy-two-hour hold."

"You aren't planning to charge her, are you, sir?" Sam asked.

"AUSA Miller is considering charges."

"If I may, sir," Sam said. "While no one would mistake Destiny Johnson for mother of the year, I have no doubt her heartbreak is genuine."

"That doesn't give her the right to threaten the life of a police officer," Farnsworth said.

"She has good reason to be pissed with Sergeant Holland and the department," Stahl said.

"Lieutenant, I find your attitude counterproductive," Farnsworth said. "You can get back to work."

"But—"

Captain Malone flipped his thumb toward the door.

With an infuriated glance at Sam, Stahl hauled himself out of the chair and waddled to the door. After it closed behind him, Farnsworth returned his attention to Sam. "We have to take her threats seriously, Sergeant. You're extremely vulnerable in the field, so until you've testified on Tuesday, we're putting you under. Limited duty, permission to work from home, no field work."

"Since I'm going to Chicago tomorrow, taking Sunday off, and attending the senator's funeral on Monday, that shouldn't be a problem."

"About the funeral…" Deputy Chief Conklin said.

"I believe the local and federal security required to bring in the president will be sufficient to protect a lowly District sergeant," Sam said with what she hoped was a confident smile.

"The Secret Service will have to be made aware of the threat and your planned presence at the service," Conklin said. "I'll take care of that."

"Appreciate it," Farnsworth said. He leaned forward to address Sam. "I want you to take this very seriously. Johnson has a lot of friends, and all of them—fairly or unfairly—blame you for what happened in that house. They don't care that you didn't fire the shot. They care that you gave the order."

"Yes, sir." Since she blamed herself, too, she could understand where they were coming from.

"AUSA Miller, has Sergeant Holland been adequately prepared for Tuesday's court appearance?"

"She has, Chief. We've been through it several times, and she's never wavered from her initial statement."

"I'll let you get back to work then," Farnsworth said. "Thanks for being here."

"No problem." With an encouraging smile for Sam, Charity got up and left the room.

"If there's nothing else, I've got a few more threads to tie up before my tour ends," Sam said.

"There's just one more thing," Farnsworth said, reaching for a file on his desk.

Sam refused to acknowledge the twinge of pain that hovered in her gut. "Sir?"

"I had lunch with your father earlier this week."

"Yes, sir, he mentioned that. I know he appreciates your visits." To the others, she added, "All of you."

"And I know you go out of your way to downplay your family's history with this department."

"I don't want nor do I expect special treatment because of the rank my father attained prior to being injured in the line."

Farnsworth replied with a hint of a smile. "Regardless, he was curious as to whether I'd gotten the results of the lieutenant's exam."

Just those words were enough to override any success she'd had in keeping the pain at bay. It roared through her, leaving her breathless in its wake. When she was able to speak again, she said, "I'm aware it's a source of embarrassment to my father and to you as my superior officers that I've been unable to pass the exam on two previous attempts."

"What I'd like to know is why the fact that you're dyslexic isn't mentioned anywhere in your personnel file."

Stunned, Sam opened her mouth and then closed it when the words simply wouldn't come.

"I've done some basic research on dyslexia and discovered that standardized tests are one of the dyslexic's greatest foes."

"Yes, but—"

"Allow me to finish, Sergeant. I have to admit this information was a relief to me." He gestured to the deputy chief and captain. "To all of us. We've been hard pressed to understand how the best detective on this force has been unable to attain a rank that should've been hers some time ago."

"I...um..."

"You passed this time," Farnsworth said. "Just barely—but you did pass."

Sam stared at him, wondering if she had heard him correctly.

He rifled through some other papers until he found what he was looking for. "With the distinct exception of Lt. Stahl, you've received outstanding superior officer recommendations, high marks on your interviews and evaluations. We also factored in the graduate degree in criminal justice you earned from George Washington. All in all, you make for an ideal candidate for promotion." He looked up at her. "Under my discretion as chief of police, I'm pleased to inform you that your name will be included in the next group of lieutenants."

"But, sir," Sam stammered, "people will talk. They'll scream favoritism."

"You met the criteria. The test score is only one element, and no one but the people in this room will know it was low."

"I'll know," she said softly.

"Sergeant, do you believe you've earned the rank of lieutenant?"

"If I didn't, I wouldn't have sat for the exam in the first place, but—"

"Then you should have no further objection to a promotion you have earned and deserve. You'll be taking command of the detective squad at HQ."

Staggered, Sam stared at him. "But that's Lieutenant Stahl's command."

"He's being transferred to internal affairs."

The rat squad, Sam thought, her stomach grinding under

the fist she had balled tight against it. "You're setting me up to have a powerful enemy."

"Lieutenant Stahl is skating on very thin ice these days," Captain Malone said. "I don't believe he'll give you any trouble, and if he does, he'll deal with us. Let me add my congratulations, Sergeant, on a well-earned and highly deserved promotion. I look forward to working with you in your new role."

"Thank you, sir," Sam said, still shocked as she shook his outstretched hand and then Conklin's.

"Ditto," Conklin said, following Malone from the room. "You've earned it."

"Thank you, sir."

When they were alone, Sam turned to the chief.

"You'll piss me off if you ask if this is because I'm your chief or your Uncle Joe," he said, his tone full of friendly warning.

"I was just going to say thank you," Sam said with a smile that quickly faded. "Will the, ah, dyslexia be added to my jacket?"

"It'll remain your personal business, provided it continues to have no bearing on your ability to do the job."

"It won't."

Farnsworth sat back in his big chair and studied her. "I have to ask how you managed to get two degrees while battling dyslexia."

"I got lucky with professors who worked with me, but everything took me twice as long as it took everyone else. And I've always choked on standardized tests. I just can't get them done in the time allotted."

"I can only imagine how much harder you've had to work to compensate. Knowing that only adds to my respect for you and your work." He stood up, came around the big desk, and offered his hand. "Congratulations."

Sam's throat closed as her hand was enfolded between both of his. "Thank you, sir. I'll do my very best to be worthy."

"I have no doubt. Let me know what you uncover in Chicago."

"I will, sir. Thank you again. For everything." She closed the door behind her, managed a nod to the chief's admin, and made for the nearest ladies' room. The relief, the sheer overwhelming relief, left her staggered. She gave herself ten minutes to fall apart before she pulled it together, wiped her face and blew her nose.

Studying her reflection in the mirror, she whispered, "Lieutenant," as if to try it on for size. For once her stomach had no comment. Taking that as a positive sign, she splashed cold water on her face and decided to leave on time for a change. The report could be written and transmitted from home. Besides, she needed to go tell the only other person in the world who would care as much as she did that she would soon become Lieutenant Holland.

CHAPTER 19

Before Sam could call for him, she heard the chair.

"What's this? Home on time?"

She went to him, rested her hands on his shoulders and was startled to encounter sharp bones where thick muscle used to be. Jarred by the discovery, she bent to kiss his forehead. Eye to eye, she said, "I should be furious with you."

"For?"

"Don't play coy with me."

"It should've been in your jacket. From day one. I've always said that."

"It wasn't for a reason. I don't want people feeling sorry for me or treating me differently. You know how I feel about it."

"That fierce pride of yours is only going to get you so far."

"And my daddy is going to get me the rest of the way?"

"I simply gave him a piece of information he didn't have. What he did or didn't do with it was up to him."

"No, Dad, it was up to *me*. I don't want you interfering in my career. How many times do I have to say it before you get the message?"

"I've been duly chastised. Now, are you going to tell me what he did with it?"

"Not until you've suffered a little first. What's for dinner?"

He followed her to the kitchen. "That's mean, Sam."

"Are you being mean to your father again?" Celia asked.

"Believe me, he deserves it. Oh, jeez, is that *roast beef*?"

"Sure is. Are you hungry?"

"Starving. I didn't even realize it until right this very minute." She peeked into a pot and groaned. "Mashed potatoes? God, my ass is growing just smelling it."

"Now you stop that," Celia said as she served the meal. "You have a lovely figure that I'd kill for. How was your day?"

"The usual chaos."

"Nothing special?" Skip asked. "Nothing different?"

Sam pretended to give that some significant thought. "Not really. Freddie and I are working the case, pulling the threads. Got a couple of good angles to pursue."

"What are they doing about Johnson?" Skip asked.

Hanging on their every word, Celia fed him and herself with a practiced hand.

"I was ordered to 'lay low' until I testify on Tuesday."

"To which you said...?"

She shrugged. "I'm fine with it. I have to go to Chicago tomorrow, I'm taking most of Sunday off, and have the funeral on Monday. I should be fine."

"Should be isn't good enough." He swallowed, cleared his throat and turned his steely blue eyes on his daughter. "Anything else happen at your meeting with Farnsworth?"

Deciding she had tortured him long enough, she said, "Oh, you mean about the promotion?"

He growled.

"I got it." She took another bite of mashed potatoes and tried not to think about the calories. "You can soon call me Lieutenant, Chief."

"Yes," he whispered. "Yes, indeed."

"Oh that's wonderful, Sam!" Celia jumped up to hug and kiss her. "That's just wonderful, isn't it, Skip?"

He never took his eyes off his daughter. "It sure is. Come give your old man a hug."

Pained that he'd had to ask and embarrassed by Celia's effu-

MARIE FORCE

siveness, Sam got up and did her best to work around the chair. With her lips close to his ear, she whispered, "Thank you."

"For?"

Sam pulled back to smile at him. "Love you."

"When you're not being mean to me, I love you, too."

Two hours later, Sam was laboring her way through the report of the day's activities on her laptop when Celia knocked on the door.

"Sorry to interrupt your work, but I thought you might enjoy some warm apple pie. It's so darned cold out."

Sam moaned. "Tell me it's fat free, calorie free and can't find an ass with a roadmap."

Chuckling, Celia handed her the plate. "All of the above. I swear."

"If the nursing gig doesn't pan out, you might consider a life of crime. You're a convincing liar."

"You've made your father very proud tonight, Sam. He's always proud of you, but he wanted this promotion for you. More, I think, than you wanted it for yourself."

"I don't doubt it." Sam used a finger to swirl a dollop of whipped cream off the pie and pop it into her mouth. "Sometimes I feel so selfish where he's concerned."

Celia lowered herself to the edge of Sam's bed. "How do mean? You're here for him every day, despite a demanding, time-consuming job."

"It would've been better...for him anyway...if the shot had been fatal. I can't imagine how he stands living the way he does, confined to four small rooms and wherever he can go in the van the union bought him. But I wasn't ready to lose him, Celia. Not then and not now. I thank God every day that bullet didn't kill him. As much as I hate the way he has to live now, I'm so grateful he's still here."

"In his own way, he's accepted it and come to terms."

"I wish you could've known him." Sam sighed. "Before."

"I did," Celia said with a smile, her pretty face blazing with color and her green eyes dancing with mirth.

"You've never told me that! Neither of you ever did!"

"I met him at the Giant, about two years before he was wounded. I helped him pick some tomatoes in the produce aisle, he asked me out for coffee and that was the start of a lovely friendship."

Sam slipped into detective mode as she narrowed her eyes. "Just friends?"

Laughing, Celia said, "I'll never tell."

"You dirty dogs! How did you slide this by me? By everyone?"

"You weren't looking," Celia said, her expression smug. "Why do you think I asked to be assigned to his case?"

"You love him," Sam said, incredulous.

"Very much. In fact, we've been talking about maybe… getting married."

Sam's mouth fell open. "Seriously? You said he's been down lately, worried about something. Is this it?"

"It's one of several things. He's been terribly upset about what happened to you in the Johnson case and fretting over your safety as well as the promotion he thinks you've been due for some time now."

"I wish he wouldn't spend so much time worrying about me."

"Sam," she said with a smile. "You're his life. His heart. He loves your sisters and their children very much, but you…"

"I know. I've always known that."

"And you've always struggled to live up to it."

Startled, Sam stared at her. "Been doing a lot more than nursing around here, haven't you?"

"I hope I haven't overstepped."

"Of course you haven't. You're already family, Celia. I don't know what we would've done without you the last two years."

"So you wouldn't mind too much if I married him?"

Sam put down the plate and reached for the older woman's hand. "If you make him happy and can bring some joy to whatever time he has left, the only thing I can do is thank you for that."

"Thank *you*," Celia said, her eyes bright with emotion. "It matters to him, to both of us, that you'd approve."

"I guess I need to get busy looking for another place to keep my clothes."

"Why?"

"You crazy kids won't want me underfoot."

"He wants you to stay. We both do. There's no reason for you to move out. I'll take one of the other bedrooms up here. We'll work it out. I'm here most of the time anyway. I don't expect much will change."

"This'll change everything for him, Celia. It'll give him a reason to keep fighting."

"Perhaps. I'll consider myself blessed for whatever time we get."

"Did he bully you into telling me?"

"He was afraid it would upset you, so I offered."

"You can tell him that not only am I fine with it, I'm thrilled for him. For both of you."

"That means a lot, Sam. I'm tired of hiding it. He's the most remarkable man I've ever known and the best friend I've ever had."

"Ditto," Sam said with a smile as Celia got up to leave. "Thanks for the pie."

"My pleasure. Don't work too hard."

When she was alone, Sam had to resist the urge to call her

sisters to share the huge scoop that had just fallen into her lap. "Not my news to tell," she muttered, deciding that maturity wasn't much fun at all.

While Celia's news had surprised her, Sam realized it shouldn't have. With hindsight, she could see there was something special between her father and his devoted nurse. Their banter, the carefree caresses Celia showered him with even though he couldn't feel them, the genuine affection.

Comforted by Celia's disclosures, Sam finished the pie and turned back to her report. She ran through it twice more before she sent it off to Freddie, who always checked them for her before she passed them up the food chain. If he wondered about the random mistakes, odd phrasings or twisted wording, he never said. Rather, he corrected the errors and returned the reports to her without comment.

Might be time to bring him into the loop, she thought. Dyslexia had cast its long net over every corner of her life, and until its diagnosis in sixth grade, she had believed herself to be as stupid as she was made to feel by teachers who had no idea what to do with her and parents who had been frustrated by her less-than-stellar performance in school.

Giving it a name had helped somewhat, but the daily struggles that went along with it were exhausting at times.

With the report finished, she finally allowed her thoughts to drift to Nick. As if floodgates had opened, she was overwhelmed by emotions and yearnings she had managed to resist all day. She had a list of questions she wanted to run by him, so she had every reason to take out the card he had given her. The call was about the case, right? There was nothing wrong with reaching out to him in a strictly official capacity. If she was also dying to tell him about her promotion and her father's pending marriage, what did that matter?

She flipped the card back and forth between her fingers for

several minutes until her stomach twisted with the start of the dreaded pain. Thinking of the case and *only* the case, she dialed his cell number.

He sounded groggy when he answered.

"Oh God, did I wake you?"

"No, no." A huge yawn made a liar out of him. "I was hoping you'd call."

Deciding to keep it strictly business, she said, "I have some questions. About the case."

"Oh."

She winced at the disappointment reverberating from that single syllable. "You sound...I don't know...kind of lousy."

"It's been a lousy day, except for the very beginning when I was with you."

Without saying much of anything he had managed to say it all. And she knew she couldn't tell him what she needed to tell him over the phone. "You're at home?"

"Uh huh."

"Do you mind if I come by? Just for a minute?"

"Are *you* at home?"

"At the moment."

"You're just going to 'drop by' all the way over here in Arlington? And only for a minute?"

"I need to talk to you, Nick. I need...Oh hell, I don't even know what I need."

"Come. I'll be waiting. And babe? You don't ever, *ever* have to ask first. Got me?"

She melted into a sloppy, messy puddle of need and want and desire. "Yeah," she managed to say. "I'll be there. Soon." Her heart doing back flips, Sam reached for her weapon, badge and cuffs. She released her hair to brush out the kinks and primped for a few more minutes before she headed downstairs to tell her dad she was going into work for a while. Celia told her he was already asleep.

"He was especially tired tonight." She held Sam's coat for her. "You'll be careful, won't you?"

"Always." Impulsively, she turned to kiss Celia's cheek on her way to the front door. "See you."

He'd turned on the outside light for her. A simple thing, but it evoked such a powerful sense of homecoming that Sam sat there for several minutes reminding herself of why she was there—and why she wasn't. "It can't be about you," she whispered. "Not now. This is about finding justice for John O'Connor. Nothing more."

But when Nick came to the door looking so...well...*lost* was the best word she could think of, nothing else mattered but him.

"Nick." Closing the door behind her, she let her coat drop to the floor and reached for him.

They stood there, arms wrapped around each other, comfort seeping through to warm the chill she had brought in with her.

Raising her hands to his face, she looked up at him. "What is it?"

Shrugging, he said, "Everything." He leaned his forehead against hers. "I've gone from having every minute of every day programmed to not knowing what the hell to do with myself, which gives me way too much time to think."

Even after what she had learned that day about John O'Connor, she was still able to feel Nick's pain over the loss of his friend and boss. Used to his unflappable, polished demeanor, seeing him disheveled in a ratty Harvard T-shirt and old sweats was jarring. Sometime in the course of that long day, the shock apparently wore off and gritty grief set in.

"I'm glad you're here." He shifted to press her against the

closed door. "I've been worried about you. That stuff in the paper…"

"We're handling it."

"I don't like the idea of you being unsafe." The light caress of his hand on her cheek caused her heart to lurch. He leaned in, bringing with him the scent of spice and soap.

"Nick, wait—"

His lips came down hard and insistent on hers, sucking the breath from her lungs and the starch from her spine. If he hadn't been holding her up with the weight of his body, she might have slid to the floor. Somehow he maneuvered them so her legs were hooked over his hips, his hands were full of her breasts and his tongue was tangled up with hers—all in the scope of thirty seconds.

Having forgotten everything she'd vowed in the car the moment she saw his grief-stricken face, Sam wove her fingers through his damp, silky hair and pressed hard against his straining erection. Then they were moving, falling. She yelped against his lips and clung to him as he lowered them to the sofa.

Tearing at clothes, desperate for skin, for contact, for relief, they wrestled through layers until there was nothing left between them but raging desire.

"You're just like I remembered." His tongue darted in circles around her nipple, and his hands seemed to be everywhere at once. "Tall and curvy and strong…soft in all the right places." Nick gazed with reverence at breasts that had always seemed too big to her, but he appeared to like what he saw.

Need zipped through her, leaving her desperate and panting. "Nick…" She tugged at him to align them for what she wanted more than the next breath. "Now."

"Condom," he said through gritted teeth. "Wait a sec."

She stopped him from getting up. "I'm on the pill. We get tested—"

"So do we." He slid one arm under her shoulders while his other hand cupped her bottom and tilted her into position to receive him.

Overwhelmed by desire, Sam let her legs fall open to take him in.

He held her gaze as he entered her with one swift stroke.

She cried out as an orgasm ripped through her with more force and fury than anything she'd ever experienced.

He froze. "Oh, God, did I hurt you?"

"No, *no!* Don't stop. *Please.*"

Watching him, feeling him, there were no recriminations. There wasn't room for thoughts of anything but him as he began to move, slowly at first and then faster as his closely held control seemed to desert him. She remembered that from the last time, how he'd let go with her, in a way she suspected he didn't often allow himself.

With his arms wrapped tight around her, he pounded into her, the smack of flesh meeting flesh the only thing she could hear over the roar of her own heartbeat.

Sam met each thrust with equal ardor, and when he sucked hard on her nipple, she cried out with another climax that took him tumbling over with her.

"Jesus," he whispered when he'd recovered the ability. "Jesus Christ. I didn't even offer you something to drink."

She laughed and tightened the hold she had on him, letting one hand slide languidly through soft hair still damp from an earlier shower. "What kind of host does that make you?"

"A crappy one, I guess," he said, turning them over in a smooth move.

Stretched out on top of him, still joined with him, Sam breathed in his warm, masculine scent and reveled in the comfort of strong arms wrapped tight around her. It was almost disturbing to accept that she had never experienced anything even remotely close to this, except during the one night she spent with him so many years ago. How foolish she had been then to assume that what she'd shared with him would show up again with someone else. She was wise enough now, old enough, jaded enough, to know better.

But even as the woman continued to vibrate with aftershocks and tingle with the desire for more, the cop resurfaced with disgust and dismay. "This was a very bad idea," she muttered into his chest.

He curled a lock of her hair around his finger. "Depends on your perspective. From my point of view, it was the best idea I've had in six years."

Sam studied him. "It must be the politician in you."

Eyebrows knitting with confusion, he said, "What must?"

"The way you always seem to have the right words."

He framed her face with his big hands. "I'm not feeding you lines, Sam."

His sweet sincerity made her heart ache with something she refused to acknowledge. "I know." The emotions were so overwhelming and new to her, she did the first thing that came to mind. She tried to escape.

His arms clamped around her like a vise. "Not yet." He brushed his lips over hers in a gesture so tender it all but stopped her heart. Her eyes flooded with tears that she desperately tried to blink back.

"What?"

She shook her head.

"Sam."

Letting her eyes drift up to meet his, she said, "I like this. I know I shouldn't because of everything…but I like it."

"Sex on the sofa?"

"This." She had to look away. It was just too much. "You. Me. Us."

"So do I." He kissed her softly. "So does this mean we're together now?"

A stab of fear went through her. She just wasn't ready for the magnitude of what this had the potential to be. "Why does it need a label? Why can't it just be what it is?"

Once again, the flash of pain she saw on his face bothered her more than it should have. "And what is it exactly, Sam? I want far more from you than just a sex buddy."

"That might be all I can give you right now."

He sighed. "I suppose I'll take whatever I can get." When his lips coasted up her neck, he made her shiver. "We could move this somewhere more comfortable. There's a big soft bed in the other room."

Her stomach ached as reality stepped in to remind her of why she'd needed to see him. "There're things we need to talk about. Stuff about the case."

"We'll get to it. Can I just have a few more minutes of this first?"

Because he seemed to need it so much, she said, "Okay."

CHAPTER 20

The bed, as advertised, was big and soft. How he managed to coax her into it was something she planned to think about later when she reclaimed her sanity. It would be so easy, so very easy indeed, to curl into him and sleep the sleep of the dead. But the grinding sensation in her gut was an ever-present reminder of the conversation she needed to have with him.

"What's wrong?" he asked as his talented hand worked to ease the tension in her neck.

"Nothing, why?"

"I had you on the way to relaxed, and now you're all tight again."

"We need to talk."

"So you've said. I'm listening."

"I can't do cop work naked."

Laughing, he said, "Is that in the manual?"

"If it isn't, it should be."

Sitting up, he reached for the pile of their clothes he had deposited on the foot of the bed, found the T-shirt he'd been wearing when she arrived, and helped her into it. "Better?"

Engulfed in the shirt that carried his sexy, male scent, she was riveted by his muscular chest. "Um, except you're still naked."

"I'm not the cop." He reached for her hand, brought it to his lips. "Talk to me, Sam."

The dull ache sharpened in a matter of seconds.

"Something's wrong," he said, alarmed. "You just went totally pale."

"It's nothing." She tried and failed to take a deep breath. "Just this deal with my stomach."

"What deal?"

"It gives me some grief from time to time. It's nothing."

"Have you had it checked?"

"A couple of times," she squeaked out.

"Babe, God, you're in serious pain! What can I do?"

"Gotta breathe," she said as the pain clawed its way through her, making her feel sick and clammy. "Sorry."

"Don't be." He fitted himself around her, held her close and whispered soft words of comfort that eased her mind.

She closed her eyes, focused on the sound of his voice and drifted. The pain retreated, but the episode—worse than most—left her drained and embarrassed. "Sorry about that."

"I told you not to apologize. You have to do something about that. You might have an ulcer or something. I can get you in with my friend. He's awesome."

"It seems to crop up whenever I'm nervous about something, which I'm finding is fairly often."

"You're nervous about what you have to say to me?"

She tilted her head and found his pretty hazel eyes studying her intently. "I guess I am."

He sat up, propped the pillows behind him and snuggled her into his chest. "Then let's get it over with."

"Cops don't snuggle."

"Make an exception."

"I think I've already made quite a few," she said dryly.

"Make another one."

Before the pain could come back to remind her she was powerless against it, she took the plunge. "I have to ask you something. It's probably going to upset you, and I hate that, but I have to ask."

"Okay."

"Is there any chance John was gay? Or maybe bi?" She felt the tension creep into his body, and then just as quickly it was gone.

He laughed. He actually *laughed*. "No. Not only no, but *no fucking way*."

"How can you know that for sure? Some men hide it from their friends, their families…"

"I would've known, Sam. Believe me. I would've known."

"You didn't know he had a son."

And just that quickly he was tense again. "You don't know that, either."

"I'm all but certain of it. The picture?"

"What about it?"

"His parents lied. His cousin Thomas, the son of Robert O'Connor? He's thirty-six, dark hair, dark eyes." She sat up straighter and shifted so she could see his face. "Surely you must have heard him talk about a cousin who was the same age as him?"

Nick mulled that over. "I can't say I ever did. Maybe they weren't close. I don't think Graham and his brother are."

"Either way, the kid in the picture isn't his cousin. His mother lied to me today, and his father didn't refute it. The monthly payments—stretching twenty years—the weekly phone calls, catching his parents in a big, fat lie, the startling resemblance to the senator…It doesn't take a detective to add it all up, Nick."

"But why…wait." He went perfectly still. "One weekend a month."

Baffled, she said, "Excuse me?"

"He required one weekend a month with no commitments.

Usually the third weekend. Never would say what he did with the time. In fact, he was always kind of weird about it, now that I think about it."

"And you just thought to mention this now? What the hell, Nick?"

"I'm sorry. It was just so much a part of our routine that I didn't think anything of it until right now."

"I bet if I do some digging, I'll find him booked on a regular flight to Chicago."

All the air seemed to leave Nick in one long exhale. "Why didn't he tell me? Why would he keep something like this hidden from me? From everyone?"

"I don't know, but I'm going out there tomorrow to find out."

"You are?"

"I'm on an eleven o'clock flight."

"Does she know you're coming?"

Sam shook her head. "Element of surprise. I don't want to give her time to put away the pictures or send the kid out of town."

"And you think this has something to do with his murder?"

"I can't say for sure until I've spoken to the mother, but for some reason they've kept him hidden away for twenty years. I want to know why."

"Politics, no doubt."

"How do you mean?"

"A teenaged son with a baby would've been a political liability to the senator. I should know. As the offspring of teenaged parents, I can attest to the embarrassment factor in a family with zero public presence."

Sam ached from the pain she heard in his voice.

"Graham O'Connor would've wanted this put away in a closet," he concluded.

"His own grandchild?"

"I don't think it would've mattered. The O'Connor name wasn't always the powerhouse it is now. He had a few contentious campaigns around the mid-point of his career. If the timing coincided, this could've ruined him. He would've acted accordingly."

"At the expense of his own family?"

"Power does strange things to people, Sam. It can be addicting. Once you get a taste of it, it's hard to give it up. I've always found Graham to be a kind and loving—albeit exacting—father, but he's as human as the next guy. He would've been susceptible to the seduction of power." Nick paused, as if he was pondering something else.

"What are you thinking?"

"I'm wondering how, considering you're certain he had a son, you also think he might've been gay."

"Just a vibe we've picked up on the investigation. Nothing concrete. I've told you my gut says it was a woman he'd wronged, but then Freddie goes and ruins that by pointing out that it could've just as easily been a love affair gone wrong with a guy."

Nick shook his head. "I can't imagine it. There was never anything, *anything* in almost twenty years of close friendship that would make me doubt his orientation. Nothing, Sam. He was a skirt-chasing hound."

"So I've discovered. But he wouldn't be the first guy to use that as a front to hide his real life."

"I suppose."

"You're upset. I'm sorry."

He shrugged. "It's just…you think you know someone, really know them, only to find out they had all these secrets. He had a son. A *child*. And in twenty years, he never mentions that to his closest friend? It's disappointing at the very least."

It was also a betrayal, she imagined. That the family he'd considered his own—his only—had kept something of this magnitude from him.

As if he could read her thoughts, he said, "Did they think I'd tell anyone?"

"You shouldn't take this personally, Nick. It won't do you any good."

"How else should I take it?"

Looping an arm around him, she bent to press her lips to his chest and felt the strong, steady beat of his heart. "I'm sorry this is hurting you. I hate that."

He enfolded her in his arms. "It goes down easier coming from you." Tilting her chin, he fused his mouth to hers.

"I should go," she said when they resurfaced.

"Stay with me. Sleep with me. I need you, Samantha." He dropped soft, wet kisses on her face and neck. "I need you."

"You're playing dirty."

"I'm not playing."

Something other than pain settled in her gut, something warm and sweet. This was a whole new kind of powerlessness, and it felt good. Really good. She let her hand slide over the defined chest, the ripped abdomen and below. Finding him hard and ready, her lips followed the path her hand had taken. His gasps of pleasure, his total surrender, told her she had succeeded in taking his mind off the pain and grief, which made everything that was wrong about this feel right.

They began the next day the same way they finished the one before.

As her body hummed with rippling aftershocks, she pressed her lips to his shoulder. "This is getting out of hand."

"We've got six years of lost time to make up for."

His lips moving against her neck made her tremble. "I need

to go soon," she said. "I have to shower and change and get to the airport."

"I'm taking the staff to Richmond today to see John," he said with a deep sigh. "I'd rather be going with you."

"I wish you could." She reached up to caress his face and found the stubble on his jaw to be crazy sexy. Replacing her hand with her lips, she said, "I forgot to tell you my news."

"What news?"

"I made lieutenant."

His face lit up with pleasure. "That's awesome, Sam! Congratulations."

"It won't be official for a week or so." For a moment, she thought about telling him how it happened but decided against it. "And my dad is marrying one of his nurses."

"Wow. Do you like her?"

"Yeah. A lot."

"Where's your mother?"

"She lives in Florida with some guy she hooked up with when I was in high school. They ran off together the day after I graduated. Nearly killed my dad. He had no idea."

"Ouch. That sucks. I'm sorry."

"Yeah, I guess I should be grateful that she stuck around long enough to get me through school, but it wasn't like she was *there* for me or anything."

"I saw my mother three times when I was in high school."

Sam cursed herself for being insensitive. "I'm sorry. I didn't mean to complain."

He shrugged. "It was what it was."

"At least you had your grandmother."

"And she was a real treat," he said with a bitter chuckle.

Intrigued, she shifted so she could see him. "She wasn't good to you?"

"She did what she could, but she always made it clear that

I was a burden to her, that I was keeping her from traveling and enjoying her retirement." He paused, focused on her fingers. "When I was about ten, I heard her talking to my dad—her son. She said she'd done enough, and it was time for him to step up and take over, that he was an adult now and there was no reason he couldn't take care of his own child. He said he would, and I got all excited, thinking I was going to get to go with him."

Her stomach twisted with anxiety for the ten-year-old boy. "What happened?"

"I didn't see him again for a year."

"Nick...I'm sorry."

"He sent money—enough for me to play hockey, which I loved. I poured all my energy into that and school. Ended up with an academic scholarship to Harvard and played hockey there, too. That was my escape."

Listening to him, she wanted to give him everything he'd been denied as a child and wished she had it to give.

"Anyway," he said, running a hand through his hair, "someday hopefully I'll have my own family and it won't matter anymore."

And that, she thought, *is my cue to go.* She sat up and reached for her clothes at the foot of the bed.

"It's only seven. You've got time yet." His hand slid from her shoulder to land on her hip. "I could make you some breakfast."

"Thanks, but I've got to go home, take a shower, get changed, check in at HQ," she said as she jammed her arms into her shirt and dragged it over her head. *Air and space*, she thought, *and we're not talking about the museum. That's what I need. Some air, some space, some perspective. Distance.*

Twirling her bra on his index finger, his full, sexy mouth twisted into a grin. "Forget something?"

She snatched it away from him and jammed it into her pants pocket.

Laughing, he reclined on the big pile of pillows.

She felt the heat of his eyes on her as she ducked into the bathroom. Re-emerging a few minutes later, she found him out of bed and wearing just the sweats he'd had on the night before. The pants rode low on narrow hips, and that chest of his...It should've been gracing the covers of erotic romance novels rather than spending its days hidden behind starched dress shirts and silk ties. Tragic. Truly a waste of good—no, *great*—man chest.

"You're staring."

"And you're hot. Seriously. Hot."

"Well, um, thanks. I guess."

His befuddlement amused and delighted her until she remembered that she'd been plotting her escape. Suddenly, morning-after awkwardness set in, leaving her tongue-tied and uncertain as she tugged on her sweater. "Good luck with your staff. Today. In Richmond."

"Thank you." He reached for her hand, brought it to his lips. "Will you tell me what happens in Chicago?"

"If I can, I will. That's the best I can do."

"That's all I can ask." Releasing her hand, he caressed her cheek. "When will I see you?"

Before she knew it the words were tumbling from her face as if her mouth was on autopilot. "There's this thing tomorrow. Family dinner at my dad's. If you want to come." All but stuttering now, she added, "I'd understand if you didn't want to because there're so many of us—"

He stopped her with a finger to her lips. "What time?"

"Dinner's at three." Her cheeks grew warm with embarrassment. "But if you want to come earlier, we could take a walk. Check out the market. If you want."

"I want." He slid his arms around her waist and brought her in snug against him. "I really want."

She should've been prepared by then for the way her legs turned to jelly when he kissed her in that particular proprietary way, but the sweep of his tongue, the pressure of his hands on her ass holding her tight against his instant arousal...no way in hell she could prepare for that.

"So," he asked, peppering her face and lips with kisses, "does *this* mean we're together? I mean, *you're* asking *me* to do stuff." His teasing grin did nothing to offset the serious look in his eyes.

With her hands on his chest, she managed to extricate herself. At the bedroom door, she paused and turned back to him. "I've crossed every line there is to cross here, Nick."

"I know that," he said, his expression pained.

"If the job requires it, I won't hesitate to cross back."

"I wouldn't expect anything less."

Satisfied that he understood, she left him with a nod and a small smile.

He followed her downstairs. "Sam?"

She swung open the inside door. "Hmm?"

Framing her face with his hands, he said, "Fly safely."

She winced.

"What?"

"I hate to fly. Hate it with a passion. I've been trying not to think about it."

Grinning, he leaned his forehead against hers. "Just close your eyes and try not to think about it."

"Yeah, right," she said, rolling her eyes. "Okay, I'm going now."

"Okay, I'm letting you." Except he didn't. He hung on for a moment longer. "Be safe. This thing with that Johnson woman...Be careful." He kissed her. "Please."

"I always am."

"Guess what?"

"What?"

His lips landed on hers for another mind–altering kiss. "You're pretty damned hot yourself."

Sam gave herself one last minute to sink into the kiss.

With what appeared to be great reluctance, he finally released her.

CHAPTER 21

Nick stayed at the door to watch her walk to her car. *Damn*, if the woman didn't make his mouth water with that curvy body and long-legged gait. The whole package was a huge turn-on. He acknowledged they were walking a fine line that was causing her great ethical conflict, but Nick could only be grateful for the second chance they'd been given. And despite her reluctance to acknowledge that this was an actual relationship, he had no intention of messing it up this time.

Long after she should have driven away, she sat at the curb. He wondered if she was on the phone. Tipping his head so he could better see her face, he noticed it was tight with frustration. He cracked the door, heard the unmistakable click of a dead car battery and waved at her to come back in.

Furious, she got out, slammed the car door and started back up the stone pathway to his door. She was halfway there when the car exploded.

The blast was so strong it shattered the storm door and propelled him backward onto the floor. His head smacked hard on the tile, but he fought through the fog to remain conscious so he could get to her.

Barefooted, shirtless and panic-stricken, he crawled through the glass calling for her. The quiet neighborhood had descended into bedlam. He heard people screaming and could smell the acrid smoke coming from the burning car. "Sam! Sam!"

Blood flowed from a cut on his forehead. He swiped at it

and started down the stairs, ignoring the pain of jagged glass under his feet. *"Samantha!"* Frantically, he scanned the small front yard, the street, the neighbors' yards.

A moan from the bushes behind him caught his attention. "Sam!" He rushed to the huddled form in his garden and had the presence of mind to realize that the miniature evergreens he had planted the summer before had most likely saved her life. "Sam! Sam, look at me." With the scream of sirens in the distance, he gently turned her head. Other than a knot on her forehead and a shocked glow to her eyes, he didn't see any obvious injuries.

"Bleeding," she whispered. "You're bleeding."

"I'm fine." He picked branches from her hair, brushed dirt from her cheek. "Do you hurt? Anywhere?" Releasing a long deep breath, he swayed with lightheadedness. "Babe. Jesus." Sitting with her in the garden, he did battle with the blood pouring from his forehead. He held her tight against him and whispered soothing words as she trembled in his arms.

"Need to call. HQ. Report it."

"I'm sure someone called 911. Just stay still until we get you checked out."

"My ears are ringing."

"Mine, too. You didn't hurt anything else?"

"Chest hurts." She trembled. "God, Nick. Oh my God." Clutching her stomach, she rocked in his arms.

He tightened his hold on her. "Shh, babe." The blood coming from the cut on his forehead seemed to finally be slowing. "Breathe. Deep breaths."

An Arlington police officer approached them. "Are you folks all right?"

"I'm on the job." She showed him the badge she pulled from her tattered coat pocket. "Detective Sergeant Holland. Metro."

"Are you hurt, Sergeant?"

"I don't think so, but it was my car that went up. I need to get word to my brass."

"I'll call it in for you." Until the cop handed Nick a blanket, he'd forgotten he was wearing only the now-torn sweats. "And I'll send the paramedics right over."

"Thank you, Officer…"

"Severson."

"Thank you," Sam said again. When they were alone, she glanced at Nick. "I'm sorry."

"What the hell for?"

"For bringing this to your home." She sniffed and wiped her nose. "I never thought they'd really try to kill me. I never imagined they had the balls."

"Don't you dare apologize to me, Samantha. You're a victim here."

"Your windows are broken. Your neighbors', too."

"Screw that. It's glass. It can be replaced. But you…" His voice hitched with emotion. Brushing his lips over the lump on her forehead, he took a deep shuddering breath. "There's no replacing you. I ought to know. I tried for six years."

"Nick," she said, haltingly, "I'm supposed to hold it together and do my job, but this…" She fixed her eyes on the firefighters hosing down what was left of her car.

"Nothing's going to happen to you. I won't let it."

Smiling now but still shaky, she turned to him and wiped the drying blood from his brow. "And how do you intend to do that?"

"By not letting you out of my sight."

"Nick—"

"Sergeant Holland?" Officer Severson said. "The paramedics are ready for you."

"We're not finished," she told Nick as she gestured the paramedics over. "We'll talk about this later."

"You bet your fine ass we will."

Remarkably, Nick's injuries were more serious than Sam's.
He required five stitches to close the cut over his left eyebrow
and stitches in his right foot after doctors removed several sliv-
ers of glass. In addition, he had a slight concussion and a minor
case of hypothermia from the hour he spent half-dressed in
the cold.

Sam, on the other hand, had only a bump on the head and
an ugly bruise on her breastbone where she'd connected with
the bushes. When she allowed her mind to wander to what
could've happened, she was beset by the shakes. She decided it
was better if she didn't think about it until she had to. Standing at Nick's bedside, watching the plastic surgeon stitch his
forehead, Sam's knees went weak as the needle passed through
his flesh. Nothing freaked her out more than needles—not
even airplanes.

The TV was tuned to John's public wake in Richmond,
with special coverage of the O'Connor family's poignant visit
the day before. Nick was riveted to the coverage, but Sam was
riveted to the needle.

"You'll have a scar," she whispered.

"No way," the doctor protested. "He'll be good as new."

"Damn," Nick said with a grin. "I was hoping for a gnarly
scar."

"It's not funny," Sam snapped.

"Hey." He squeezed her hand. "Why don't you wait outside? You're pale as a ghost."

"I'd rather stay in here where there're needles than face
what's waiting for me out there."

"And that would be?"

"I heard the lieutenant and the captain are here, no doubt media, too. It'll be all over the news that I spent the night with you."

"We'll deal with it, babe."

"*I* will deal with it. *You* will say nothing, you got me?"

"I'm not going to let you get reamed for something we both had a hand in."

"You're a *civilian*. You won't help me if you try to fight my battles for me, Nick. You have to promise me you'll resist the urge to speak."

"Or?"

"I'll have Freddie toss you in the can until the dust settles."

"You wouldn't dare."

"Oh no?" She leaned in close to his battered face, but not too close to the needle. "Try me."

The doctor smiled. "I think I'd listen to the lady if I were you—unless you want to be back for more stitches."

"The *lady*," Nick said, never taking his eyes off Sam, "is sadly deluded if she thinks she can order me around like one of her collars."

"*Ohhh,*" Sam said. "Listen to him spewing cop talk." Reaching behind her, she grabbed her cuffs and snapped them on him and the bed rail so fast he never saw it coming.

"*What the fuck?*" He tugged on the cuffs, clanked them against the metal rail. "*Goddamn it, Sam!*"

"Ah, you need to stay still unless you want a needle straight through to your brain," the doctor said.

"I'll be back to get him after I've dealt with my bosses," Sam said to the doctor. "Keep him quiet until then."

"Yes, ma'am," the doctor said, seeming awestruck by her brassiness.

"You're going to pay for this, Samantha," Nick growled.

She brushed a kiss over the uninjured side of his forehead.

"Be back soon." Over her shoulder, she added, "Behave." As she walked away, the furious clatter of cuffs made her smile. "That'll teach him to screw with me." Her smile faded when she encountered Lieutenant Stahl's angry scowl in the waiting room. Realizing she was still braless, she pulled her tattered coat closed and crossed her arms.

Stahl gestured her to a deserted corner. Captain Malone followed them.

"Sergeant," Stahl said. "I'd like an explanation for what you were doing at the home of a material witness—overnight."

"Yes, sir, Lieutenant, I'm fine. Thanks for asking."

"How about we add a rap for insubordination to your growing list of problems?" Stahl retorted.

"Lieutenant," Captain Malone said, the warning clear in his tone. To Sam, he said, "Your injuries were minor?"

"Yes, sir. Bump on the head, bruised sternum."

"And your companion?"

Sam gave him a rundown of Nick's injuries. "Was anyone else hurt?"

"No. The street was deserted. Luckily, it was a weekend."

Yes, luckily, Sam thought, feeling a tremble ripple through her as she realized how truly lucky she—and Nick—had been. "Has Explosives gotten anything on the car?"

"They're there now. Our people are bumping heads with Arlington. The chief was on the phone with their chief asking for some latitude when I left."

"I'm sorry to have caused all this trouble, sir."

"You start down that path, you're gonna piss me off."

"What were you doing with Cappuano?" Stahl asked.

This time, Malone didn't bail her out. Rather, he watched her with wise gray eyes that she knew from experience didn't miss a thing.

"We're friends," she said haltingly. "We met at a party six

years ago. I hadn't seen him again until the, ah, until the senator was murdered. Cappuano has been cleared of any involvement and has been a tremendous asset to the investigation in a civilian capacity. Sir."

"I'm taking you off the O'Connor case, effective immediately," Stahl said, puffed up with his own importance.

"But—"

"Not so fast, Lieutenant," Captain Malone said.

"This is my call, Captain," Stahl huffed. "She's *my* detective."

"And I'm *your* captain." Malone dismissed Stahl by turning his back to him.

The foul look Stahl directed at Sam would have reduced a lesser woman to tears. Fortunately, Sam wasn't a lesser woman. She directed all her attention and focus on the much more rational captain.

"Sergeant, I'm disappointed in the judgment you've exhibited by getting involved with a witness," Malone said.

"Exactly—" Stahl sputtered.

"Lieutenant!" the captain roared. "Get back to your squad." When Stahl didn't budge, Malone added a fierce, *"Now."*

With one last hateful glance at Sam, Stahl stalked out of the emergency room.

"As I was saying," Malone continued, "you've shown poor judgment with this involvement, but in the more than twelve years you've been under my command, I've never once had reason to question your judgment. I know you, Holland. I know how you think, how you operate and have had many an occasion over the years to appreciate your high ethical standards. So, the way I see it, the only way you hook up with a witness in the midst of the most important case of your career is if it's serious."

Sam might've swallowed her tongue—if she could've opened her mouth. "Sir?" she squeaked.

"Are you in love with this guy? Cappuano?"

"I…ah…I…"

"It's a simple yes or no question, Sergeant."

"Don't be ridiculous. Of course I'm not in love with him," Sam sputtered, but the words rang hollow, even to her. Apparently, they did to him, too.

Looking satisfied, he studied her again, long and hard. "I'm going to give you the benefit of the doubt. I'm going to assume you've done nothing to compromise this investigation, that when you say Cappuano has been invaluable to you, you're being completely aboveboard with me."

"I am, sir."

"In that case, for now you're to have no comment to the press about your relationship with him. We'll let the media folks spin it. I'll take care of that." He sat and gestured for her to take the chair next to him. "As for the bombing—"

"If you take me off O'Connor, you're going to have to take my badge, too."

"Sergeant, there's no need for ultimatums. You've been through a traumatic thing."

"Yes, I have, and by tomorrow morning, everyone in the city will know who I'm sleeping with. They'll know Destiny Johnson meant it when she said she'd get even with me for what happened to her kid. They'll know I'm no closer to a suspect in the O'Connor case today than I was the day it happened. They'll know all that, and then they'll hear that my own command didn't have enough confidence in me to let me close this case. Where will that leave me?"

"You're a decorated officer. Soon to be a lieutenant. This is a setback. That's all it is."

"On top of another setback. You want me to take command

of the detective squad. I won't have an ounce of authority left if you take this case away from me."

"Your safety has to be a consideration. They've come at you once. They'll come at you again."

"Next time, I'll be ready. I screwed up this time because I didn't take her seriously. I know better now."

"I've got to talk to the chief about this. He's having a fucking cow. Gonzo and Arnold have Destiny Johnson in interview right now. Because we've had her in lock-up since yesterday, she's playing dumb on the bombing."

Freddie came rushing into the Emergency Room, looking pale and panicked. "Oh, thank God," he said when he saw Sam talking with Malone. "Thank you, Jesus."

"If you hug me, I'll have you busted down to patrol," Sam snarled at him.

Freddie stopped just short of the embrace, bent at the waist and propped his hands on his knees. "I heard it on the radio," he panted. "Scared the freaking shit out of me."

"He's swearing," Sam commented to Malone. "He only does that in extreme circumstances. I'm honored."

Freddie tipped his face, met Sam's eyes. "You almost got blown up. I'm sorry if I don't find that funny."

"I'm fine, Cruz," she said, touched by his concern. "You can relax."

"What are we doing?" he asked Malone, his eyes hot with anger and passion. "What can I do?"

"Gonzo's got Destiny in interview," Sam told him.

"I was thinking on the way over here," he said, still breathing heavily. "What if it's not Johnson?"

"How do you mean?" Malone asked.

Freddie stood up straight. "Destiny spews in the paper yesterday, right?"

Sam and the captain nodded.

"So say someone wants to hose up the O'Connor investigation? What's the fastest way?" Before they could answer, he said, "Take out Sergeant Holland and have the full wrath of the department focused on Johnson. Presto. O'Connor is back burner. Senator or not, no one takes precedence over a dead cop."

"That's an interesting theory, Detective," Malone said, clearly impressed.

Sam was filled with pride. Young Freddie was coming along very well. Very well, indeed.

"You think it's possible?" Freddie asked, full of youthful exuberance.

"It's solid, Cruz," Sam said. "Good thinking." She paused, thought for a moment and decided. "I want you to go to Chicago and talk to Patricia Donaldson. I want to know if her kid is John O'Connor's son. I want the whole story. Tell her she can either spill it to you, or we'll get a warrant for DNA. Don't come back until you know every detail of her relationship with O'Connor. He went out there the third weekend of every month. I want to know if he was banging her. I want to know how. You got me?"

"Without you?" His normally robust complexion paled again.

"A bomb just blew off your training wheels, Detective." Sam winced at the pain in her chest as she rose. "Get your ass to Chicago." She grabbed the lapels of his ever-present trench coat and pulled him down so his face was an inch from hers. "You get yourself hurt in *any* way, and I'll kill you. You got me?"

"Ma'am." He swallowed hard. "Yes, ma'am."

She retrieved the paper with her ticket information from her purse. "Be on that eleven o'clock flight and get back here as fast as you can. Report in tonight."

"Watch your back, Cruz," Malone added. "If they've got eyes on Sergeant Holland, they're on you, too."

"Yes, sir." Freddie stood there for a second longer, beaming at the two of them.

"What the hell are you standing there grinning like a goon for?" Sam asked.

"I'm going. I won't let you down. I'll call you as soon as I've got anything."

"*Go!*" After he scrambled through the ER doors, she glanced at Malone. "Sheesh, was I ever that green?"

"Nope," he said without hesitation. "You came in with the sensibilities of a captain. Why do you think I've been watching my back all these years?"

Staggered by the compliment, Sam stared at him. "I'm sorry if I've let you down."

"I'll bet your friend is wondering where you are. Why don't you go on back and check on him? I'll give you both a lift when he's sprung."

She rested a hand on his arm. "Don't let them take me off O'Connor, Captain. Don't let them."

"I'll do what I can."

CHAPTER 22

Sam made her way back down the long hallway, pausing just before Nick's room to lean against the wall and collect herself. She couldn't stop thinking about what Malone had said. Was she in love with Nick? Is that why she'd allowed things with him to progress even though she knew it was wrong and could get her into a shit load of trouble? Had she maybe always loved him? Way back to the first time they met?

With a soft groan, she tipped back her aching head. She hadn't loved Peter but discovered that far too late. When Nick failed to call her after their night together—or so she thought—she'd been seriously depressed. Peter came to the rescue, offering a shoulder to cry on and a friend to lean on. It had been easy, too easy she later realized, to get swept up by him.

Now, on top of everything else she'd learned about him, she knew he intercepted Nick's calls while pretending to offer comfort, proving he was an even bigger asshole than she had given him credit for being. He had robbed her of a lot more than four years of her life. He had taken her self-esteem, caused her to question her judgment, stolen her self-respect and left her confidence in tatters.

A smart woman would be leery of making another mistake after the whopper she'd made with Peter. A smart woman would go slow with Nick, would take her time, would make sure she was doing the right thing. As the clank of metal against metal reminded her she had a very angry man to deal with, she decided she clearly wasn't as smart as she'd always thought.

Pasting a big smile on her face, she stepped into the room, her stomach aching from the tension. "Great! You're all done."

All but smoking with rage, Nick said, "Get these things off me, Sam. Right now."

"I'd be happy to." She dug the key out of her pocket and dangled it in front of him. "But before I do, let's get one thing straight. I need you to stay out of my work stuff. Agree to that, and I'll let you go."

"How do you know I don't plan to let *you* go once you unlock me?"

The question sent a surprising jolt of fear through her. "Well, I guess that'll be up to you, won't it?" she said with more bravado than she felt.

"Unlock me. Now."

"Not until you agree."

"I'm not agreeing to anything while I'm locked to a bed. If you want to unlock me and talk this through like rational adults, then that's fine."

She studied his furious, handsome face for a long moment. "You're awfully sexy when you're pissed." Leaning down, she kissed the bandage over his left eye.

The kiss seemed to defuse him, but only somewhat.

"I'm sorry I locked you up." When his face twisted with skepticism, she said, "I *am* sorry. But you have no idea how difficult it is to be a woman in this profession or the daughter of a fallen hero. The last thing I need is some guy on a white horse riding to my rescue as if I can't handle things myself. As it is, I spend most of every day waiting for it all to blow up in my face."

"Like it did today?"

"A joke?" she asked, incredulous. "You're joking about a bomb?"

"Sorry," he said with chagrin, "it was too good to pass up. Doesn't mean I think it's funny. Quite the contrary." With his free hand, he captured one of hers and brought it to his lips. "Unlock me. I promise not to kill you."

Knowing that was the best she was going to get and encouraged by the tender gesture, she released the cuffs.

He made a big dramatic show of rubbing his sore wrist for a minute before he got up to reach for his jeans and sweater.

Still uncertain about just how angry he really was, Sam stayed on the far side of the bed while he got dressed. She winced at the flash of pain that crossed his face as he slid his injured foot into an old running shoe the cops had brought from his house.

"Um, Captain Malone is going to take us...well...I guess to my house if you don't mind."

"I don't mind," he said in a testy tone.

Swallowing the lump in her throat, she added, "I'd appreciate it if you don't discuss what happened earlier with him."

"What? That my girlfriend or sex buddy or whatever you are was nearly blown to bits in my front yard? I shouldn't mention that?"

She rubbed at eyes gone gritty with exhaustion. After an almost-sleepless night with him, she'd planned to catch a couple of hours on the plane if her nerves allowed it. "I'm asking you to do this for me. He was a lot cooler about me getting caught with you than I expected him to be. It would just be better if you stayed out of it."

He came around the bed and backed her up to the wall. "You want me to stay out of it?"

"Um, yeah, that would help." Only her hands on his chest kept him from completely invading her space.

"Let's get one thing straight, Samantha. I've been the guy behind the guy my whole career, and that's fine with me. But if you think, for one second, I'm going to ride shotgun in my personal life, you've got the wrong lapdog on your leash."

While she should have been pissed at a comment like that, she was ridiculously turned on. She looped a hand around his neck and brought him down for a kiss intended to make him forget all about being mad with her.

With his hands on her hips, he jerked her tight against him.

"I don't want a lapdog," she said when she finally came up for air. "That's not what I'm asking you to be."

"What *are* you asking me to be?"

"Do we have to decide that right now? It's bad enough the whole town's going to know we're sleeping together."

"Damage done," he said with a bitter laugh that jangled her already frazzled nerves.

"That's easy for you to say. Your job isn't on the line."

"No, it's not. I lost my job when my boss got himself murdered. Remember?"

"I don't want to do this. I don't want to be sniping with you when we've got so many bigger things to deal with."

"See what you just said there? *We* have so many bigger things to deal with? You just made my point."

She studied the floor for a moment before she found the courage to bring her eyes back up to meet his. "I'm not used to *we*."

He laughed, but at least the anger seemed to be gone. "And you think I am? This is all new ground for me, too, babe."

"I'm sorry we're being forced to go public before we're ready."

"Something tells me that nothing about you and me is going to be simple or easy. We may as well get used to it. At least you're calling us 'we' now. That's progress."

Ignoring that, she said, "So you'll be cool with the captain?"

"I'll be cool."

With her eyes fixed on his, she kissed him softly. "You really are super sexy when you're all steamed up."

"Is that so?"

She loved how embarrassed he got when she said stuff like that. "Uh huh." After patting his face, she headed for the door.

"Samantha?"

She turned back.

"You owe me twenty-six minutes in handcuffs, and I fully intend to collect."

Damn him! When all her attention and focus was needed to deal with the captain and whatever was waiting for her at home, all Sam could think about was being cuffed and at Nick's mercy for twenty-six minutes. Her whole body tingled with anticipation.

Turning to glare at him, she was rewarded with a shit-eating grin that told her he knew he had rattled her.

"You really are super sexy when you're all steamed up," he whispered, earning another furious glare. When he tried to hold hands with her, she tugged hers free and jammed it into her coat pocket where she encountered the cuffs and her bra. Her head pounded, and she began to believe it was possible for a head to actually blow off a neck. As they approached the waiting area, her stomach took a nasty dip that caused her to gasp with pain.

"What?" Nick asked, taking her arm to stop her.

"Stomach."

"Why don't we get someone to look at that while we're here?"

She tugged her arm free. "It's been checked."

"It needs to be checked again," he said, rubbing his hands up and down her arms.

"It's better." She stepped out of his embrace. "No PDA in front of the captain or anyone else."

"You're not giving me orders, remember?"

"Nick—"

"Sam."

With a growl of frustration, she marched into the waiting room several strides ahead of him.

Captain Malone put down the *Time* magazine he'd been flipping through and stood up. "Ready?"

"Yes, sir. Ah, this is Nick. Nick Cappuano." Gesturing to Nick without looking at him, she added, "Captain Malone."

While Sam's stomach grinded, the two men sized each other up as they shook hands and mumbled, "Nice to meet you."

"On behalf of the department," Malone said, "I apologize for your injuries and the damage to your home."

"Not your fault," Nick said. "However, I'd like to know what's being done to find the person who tried to kill Sam."

Sam stared at him, her mouth hanging open. Was *that* how he planned to stay out of it?

"Let's get you two out of here, and we'll talk about it on the way." He waved his hand and two uniformed officers appeared. "We've got press up the wazoo outside the E.R., so Officers Butler and O'Brien are going to get you out through the main door upstairs. I'll get my car and meet you there."

"Thank you, sir," Sam said. The moment the captain was out of earshot she pounced on Nick. "*That's* you staying out of it and being cool?"

"What? He knows we're sleeping together. Wouldn't I look like a jerk if I didn't even ask? Do you want him to think I'm a jerk? Wouldn't it be better for you if he likes me? If he can see why you'd risk so much to be with me right now?"

"Ugh!" She stalked after the uniforms, pretending not to hear him laughing behind her.

By the time they had parked in front of her father's Capitol Hill home, Nick was the captain's new best friend. They'd bonded over their shared concern for Sam's safety as well as their passion for the Redskins, politics and imported beer. If Sam hadn't already been on the verge of puking, she would be now for sure.

She suspected they were using the small talk to mask the underlying tension that surrounded them all as they contemplated what could have happened that morning and the staggering array of implications they were left to contend with. For that reason, and that reason only, she decided not to kill Nick for defying her.

Her stomach clutched when she saw the chief's car parked on Ninth Street. No doubt he and her father were in there concocting a plan to lock her up somewhere until she testified.

As they approached the house, Sam glanced at Captain Malone. "Um, sir, could you give us just a second?"

"Sure. I'll see you in there."

After he had gone inside, Nick turned to her. "I know what you're going to say, but I was just trying to make conversation—"

She went up on tiptoes to plant a kiss on him.

Startled, he said, "What was that for?"

"Just wanted to."

"Are you intentionally trying to keep me off balance?"

"It's not intentional, but if it's working…"

"I figured I was in for another tongue-lashing—and not the good kind."

She smiled. "I just wanted to tell you that my dad has some feeling in his right hand, so when I introduce you…"

She shrugged. "If you wanted to squeeze his hand, it'd mean something to him. And to me."

Nick put his arms around her, drew her in close and kissed the top of her head. "Thank you for telling me."

"He's going to be all wound up about the bomb and stuff, so he might not even notice you. Don't be offended by that."

"I won't."

"I hope you didn't use up all your charm on the captain," she said, rubbing her belly, "because my dad's the one who counts. You know that, right?"

"Of course I do. It's going to be fine, babe. Don't worry or your stomach will start up."

She eyed him with amusement. "Starting to see the pattern?"

"Yep. Let's get this over with before you work yourself into a full-blown episode."

"Might be too late," she muttered. Taking one last deep breath, she led him up the ramp to the front door and stepped into a room full of cops.

Celia pounced on her. *"Oh my God, Sam!"* Her tears dampened Sam's cheek. Stepping back to run her hands over Sam as if to take inventory, Celia said, "Are you all right?"

"I'm fine." She did a little spin. "See? Everything still attached and working."

Celia raised an eyebrow. "You lied to me last night when you said you were going to work."

Sam squirmed under her future stepmother's stern glare. "Um, yeah, I do that every now and then. Lie, that is. Is that going to be a problem for you?"

Celia cast an appreciative glance at Nick over Sam's shoulder and smiled. "If he's the reason, I guess I can forgive you. This one time."

Sam introduced her to Nick, and when she couldn't avoid it

for a second longer, she met her father's steely stare from across the room. She went over to him and bent to kiss his cheek. "I'm sorry you were worried."

"I went past worried about three hours ago, but we'll get to that. Who've you got with you?"

Knowing her father was already fully aware of who Nick was, Sam nodded to Nick anyway. "Dad, this is Nick Cappuano."

As instructed, Nick squeezed Skip's right hand. "Pleased to meet you, Deputy Chief Holland."

"Excellent sucking up. I'd say someone prepared you well to meet her old man."

"I wouldn't know what you mean, sir."

Skip's eyes danced with mirth. "That from this morning?" he asked, referring to the bandage over Nick's eye.

"Yeah, but I'll live."

Sam re-introduced Nick to Chief Farnsworth.

"Detective Higgins, ma'am," the other cop said to Sam. "Explosives."

"I've seen you around," Sam said, although she couldn't believe he was a detective. With his sandy hair cut into a flat top over a baby face, he barely looked old enough to be out of the academy. "What'd you find?"

"Two EDs on your car." For the benefit of Nick and Celia, he added, "Explosive devices—one on the ignition and a backup. Only one detonated. Both of them go, we're not having this conversation."

Sam swallowed hard and didn't object when Nick's hand landed on the small of her back.

"That's not all," Higgins said. "When we did a sweep of the other cars in the area, we found two more attached to a black BMW."

Nick and Sam gasped.

"Registered to you, Mr. Cappuano."

As if all her bones had turned to mush, Sam sank to the sofa. "Why?" she whispered. "Why would they target him?"

"We were just discussing that when you came in," Chief Farnsworth said. "If it's Johnson or their pals, the best theory I've heard yet is 'you take mine, I'll take yours.' Revenge, pure and simple. Johnson wanted you either dead or decimated. How would they've known his car?"

"I've been in it," Sam confessed. "Recently. And I've had the feeling someone was watching me a few times."

"Detective Cruz suggested a link to O'Connor rather than Johnson," Malone said. "Worth looking into, especially since they targeted Nick, too."

Farnsworth turned to Nick. "Do you know of anything Senator O'Connor was involved in that had ties to terrorists or terrorism?"

"He was on the Homeland Security Committee, working mostly on the immigration issue, but he was briefed on counterterrorism initiatives. We both were."

"I want to take apart that bill he was sponsoring, line by line," Sam said. "Maybe I've totally missed the boat on this. I've been thinking jilted lover, but they don't tend to plant bombs."

"No," Malone agreed. "They tend to dismember."

"Which is why I've focused most of my attention on his love life." Sam got up to pace. "We've uncovered a slew of recent ex-lovers, a few with complaints about some of his, um, fetishes." She sent a sympathetic glance to Nick since he was hearing this for the first time. "But maybe Cruz is right. Maybe the Lorena Bobbitt was intended to throw us off."

"He was *dismembered?*" Higgins squeaked, his baby face gone pale.

"A detail we've managed to keep out of the press," Farnsworth said with a pointed look at his detective.

"Yes, sir." Higgins got up to leave. "I need to get back to the lab where it's safe."

Sam rolled her eyes. "Run back to your cave, Higgins, and leave the dirty work to those of us in the field."

"You can have it. I'll send you details on the EDs when I have more, but I can tell you they were crude and you got lucky, Sergeant. Damned lucky."

"Yeah," Sam said. "I know." She saw him out and turned to find every man in the room focused on her.

No doubt sensing a battle royal in the making, Celia stepped into the kitchen.

"Before you all get going," Sam said, "I have something I want to say, and I want you to listen to me without interrupting."

When they agreed with their silence, she pushed her fist into her aching gut and took a second to look each of them in the eye—Dad, her hero and her rock; Chief Farnsworth, beloved friend and respected leader; Captain Malone, boss and mentor; and Nick, quickly becoming more important than anyone. All of them cared about her. She had no doubt about that, just as she had no doubt they'd go to any lengths to keep her safe.

"I'm sure you two have cooked up a plan to toss me into a safe house for the weekend," she said to her father and the chief, "but that's not going to happen." Before they could protest, she held up a hand to stop them. "I'm going to continue to work this case until I close it, and I'm not going to let punks or terrorists or whoever strapped an ED to my car and Nick's take me off the streets. The minute they think they have that kind of power over me, I'm done on this job and you know it."

Pausing, she made eye contact with each of them again. "I know you're worried, and I know you care. But if you care about me at all, don't ask me to be a coward. I won't deny that bomb scared the shit out of me." She let her gaze fall on Nick. "When I saw your face covered with blood, my heart almost stopped. So I'm going to get them. If for no other reason than they hurt you, and that's simply unacceptable to me."

Nick's hard expression softened into a smile that engaged his eyes and filled her heart with emotions she had never experienced quite so strongly before.

To Farnsworth, she said, "Let me do my job. I'll take every precaution I can. I'll run things from here, stay as close to home as I can, but I won't hide out. I dare any of you to tell me you wouldn't rather go down in the line than run scared from scum who think they can take us out like yesterday's garbage."

A full minute of silence ensued, during which she noticed Farnsworth and Malone watching her dad and understood they were going to take their cues from him.

"I'd like to see that immigration bill," Skip finally said. He glanced at Nick. "I'm a political junky in my spare time. I might catch something in there we can use."

"I'll get it for you." Nick checked his watch as he stood up. "My staff should be back from Richmond by now, so let me make a call. What format do you prefer?"

"A fax would work. We can pop it right into my reading device. I can see two pages at once that way." Skip rattled off the number and followed Nick into the kitchen.

"I'm going to go lean on the lab to speed things up with the boomer," Malone said as he pulled on his coat.

Sam was left alone with the chief. "I know what you're going to say."

"Do you?"

She squirmed under the heat of his stare. In a rush of words, she said, "I'm sorry I lied to you about Nick. But I was so afraid you'd take me off the case, and after Johnson I *needed* it. You know I did. I tried to fight what was happening between us, but he was just *there* for me, every step of the way and I, um... Why are you smiling?"

"In some ways, you're exactly the same as you were at twelve, you know that?" He took a step closer to her, the smile fading. "But if you ever, *ever* lie to me again, Sergeant, I'll have your badge. Are we clear?"

"Crystal," she said, swallowing hard. "Sir."

"Get O'Connor cleaned up—and fast. I don't want any more bad publicity for you or the department."

"Yes, sir."

He called out his good-byes to Skip and Celia before donning his coat.

"Chief? Thank you for understanding why I have to do this."

"I would've done the same thing myself. In fact, your dad predicted your little speech almost down to the last vowel. We were ready for you."

"Well, sheesh," she huffed. "Here I was thinking I'd handled you, and *I'm* the one being handled?"

"You gotta get up a lot earlier in the morning to get one past a couple of crusty old vets like us. Truth is, we would've been disappointed if you'd done it any other way. You're a chip off the old block, Holland."

"Thank you, sir. You couldn't pay me a higher compliment."

"I know." He glanced toward the kitchen. "You think about what it would do to him if something happens to you. It'd be the end of him. You think about that."

"Yes, sir," she whispered as she watched him go down the ramp.

CHAPTER 23

With Nick outside on the phone, Sam went into the kitchen where her dad was reading the bill.

She bent to kiss his cheek. "Thanks for the help. I hate feeling like I've totally missed the point on this one."

"Don't know for sure yet that you have. Just because it's taken a few twists and turns doesn't mean you aren't on the right path."

"That's true."

"Seems like a nice kid."

"Who? Higgins?"

"No," he said grinning. "Nick."

"Oh, right." She wasn't ready to go down *that* path with him just yet. "So, hey, I hear you've been keeping secrets."

"You're one to talk, and which secrets are you referring to?" Sam raised an eyebrow as she slipped into a kitchen chair.

"Oh. Celia."

"Uh huh," Sam said, delighted by the faint blush that appeared on his ruddy cheeks.

"Well, I was going to tell you."

"Except you were too chicken so you got her to tell me."

"Something like that."

Sam laughed. "I'm happy for you."

"Really? You are?" His relief was almost as comical as his embarrassment.

"Of course I am. She's terrific. What would we have done without her the last couple of years?"

MARIE FORCE

"No kidding. Thing I can't understand is why she'd want to shackle herself to this?" With his eyes, he took in his useless body, the chair, the whole situation.

"She loves you. I think it's that simple."

"She's not in it for the house or the pension, in case you wondered."

"I didn't."

"Sure you did, because I've trained you to be as cynical as I am."

"Well, maybe it crossed my mind for an instant, but listening to her talk about you…she's genuine."

"I think she is," he said, seeming incredulous. "In fact, she wants to sign something that says she gets nothing, you know, after…"

"Which says to me she should get it."

"See? That's what I think, too. It wouldn't bother you or your sisters if she got a cut?"

Sam stood up to rest her hands on his shoulders and brought her face down to his. "All I want is you, here with us, for as long as we can have you, for as long as you want to be here."

"You haven't forgotten, have you? About our deal?"

Sam thought of the prescription bottle she had stashed in a safety deposit box. "No."

"And you're still willing? If the time comes…"

Fighting back the sting of pain in her belly and her heart, she kept her voice steady when she said, "If the time comes."

He released a long deep breath. "Good. Okay. Let me get back to this. I'll report in if anything jumps out, Sergeant— or should I say Lieutenant?"

"Not quite yet." She kissed his forehead. "Thanks for the help."

"My pleasure."

And she could see that it was. He seemed more vital, more

alive in that moment than he had in a long time. She should've been bringing him into her cases on a more formal basis all along and vowed to do so going forward. His mind was as sharp as ever, and if using it gave him a reason to stay in the fight, then she'd use it and no doubt benefit from it.

Nick ended the call with Christina and stashed the cell phone he'd borrowed from Sam in his pocket. He rested against the porch rail and let his eyes wander up and down the quiet street. Some of the townhouses were painted in a variety of bright colors while others were fronted by brick or stone. The red brick sidewalks sloped and curved over tree roots. Black wrought-iron gates added a touch of class to the Capitol Hill neighborhood.

Was someone out there right now watching him? Hoping to get another shot at Sam? Or at him? The thought sent a chill chasing through him as he contemplated the sudden changes in his life. Last Saturday, he spent the morning in the office and then played in a pickup basketball game at the gym. He went out for a few beers with the guys he'd played with and went home alone.

Now, a week later, John was dead, he was in love with Samantha Holland and someone had tried to kill them both. Any doubt that he was in love with her had evaporated during the interminable trip through shattered glass to get to her after the bombing. He'd had just enough time to imagine a return to the empty existence his life had been without her to be certain he loved her.

Three doors down on Ninth Street, a metal "For Sale" sign caught his attention as it banged against a brick-front townhouse. The creepy sound reminded Nick of ghost towns and spaghetti Westerns. Another trickle of fear crept along his spine as he took a long look up and down the deserted street.

"What're you doing out here in the cold?" Sam asked as she joined him on the porch.

"Nothing much." He extended a hand to her. "Where's your coat?"

"I'll share yours." She slipped her arms around his waist and burrowed into his coat. "Mmm. Warm."

As Nick held her close, he wondered how he had survived, how he had lived without her for all the years since he first met her. He closed his eyes and rested his cheek on the top of her head.

"What are you thinking about?"

He couldn't tell her he loved her. Not now. Not in the midst of murder and chaos and not when she wasn't ready to hear it. Later, he decided. There'd be time. He would make sure of it. "That you showed a lot of spine before, letting them know you planned to stay on the case."

"Yeah, well, apparently they predicted that's what I'd say and had planned for it." She looked up at him. "I just cashed in every good judgment and sterling moral code chip I've earned in twelve years on the force to bring you into my life." With a coy smile, she added, "I hope you're going to be worth it."

Realizing the huge step she was taking, he framed her face with his hands and kissed her. "I will be. I promise."

"I was kidding."

"I wasn't."

She brought him down to her and sucked the breath out of his lungs with a passionate kiss.

"Sam," he gasped, burying his face in the elegant curve of her neck. "God."

"What? What is it?"

"When I think about what might've happened." He raised his head, met her sparkling blue eyes and was grateful. So very grateful. "I know this is all so new, but the thought of losing you...again...I don't want to lose you."

"You won't. Nothing's going to happen to me."

"They could take a shot at you right now. We're totally exposed standing out here."

She reached up to caress his face. "You can't do this. If you're going to be with me—"

"*If?*"

She smiled. "I get hurt every now and then. I have close calls—not like I did today—but stuff *happens*. You can't let fear rule you. That's no life for you—or me." She hesitated, as if there was something else she wanted to say.

"What?" He sensed her tension before he felt it. "Babe. What?"

"When I was married," she said haltingly, "Peter obsessed about my safety, my whereabouts, my cases. It wasn't healthy, and while it wasn't the only problem we had, it made a bad situation much worse. It was totally suffocating."

"I hear what you're saying, and I understand. I really do. I'll do my best to give you room to breathe, but you've got to give me some time to adjust, okay? I'm not used to the woman I care about being nearly blown up in my front yard. It's going to take me a while to get used to the dangers that go with your job."

"Fair enough."

He brushed his thumbs over the deep, dark circles under her eyes and pressed a gentle kiss to the lump on her forehead. "You're whipped. Do you think you could sleep for a bit?"

"I guess I could try, but my mind is racing. I want to get everyone here later when Freddie gets back to start all over again. We're missing something. I know we are."

"You won't be any good to anyone if you run yourself into the ground. How about a nap to recharge?"

She flashed that coy smile he'd come to love. "Only if you join me."

"*Here?* With your dad in the house?"

"He can't shoot you."

"That's not funny. He can have me killed. Easily."

"I was married, Nick. He knows I've had sex."

"Not with me."

"I'll bet he doesn't think we were baking cookies last night."

"That's what we were doing. If he asks, that's *exactly* what we were doing. Baking cookies—all night long."

Laughing, she took his hand to lead him inside. "We're going to crash for a bit," she said to Celia. "Freddie is due back later tonight. If we conk out big time, will you wake us up when he gets here?"

"I sure will, honey. Can I get you two something to eat?"

"I don't think I could eat yet," Sam said, running her hand over her belly.

"Me either," Nick said. "But thanks anyway." He glanced at the kitchen where Skip was still engrossed in the immigration bill. "If you could fail to mention to Chief Holland that I'm upstairs, too, that'd be cool. In fact, I'd pay you."

Celia chuckled and waved them up. "I'll see what I can do."

Feeling like a teenager sneaking into his girlfriend's room— a goal he'd never managed to achieve back then—Nick followed Sam up the stairs.

She closed the bedroom door and pulled off her sweater.

He winced at the ugly purple bruise on her chest. If he hadn't stopped breathing, he might've enjoyed watching her strip. "I agreed to a nap. I didn't agree to nudity."

"You want me to sleep, right?"

"Uh huh."

She wiggled out of her jeans and panties and came at him with intent in her eyes. "I sleep best in the nude."

He took a step back and encountered wall. "He's going to know. If a babe like you is my daughter, I've got her room bugged to make sure guys like me don't get in." Without allowing his eyes to leave her face, he said, "So he's going to know I'm up here with his daughter—his beautiful, sexy, *naked* daughter—and he'll call some of his cop buddies. They'll drag me into a dark alley to rip the limbs from my body one by one, and then toss what's left of me in the Potomac."

Laughing, Sam slipped her hands under his sweater and eased it up and over his head, catching him off guard when she nuzzled his nipple. That's all it took to make him rock hard.

"With an imagination like that, you should consider a career in fiction."

He kept his hands limp at his sides. Maybe if he didn't leave prints on her he'd walk away with his life.

"You really think you can resist me?" she asked, trailing kisses from his jaw to his collarbone as her breasts rubbed against his chest.

"My life depends on it."

Her lips glided over his chest to his belly. "All that tough talk from before…" She unbuttoned his jeans, pushed them down and sank to her knees in front of him. "I think I'm about to make you my lapdog."

Sensing where this was going, he tried to escape.

In a move that both startled and stirred him, she pinned him to the wall.

He groaned, his fingers rolling into fists as her hot mouth closed around him. "Sam…*please*. I thought you liked me."

"I do," she said, dragging her tongue in circles that made his head spin. "I really do."

A bead of sweat rolled between his shoulder blades, straight down his spine. "He'll *know*, and he'll kill me."

She managed to laugh as she sucked. Hard.

"Jesus." His breathing became labored, the heat of her mouth unbearable. "Sam, honey, come here."

"So you're willing to play now?"

"Yeah." He helped her up, lifted her and sank into her in one easy movement. "Hell, you only live once, right?"

She gasped from the impact.

"Okay?" he asked.

Her arms encircled him, and he bit back a moan when she made contact with the bump on the back of his head. "Yes," she sighed. "*So* okay."

If he had to suffocate, he decided, he wanted to do it between Samantha Holland's spectacular breasts, engulfed in her jasmine and vanilla scent. Dropping a gentle kiss on the bruise, he walked them—carefully, since his jeans were still twisted around his ankles—to the bed and lowered her.

"Nick."

"What, babe?"

"Fast." She clung to him. "I want it fast."

His heart staggered, and he had to bite his lip to keep from losing it right then and there. Knowing she could be noisy, he captured her mouth as he gave her what she wanted. Had *anything* ever been this good? No. Nothing. Ever. She was tough and courageous on the job, yet here with him she was all girl—warm, soft, fragrant girl. Her moan echoed through her and into him the instant before she lifted off.

He muffled her cries, or at least he hoped to God he did, before he pushed hard into her one last time and let himself go.

CHAPTER 24

Freddie sat in front of Patricia Donaldson's two-story home for a long time. He couldn't imagine asking her the questions he needed to ask but knew it was long past time he got over the queasiness that struck him whenever he had to ask people personal questions—especially about their sex lives.

Perhaps if he got a sex life of his own, then he wouldn't be so put off by asking about what other people did in their bedrooms. He'd been raised a Christian, had taken his religion seriously and had saved himself for marriage. That's how he ended up a twenty-nine-year-old virgin, a fact he had shared with no one, lest he be ridiculed by his colleagues.

He'd had plenty of girlfriends and had done his share of fooling around, but he'd yet to have the full experience. Lately, he'd been thinking too much about what he was missing. And with no marital prospects on the horizon, he wondered how much longer he could hold out.

Since they'd interviewed that personal trainer the other day, Elin Svendsen, he had fantasized about her obsessively. The way she hinted at the nasty stuff she had done with Senator O'Connor...What Freddie wouldn't give for one night with her. Maybe once they cleared the case, he'd be in the market for some personal training of a different sort.

In the meantime, he needed to go into that house and ask Patricia Donaldson if her son was John O'Connor's son, if she'd continued a sexual relationship with the senator and if so, what kind of sex she'd had with him. The thought of asking those questions of a woman he'd never met made him sick.

Even if he sat there all night, he'd never be fully prepared. And since Sam was waiting for him to get this information and get it back to her, Freddie emerged from the rental car and headed up the flagstone walkway. With one last deep breath to settle his nerves, he rang the bell. Chimes echoed through the house. He waited a full minute before a fragile-looking blonde opened the door. Her blue eyes were rimmed with red, her pretty face ravaged with exhaustion. If this woman hadn't recently lost someone she loved, Freddie would turn in his badge.

"Patricia Donaldson?"

"Yes?"

"I'm sorry to disturb you, ma'am. I'm Detective Freddie Cruz, Metro Police, Washington, D.C." He showed her his badge.

She took the badge from him, examined it and handed it back to him. "This is about John."

"Yes, ma'am. I wondered if I might have a few minutes of your time?"

With a weary gesture, she stepped aside to let him in.

Freddie followed her to a comfortable family room, noting the photos of the handsome blond boy scattered throughout the house. The place appeared to have been professionally decorated, but had retained a warm, cozy atmosphere.

When he was seated across from her, Freddie said, "You were acquainted with Senator John O'Connor?"

"We've been friends for many years," she said softly.

"I'm sorry for your loss."

Her raw eyes filled with tears. "Thank you." She brushed at the dampness on her cheeks.

"You were just friends?"

"Yes," she said without hesitation.

Freddie reached for a framed photo on an end table. "Your son?"

"Yes."

"Handsome boy."

"Thank you."

"I can't help but notice his striking resemblance to the senator."

She shrugged. "Maybe a little."

Freddie returned the photo to the table. "Is your son at home?"

"He went to do an errand at school. He's a junior at Loyola."

Relieved to know the boy wasn't in the house, Freddie pressed on. "In the course of our investigation, we've uncovered a series of regular monthly payments Senator O'Connor made to you for the last twenty years." Even though he knew the facts by heart, Freddie consulted his notebook. "Three thousand dollars, paid by check, on the first of every month."

Her hand trembled ever so slightly as she reached for the gold locket she wore on a chain around her neck. "So?"

"Can you tell me why he gave you the money?"

"It was a gift."

"That's a mighty big gift—thirty-six thousand dollars a year, totaling more than seven hundred thousand over twenty years."

"He was a generous man."

"Ms. Donaldson, I realize this is a very difficult time for you, but if you were his friend—"

"I was his best friend," she cried, her hand curling into a fist over her heart. "He was mine."

"If that's the case, I'm sure you want us to find the person who killed him."

"Of course I do. I just don't see what you need from me."

"I need you to confirm that your son Thomas is John O'Connor's son."

"Do you, Detective?" she asked softly. "Do you really need me to confirm it?"

Her easy capitulation flustered Freddie. He'd expected to have to work for it. "I'd appreciate if you could tell me about your relationship with the senator, from the day you met him through to his death."

She paused for a long moment, as if she were making a decision, and then began to talk so softly that Freddie had to strain to hear. "My family moved to Leesburg the summer before eighth grade. I met him on the first day of school. He was nice to me when no one else gave me the time of day, but that was John. It was just like him to make the new girl feel welcome." Lost in her memories, she seemed to have forgotten Freddie was there.

He took notes, knowing Sam would expect every detail.

"We became friends—unlikely friends."

"Why unlikely?"

"His father was a United States senator, a multi-millionaire businessman. Mine worked at the post office. We weren't exactly from the same universe, but John was the least status-conscious person I ever knew. He couldn't have cared less about his father's position, which of course drove his father crazy.

"Over time, our friendship grew and blossomed into love. His parents never liked me, never welcomed me into their home or their family. That made John sad, but it didn't keep us apart. He was the love of my life, Detective, and I was the love of his. We knew it at fifteen. Can you imagine?"

"No, ma'am." He couldn't imagine it at twenty-nine. "I can't."

"We were overwhelmed by what we felt for each other and determined to be together forever, no matter what it took."

She glanced down at her lap, her fingers twisting nervously. "I was sixteen when I got pregnant. My parents were devastated, but his were outraged. His father was in the midst of an ugly re-election campaign, and all they cared about was the potential scandal. They offered me a hundred thousand dollars to have an abortion."

Freddie kept his expression neutral.

"I refused to even consider it. I was under the illusion that John and I would find a way to be together, to raise our child together. I had no idea then how far people with power could and would go to get what they wanted. Within a week, my father was transferred to a post office in Illinois."

"What did John say about this?"

"What could he say? He was going into his senior year of high school. His parents still had him under their thumb."

"Did he see the baby?"

She nodded. "He and his parents came out for a day when Thomas was born. The senator pitched a holy fit when I named him Thomas John O'Connor, but they had taken John away from me—away from us—they weren't going to deny my son his father's name. I had my limits, too."

"What was your relationship with John like after the baby was born?"

"We talked on the phone as often as we could. We made plans to be together." Her hands trembled in her lap. "After he graduated from high school, his father got him an internship in Congress for the summer and then they shipped him off to Harvard. It was more than a year before we saw each other again."

"He was an adult by then. Why didn't he stand up to his parents?"

"They controlled the money, Detective, the money he was

using to support his son while he was in college. He did what he was told."

"And after college?"

"His father threatened to disown him if he married me, because if he did, people would find out about 'the kid' as Graham called him, and there'd be a scandal." Her voice had gone flat and lifeless. "As much as John loved me and Thomas, he wouldn't have been able to live with being disowned by his father." She leaned forward. "Don't get me wrong, Detective. I hate Graham O'Connor for what he denied me, what he denied Thomas and mostly what he denied John. But John loved his father, and more, he respected him despite everything he had done to us. John was a good man, the best man I've ever known, but he didn't have it in him to turn his back on his father. He just didn't. I accepted that a long time ago and learned to be satisfied with what I had."

"Which was what exactly?"

"We had one weekend a month to be a family, and we made the most of it. John was a wonderful father to Thomas. Between visits, he was completely available to him, and they talked most days. My son is devastated by his father's death."

"And no one ever questioned his resemblance to the senator in light of the fact that he had his name?"

"No," she said. "Amazingly, we got away with it. The O'Connors managed to thoroughly bury us here in the Midwest. During John's campaign and the first few months he was in office, we played it cool and didn't see much of each other. Once the attention faded, we were able to pick things up again. The media never caught so much as a whiff of us."

"I'm curious as to why he sent you monthly payments, rather than giving you a lump sum. His parents had money, and he became a wealthy man himself when he sold his company."

"He took good care of us, but he liked sending the monthly

payments. He said it made him feel connected to Thomas and to me."

"I apologize in advance for what I'm about to ask you…But I need to know where the senator slept when he was here."

Her eyes flashed with anger and embarrassment. "Where do you think he slept?"

"Was he involved with other women?" Freddie hated the pain his question obviously caused her.

"Yes," she said through gritted teeth. "But my son doesn't know that, and I'd prefer to keep it that way."

"It didn't bother you? That he was with other women?"

"Of course it bothered me, but I didn't expect him to be celibate the other twenty-seven days a month."

"Did you discuss the other women in his life?"

"We did not."

"Not even when he was with Natalie for three years?"

"He had his life, and I had mine," she snapped. "One weekend a month, we belonged to each other."

"Have you ever been married?"

She laughed. "Where do you think I would've stashed my husband on the third weekend of every month when my long-time lover came to visit?"

"So that's a no?"

"I've never been married."

"When he was here," Freddie said, trying not to stumble over the words, "you had sexual relations with him?"

"I don't see how that's relevant to the case."

"It's relevant, and I need you to answer the question."

"Yes, I had sex with him! As much and as often as I could! Are you satisfied?"

"Was there anything, um, unusual about the kind of sex you had with him?"

She stood up. "We're finished here. I won't allow you to

come into my home and debase the most important relationship in my life."

Freddie stayed seated to give her the perceived advantage as he dropped the final bomb. "Did he ever try to get you to have rough sex or anal sex with him?"

She stared at him, astounded. "I want you to leave. Right now."

"I'm sorry, ma'am, but you can answer the question here or I can take you back to Washington so you can answer it there. It's your call."

Her hands on her hips, her eyes shot daggers at him. "John O'Connor was never anything but a perfect gentleman with me. Every woman should have a lover as gentle and sweet. Now if there's nothing further, I want you to leave my home."

"Will you be attending the funeral in Washington?"

"Since there's no longer an O'Connor in office, I can't see any reason for my son and me to hide out anymore. We're planning to go. John's attorney called me today to tell me we need to be at the reading of the will the day after the funeral. I'm sure Graham and Laine are thrilled about that."

"Have they ever had any contact with Thomas?"

"Not since the day after he was born."

"The media will be all over you."

He admired the courageous lift of her chin. "John suffered over the fact that he couldn't acknowledge his son. The least I can do for him is rectify that now that he's gone."

"I'm sorry again for your loss, Ms. Donaldson, and I'm sorry to have upset you with my questions."

She shrugged off his apology. "If it helps the investigation, then I guess it will have been worth it."

"You've been a big help."

At the door, she said, "Detective? Get the person who did this to my John." Her eyes filled with new tears. "Please."

"We're doing everything we can."

CHAPTER 25

The Watergate lobby was mobbed, but when Nick walked in the mob went silent, parting to allow him passage to the elevator. He recognized some of the faces—his grandmother, his father, Mr. Pacheco from seventh grade science, Lucy Jenkins who'd lived next door and Graham O'Connor. Why was he here? With the vote this afternoon, John wouldn't have time for one of their regular lunches.

Nick tried to tell him John was busy, but Graham wouldn't listen. He just smiled, like he knew something Nick didn't know. Behind him, was that...Sam? Sam Holland? She hadn't returned his calls, but that was a long time ago. He'd always wanted to see her again. Reaching out, he tried to get to her.

She smiled and slipped away.

"No! Not again. Come back. Sam!"

John's sister Lizbeth cried and clawed at him, her face red and swollen. "John's hurt! Help him, Nick. Help him!"

Nick ran for the elevator, pushed the up button frantically, but the doors wouldn't open. Banging on the metal doors until his hands were bruised, he finally bolted for the stairs and ran up six flights. Gasping for air, he emerged into the hallway. A woman dashed from John's apartment carrying a bloody knife, her face covered by a knitted scarf.

"John!" Nick sprinted into the apartment.

"Hey, Cappy," John said, emerging from the bedroom, blood coursing from the open wound in his neck. "What's up?"

"John..." Nick pressed his hands against John's neck, trying to make it stop. How could he lose this much blood and stay conscious? "Help! Somebody help us!"

"It's okay, Cappy." John's hand landed on Nick's shoulder. "I'll be all right."

Nick looked up to find John's face morphing into a smiling skeleton. He screamed.

"Nick," Sam said. "Wake up. Babe, wake up."

His head ached, his mouth was dry, his eyes gritty. "What?"

Sam brushed the hair off his forehead and kissed his cheek. "You were dreaming."

Nick rested a hand over his racing heart. "John was there. He was still alive. There was so much blood. I tried to make it stop." His throat tightening, he closed his eyes. "I couldn't stop it."

She held him close, running her fingers through his hair. "You couldn't have stopped it," she whispered.

"The stuff I've found out about him…since it happened… None of it matters. He was my friend."

"Yes." She pressed her lips to his forehead. "That'll never change."

"He was the closest thing to a brother I've ever had. We had this…language. It was all ours. The staff used to shake their heads when we'd get going. They had no idea what we were talking about. But we did. We always did."

Sam tightened her hold on him.

"I miss him," he whispered. "I really miss him. I just can't believe I'm never going to see him again."

"I'm sorry. I wish there was something I could say."

"You're helping." He raised his head, met her eyes.

She leaned in to kiss him. "I want to get the person who did this for his parents and his family. But mostly I want it for you."

"I'm apt to be a bit of a mess for a while."

"That's all right."

He rested his hand over the hideous bruise on her chest. "This is a hell of a time for us to be starting something. You know that, don't you?"

"Worst possible time."

"So it stands to reason we'll be able to deal with just about anything if we can get through this."

"I guess we'll find out." She smiled and caressed his face. "I need to get back to work."

"I know. Did you sleep?"

"Big time. I didn't think I would."

"You needed it. We both did." He leaned in to kiss her once more. "Are you or your dad going to mind that I plan to stay here with you until this is over?"

"No. I like having you here, and he doesn't really care, despite the grief he might give you."

"I need to go home at some point to get some clothes and make sure the condo association took care of getting the windows fixed."

"We can arrange that." She sat up and stretched. "I'm going to grab a shower. Care to join me?"

"I'd love to, but I'm not going to push my luck. I'll go after you."

"Wimp."

"Yep."

She laughed as she slipped into a robe, and the sound warmed him. He was surprised to realize she had made him feel better, even as the sickening images from the dream lingered. After Sam went into the bathroom, he sat up, gripping his pounding head. The concussion they'd called minor was making a major statement, and whatever they'd used to numb the cut over his eye had worn off, leaving a dull, throbbing ache.

He felt kind of foolish about unloading on Sam, but she

hadn't seemed to mind. Having someone to share the ups and downs with was something he could get used to—as long as that someone was her.

He stood up and groaned when his injured foot protested. Reaching for his jeans, he pulled them on and took a good look around the messy room. Sam had a way of exploding into a space, which was in direct conflict with his need for order. Beginning with the clothes piled on the floor, he went to work on the clutter. By the time she emerged from the bathroom fifteen minutes later, the place was almost livable.

Her eyes all but popped out of her skull. "It's like you can't help yourself!"

"Just straightening up. No biggie."

"I won't be able to find anything!"

"You couldn't find anything before."

"I knew *exactly* where everything was."

"No way," he scoffed. "You're a slob, Samantha." He bunched the towel she had wrapped around her into his fist and tugged her close enough to kiss. "A sexy, gorgeous slob, but a slob nonetheless."

Pouting, she tried to break free of him. "Just because I'm not an anal retentive freakazoid, doesn't mean I'm a slob."

"Freakazoid? I'm hurt." With another hard kiss he released her so she could get dressed. "This is going to be a problem when we live together."

"*Live* together?" she sputtered, choking on the words. "Where the hell did *that* come from?"

"You don't have to act like the idea is totally repulsive."

She shoved her long legs into jeans. "We haven't even been together a week, Nick. I mean...come on."

Not wanting her to see that she'd hurt him by being so dismissive, he turned away from her to look out the window. He churned with things he'd like to say to her, arguments and persuasions she was clearly not ready to hear. As he stared out into the darkness, a shadow across the street caught his eye. Zeroing in for a closer look, he realized someone was watching the house. He ignored the screaming pain in his foot and the pounding in his head when he bolted for the door and flew down the stairs.

Sam called out to him.

Blasting through the front door and down the ramp, he was almost hit by a car as he ran into the street. The blare of the car's horn startled him, taking his attention off the shadow for just an instant, but that was all it took.

"Watch out, asshole!" the driver yelled out the car window.

By the time Nick recovered his bearings the shadow was long gone.

"*Shit!* Son of a bitch!"

"What're you doing?" Sam screamed from the porch.

"Someone was there," he said, his breath coming out in white puffs in the cold air. "I saw him. Watching the house."

"So you just run out half-cocked, not to mention half-dressed?"

"What else was I supposed to do?"

She had her hands on her hips in a gesture he recognized by now as her seriously pissed stance. "Um, I don't know. Maybe tell the *cop* who was in the room with you?"

He limped back to the ramp and started up to where she waited for him. "I didn't think of it. All I thought about was getting him."

"And what were you going to do with him once you got him?"

Squirming under the heat of her blue-eyed glare, he shrugged. "I would've figured something out."

"That's *exactly* how civilians get themselves killed by the hundreds every year, thinking they can take the law into their own hands."

"I don't need you to lecture me or to keep using the word *civilian* like it's some kind of vermin."

"Vermin's got to be smarter than you just were."

"I almost had him."

"You almost got flattened by a car!"

Fuming, they stood there spitting nails at each other.

"Um, 'scuse me, but, ah, I'm back," Freddie said from the sidewalk. "You said I should come here and, um…"

"Come up," Sam said, never taking her eyes off Nick. "Go in. I'll be right there."

"Gotcha, boss," Freddie said with a sympathetic smile for Nick as he went by them. "Good to see you again, Mr. Cappuano."

"Likewise," Nick said, still focused on Sam. "And you can call me Nick."

"You should've told me what you saw," Sam said after the door closed behind Freddie. "If you had, I could've called it in, and maybe we would've nabbed him. Instead, you go off on a Rambo mission that yielded squat."

Nick contemplated that. "You might have a point."

"I *might?* Really? Wow, thanks."

"I'm sorry, all right?" He ran a hand through his hair in frustration. "I just reacted. So shoot me for wanting to get whoever is stalking you."

"How do you know they're not stalking *you?*"

"Because I'm a whole lot more boring than you are."

"You're not boring. Stupid occasionally, but never boring."

"Thank you. I think."

"Did you get a good look at him?"

He shook his head. "Nothing but a shadow, but that shadow was definitely watching this house."

"If you see him again, *tell me*." She pinched his chest hair and tugged just hard enough to raise him to his tiptoes and bring tears to his eyes. "Don't you *dare* risk yourself like that again. You got me?"

"I got it," he said through gritted teeth. After she released him, he rubbed a hand over his chest. "I only let you get away with that shit because I was taught it's bad manners to flatten a woman, even if she deserves it."

"Whatever," she retorted on her way back into the house where Skip, Celia and Freddie waited for them.

Skip's sharp eyes skirted over Nick's bare chest and feet.

"Um, I'm going to go find a shirt," Nick said, starting up the stairs.

"Might not be a bad idea," Skip said.

"Leave him alone, Dad," Sam said. "He's already convinced you're going to have him killed."

"Also not a bad idea. Why didn't I think of it?"

"*Dad...*"

"Relax and let me have some fun with the boy, will you? I so rarely get to have any fun these days."

Freddie smirked.

"What're you smiling at, Cruz?"

The smile faded. "Not a thing, ma'am. Not one thing."

"I assume you're not just here to bum another meal. What've you got for me?"

"Some of the others are heading over from HQ to help out," he said. "Want me to wait and brief everyone at the same time?"

"Give me the highlights."

By the time he had run through it, she had paced a path in the living room rug.

"I was thinking on the plane ride home," Freddie said, "that the other women he dated were like substitutes for the one he couldn't have. All of them resemble her in basic features, and I'm no shrink, but maybe he turned on the kink with them because he was frustrated he couldn't be with the one he wanted."

"That's probably why he freaked when Natalie pressured him about getting married. In his own twisted way, he felt like he was already married, even if he was unfaithful to her. I mean, how does he marry someone else when she's off raising his kid in Siberia?"

Nick came down the stairs, his hair wet from the shower.

"You heard all that?" Sam asked, alarmed by his pale face and flat eyes.

"Enough to get the gist."

"I'm sorry," she said, surprised when he shook off her sympathy.

"Don't protect me. Do your job. Find out who did it."

"Okay," she said, understanding that he was absorbing the blow the best way he knew how. Turning back to Freddie, she was interrupted when the front door swung open. In flooded most of the HQ detectives, carrying platters of food, six packs of beer and soda, and armloads of chips. Each of them paused to squeeze Skip's hand on their way into the kitchen to deposit the food.

"What the hell is this?" she asked Gonzo.

"They take a stab at you, they take one at all of us," he said, his chocolate brown eyes fierce. "Everyone's on their own time. Give us something to do."

Touched and on the verge of choking up, she said, "Thank you."

"They posted the LT list today. Congratulations."

"You'll be there soon enough," she said with a twinge of guilt over how she'd gotten there. Gonzo made detective a couple of years after her, so at least she hadn't snagged a spot from him. "For sure."

He shrugged. "We'll see."

"There was someone out there." She gestured to the door. "Nick saw him watching the house. He went vigilante on me and scared the guy off."

"I'll call it in and get someone posted outside."

"If it was just me, I wouldn't want it. But my dad's here and Celia…"

"Say no more. We're on it." He glanced over at Nick. "So. You and the witness, huh?"

She winced. "Don't."

Gonzo's handsome face lit up with amusement. "I won't, but others will. You have to know that."

"Hopefully, the gossip mill will run its course and the story will die a natural death when someone else fucks up."

"Not before you take some serious abuse."

"I can handle it."

"Sam?" Nick said. "Why don't you come have something to eat?"

"He likes to feed me," she whispered to Gonzo.

"Nothing wrong with that."

Thirty minutes later, after everyone had eaten, Sam called them into the living room. "Let's get back to work."

"Before we do that," Freddie raised his Coke bottle in salute to Sam, "a toast to my partner, soon-to-be *Lieutenant* Holland."

As Sam glared at him and plotted his slow, painful death, the room erupted into applause and whistles. She glanced at her father and found him watching her, his eyes bright with emotion.

He nodded with approval and pleasure—more pleasure than she'd seen on his face in two years.

"All right," she said, putting a stop to the merriment before they forgot they were there to work on a homicide. "Thanks for the food, the toast and the help. I appreciate it. Before we go any further, I need to ask if you all mind that Nick is here. He's been very helpful to us on the investigation—"

"He's been critical," Freddie said.

Sam sent him a grateful smile. "Still, if anyone's uncomfortable…"

"No problem for me," Gonzo said.

The others mumbled their agreement.

Sam released a breath she hadn't realized she'd been holding and turned to Freddie. "In that case, Cruz, let's hear what you found out in Chicago."

"You got it, boss."

CHAPTER 26

"I also dug into the girlfriends like you asked me to," Freddie said, consulting his notebook. "Tara Davenport has no tattoos or unusual piercings. The people she says she was with on the night of the murder confirm her story, and security tapes show her arriving home at 10:18 and leaving again at 9:33 the next morning. Elin Svendsen's date, Jimmy Chen, a major muscle head, confirmed they had dinner and went to a dance club for a couple of hours. He dropped her off at her apartment just after two in the morning. The building has minimal security and no video, so I couldn't confirm that she stayed in for the rest of the night. She has a tattoo on her left breast—a heart with a Cupid's arrow—and both nipples are pierced."

"I don't even want to *know* how you found that out," Sam said, drawing chuckles from the other detectives.

"Not the way I would've preferred, that's for sure."

"Go, Cruz!" Detective Arnold said with a bark of laughter.

"Aw, our little boy's growing up," Gonzo said, dabbing at a pretend tear.

"Up yours, Gonzo."

In deference to her partner, Sam stifled the urge to laugh. "Is that it?"

"You didn't tell me to," Freddie continued, "but I dug a little deeper on Natalie Jordan. St. Clair was her maiden name, and I got a hit on that. Apparently our girl Natalie lost her college boyfriend in a suspicious fire in Maui about fifteen years ago."

"You don't say." Blood zipped through Sam's veins as pieces began to fall into place. Whether they were the right pieces, she'd soon find out.

"She and the senator had been broken up for years when he was killed," Skip said. "Hardly the same thing."

"True," Sam said. "Give us the details on the fire, Cruz."

"Brad Foster, age twenty-one, killed in a suspicious house fire while on a two-week vacation in Maui with Natalie St. Clair."

"Two weeks in Maui for a couple of college kids?" Gonzo asked with a low whistle.

"Apparently, Foster's family was loaded. His parents owned the beach house. Anyway, from the reports I found in the newspaper, Natalie went out for a morning walk and while she was gone the house went up. Police suspected arson but couldn't prove it. Her alibi for the time of the fire was flimsy. They looked really closely at her but never charged her with anything."

"Good work, Cruz," Sam said. "We'll have another chat with Mrs. Jordan tomorrow."

"I should also add that I found no unsolved dismemberment cases in the District, Virginia or Maryland," Freddie said. "I can widen the search if you think it's worth it."

"Hold off on that for now. Gonzo, what do you have from the search of O'Connor's cabin?"

"Nothing other than some additional references to the kid, Thomas—cards, letters, artwork from when he was younger—but you've already got that."

"What about the immigration bill, Dad?"

Skip took them through the finer points of the proposed law. "There's a lot of passion on both sides of this issue. There are those who feel that keeping our borders open to people in need is what this country is all about—'give me your tired, your poor, your huddled masses..."' When he was greeted with blank stares, he added, "Emma Lazarus? The poem engraved on the Statue of Liberty? Did you people go to school?" Rolling his eyes, he continued. "The other side argues that immigrants are a drain on the system, that charity should begin at home and we can't take care of the people who are already here."

"Would killing the senator kill the bill, too?" Sam asked Nick.

"That's exactly what it did. We had it sewn up by one vote. The Senate's in recess until January. Depending on who they get to take John's seat and whether he or she supports the bill, we might get lucky and get it back to the floor for a vote sometime next year. But either way, the supporters will have to start all over to make sure they have the votes. Even a month is a long time in politics—plenty of time for people to change their minds."

"So if someone was out to stop it altogether, killing him would accomplish that," Sam said.

"It'll certainly delay it indefinitely. Getting a bill through committee and on to the floor for a vote is no simple process. It took more than a year of writing, rewriting, compromising, meetings with various lobbies and interest groups, more compromise. Not simple."

Listening to him, Sam had a whole new appreciation for how John's death had affected Nick's professional life. The failure to pass the immigration bill had to be a bitter defeat on top of the personal tragedy. "In that case, his murder seems too well timed to be coincidental."

"Someone couldn't bear to see him get this win, you mean," Freddie said.

"Which takes us right back to his brother Terry," Sam said.

Nick shook his head.

"Speak," Sam said.

"I've said this before—Terry doesn't have the balls to kill his brother. He's an overgrown boy trying to live in a man's world. This would take planning and foresight. Terry's idea of making a plan is deciding which bar to hit on a given night."

"Still," Sam said, "he had motive, opportunity, a key and can't produce his alibi. I want to bring him in tomorrow morning for a formal interview."

"Can't that wait until after the funeral?" Nick asked, beseeching her with those hazel eyes of his.

"No. I'm sorry. I wish I could spare the O'Connors any more grief, but the minute they lied to me about Thomas, they lost the right to that courtesy. In fact, I could charge them with obstruction of justice."

"But you won't," Nick said stiffly.

"I haven't decided yet."

"I noticed Terry never completed the court-ordered safe driving school after his DUI," Freddie said.

Sam smiled as she turned to Gonzo and Arnold. "Will you pick up Terry O'Connor in the morning? While he's our guest, we'll have another chat with him about his alibi. Coordinate with Loudoun County."

"Can do," Arnold said.

"You're barking up the wrong tree," Nick said, frustration all but rippling from him.

"So noted." To the others, she said, "What've we got on the bombing?"

Higgins gave them an in-depth analysis of the four crude, homemade bombs they'd found attached to Sam's car and Nick's. "We got a partial print off one of the EDs on Mr. Cappuano's car, and we're running it through AFIS now," he said, referring to the Automated Fingerprint Identification System.

"We've worked our way through the Johnson family and

the majority of their known associates," Detective Jeannie Mc-
Bride said. "For the most part, they were hardly sympathetic
to hear you'd nearly gotten blown up but were adamant that
they had nothing to do with it." With a chagrinned expression, she added, "A few said they wished they'd thought of it."

"Nice," Nick muttered.

"We didn't pick up any vibe that an actual order had come
from either of the Johnsons," McBride said.

"And it would have," Sam said. "After six months undercover with them, I can tell you nothing happens without one
of them ordering it."

"Agreed," McBride said.

Sam ran her fingers through her hair, which she had left
down the way Nick liked it. "I've got a bunch of shit running
around in my head, so I want to go through it from the top
if no one minds."

When the others nodded in agreement, she began with
Nick finding the senator's body in his apartment. "He's murdered on the eve of a vote that would elevate his standing in
the Senate by passing legislation on a hot-button issue. The
murder itself, at least on the surface, is personal, with all the
trimmings of a love affair gone wrong. However, as Detective Cruz correctly pointed out, the dismemberment could've
been intended to throw us off, to send us down the personal
road. Keep in mind there was no forced entry and no sign of a
struggle, leading us to believe the killer was someone he knew,
someone he was comfortable with and not surprised to see."

"And someone who had one of the many keys he'd given
out," Freddie interjected.

"Yes. We've interviewed three of his past lovers, discovered he had a few fetishes, and uncovered a son his family
kept hidden from the public for twenty years. The mother of
that child appears, for all intents and purposes, to have been

the love of his life and, for some reason, the only one who didn't experience his wilder side. It would stand to reason that his often-cavalier treatment of other women and his fixation with Internet porn stem directly from the stymieing of the most important sexual relationship in his life. That it wasn't allowed to flourish or take its natural course, set him up for all kinds of psychological issues that he worked hard to keep hidden from even the people closest to him." She glanced at Nick and found him staring at the wall, his face impassive.

"The senator's relationship with his parents, his father in particular, was complicated by the teenage pregnancy and the resulting child. When John reached adulthood, his father threatened to disown him if he married Patricia Donaldson or acknowledged his son. If Ms. Donaldson is to be believed, protecting his political career and reputation was more important to Graham O'Connor than his own grandchild." She looked to Freddie for confirmation. With his nod, she continued. "On the same night he discovered the senator's body, Mr. Cappuano reported an intruder in his house, which the Arlington police investigated. Toss in Destiny Johnson's threats in yesterday's paper and the bombing today. Is that everything?" She looked to Freddie. "Am I forgetting anything?"

"Stenhouse."

"Right—the O'Connors's bitter political rival. His motive would be derailing the bill and deflecting the accompanying glory that would have fallen on John, the son of a man he told us he hated."

"But he would've had no way into O'Connor's apartment," Freddie said. "Or at least he wouldn't have had a key."

"Which keeps him at the bottom of the list, but still a person of interest," Sam said. "A man in his position could probably get a key if he wanted one badly enough. So how's it all related? How's our dead senator related to a break-in at his chief of staff's house? If we've ruled out Johnson, how's it related to a bombing at the same location?"

"Maybe it isn't," Skip said.

All eyes turned to him.

Sam's brows knitted with confusion. "What do you mean, Dad?"

"Goes back to timing. What else has happened this week?" Before Sam could reply, he said, "In the course of the investigation, you've rekindled an old flame." He glanced at Nick. "Who might be put out by that?"

"We're both single, so other than my superiors, I can't think of anyone," she said, wondering where he was going with this.

"Are you sure?"

And then, all at once, she knew exactly what he was talking about—or rather *whom*. "Peter," she gasped. "Oh my God." Curling her fist into her stomach, she had to sit when her legs would have buckled under her.

The room fell silent. Her rancorous divorce, complete with restraining orders and accusations of mental cruelty and emotional abuse, was hardly a secret to any of them.

Nick sat next to her, and Sam didn't object when his arm slid around her shoulders.

"He was outside the house," she whispered. "That was him before. He was watching us that night after we had pizza. I felt *something*, but I blew it off, chalked it up to nerves. I'll bet he was in your house, too."

"What would he want there?"

"First rule of combat," she said softly. "Know your enemy."

Nick turned to Skip. "What do we do?"

Skip shifted his furious eyes to Gonzo. "Call Malone. Report in, and then pick up Gibson."

"Yes, sir." Gonzo signaled to Arnold, his partner, and they left.

"I'm going with you," Freddie said, following them.

Sam got up and grabbed her coat off a hook by the door. "I just need some, ah, air." She rushed through the front door.

Nick was right behind her.

She struggled against his efforts to embrace her. "Just leave me alone, will you?"

"The hell I will." He pulled her in close and tightened his arms around her. "Don't push me away, Samantha."

"*He was watching us!* He was in your house! Because of *me!*"

"It's not your fault. Don't take it on."

"*How can I not?* He's obsessed." Another thought occurred to her all of a sudden.

"What?"

"The EDs," she whispered, the ramifications so huge, so monstrous it was almost too much to process.

"You don't think..."

She looked up at him. "That he'd rather kill me than see me with you? Yeah, I do, and if he couldn't take me out, getting rid of you would be the next best thing."

"Jesus."

"I told him everything about you after that night we spent together. When you didn't call, I told him about the connection we'd had, how I'd never had that before with anyone else. I thought he was my friend." She took a deep, rattling breath to stave off the pain circling in her gut. "He'd remember that. He'd know you were important, a real threat. The first real threat since he and I broke up."

"He'd be jealous enough to want to kill us both?"

"Destiny Johnson handed him the perfect opportunity with her tirade in the paper yesterday," Sam said as the whole thing clicked into focus with such startling clarity she wondered how she could've missed it. "If it had worked, the cops would naturally blame her or her friends. No one would've thought to look at him. It was so easy. He wouldn't have been able to resist." The pain gnawed at her insides, making her sick and weak.

"Would he know *how* to build a bomb?"

"You can get how-to instructions for just about anything on the Internet these days." She winced at the claws stabbing her gut. "Higgins said the EDs were crude. I guess we were lucky Peter screwed it up."

"You're in pain."

"Just need to breathe," she panted.

He loosened his hold on her. "What can I do? You're scaring me, Sam."

Clutching her midsection, she looked up at him. "I've dragged you into a nightmare."

"I'm exactly where I want to be—where I've wanted to be since the night I met you. And if I get my hands on that ex-husband of yours before you do, I'll be sure to let him know that he might've sent us on a long detour but we found our way back to each other." He kissed her, gently at first and then with more passion when she responded in kind. "Despite him, we found our way back, and nothing's going to get in our way this time. Nothing and no one."

"Especially not a couple of bombs," she said with a weak smile.

"That's right." He returned her smile. "How's the belly?"

"Better," she said, surprised to realize it was true.

"We're going to do something about that. As soon as this case is closed, you're going to see my doctor friend Harry."

"You and what army will be taking me?"

"You'll find out if you don't go on your own."

Her heart hammered in her chest as she studied him. "There're things...about me...that I need to tell you, stuff you should know before you decide anything."

Cradling her face in his hands, he looked down at her with

his heart in his eyes. "There's nothing you could tell me that would make me not want to be with you. Nothing."

"You don't know that—"

His mouth came down hard on hers, stealing the words, the thoughts, the air and every ounce of reason. When he had kissed her into submission, he said, "I do know that."

"But—"

"I love you, Samantha. I've loved you from the first instant I ever saw you across a crowded deck at that party and for all the years since. Having you back in my life is the single best thing that's ever happened to me. So there's nothing, nothing at all, you could tell me that would change my mind about you or what I want from you."

Sam rarely found herself speechless, but as she looked up at his beautiful, earnest face—the face she had dreamed about during her miserable marriage—she simply couldn't find the words.

Without breaking the intense eye contact between them, he brushed his lips over hers in a kiss so sweet and undemanding that her knees went weak.

"Later," he said. "We'll have all the time in the world. I promise."

CHAPTER 27

They borrowed Celia's car to go to Arlington. After an upsetting day, the neighborhood had returned to tranquility, and the media had thankfully moved on to the next story. At Nick's house, the windows had been repaired, but broken glass crunched under their feet in the foyer and upstairs in his bedroom. "I'll still be cleaning up glass a year from now," he joked, attempting to make light of it since he could feel the distress radiating from her.

"I'm sorry."

"Don't go there, Samantha." He threw jeans, sweaters, underwear, T-shirts and socks into a large duffel bag. With the funeral scheduled for Monday, he packed a dark suit, dress shirt and tie into a garment bag and tossed a pair of wingtips into the duffel. In the bathroom, he grabbed what he needed as fast he could, not wanting her to be there any longer than necessary after what happened earlier.

He'd told her he loved her. Just blurted it out because he thought she needed to hear it right then. He told himself it didn't matter that she hadn't said it back. She would. Eventually. But what if she didn't? What if she'd been swept up by the craziness of the investigation, and he'd read her all wrong? No. That wasn't possible. Couldn't be possible.

"Nick?"

"What, babe?"

"You just went all still. What're you thinking about?"

He cleared the emotion and fear from his throat. "I'm wondering if they found Peter."

"They'll call me. They know he's mine once they bring him in."

"You're going to confront him?"

"I'm going to nail him."

"Why don't you let someone else do it? Why does it have to be you?"

"Because it does."

"That's it?"

She shrugged. "Yeah."

"What if I ask you not to?"

"Don't."

"Would it matter? If I did ask?"

"It would matter. And I'd take that in with me, and it'd throw me off. I want to be at one hundred percent when I confront that miserable excuse for a human being. So don't send me in there dragging baggage. Don't do that to me."

"Is that what I am? Baggage?"

"What the hell happened between my house and here?"

He zipped the duffel. "Nothing. Not a goddamned thing."

She grabbed his arm and spun him around to face her. "Are you mad that I didn't say it back?"

"What're you talking about?" he asked, his heart aching.

"You know." Her tone softened as she raised her hands to his face. "Everything is so insane—the investigation, my psychopathic ex-husband, your loss and your job situation, my stomach…even the freaking holidays are bearing down on me. After what I went through with Peter, I'm different than I used to be. I'm more cautious. I haven't been cautious with you, though, and that scares me." She laughed. "It terrifies me, actually."

"You have nothing to fear from me."

"I know that, but I've screwed up so badly in the past. I need time, when I don't have fifty other things on my mind, to think and to process everything that's happened this week. I can't do that right now. But if it helps at all, I can tell you I'm moving in the same direction you are."

"It does help to know that." He reached for her hands and brought them to his lips. "Will you promise me one thing?"

"If I can."

"Will you spend Christmas Eve with me here? No matter what happens in the next few days, will you save that one night for me?"

"We usually go to my sister's…"

"We can do whatever you want on Christmas Day."

"All right."

"Promise?"

"I promise." She went up on tiptoes to kiss him. "I can't believe Christmas is Wednesday, and I haven't bought a thing for anyone. What about you?"

"Not too many people on my list. I usually get something for Christina, the O'Connors, my dad's twins, John…"

"I'm sorry. I wasn't thinking. About your family situation."

"Don't sweat it." He shut off the light in the bedroom and led her downstairs.

She stood in the living room with her hands jammed into her coat pockets. "What you said earlier, about us living together?"

"Too much, too soon. I get it."

"What I was going to say is if, you know, we get to that, I couldn't live here. It's too far from the city and my dad."

"Okay."

"That simple?"

"It's just a house."

She studied him. "When are you going to turn into a jerk?"

"Any minute now. I've been meaning to get to that."

Her cell phone rang, and she pulled it from her pocket. "It's Freddie." She put it on speaker so Nick could hear. "What've you got?"

"No sign of him at his place, but we found wires, plastic and fertilizer sitting right out on the table. Gonzo requested a warrant for a full search, and we're just waiting on that now."

She sat down. "I was hoping it wasn't him. I was really hoping…"

"I'm sorry. We've issued an APB. Every cop in the city is looking for him. We'll get him, Sam."

"Thanks. Go on home. Get some sleep. Meet me at HQ at eight. We'll put in a half day."

"I'll be there. Are you okay?"

"Overall, I've had better days, but I'm okay. See you in the morning."

Nick dropped the duffel and suit bag by the front door and joined her on the sofa.

"I was so hoping he was just stalking me and we wouldn't be able to pin the EDs on him. I didn't want it to be him."

Nick put his arm around her and brought her in to rest against him. "I know, babe."

"The papers tomorrow will be all about me—the bomb, my relationship with you, my psycho ex-husband. They'll rehash Johnson, run through my dad's unsolved case." She scrubbed at her face. "I hate when the story is about me. It's been about me too often lately."

"You're so tired," he said, kissing her brow. "Do you want to sleep here tonight?"

"I'd rather stay close to home until we get Peter. He knows my dad is an Achilles heel of mine."

Standing, Nick held out a hand to help her up.

She surprised him when she wrapped her arms around him. "Can we just do this for a minute?"

He kissed the bruised bump on her forehead. "For as long as you want."

They were interrupted several minutes later by a knock on the door.

"Wonder who's here at this hour." Nick swung the door open and was startled to find Natalie Jordan on his doorstep. "Natalie? What're you doing here?" He wouldn't have thought she even knew where he lived.

Her eyes rimmed with red, she said, "May I come in for a minute?"

Nick glanced back at Sam, who nodded. He showed Natalie into the living room.

"I was hoping you'd be here," Natalie said to Sam. Her face was splotchy, as if she'd been crying for hours.

"What can I do for you?" Sam asked.

To Nick, Natalie said, "Would it be possible to get a glass of water?"

Nick made eye contact with Sam. "Sure." When he returned with the water, Natalie had taken a seat on the sofa and was focused on her hands in her lap.

Sam looked at him and shrugged.

"Here you go," Nick said, handing Natalie the glass of water.

"Thank you."

"It's really late, Natalie," Nick said. "Why don't you tell us why you're here?"

"It's so unreal," she said softly. "I still can't believe it..."

"Mrs. Jordan, we can't help you if we don't know what you're talking about," Sam said.

Looking up at them with shattered eyes, Natalie said, "Noel. I think he..."

"What did Noel do?" Nick asked, his heart beating harder all of a sudden. He wanted to take Natalie by the shoulders and shake it out of her. "What did he do?"

"He might've killed John."

"Why do you say that?" Sam asked.

Nick noticed that she'd slipped into her cop mode, all signs of her earlier dismay over Peter gone.

"He's been acting funny, leaving at odd hours, long silences. He seems very angry, but he won't tell me why."

"When I talked to you earlier in the investigation, you didn't mention any of this."

"I hadn't put two and two together yet."

"Tell me what you think you've put together."

"That night," Natalie said haltingly, "the night John was killed, we went to bed together, but I woke up in the middle of the night and he was gone."

"You never mentioned that before."

"He's my husband, Detective." Natalie's eyes flooded with new tears. "I couldn't believe it was even possible. I didn't want to believe it's possible."

"So what changed?" Nick asked. "Why did you come here?"

"You were John's friend," Natalie said to Nick. "I thought you'd want to help find the person who did this to him."

"Of course I do! But I want the truth!"

"So do I! I loved him! You know I did. Noel was jealous of him. I couldn't even mention John's name without setting him off."

"What do you think set him off enough to want to kill him?" Sam asked.

"We saw John a couple of weeks before he died. It was at a cocktail party the Virginia Democrats had at Richard Manning's house." Natalie wiped new tears from her cheeks. "John came over to me, gave me a friendly hug and kiss. We talked for a long time, just catching up on each other's lives. It was nothing. But I looked over at one point and saw Noel watching us. He looked like he could kill us both on the spot."

"Why didn't you mention any of this to us the other day?" Sam asked.

"I didn't want to believe it."

"You still haven't said what changed your mind."

"I asked him." She ran a trembling hand through her disheveled hair. "Straight out. 'Did you kill John?' He denied it of course, but I don't believe him." To Nick, she said, "I didn't know what to do, so I came over here, hoping you'd put me in touch with Detective Holland."

"Do you have somewhere you can go where you'll be safe?" Sam asked.

Natalie nodded. "My parents' home in Springfield."

"Give me some time to look into this," Sam said.

"He's powerful," Natalie said. "You'll never be able to pin this on him."

"If he did it, I'll pin it on him," Sam assured her.

Natalie stood up to leave. "I'm sorry to barge in on you. I heard about what happened earlier. I'm glad you weren't seriously hurt."

They walked her to the door. "Tomorrow, I'll want to get all of this on the record." Sam pulled her ever-present notebook from her back pocket. "Write down your parents' address and a phone number where I can reach you."

Natalie did as she asked. "Thank you for listening." To Nick, she added, "I know I was never your favorite person—"

"That's neither here nor there."

"Anyway, thank you."

They watched her walk to her car.

"She's full of shit," Nick said, his eyes intensely focused

on Natalie's car as it drove away. "I don't believe her for one minute."

"What don't you believe? That her jealous husband could've killed the man his wife never stopped loving? That's as good a motive as I've heard yet."

"I know Noel Jordan. He's not made of that kind of stuff. If you ask me, she is, though. I could very easily see her losing her shit with John and killing him for not loving her enough. After what we heard earlier about her ex-boyfriend dying in a suspicious fire, you believe it's possible, too."

"Why would she come here, seeking out the lead detective on the case, if she was the one who did it? Think about that, Nick."

"Why didn't you ask her about what happened to her boyfriend in Hawaii?"

"I didn't want to tip my hand on that just yet. As long as she thinks we don't know about it, she might be more forthcoming."

"I don't like her. I've never liked her, and I don't care what you say, she's lying. She'll do anything it takes to advance her agenda, even if it means tossing her husband under the bus."

Sam checked her watch. "I wonder what time Noel goes to bed."

"You're actually going to do something with that pile of bullshit she just fed you?"

"Of course I am. This could be the break we've been waiting for."

He ushered her out of the house and locked the door behind them. "You're wasting your time."

"It's my time to waste."

"It's almost midnight."

"I know what time it is. If you'd rather stay here, I can go by myself."

"You're not going anywhere by yourself as long as your ex-husband is out there waiting for another chance to kill you."

"I don't need you to protect me, Nick. I'm more than capable of taking care of myself."

Silently, he ushered her into the car and a few minutes later took the exit for the George Washington Parkway, heading toward Alexandria. "You really think I could go home and go to bed and actually *sleep*, knowing you're out here by yourself confronting a potential killer while your ex waits for his next opportunity?"

"I've been in tighter spots."

"That was before."

"Before what?"

"Before me."

"I'm not one of those women who finds this whole alpha-male act sexy. In fact, it's a major turn-off."

"Whatever."

They rode to Belle Haven in stony silence. Sam didn't speak until she had to direct him to the dark house. She retrieved her gun and badge from her purse and tucked them into her coat pockets. "Wait here."

As if she hadn't spoken, Nick emerged from the car and followed her up the walk.

"I told you to wait!"

"You're not going in there alone, Sam. It's either me, or I call 911." He held up his cell phone defiantly. "What's it going to be?"

They engaged in a silent battle of wills until Sam finally said, "Don't say a word. Do you hear me? Not one freaking word." She spun around and marched up the front stairs to ring the bell. It echoed in the big house. They waited a couple of minutes before a light went on upstairs. Through the beveled windows next to the door, Sam watched Noel come down the stairs.

He peeked through the window before he opened the door. "Sergeant Holland?" Blinking, he glanced at Nick.

"Yes," Sam said. "I'm sorry to call on you so late." Begrudgingly, she added, "I believe you know Nick Cappuano."

"Of course. Come in." Noel's blond hair stood on end. He wore a T-shirt from a road race with flannel pajama pants and hardly resembled the second-ranking attorney at the U.S. Department of Justice she had met the other day.

Nick and Noel shook hands as he ushered them into the house.

"What can I do for you?"

"Is Natalie here?" Sam asked, feeling him out.

Noel's genial expression faded. "She flew out of here in a rage after we had a fight earlier. She must be at her parents' house."

"Is that something that happens often?" Sam asked. "The rages?"

"It's not the first time, but I think it's going to be the last. I can't believe what she accused me of! She thinks I could actually *kill* John O'Connor. Can you even imagine?"

"People have killed over jealousy before."

"I see that she's voiced her suspicions to you." Noel ran his hands through his hair. "What do you want, Detective?"

"Why did you tell me that you attended the Big Brother/ Big Sister event the night John was killed?"

"Because I had it in my date book."

"Your date book was off by a week."

Noel seemed startled to hear that. "My secretary keeps it up for me." He thought for a moment. "You know, you're right. It was two weeks ago. I'm really sorry about that. Things have been insane at work lately, and at home…"

"What's been going on at home?" Nick asked.

Sam glowered at him. "I'll ask the questions." Turning back to Noel, she said, "Things have been tense between you and Natalie?"

"More so than usual since we saw John at a fundraiser a couple of weeks ago. She knows how I feel about her talking and flirting with him in public, so what does she do? Flaunts her 'friendship' with him right in front of my face—and everyone in the room is talking about the two of them. How do you think that makes me feel?"

"Disrespected?" Nick said.

"I said to be quiet!" Sam hissed.

Noel directed an ironic chuckle at Nick that infuriated Sam.

"I guess you can relate, huh?" Noel said to Nick.

They followed Noel into the living room where he poured himself a drink from a crystal decanter.

Sam shook her head when he offered them one.

"Don't mind if I do," Nick said, earning another glare from Sam.

"Were you jealous of John?" Sam asked, anxious to wrestle the interview back from the old boy's club.

Noel handed Nick a drink and took a seat on the sofa. "I was sick of him. I was sick of hearing about him, sick of running into him. Mostly, I was sick of being her consolation prize."

"Why didn't you tell me any of this the other day?" Sam asked.

Swirling the amber liquor around his glass, Noel glanced at her. "Because I love her." He smiled, but it didn't reach his eyes. "Pathetic, huh? She has almost no regard for me or my feelings, yet I love her anyway."

"Were you sick enough of John O'Connor to kill him, Mr. Jordan?"

"No! Of course not. I didn't kill him."

"I'd like to give you a polygraph in the morning," Sam said.

"Fine. I have nothing to hide."

"Natalie said she woke up in the middle of the night John was killed and you were gone?"

"I was out running. I do that when I can't sleep."

"Do you think Natalie continued to see John after you were married?"

"We ran into him quite frequently. I've told you that."

"I don't mean in public."

Sam watched as her meaning dawned on him.

"You're not suggesting…"

"I'm not suggesting anything. I'm just asking."

"If she'd been seeing him, it's certainly without my knowledge." He took a long sip of whiskey, and Sam noticed a slight tremble in his hand.

"Do you think there's any way she killed him?"

"I'd like to say no way, but I honestly don't know anymore what she's capable of. I used to think I knew her. All I can say is she's been genuinely distraught since we heard he was dead. No doubt she's more upset than she would've been if it had been me who'd been murdered. And I'm the one who actually married her."

"Do you know about her ex-boyfriend who died in Hawaii?"

He nodded. "Brad. She's had more than her share of heartbreak, that's for sure."

Sam stood up. "I'm sorry to have disturbed you, but I appreciate your candor. I'll have someone contact you in the morning about the polygraph."

At the door, Noel said, "I didn't kill him, Sergeant. But it doesn't break my heart that someone else did."

"I know you're dying to tell me what you think," Sam said as they crossed the 14th Street Bridge on the way back to Capitol Hill.

"I was told to be quiet."

"I don't want to fight with you, Nick. That's the last thing I need right now."

"I don't want that, either. But you're asking a lot expecting me not to worry about you. He tried to *blow you up*."

"We're both kind of raw today," she said, reaching for his hand. "I really do want your impression of Noel."

"So you value my opinion?"

"Yes!"

Laughing, he curled his fingers around hers.

Right away, Sam felt better.

"He didn't do it," Nick said, "but he's not a hundred percent certain that she didn't."

"My thoughts exactly."

"I still say she's the one. She wanted John, he rejected her and she's never gotten over that."

"So why now? What sent her over the edge?"

"Maybe she didn't want to see him get the big win with the immigration bill."

"Why would she care about that? I keep coming back to that, to the timing of it all on the eve of that vote. *Why then?*"

"I can't see how the bill would have any impact whatsoever on Natalie," Nick said.

"Maybe the bill has nothing at all to do with his murder."

"I find that hard to believe."

"Yeah," Sam said, staring out the window. "Me, too."

CHAPTER 28

Sam tossed and turned. She dreamed about Peter, Quentin Johnson and Natalie Jordan, and for once she actually remembered the dreams when she awoke with a start, her heart racing. Glancing at the bedside clock, she saw it was just after three and realized Nick wasn't in bed with her. Her eyes darted around the dark room and found him standing at the window, the glow of a street light illuminating his tall frame.

Taking a moment to appreciate his muscular back, she remembered him telling her he loved her and was filled with a warm feeling of contentment and safety that was all new to her. Then she remembered arguing with him over Noel and Natalie, and her stomach took a sickening dip. The soaring highs and crushing lows were just one reason why she'd stayed away from men since she broke up with Peter, who never would've been as civil as Nick had been during a fight. Even though they'd disagreed, Sam didn't doubt for a minute that he loved her. That made him as different from Peter as a man could get.

She got up and went to Nick. Slipping her arms around him from behind, she pressed her lips to his back. "What're you doing up?"

He rested his hands over hers. "Couldn't sleep."

"He's not stupid enough to come back here. By now he knows we're looking for him."

"I think I could kill him if I got my hands on him. I really think I could. Not just because of the bombs, but all those years ago, too. All the years we could've had."

"He's not worth losing sleep over, Nick." She turned him so he faced her and shivered with desire when he ran his hands over her while looking down at her with hot, needy eyes. Looping her arms around his neck, she gasped when he lifted her and carried her back to bed. "I thought you were mad with me."

"I am," he said in an unconvincing tone as he snuggled her against him and pulled the comforter up around them. "Try to get some sleep."

She dragged a lazy finger from his chest to his belly and smiled when he trembled under her touch.

"*Sleep*, Samantha."

"What if I don't *want to*, Nick?" she asked, curling her hand around his erection.

"I'm sleeping," he said with an exaggerated yawn. "And I'm mad with you."

Laughing, she clamped her teeth down on his nipple.

"*Ow!* That hurt!"

"But you're not asleep anymore," she said with a victorious smile as she raised herself up to plant wet kisses on his belly while continuing to stroke him.

His fingers combed through her hair. "You're going to be tired again tomorrow."

"Then I'd better make it count." She straddled him and teased him by sliding her wet heat over his hard length, her nails lightly scoring his chest.

He arched his back, seeking her.

"Maybe you're right," she said, stopping. "We should get some sleep."

Growling, he surged up and entered her with a hard thrust that took her breath away.

"Mmm," she sighed, closing her eyes and letting her head fall back in bliss. "All right, if you insist."

"I insist. Sleep is highly overrated." He brought her down to him and fused his lips to hers, his tongue flirting and enticing.

When she needed to breathe, Sam broke the kiss and moved with painstaking slowness, rising up until they were barely connected, and then taking him deep again. If his sharp intake of air was any indication, he liked it. A lot. So she stopped. "Are you still mad at me?"

"Yes." With his hands on her hips, he tried to control the pace, but she wouldn't be controlled. "Sam…" He moaned, his eyes closed, his jaw tight with tension. "Babe…" Overpowering her, he held her in place and pumped into her. "Come for me. Now."

She rolled her hips, but the orgasm hovered just out of reach. "I *can't*," she whimpered.

Without losing their connection, he turned them over and gave it to her hard and fast, the way she'd told him she liked it, as he sucked her nipple into his mouth and flicked his tongue back and forth.

She cried out when she reached the climax that had eluded her.

Calling out her name, he went with her.

Her fingers danced through the dampness on his back. "You didn't have to do that."

He raised his head and found her eyes in the milky darkness. "Do what?"

"Wait for me." Her cheeks burned with embarrassment, and she was grateful for the dark.

He kissed her. "I'll always wait for you."

"It doesn't always happen."

"It has with me unless you've been faking."

She smacked his shoulder. "I haven't!"

"I know," he said, laughing as he rolled to his side and brought her with him.

"It's been an issue…in the past."

"It's not an issue now."

Reaching up to caress his face, she pressed her lips to his neck and breathed in the warm spicy scent she was quickly coming to crave. "I guess the right partner makes all the difference, even when he's mad with you."

"Especially then." His fingers danced over her hip, sending a new shiver of desire racing through her. "Want to try for a two-fer?"

"That *never* happens."

He eased her onto her back and kissed his way down the front of her. "Baby, I *love* a challenge."

Sam skipped through her morning routine with far more energy than she should have had. Multiple orgasms had multiple benefits. Who knew? With one last glance at Nick sleeping on his belly, she went downstairs in desperate need of a soda. As the first blessed mouthful cruised through her system, she realized she had no way to get to HQ.

Laughing softly, she called Freddie and asked him to pick her up. Since her dad wasn't up yet, she decided to wait for Freddie on the front porch. She surveyed the quiet street, wondering if Peter was out there somewhere watching her and waiting for his next opportunity. They would've called her if they'd found him, so she knew it was possible he was watching her.

"Come and get me, you bastard. You won't catch me off guard a second time."

As she took another long drink of soda, Freddie's battered Mustang came around the corner with a loud backfire.

"Gonna wake up the whole freaking neighborhood," she grumbled.

He pulled up to the house and leaned over to unlock the passenger door.

"Do I need a tetanus shot before I ride in this thing?"

"What's that they say about beggars and choosers?"

She battled with the seatbelt. "I've got to requisition a new ride."

"I'll take care of that for you, boss." He offered her one of the powdered donuts from the package on his lap.

With a scowl, she took one and turned so she could see him. "You've done some good work on this case, Cruz. Damn good."

His face lit up with pleasure. "Thanks. So after I got home last night, I was kinda wired and couldn't sleep, ya know?"

"Uh-huh." Her face flushed when she thought of how she'd worked off her own tension.

"I got to thinking that maybe there's some sort of connection besides the sexual kind between O'Connor and one of our people of interest."

"What kind of connection?"

"A domestic—cook, caterer, cleaning lady, gardener."

"Possible. Where you going with it?"

"I know this is way out there, but what if one of the domestics found out about the kid, Thomas, and told someone who'd be infuriated by it?"

"Worth looking into."

"You think?"

"When are you going to start having some faith in yourself and your instincts?"

"I don't know. Soon. I hope."

"So do I, because you're starting to piss me off."

"You know what pisses me off?" He took his eyes off the road long enough to glance at her. "Your scumbag ex-husband. He pisses me off."

"Yeah," she sighed. "Me, too."

"It's all over the papers."

"I knew it would be."

"I have it there. In the backseat if you wanted to…"

Her stomach twisted in protest. "That's all right. Thanks."

"He had pictures of you all over his place. It was totally creepy. There were shots of you from a distance working crime scenes, and he even had a police scanner."

Sam's stomach took a dive at that news. "I should've known he wouldn't just give up and go away. I should've known that."

"This isn't your fault," he said fiercely.

"So Natalie Jordan paid us a visit last night," Sam said, anxious to change the subject. She relayed what Natalie told them and went over their visit with Noel. "I don't think he did it, but I want to get him on a polygraph today. Will you set that up?"

"Sure thing. I don't see Noel for it, either. Nothing about him screamed 'murderer' to me. Natalie, on the other hand, she's a cool customer."

"Nick said she's lying about Noel, but he's never liked her."

"He's got good instincts, though," Freddie said.

"Do me a favor when we get in, ask Gonzo and Arnold to check out this address." She gave him the slip of paper with Natalie's parents' address. "And have them go by Noel Jordan's house in Belle Haven. Get me a couple of hours of surveillance on him before you bring him in."

"Got it. Will do." As they pulled up to the last intersection before the public safety building, he said, "Shit." He pointed at the street leading to HQ, lined with TV trucks bearing satellite dishes.

"Goddamn it."

He scowled at her choice of words. "Let's go in through the morgue."

"Good plan."

They parked on the far side of the building, entered through the basement door and took a circuitous route to the detectives' pit where Gonzo and Arnold waited for them.

"We've got Terry O'Connor in lockup. He's lawyering up."

"Figured."

"They filmed us bringing him in," Arnold said. "It'll be the lead story this morning."

Captain Malone burst through the door. "The chief just got off the phone with a very angry Senator O'Connor. He's threatening to call the president."

"He can call anyone he wants," Sam said. "His son had motive, a key and can't produce his supposed alibi. If he was anyone else, we would've had him in here days ago, and you know it. I need to rule him out."

They stared each other down for a long moment before Malone blinked. "Get him into interview and either charge him or let him go. And do it quickly."

"Yes, sir." To Gonzo, she added, "Bring him up."

CHAPTER 29

When Sam and Freddie entered the small interrogation room, Terry O'Connor leaped to his feet. "I didn't kill my brother! How many times do I have to tell you that?"

She pretended to gaze intently into the file she had carried into the room with her. "The reason you're here is you failed to attend the safe driving course the judge ordered after your DUI."

"You aren't serious."

Sam glanced at Freddie.

"She's serious," Freddie said.

"I meant to," Terry stammered.

"Why don't we talk about why we're really here?" the attorney said.

"Give me a lie detector."

Grabbing Terry's shirt, the attorney yanked him into a chair. "Shut up, Terry."

"Mr. O'Connor, have you been advised of your rights?" Sam asked.

"The cops you sent to haul me out of my parents' house before dawn went through all that," he spat back at her.

"Do we have your permission to record this interview?"

"At the advice of counsel," the attorney drawled in a honeyed Southern accent, "Mr. O'Connor will cooperate with this farce—within reason."

"Isn't that good of him?" Sam asked Freddie.

"Real good," Freddie agreed as he turned on the recorder and noted for the record who was in the room and why.

"It's now been ninety-six hours since your brother's body was discovered in his apartment," Sam said. "You say you spent the night of the murder with a woman you met in a Loudoun County bar. Can you give me her name?"

"No," Terry said, dejected.

"Have you found anyone who can confirm you left the establishment with this imaginary woman?"

"She wasn't imaginary!" he cried, slapping his hand on the table.

"Witnesses?"

He slumped back into his chair. "No."

"That kind of puts you in a bit of a pickle, doesn't it?" she asked as Nick's words echoed through her mind—*you're barking up the wrong tree with Terry.* She had to admit that the buzz she got from knowing she had a suspect's nuts on the block and all she had to do was lower the boom was missing here.

"Is there a relevant question coming any time soon?" the attorney drawled.

Sam hammered Terry hard for ninety minutes, reduced him to a whimpering, sniveling baby, but he never deviated from his original statement. Finally, needing to regroup, she asked for a word with Freddie in the hallway.

Malone waited for them outside the observation room door. "Spring him."

Frustration pooled in her aching belly. She nodded to Freddie. "Tell him to stay local and to get that safe driving class done within thirty days."

"Got it."

When they were alone, she looked up at Malone. "I had to rule him out."

"And you all but have." He lowered his voice. "They brought Peter in thirty minutes ago."

"He's mine."

"No one's saying otherwise. But you know we can take care of him if you aren't up to it—"

"I'm up to it—after he chills in the cooler for a little while longer."

"As a courtesy, I let Skip know we had him."

"Thanks."

"The partial print off the ED on Cappuano's car had similarities to Peter's, but they couldn't make a definitive ID."

"I'll get him to confirm the print is his," she said, more to herself than to Malone.

"With what we found in his apartment, we've more or less already got him." He handed her a rundown of what the warrant had yielded and a folder full of photos that made her sick.

"But he doesn't know that," she said.

"Nope."

She looked up at the captain. "I think I'm going to enjoy this. Does that make me a bad cop?"

"No, it makes you human. Arlington will want him when we're done with him."

With a nod, she left him to go buy another soda and took it back to her office. Closing the door, she dropped into her chair suddenly exhausted and drained. She hadn't seen Peter, except for in court, in almost two years. Their last explosive argument over the time she was spending with her newly paralyzed father had put the finishing touches on what had been a horrible four years for her. The next day, she'd moved her essentials into her father's house and put the rest of her belongings in storage where they remained.

In the ensuing months, Peter had popped up with such annoying regularity that she'd been forced to get a restraining order to keep him from coming around while they hurled accusations back and forth. Since then she'd often had the sensation of being watched or followed, little pinpricks of awareness on the back of her neck that had never materialized into an actual confrontation. In fact, it hadn't occurred to her that he'd still be so invested in her. She should've known better. What made her truly sick was that she had endangered Nick just by spending time with him.

Imagining Peter locked up in a cell in the basement, she smiled. "Let him sit there for a while longer wondering how much we know." The idea infused her with joy as she drank her soda and returned her attention to the O'Connor case.

Nick woke up alone in Sam's bed and shifted onto her pillow to breathe in the scent she'd left behind. He contemplated whether he should stay there until she got home or get up to face her father. Staying in bed all day was definitely the more appealing of the two options. But since he didn't want her to think he was a total coward, he got up to take a shower.

He took his time getting dressed in jeans and a long-sleeved polo shirt. How ridiculous was it that he was afraid to go downstairs to face a man in a wheelchair?

"You're being an ass," he said to his bomb-battered reflection in the mirror. Still, he took another ten minutes to make the bed and straighten up the room while marveling that one woman could own so many shoes. When there was nothing left to do, he finally started down the stairs and almost groaned when he found Skip by himself in the kitchen. Couldn't even Celia have been there to provide a buffer?

"Morning," Nick said.

"Morning," Skip muttered. "There's coffee."

"Thanks." As Nick filled a mug that had been left by the

pot, he felt the heat of the other man's eyes on his back. "Sam got an early start."

"I heard her leave about seven-thirty. Celia's downstairs doing laundry, but she made bacon and eggs. Plates are up there in the cabinet."

"That sounds good." Wondering if he'd be able to eat under the watchful eyes of Sam's dad, Nick brought the plate and coffee to the table. They sat in awkward silence for several minutes before Nick put down his fork and worked up the courage to look over at the older man. "I love her."

"If I thought otherwise you wouldn't have slept in her bed last night. I don't care how old she is."

Taken aback, Nick stared at him. "I wanted to go with her today."

"She wouldn't have let you."

"Still, until this thing with Peter is cleared up…"

"They snagged him this morning at Union Station, buying a one-way ticket to New York."

"Is that so?"

"Yep."

"Well, that's a relief."

"She's gonna have a go at him. I don't know about you, but I'd kind of like to see that."

"How about I drive you?"

Sam took a series of deep breaths to calm her churning stomach before she picked up the folder of material gathered from Peter's apartment, opened her office door, signaled to Freddie, and headed for the interrogation room where she'd asked the uniforms to put Peter. The quiet in the normally buzzing detectives' cubicles told her she'd have a good-size audience watching in observation.

"He's apt to come at me," Sam said to Freddie before they went in. "Don't stop him."

"Are you out of your freaking mind?"

"Let me handle this my way, Cruz."

"Fine, but if it appears he's about to kill you, you'll have to excuse me if I get in the way of that."

"Deal." With a small smile for Freddie, she stepped into the room. Peter had aged since she last saw him. His sandy hair was now shot through with silver, and the face she'd once found handsome was hard and lined with bitterness.

Nodding to release the officer guarding him, Sam stepped up to the table.

"I want someone else," he said without looking at her.

"Tough."

"This is a conflict of interest."

"We're not married anymore, so no it isn't. Detective Cruz, please record this interview with Peter Gibson."

Freddie clicked on the recorder and returned to his post by the door, sending the signal that this one belonged to Sam.

"You've been advised of your rights, including your right to an attorney?"

"Don't need one. You've got nothing on me." Peter raised his cuffed hands. "Is this really necessary?"

"Detective Cruz, please un-cuff Mr. Gibson." When Freddie didn't immediately comply, she said, "Detective."

Freddie stalked past her and released the cuffs. Scowling at her, he returned to the door.

Peter rubbed his wrists. "Kind of a lot of drama over nothing, Sam," he said in the patronizing tone he'd often used on her when they were together.

"Nothing?" She laid out each of the photos of her that had been found in his apartment, hearing the loud nuts-on-the-block buzz that had been missing with Terry O'Connor. "What do you call this?"

"Amateur photography. Is that a crime these days?"

"No, but stalking is."

He shrugged. "A misdemeanor. So charge me."

"Thanks, I will. Hanging around outside my house? Kind of pathetic, even for you."

His genial blue eyes hardened. "I wasn't outside your house."

"Yes, you were. It's sad that you'd rather stalk the woman who divorced you than find someone new to control. Pathetic, isn't it, Cruz?"

"At the very least," Freddie said. "I'd say it's kind of sick *and* pathetic to be fixated on your ex, especially when she's made it crystal clear to the world that she wants nothing to do with you."

If looks could kill, Freddie would've been a goner.

Sam moved around the table so she was behind Peter. "Pissed you off that I didn't want you anymore, didn't it?"

"I didn't want you, either. You were a shitty wife and lousy in bed." He looked up at the dark glass that masked the observation room. "You hear that?" he yelled. "She sucks in the sack!"

"Nick doesn't think so."

Peter tried to surge to his feet, but she shoved him back down.

"I guess you've figured out that we compared notes and discovered you didn't give me his messages six years ago when you were pretending to be my friend."

"That's not a crime."

"No, but it *is* pathetic. Must've pissed you off this week to see me with him."

"Like I care."

"Oh, I think you do." She leaned in to speak close to his ear. "I think you care a whole lot."

In a jerky motion, he shrugged her off. "Giving yourself a lot of credit, aren't you?"

Returning to the other side of the table, she laid a photo of the bomb-making materials in front of him.

"What's that?" he asked.

"Why don't you tell me?"

A bead of sweat appeared on his upper lip. "I have no idea."

"I think you do." Sam rested her hands on the table and leaned toward him. "You disappoint me, Peter. Four years of living with a cop and you didn't learn a goddamned thing. If you're going to try to kill your ex-wife and her boyfriend, you should know better than to leave fingerprints on the bombs."

"I didn't leave any prints!"

She smiled. Bingo.

His face went purple with rage. "You fucking cunt. Spreading your legs for that asshole ten minutes after you see him again."

Sam leaned closer to him, her stomach burning. "That's right. And guess what?" She lowered her voice so only Peter— and maybe Freddie—could hear her. "When I fuck him, I come every time—sometimes more than once. So it turns out that despite what you always tried to make me believe, *you* were the one who sucked in the sack."

He lunged at her, grabbed her throat and squeezed so hard she saw stars in a matter of seconds.

She heard Freddie moving toward them as she rammed the heel of her hand into Peter's nose, sending him flying backward, blood bursting from his face.

"You *fucking bitch*! You motherfucking frigid whore! You broke my fucking nose!"

"Book him, Cruz." Sam's hand shook as she brought it up

to her throat. "Two counts attempted murder, assaulting a police officer, stalking a police officer, possessing bomb-making materials, breaking and entering, violating a restraining order, and anything else you can think of."

Freddie hauled Peter up off the floor and snapped cuffs on his wrists. "With pleasure."

"Does he know you're only half a woman?" Peter screamed. "Did you tell him you're barren?"

Sam's heart kicked into overdrive as pain shot through her gut. "Get him out of here."

Long after Freddie dragged the shrieking Peter from the room, Sam stood there trying to get her shaking hands under control. Finally, she turned to leave the room and found a crowd of coworkers waiting for her.

Captain Malone stepped forward. "Well done, Sergeant."

"Thank you," Sam said, her voice shaky. She heard the whir of the wheelchair before she saw it. *Oh God*, she groaned inwardly at what her father must've heard. The crowd parted to let him through, and her heart almost stopped when she saw Nick with him. "So you heard all that, huh?" Sam said to her dad after the others left them alone.

"Uh-huh."

"I'm sorry," she said, her cheeks burning. "It must've been embarrassing for you—"

"That was the most entertaining fifteen minutes of my life—right up until he grabbed you. You should put some ice on your neck. Those bruises are gonna hurt."

"I will." She bent down to kiss his cheek.

"Proud of you, baby girl," he whispered.

She rested her head on his shoulder. How she wished he could wrap his strong arms around her the way he used to. "I think it's finally over."

"I think you're right. Since I'm here, I'm going to go do some visiting. I'll be back in a bit, Nick."

"I'll be right here," Nick said.

"That's what I figured." Skip turned his chair and started down the long corridor, no doubt heading for Chief Farnsworth's office.

Nick held out a hand to her. That he did just that and nothing more finally did it for her. Curling her hand around his, she fell the rest of the way into love with him.

CHAPTER 30

"I'm sorry," Sam said when they were in her office.

"What the hell for?" Nick asked.

"For using you and our relationship to stick it to him. I didn't know you were there. I hate that you heard it."

"You think that bothers me?" His hazel eyes were bright with emotion. "You nailed him. That's all that matters. So what did you say that made him go ballistic?"

"It doesn't matter."

"It matters to me."

Reluctantly, Sam told him what she'd said. "I don't want you to think…"

As if he could no longer resist, he put his arms around her. "What?"

Again her cheeks burned with embarrassment and discomfort, but this had to be said. "That I think of what we do… together…as fucking."

"Baby, come on. I know that."

"Because it's so much more than that," she said, looking up at him.

"Yes." He brushed his lips over hers. "It is."

"I love you, too."

He went perfectly still. "Yeah?"

Pleased to have caught him off guard, she nodded. "Since that night at the party for me, too. I shouldn't have married Peter for many reasons, but mostly because I always loved you. Always."

"Samantha," he whispered, leaning in for a deep, passionate kiss.

"No PDA on duty, or any other time," she mumbled when she came to her senses and remembered where they were.

"Very special occasion." His hands slid down to cup her ass and pull her tight against his erection. "Does that door have a lock?"

With her hands on his chest, she tried to push him back. "Don't even think about it."

"I'm way past thinking."

She went up on tiptoes to roll his bottom lip between her teeth. "I'll make it up to you. I promise."

Groaning, he released her. "I'll hold you to that."

"Um, what he said about me...at the end...We should probably talk about that."

Nick rested a finger on her lips. "Later."

Grateful for the reprieve, she took a deep breath. "So what's with you and my dad?" she asked, grabbing a half-empty bottle of soda from her desk.

"We've reached an understanding of sorts."

Raising a suspicious eyebrow, she studied him. "What sort?"

"That's between me and him."

"I don't like the sound of that."

He tweaked her nose. "You don't have to."

A knock on the door startled them.

"Enter," she called.

Gonzo opened the door. "Um, sorry to interrupt—"

"You're not interrupting anything," she said with a meaningful glance at Nick. "What's up?"

"There's a woman here to see you. Wouldn't give her name, insists on seeing you and only you. Looks shook up."

"All right. Bring her in." To Nick, she said, "Do you mind taking my dad home? I'll be along soon."

"Sure." He leaned in for one last kiss.

"Don't talk about me with him."

"Dream on," he said, laughing as he left the room. "Put some ice on that neck."

Sam took in the view of his fine denim-clad ass and sighed with delight. That he was hers, all hers, was something she still couldn't believe. She wished she had time to indulge in the happy dance that was just bursting to get out.

Gonzo accompanied a distraught woman to the door and showed her in. "This is Sergeant Holland."

"Have a seat." Sam gestured to the chair and dismissed Gonzo with a grateful nod. "What's your name?"

The woman's manicured fingers fiddled with her designer purse as she looked at Sam with dark, ravaged eyes. "Andrea Daly."

"What can I do for you, Ms. Daly?"

"It's *Mrs.* Daly." She looked down at the floor, sobs shaking her petite frame. "I've done an awful thing."

Sam came around her desk and leaned back against it. "If you tell me about this awful thing, maybe I can help you."

Andrea wiped the tears from her face. "The night the senator was killed…"

The back of Sam's neck tingled. "Did you know him? Senator O'Connor?"

Andrea shook her head. "I've never done anything like this. My family means everything to me. I have children."

"Mrs. Daly, I can't help you if you don't tell me what it is you think you've done."

"I was with Terry O'Connor," she whispered. "I spent that whole night with him at the Day's Inn in Leesburg." She wiped her runny nose. "When I saw him on the news being brought in this morning…I couldn't let that happen. He didn't do it."

"I know."

Incredulous, Andrea stared up at Sam. "I risked my marriage and my family and you *already knew?*"

Sam reached out to her. "You did a brave thing coming here. It was the right thing."

"A lot of good that'll do me when my husband reads about it in the paper."

"It won't be in the paper. If your husband finds out, it'll be because you tell him."

"Do you mean that?"

"Terry O'Connor doesn't remember you. He was so drunk he couldn't even offer a description of the woman he said he'd been with. I'm sorry if that hurts you, but it's the truth. So the only two people who know he was with you are in this room. I know what I'm going to do with the info. What you do with it is up to you."

Overcome, Andrea bent her head. "I've never been unfaithful to my husband before. In nineteen years, I've never so much as looked at another man. But he travels a lot, and we've drifted apart in the last couple of years. I was lonely."

"I understand that feeling—better than you can imagine." Sam raised her fingers to cover bruises on her throat that were starting to hurt. "But if you love your husband and want to make your marriage work, stay out of the bars, go home and fix it. You're lucky this was the worst thing that happened."

"Believe me, I know." She stood and offered her hand. "Thank you."

Sam held Andrea's hand between both of hers. "Thank *you* for coming in. You did the right thing. I had him ninety-nine percent eliminated. You just gave me the one percent I still needed."

"In that case, I guess it was worth it."

"Good luck to you, Mrs. Daly."

"And to you, Sergeant. Senator O'Connor was a good man. I hope you find the person who did this to him."

"Oh, I will. You can count on that." Sam stood at her doorway and watched Andrea leave.

"What was that all about?" Freddie asked.

"Terry O'Connor's alibi."

Freddie's eyes lit up. "No shit?"

"Nope."

"Did you get an official statement?"

"Nope."

"Why not?"

"Because I had nothing to gain, and she had everything to lose. She gave me what I needed. That was enough."

"I continue to be awed not just by your instincts but by your humanity."

"Fuck off, Cruz," she said, rolling her eyes. "Did you get Peter put on ice?"

"Yep. Sent the EMTs down to take a look at his busted schnoz. He's screaming police brutality."

"Self-defense." The fact she had taunted Peter into attacking her wouldn't matter to the U.S. Attorney in light of the evidence they had implicating him in the bombings.

"Damn straight it was."

"What're you hearing from Gonzo and Arnold?"

"Natalie's mother told them she's in seclusion and couldn't come to the door. They didn't push it because all you wanted was confirmation that she was there, and they saw her looking out an upstairs window. Noel spent the day working in his yard and washing his car. No sign of her at the house. Gonzo just took him in for the polygraph."

"Let's set one up for her for tomorrow, after the funeral."

"Got it."

"So where does that leave us?" Sam unclipped her hair and

ran her fingers through it. "Our two prime suspects, both with motive and opportunity pointing the finger at each other, but nothing about them is jumping out at us."

"Except her dead boyfriend. That's a red flag."

"If she had anything to do with that, would her husband know about it? Would she have told him all about the boyfriend who'd tragically died in a fire?"

"Hard to say. Murderers can be an arrogant lot. They often want people to know what they've done so they get the credit."

"I didn't get that vibe from Noel. It was more of a 'she was heartbroken' vibe." Sam checked her watch and saw it was after one. "I wanted another go with her, but I think I'll wait until after we polygraph her to see if I need to show my cards on the dead boyfriend. Have Gonzo get her suspicions about her husband on the record at some point today. I'm not liking him for a suspect, but I want it in the file."

"Sounds like a good plan. Do you think it's possible that neither of them had anything to do with it, and she's just trying to get rid of a husband she never should've married?"

"At this point, I'd say anything is possible, but I'm still left without a primary suspect three days into the investigation. That'll really please the chief."

"How about I write up the reports from this morning?"

"I'd appreciate that." She thought for a moment and realized this was as good a moment as there was likely to be. "Can you come in for a minute?"

"Sure." He shut the office door behind him. "What's up?"

"You know I appreciate your help with the reports, right?"

"It's no problem."

"Well, for me it kind of is." She rubbed a hand over her belly. In a rush of words, she said, "I'm dyslexic. I've struggled with it all my life, and it's mostly under control, but I know you must wonder about the weird mistakes and stuff."

"Why didn't you tell me before? I could've been doing all the reports."

"I don't want that. It's enough that you help me as much as you do."

"You still should've told me. We're partners."

"Do I know everything there is to know about you?"

He squirmed under the heat of her glare. "Most everything."

"We've all got our secrets, Cruz, and the last thing I want is special treatment. I don't expect anything to change now that you know."

"Asking for help doesn't make you weak, Sam. It makes you human."

"That's the second time today someone told me what it means to be human. Don't tell anyone about the dyslexia, all right?"

"Who would I tell?" he huffed. "If you don't know by now that you can trust me—"

"If I didn't trust you, I wouldn't have told you." She paused before she said, "I'm sorry you had to hear that stuff I said to Peter. I know it was embarrassing for you."

"You got him to implicate himself, which is the goal of any interrogation."

"Still..."

"I'm a big boy, Sergeant. I can handle it."

She looked at him with new appreciation. "Copy me on those reports, and you can run your domestic angle in the morning while I'm at the funeral."

"Got it."

"Go home after you finish the paperwork."

He held up a set of keys. "Your new ride, madam."

"Ohhh, what'd you get me? One of the new Tauruses?"

"Yep. Navy blue." He rattled off the parking space number.

"Nice. Thanks."

"I might come by to watch the game later. I mean, if that's all right with you."

"My dad invited you, didn't he?"

"Well, yeah, but…"

"But what?"

He smiled. "Nothing."

She pulled on her coat. "I'll see you later, then. Oh, and thanks for having my back with the scumbag."

"No problem." He followed her out of the office and closed the door behind him. "Sergeant Holland?"

She turned to him, perplexed by his formality.

"It's a great pleasure to work with you."

"Back atcha, Detective. Right back atcha."

On her way out of the detectives' pit, she stopped to peek into the office that would soon be hers. Since the day she made detective, she'd had her eye on the lieutenant's spacious corner office. However, because of her struggles with dyslexia, she hadn't really allowed herself to hope.

She turned to leave and ran smack into Lieutenant Stahl.

"Would you jump in my grave that fast, Sergeant?"

Taken aback by his sudden appearance, Sam stepped aside to let him in and noticed he carried a box.

"You must be feeling quite satisfied." He flipped on the lights and dropped the box on the desk. "Shagged a witness, made lieutenant, stole my command and got away with it—all in the same week."

Sam leaned against the doorframe and let him spew, fascinated by the way his fat chin jiggled in time with his venomous words.

"I mean do you *honestly* think you'd have gotten away with screwing a witness if your daddy wasn't the chief's buddy?" He tossed pictures and mementos into the box. "You can bet internal affairs will be interested in taking a closer look at that. In fact, you might just be my very first order of business."

Sam pretended to hang on his every word while she planned where to put her own things in the space.

"This isn't over, Sergeant. I refuse to turn a blind eye to blatant disregard for basic rules by someone who's gotten where she is because of *who* she is."

Her hand rolled into a fist that she'd love to plant smack in the middle of his fat face, but she wouldn't give him the satisfaction. Instead, she pulled her notebook from her back pocket and reached for a pen.

His eyes narrowed. "What are you writing?"

"Just a note to maintenance. They need to do something about the smell in here." As little red blotches popped up on his fat face, she returned the pad to her pocket. "Good luck in the rat squad, Lieutenant. I'm sure you'll fit right in." Turning, she took her leave.

"Watch your back, Sergeant," he called. "Daddy won't always be there to clean up your messes."

She turned around. "If you so much as look at my father with crossed eyes, I'll personally break your fat-assed neck. Got me?"

He raised an eyebrow. "A threat, Sergeant?"

"No, Lieutenant. A promise."

CHAPTER 31

Following the confrontation with Stahl, Sam's stomach burned as she headed for the morgue exit, anxious to avoid the press and get home to Nick. The prospect of a boisterous Sunday dinner with her sisters and their families was looking better all the time. She was on her way to a clean escape when Chief Farnsworth stopped her in the lobby.

"I'm glad I caught you, Sergeant. You need to give the media ten minutes."

She groaned.

"In the aftermath of the bombing, you have to show the public you're alive and actively engaged in the O'Connor case—and you've got to let them know you've cleared Terry O'Connor before the president himself starts calling for my ass in a sling."

"Yes, sir."

"They'll ask about Nick."

Rubbing her hand over her gut, she looked out at the media circus that had taken over the plaza. "I can handle it."

"I'll be right there with you."

"Thank you," she said, knowing his presence would send the signal that the department was firmly behind her.

"You're pale. Do you need a minute?"

"No." She breathed through the pain and buttoned up her coat. "Let's get it over with." The chief followed her into the maelstrom.

The reporters went wild, screaming questions at her.

Chief Farnsworth held up a hand to quiet them. "Sergeant Holland will answer your questions if you give her the chance."

As Sam stepped up to the microphone, the crowd fell silent. "Today, we ruled out Terry O'Connor as a suspect in his brother's murder. We have a number of other persons of interest we're looking at closely." She really wished that was true, but she couldn't exactly tell the media that the investigation had hit a dead end.

"Can you tell us who they are?"

"Not without compromising the investigation. As soon as we're able to give you more, we will."

"Is there anything else you can tell us about the O'Connor investigation?"

"Not at this time."

"How close are you to making an arrest?"

"Not as close as I'd like to be, but it's far more important that we build a case that'll hold up in court rather than rush to judgment."

"Why did Detective Cruz go to Chicago?"

"No comment." No way was she handing them Thomas O'Connor. They would have to figure that one out for themselves.

"Did the Johnson family play a role in yesterday's bombing?"

"No. We've made an arrest that's unrelated to the Johnsons." She looked down and summoned the strength to get through this. "My ex-husband, Peter Gibson, has been charged with two counts of attempted murder—among numerous other charges—in the bombing."

"Why'd he do it?" one of the reporters shouted.

"We believe he was enraged by my relationship with Mr. Cappuano."

"Did you know Mr. Cappuano before this week?"

Gritting her teeth, she forced herself to stay calm and to not make their day by getting emotional. "We met years ago and had a brief relationship."

"Did you tell your superior officers that you'd had a past relationship with a material witness?" asked Darren Tabor from the *Washington Star*. He'd been particularly harsh toward her in his reporting after the Johnson disaster.

Sam's fingers tightened around the edges of the podium. "I did not."

"Why?"

"I was determined to close the O'Connor case and believed Mr. Cappuano's assistance would be invaluable, which it has been. Thanks to his help, I'm much further along than I would've been without it."

"Still, aren't you walking a fine ethical line especially in light of the publicity you received after the Johnson case?" Tabor asked with a smirk.

"If you examine my more than twelve-year record, you'll find my behavior to be above reproach."

"Until recently."

"Your judgment," Sam said, working to keep her cool while making a mental note to check on his unpaid parking tickets. Issuing a warrant for his arrest would give her tremendous joy.

"Is it true Mr. Cappuano is the beneficiary of a sizable life insurance policy taken out by the senator?" Tabor asked.

Sam clenched her teeth. How the hell had *that* leaked? "Yes."

"Doesn't that give you a motive?"

"Maybe if he had known about it."

"You believe he didn't?"

"He was as surprised by it as we were. Mr. Cappuano has been cleared of any involvement in the senator's murder."

"Is it serious between you and Cappuano?" Sam wanted to groan when she recognized the bottle-blonde reporter from one of the gossip rags.

"It's been a week," Sam said, laughing off the question.

"But is it *serious?*"

What is this? Sam wanted to shoot back at her. *High school?* "Would I have gotten involved if it wasn't? Next question." She looked away from the reporter's satisfied grin, sending the signal that she was finished with the discourse into her personal life.

"Are you concerned by Destiny Johnson's threats?" another reporter asked.

Relieved to be moving on, Sam made eye contact with the new reporter, a woman she recognized from one of the network affiliates. "Mrs. Johnson is a grieving mother. My heart goes out to her."

"How about Marquis Johnson?"

"As I'm due to testify in his probable cause hearing on Tuesday, I have no comment."

"Sergeant, the second anniversary of your father's shooting is coming up next week. Are there any new leads in his case?"

"Unfortunately, no, but it remains an open investigation. Anyone with information is urged to come forward."

"And how's he doing?"

"Very well. Thank you for asking."

Chief Farnsworth stepped forward to rescue her.

Sam held up her hand to stop him. "I just want to say…" She cleared the emotion from her throat. "That it's an honor to serve the people of this city, and while you've taken your digs at me lately, there's nothing I wouldn't do, no risk I wouldn't take, to protect our citizens. If that's not enough for you, well then you can continue to make me the story rather than focusing on real news. That's it."

As they hollered more questions at her, she pushed through them to the staff parking lot where her gleaming new car waited for her. Only when she was safely inside could she begin to breathe her way through the pain.

Sam called Nick from the car.

"Hey, babe," he said.

She took a moment to enjoy the easy familiarity they had slid into, as if they'd been together for years rather than days.

"Sam?"

"I'm here."

"Everything all right?"

"It is now that I'm talking to you. What're you doing?"

"I'm sitting on your bed trying to write what I have to say at the funeral tomorrow. It's just dawned on me that I have to speak in front of the president and most of Congress."

Sam released a low whistle. "I don't think I could do it."

"Sure you could. You just took on the Washington press corps."

"You saw that, huh?"

"Yep. I heard it's serious between us. Did you know that?"

Laughing, she said, "I've heard that rumor."

"Say it again, Sam," he said, his voice gruff and sexy.

Her heart contracted. "Say what?" she asked, even though she knew exactly what he was after.

"Don't play coy with me. Say it."

"When I see you."

"And when will that be?"

"I'm almost home. Want to meet me outside and go for a walk? I promised I'd take you to the market."

"So you did. Was that *only* yesterday?"

"Sure was. Meet me on the corner in five? If I come in, I'll get trapped, and I need some air."

"I'll be right there."

534 MARIE FORCE

★ ★ ★

He was waiting for her when she parked in front of the house and set out toward the corner.

Her heart skipped a beat at the sight of him in jeans and a black leather jacket, and she couldn't help but break into a jog to get to him faster. She hurled herself into his outstretched arms and squealed when he lifted her right off her feet.

His mouth descended on hers for a hot, breathtaking kiss.

"Mmm," she said against his lips. "I missed you."

"You just saw me a couple of hours ago."

"Long time." She burrowed into his neck to nibble on warm skin.

He trembled and tightened his hold on her. "What happened to your ban on PDA?"

"Momentary lapse."

"I like it." He returned her to terra firma and tipped her chin up. "There was something you were going to tell me?"

She thought about playing coy again, but as she looked up at his handsome face, she found she couldn't do it. "I love you. Big."

His hazel eyes danced with delight. "Big, huh?"

"Scary big."

"Not scary." He hugged her. "Because I love you bigger."

"Not possible."

"Bet?" Laughing at the face she made at him, he slipped his arm around her shoulders for the walk to the market.

A melting pot of crafts, colors, nationalities, smells and textures, Eastern Market was mobbed with last-minute Christmas shoppers braving the damp chill to bargain with bundled-up vendors.

"You aren't going to believe this, but I've never been here," he confessed as they passed a row of fragrant Christmas trees.

She stared up at him. "Are you serious? You've worked a few blocks from here for how long?"

"Well, I worked for a congressman before John, so I guess almost fourteen years."

"That's sad, Nick. Truly pathetic. The flea market is open every weekend, year round."

"So I've heard," he said with a sheepish grin. "I figured, you know, flea market—junk. I never expected all this hand-crafted stuff."

"You can get anything here, and it's usually better than what you can buy in a store."

"I can see that."

"Hey, Sam," one of the vendors called.

"How's business, Rico?"

"Booming, thank God. Heard about you on the news last night. You okay?"

"Just fine. No worries."

"Glad to hear it. Bring your dad down one of these week-ends."

"I will."

After several similar exchanges, Nick said, "Do you know *all* these people or does it just seem that way?"

She shrugged as she sorted through a table of fluffy knit-ted scarves. "This is my hood. I'm a regular." Twisting a hot pink scarf around her neck, she pirouetted in front of him. "What do you think?"

He turned up his nose. "Not your color, babe."

"My niece Brooke firmly believes that no one over the age of four should wear pink."

"That's funny. How old is she?"

"Fifteen going on thirty. You'll meet her later." Return-ing the scarf to the table, she glanced over at the next kiosk and spotted a beautifully framed painting of the Capitol that she had to have for him. Dying to get a closer look at it, she rubbed her hands together and blew into them. "Do you feel like some hot chocolate?"

"Sure."

"They're selling it right over there."

Eyeing her suspiciously, he looked over to where she pointed. "All right."

Flashing a brilliant smile, she went up on tiptoes to kiss him. "Thank you, honey."

"What're you up to?"

"Nothing." She gave him a little push. "Go."

The moment he crossed the street, she spun around and pounced on the unsuspecting artist in the neighboring booth. "That one. Right there. How much?"

"Three-fifty."

"Sold. Will you take a check?"

"With a license."

"Be quick."

They completed the transaction in record time, and Sam accepted the package wrapped in brown paper moments before Nick returned with two steaming cups of hot chocolate.

"What did you buy?"

"Something for my dad."

"You're a terrible liar, Samantha. Does this mean I have to buy something for you, too?"

"Only if you plan to get lucky in the New Year," she said with a saucy smile.

"In that case, what looks good to you? Sky's the limit."

Laughing and teasing, they were navigating the crowd on their way to the indoor food market when a flash of metal caught Sam's eye. Everything shifted into slow motion as she realized it was a gun. In the span of a second, she shoved Nick out of the way, dropped the painting and her hot chocolate, drew her own weapon and lunged at the shooter.

"Baby killer!" the woman shrieked as she fired an erratic shot.

People screamed and dove for cover as Sam wrestled the heavy-set woman to the ground and struggled to disarm her. Out of the corner of her eye, she saw Nick's black shoe.

"Get back!" she cried as the woman's elbow connected with her cheekbone.

Nick stomped on the woman's hand, and the gun clanked to the cobblestone street.

"Don't touch it!" Sam said to him as she cuffed the crying woman.

"You killed Quentin! *You killed our baby!*"

Something about the voice was familiar. "Marquis killed Quentin," Sam growled into the woman's ear as she tightened the cuffs. Flipping her over, she wasn't surprised to find Destiny Johnson's sister Dawn under her. "Was anyone hit?" Sam asked Nick.

"I don't think so." He looked down at her with a pale face and big, shocked eyes. "I heard someone call 911."

"Thanks for the assist."

"No problem."

As the market slowly returned to normal around them, Sam sat on a curb with Dawn until a couple of uniforms arrived to take statements and cart her off. Sam promised to write up her portion of the report and get it to them later.

"Nice job, Sam," one of the vendors called to her.

"Thanks," she said as Nick helped her up.

The moment she was upright, the pain she had managed to stave off during the confrontation with Dawn roared through her, leaving her breathless and weak in its wake.

"Jesus Christ, Sam," Nick muttered.

"S'okay," she said, bent in half as she took deep breaths. "Just give me a second." It took several minutes, but she was finally able to straighten only to find his hazel eyes hot with dismay and anger. "I'm fine."

"You're not fine." He took hold of her arm to steer her toward home. "And don't you ever push me out of the way again so you can dive at a gun, do you hear me? Don't ever do that again."

Startled by his tone, she stopped and turned to face him. "It's instinct and training. You can't fault me for that."

"How do you think it makes me feel, as a *man*, when the woman I love pushes me out of harm's way so she can throw herself in front of it? Huh?"

"I have no idea," she said sincerely.

"Well, let me tell you, it makes me feel like a useless, dickless moron."

"I'm not the kind of woman who needs a big strong man to protect her, Nick. If that's what you want or need, you've got the wrong girl."

"And you think I'm the kind of man who needs his *woman* to protect him? Is that what *you* want?"

"Why are we fighting?" she asked, perplexed. "I saw a shooter. I took her down. What the hell did I do wrong?"

"You pushed me out of the way!"

"Excuse me for not wanting your dumb ass to get killed. Next time I'll let her blow your head off. Would that be better?"

"Now you're just being a jerk."

Stunned and dismayed, she stared at him and said a silent thanks a lot to Dawn for turning their romantic afternoon to shit. "*I'm* the jerk? Whatever." Without a care as to whether he followed her or not, she stomped off toward home. When she got there, she heard voices in the kitchen and figured her sister Tracy's family had arrived. But rather than go see them, Sam went straight upstairs, needing a few minutes to get herself together first.

What's his problem anyway? She fumed as she shrugged off her coat, tossed it over her desk chair and flopped down on the bed. *What did I do besides try to protect his sorry ass?* The ache in her stomach was no match for the pain in her heart. This was exactly why she had stayed away from relationships since she split with Peter. If she never felt this shitty again, it would be just fine with her.

Nick came in a few minutes later, carrying the package she had abandoned in the chaos. "I believe this is yours," he said as he put it on her desk and took off his coat.

She couldn't believe she had forgotten all about the painting. "Thanks."

He sat down on the edge of the bed and brushed his fingers over her sore cheek.

Sam winced when he grazed the spot where Dawn's elbow had connected.

"You should put some ice on that." He laced his fingers through hers. "Between the bump on your head, the bruises on your chest and neck, and now this, you're quite a colorful mess."

"It's not usually like this. I swear to God, it's never this crazy."

"That's good to know, because I don't think I could handle this much drama on a daily basis." He brought their joined hands to his lips and kissed each of her fingers. "I'm sorry I overreacted."

Sam's mouth fell open. "Did you just *apologize?*"

"Yeah," he huffed. "So?"

"I didn't think guys did that. This is a first for me. You'll have to excuse me while I take a moment to enjoy it."

His eyes narrowed. "I'm about to take it back."

She laughed. "Please don't." Reaching up to touch the soft hair that curled over his ear, she studied the face she had come to love so much in such a short time. "I'm trying to understand why you got so upset."

"You did what you were trained to do, and just because I didn't like it doesn't mean you were wrong."

"Wow. This is truly quite a moment for me."

"Samantha…"

"I'll always push you out of the way, Nick. If you can't deal with that, we're going to have problems."

"We're going to have problems anyway. So how about we handle it this way? When I'm wrong, I'll say so. And when you're wrong, you'll say so."

"I will?"

"Uh-huh. That's how it works. That's the *only* way it works."

"Is this you being anal again and cleaning things up?"

"If that's how you want to see it."

"Fine," she conceded. "On the sure-to-be rare instances when I'm actually wrong about something, I'll do my best to admit it. Are you happy?"

"For some strange reason," he said, bending to kiss her, "I really am."

She slid her fingers into his hair to keep him there. "So am I."

CHAPTER 32

After dinner, Sam joined her sisters on the porch to share a cigarette. She leaned in to block the air as Tracy lit up while Angela flanked her other side. Each of them took a long drag before passing it on.

"Oh, I needed that," Tracy, who at forty was the oldest, said as she exhaled a steady stream of smoke. She shared Sam's height but had held on to ten extra pounds after each of her three children.

Angela, at thirty-six, had bounced right back to her svelte shape after giving birth to her son Jack five years earlier.

The door swung open, and Angela stashed the cigarette behind her back.

"Mom, Jack is walking back and forth in front of the TV and won't stop," whined fifteen-year-old Brooke, brimming with indignation. Her long dark hair, bright blue eyes and porcelain skin gave her a delicate beauty that was a source of great consternation to her parents as the boys began to take an avid interest in her.

"Sorry," Angela said. "I'll get him."

Tracy stopped her sister and said to her daughter, "Turn off the TV and spend some time with your cousin. All he wants is your attention."

In a huff, Brooke stomped back inside.

"Sorry about that," Angela said. "He loves being with the kids."

"Don't worry about it," Tracy said. "They watch enough TV at home. They don't need to do it here, too."

The door opened again, and this time Sam stashed the cigarette behind her back when she saw it was Nick.

"I was wondering where you all had disappeared to, and your father suggested I check the front porch where I'd find the three of you sharing a cigarette that you think no one knows about. I said, 'What do you mean, Skip? Samantha doesn't smoke.'"

Behind her back, Sam transferred the cigarette to Angela in a move they had perfected over the years. She smiled at Nick. "Of course I don't smoke. Did you need me?"

"I was going to ask if you'd mind if we go to my place tonight."

"I don't mind. I'll be in shortly, and we can take off."

"Okay."

The moment the door closed behind him, Angela took a drag off the dwindling cigarette. "Mmm. Hubba hubba."

Her sisters stared at her.

"Did you seriously just say 'hubba hubba'?" Tracy asked.

"Well, come on. He's yummy. And did he call you *Samantha?*"

Sam shrugged as her cheeks heated with embarrassment. "He likes to call me that."

"You must really dig him to put up with that," Ang said. "How's the sex?"

"Angela!" Tracy said.

"What? Don't tell me you don't want to know, too."

They waited expectantly for Sam.

"It's…you know…amazing."

"I remember amazing sex," Tracy said with a sigh. "At least I think I do."

"Stop," Angela said, bumping Tracy with her hip. "Mike's still hot for you."

"Yeah, I guess. So, Sam, I didn't want to ask in front of the kids, but this insanity with Peter...Are you okay?"

"It's kind of overwhelming to know he hates me enough to want to kill me."

"I think it's more that in his own sick, twisted way he *loves* you that much," Tracy said.

Angela nodded in agreement.

Sam told them about meeting Nick years ago and what Peter had done to keep them apart.

"Motherfucker," Angela muttered.

Sam laughed as she extinguished the cigarette. The sick feeling in her stomach and the lingering foul taste reminded her of why she'd quit smoking years ago. "Tell me how you really feel, Ang."

"I hate that bastard."

"So do I," Tracy said. "Divorcing him was the best thing you ever did. I couldn't stand the way he always had to know where you were and what you were doing. He never would've gone back inside the way Nick did just now. He would've wanted to know what we were talking about."

"I know," Sam said. "When I think about him not giving me those messages...I really wanted to hear from Nick after that night."

"You might've missed the whole Peter saga altogether," Tracy said.

"Maybe everything that happened with Peter, with the babies and stuff, would've happened with Nick and it would've screwed us up just as bad."

Her sisters each slid an arm around her.

"There's no point in going there, Sam," Tracy said.

"I haven't had a chance to tell Nick the whole story."

"It won't matter to him," Ang assured her. "He's mad about you. He never takes his eyes off you, but not in the creepy way Peter used to. More of an adoring way."

"He didn't have a family growing up, and I know he wants one."

"There're other ways, hon," Tracy said. "You know that. Don't worry about it right now. Enjoy this time with him. You deserve to be happy after everything you've been through."

"Thank you," Sam said, hugging them. "I'm so glad you guys like him."

"Hubba hubba," Ang said again, and they all laughed.

"Now how about Dad and Celia?" Sam said.

Just as Sam and Nick were getting ready to leave Skip's house, Freddie called. "We've got another body, Sergeant."

A burst of adrenaline zipped through Sam. "Who?"

"Tara Davenport."

"Oh, shit," Sam sighed, remembering the timid Capitol Hill waitress they'd interviewed. "Where?"

"Her apartment." Freddie rattled off the address. "It's bad, Sam. Whoever did this made sure she suffered."

"I'm on my way."

Nick insisted on driving her to the scene. On the way, Sam pumped him for information about Tara.

"She was so sweet," he said. "We always requested her section when we went in for lunch. I can't believe anyone would want to harm her."

"No way this is a coincidence. This has got to be tied to O'Connor. Did he tell you he was dating her?"

"He never came right out and discussed it with me, but I knew. He was so much older than her. I'm sure he thought I wouldn't approve."

"Did you?"

"Not really, but they were both consenting adults, so I kept my opinions to myself."

Since emergency vehicles had surrounded Tara's apartment building, Sam told him to double-park.

Freddie met them at the door to Tara's apartment, his expression grim. "Beaten, bound, raped and strangled."

Steeling herself, Sam followed him into the bedroom. "God almighty," she whispered at the sight of a bloodbath.

Behind her, Nick gasped.

Sam spun around. "You need to step back." Realizing he was on the verge of passing out, she rushed him into a chair and pushed his head between his knees. "Breathe."

"I'm okay," he muttered, looking up at her. His eyes glazed with shock, he shook his head. "Who could do that? Who?"

"I don't know, but I'm going to find out."

"Go ahead. Sorry to wimp out."

Sam left him in the living room and returned to the bedroom as Freddie took photos of the scene. Tara had been bound, gagged and, judging by the bloody pool between her legs, repeatedly raped.

"Who found her?" Sam asked Freddie.

"One of her coworkers got the super to let her in when she didn't show up for work for the second day in a row."

Dr. Lindsey McNamara, the medical examiner, stepped into the room. "Damn. Just when you think you've seen it all…"

"No kidding," Sam said.

One of the crime scene officers lifted a baseball bat from the floor. Blood stained the thick end of the barrel. "Looks like this was used for the beating, among other things…"

The women in the room winced.

Sam studied the young waitress who'd been so distraught over her breakup with John O'Connor. "How long has she been dead?"

Lindsey pulled on latex gloves and reached out to close Tara's eyes. "Looks like twenty to thirty hours, but I won't know for sure until I get her into the lab."

"I need a time of death ASAP so I can get a timeline going."

Lindsey nodded. "Who did this to you, sweetie?" the kind-hearted doctor whispered. "Don't you worry. We'll get them." Lindsey shifted her green eyes to Sam. "Won't we?"

"You bet your ass we will."

"Go pick up Elin Svendsen," Sam said to Freddie, working a hunch.

"Really?" The spark of excitement in his voice wasn't lost on Sam. "Will I get hardship duty pay for that?"

"Take her to a hotel and arrange for round-the-clock coverage."

"Got it—take goddess to hotel and watch over her. I think I can handle that."

Sam was relieved to hear him joking again after the hideous two hours they'd just put in at Tara's. "I'm going to send Gonzo out to Belle Haven to pick up the Jordans, too. I want her under protection."

"Noel passed the polygraph."

"Yeah, I got that word an hour ago."

"What're you thinking, boss?"

"Did Patricia Donaldson tell you where she'd be staying in the city when she came for O'Connor's funeral?"

His brows furrowing with skepticism, he said, "No, but I can try to find out."

"Do that. I could be wrong, but I'm going to pull her credit card records to see if she recently bought a plane ticket to Washington."

"Come on, Sam, you're not thinking it's her…That woman was madly in love with him."

"And he was fucking his way through the city while she raised his son in Siberia." Here was the buzz that came when all the pieces started to fall into place. "I'll pull the records, you find Elin."

Sobering, Freddie said, "You can count on me to take very good care of her."

Sam rolled her eyes. "Go easy. You might sprain something."

Emerging from Tara's apartment building, Sam found Nick leaning against her car. "Aren't you freezing?"

"The cold feels good." His face was pale, his eyes watering from the cold or maybe the emotion.

"You shouldn't have followed me in there. I told you to stay here."

"I don't know how you do it," he said softly. "How you can stand seeing stuff like that day after day? I'll never forget what I saw in there."

"I wish I could say it's the first time I've seen something like that."

He reached for her, but Sam shook him off. "No PDA when the place is swarming with cops," she growled.

Jamming his hands into his pockets, he seemed to be making an effort to bite his tongue.

Sam unclipped her hair and ran her fingers through it. "I need some computer time. Do you mind dropping me at HQ?"

"Does it have to be there? You could get online at my house."

She consulted her watch. Ten-forty. "I suppose that would work."

Nick offered to drive her car to Arlington, and Sam was tired enough after the long, draining day to let him.

"This is the time to be on the road." She gestured to the

deserted stretch of I-395 as they passed the Jefferson Memorial on their way to the 14th Street Bridge.

"If only it was like this in the morning."

She turned her head so she could see his profile in the orange glow of the streetlights. Anxious to get both their minds off the horror they'd witnessed at Tara's, Sam said, "So tell me, did my family overwhelm you?"

"What? No, of course not. Everyone was really nice."

"They liked you."

"What's the story with your brother-in-law Spencer?"

Sam smiled. "He's a bit much, huh?"

"Ah, yeah. Got a big opinion of himself."

"We only put up with him because he worships the ground Angela walks on. There's nothing he wouldn't do for her."

"Mike's a lot more normal."

"I adore him."

Nick shot her a meaningful glance.

"Not like that," Sam said, laughing. "I just give him so much credit. He's raising Brooke like she's his own—"

"She's *not?*"

Sam shook her head. "Her father was a guy Tracy dated briefly. When they found out she was pregnant he hit the road, and she never heard from him again. She met Mike a couple of years later. After they got married, he adopted Brooke."

"You'd never know she wasn't his."

"That's why I love him so much. We all do. He doesn't treat her any differently than he does Abby or Ethan."

"No, he certainly doesn't," Nick agreed. "I like him even more knowing that about him."

"He's the big brother I never had."

"Which is why he thoroughly grilled me about where I came from, where I'm going and what my intentions are toward you."

"He did *not*," Sam said, astounded.

"Yes, he did. And he made sure your father was able to hear the interrogation. In fact, I'll bet Skip put him up to it."

"I wouldn't doubt it." Turning in her seat, she leaned over to plant a wet kiss on his neck. "Thank you for putting up with that." Because he deserved it after dealing with her family, she tossed in some tongue action, too.

The car swerved. "Hello? I'm going seventy over here!"

She ran her hand up his thigh. "Want to go for eighty?"

He caught her hand the instant before it reached the promised land. "Behave."

"So what did you tell Mike?" she asked, resting her head on his shoulder.

Bringing their joined hands to his lips, he pressed a kiss to the back of hers. "That I've always loved you, and I always will."

Sam sighed with contentment. "I like hearing that."

"Do you know why I wanted to go home tonight?"

"Nope."

"I found out today that you love me, too. I wanted to be alone with you tonight."

A tremble of anticipation rippled through her. "You knew before today."

"I suspected and I hoped, but I didn't know for sure. I worried that maybe we were both caught up in the craziness of the last week."

She raised her head from his shoulder. "Did you really think that was possible?"

He shrugged. "I was afraid I wanted you too much and that somehow I'd screw it up. I almost did a few times."

"I hate knowing you felt that way." Returning her head to his shoulder, she was struck by how alone he was and how badly she wanted to surround him with the love he'd missed out on while growing up without a family. A lump formed in her throat when she thought of one thing he wanted that she couldn't give him.

They rode the rest of the way in silence, both wrapped up in their own thoughts.

Entering his house through the front door, he took her coat and hung it in the hall closet.

"What happened to all the glass?" she asked.

"I paid my cleaning lady double to come in today and deal with it, but we probably shouldn't walk around barefoot for a while."

"How's your foot?"

"Sore."

She winced. "And I had you out walking on it earlier. I never even thought about it. I'm sorry."

He leaned in to kiss her. "No worries, babe. Computer's in the office. I'll take our stuff upstairs."

"Thanks. I'll be quick."

"Take your time. I've got to finish my eulogy."

She went up on tiptoes to kiss him while wishing there was something she could say to ease his pain. But knowing only time could do that, she let him go and headed for his office. Kicking off her shoes, she sat down to boot up his computer. Before she got to the research she planned to do, she wrote the report on the incident at Eastern Market and saved it to Nick's desktop.

While she waited on the police department system to log her in, she took note of the fastidious order on the dark cherry-wood desktop. Feeling mischievous, she nudged the pile of books out of alignment, shifted the container of paperclips so it was off center, turned all the black pens in the pen cup upside down and drew a heart with an arrow through the Sam loves Nick she had written on the blotter.

Pleased with her handiwork, she turned her attention to Patricia Davidson's credit card records. Scanning through the pages, her eyes began to blur with fatigue until she stopped short on an airline charge from two days before John's death. "Well, look at you, Miss Patricia," Sam whispered, the kick of adrenaline making her heart beat faster. "Gotcha!"

She took a moment to look the woman up online get a visual on her before she called Freddie. "Have you got Elin?"

"We're on our way." He named one of the city's best hotels.

"Jeez, spare no expense, why dontcha," she muttered, imagining the grief she'd get when that expense report landed on Malone's desk.

"Just following orders, Sergeant."

"Patricia Donaldson bought a seat on a flight from Chicago to Washington the day before O'Connor's murder."

Freddie released a long deep breath. "Wow. I totally missed this one. I'm sorry."

"We all missed it."

"But I interviewed her. I should've caught the vibe—"

"Knock it off, Cruz."

"I don't see her having the strength to get that knife through O'Connor's neck. She was almost fragile."

"Rage can make people a lot stronger than normal."

"Yeah, I guess. Would she have a key to his apartment?"

"Maybe she came for conjugals once in a while. It wouldn't surprise me that she had a key—I mean who *didn't* have a key to that place?"

"Right. And don't forget, he could've let the killer in after he got home."

"I still say he was taken by surprise since he was murdered in bed. Anyway, don't let Elin out of your sight, do you hear me?"

"It's a tough job, but someone's got to do it."

CHAPTER 33

Sam ended the call and sat back in the big leather chair. Closing her eyes, she let her mind wander through the parts and pieces, hoping something would start to add up. The frustration was starting to get to her as day after day went by without the big break she needed to wrap this up. *I'm missing something. Something big. But what?*

"Everything all right, babe?" Nick asked from the doorway.

Holding out her arms, she invited Nick to join her. "We might be starting to get somewhere. Patricia Donaldson bought a ticket on a flight to D.C. the day before John's murder. We've got people trying to figure out where she's staying in the city. Nothing on the credit report shows her hotel."

"You'll figure it out." He kneeled down in front of her and leaned into her embrace. "What brought on this spontaneous show of affection?"

"I just needed it," she said, resting her cheek on his shoulder. "I'm frustrated, aggravated, pissed that it's taken me so long to hone in on her, that someone else had to die…"

"Well, I'm happy to provide comfort any time you need it." He suddenly stiffened.

"What's wrong?" she asked, pulling back to look at him.

"What did you do to my desk?"

"Nothing," she said, all innocence.

"You did, too. You moved things, and you probably did it on purpose to screw with me."

Sam dissolved into laughter. "You're *such* a freak show."

When he would've gotten up to fix it, she stopped him. "Leave it. See if you can do it." She gripped his hands. "Come on. Be strong."

"Why does it bother you so much that I require order?"

"What you require is so far beyond order the sphincter police haven't invented the word for it yet."

"Fine. If you want to make a mess and walk away, that's your problem. It doesn't bother me."

"Yes, it does," she said, laughing to herself at his definition of a mess. He hadn't the slightest idea of what she was capable of in that regard. "I bet you'll sneak down here when I'm sleeping tonight and fix it."

"No, I won't," he said, his eyes flashing with the start of anger.

"It's okay if you do," she cooed. "I'll still love you and all your anal retentive freakazoidisms."

At her words of love, he softened, but only a little.

She ran her fingers through his hair and leaned in to kiss him. "Will you do me a favor?"

"What?" he asked in a terse tone.

"Will you read my report about the shooting at Eastern Market for me? See if I made any mistakes?"

He looked at her oddly as he got up to take her place at the desk.

Sam stood behind him, hanging over his shoulder as he went through the events of earlier, making tweaks here and there. She was relieved that he found no blatant errors.

When he was done, he turned to her. "Want to tell me what that was all about?"

She pursed her lips, wanting to tell him, but feeling shy all of a sudden. "Well, you were there. I was just making sure I didn't miss anything."

He reached for her hand and brought her down to sit on his lap. "You don't need me for that. What is it, babe?"

"I'm dyslexic," she said for the second time that day. "Freddie usually checks me, but since he wasn't involved in this, I didn't feel right asking him. Plus he's baby-sitting one of John's girlfriends at the moment."

"I'm glad you asked me. I'll do it for you any time."

She attached the file to an e-mail to the arresting officer. Then she returned her attention to Nick. "Thank you," she said, pressing her lips to his for what she intended to be a quick kiss.

"You're welcome," he whispered as he ran his tongue over her bottom lip before tipping his head to delve deeper. As he kissed her, he arranged her so she straddled him and took her by surprise when he pulled back to whip the sweater up over her head.

Sam shivered as cool air hit her fevered skin. "Nick— I'm working—I can't right now." As she said the words, she reached for the hem of his shirt, but he stopped her. Moaning with frustration, she found his mouth for another frantic kiss and gasped when he released her bra. "Got to work…"

"Shh," he said, feasting on one breast and then the other.

Surrendering to the sensory assault, Sam gripped his shoulders and tried to convince herself that taking ten minutes for herself didn't make her a crappy cop.

"You have the most beautiful breasts," he whispered, trailing his tongue in circles around her nipple.

"They're too big."

"No," he said, laughing. "They're not. They're utter perfection. In fact, I could sit here all night and do nothing but what I'm doing right now until the sun comes up."

She tilted her pelvis tight against his throbbing erection. "Really? Nothing but this? All night?"

He groaned. "Maybe we could mix it up a bit." Helping her to her feet, he unbuttoned her jeans, hooked his fingers into her panties and divested her of both garments in one swift move before bringing her back to his lap.

"You're kind of overdressed," she said, tugging at his shirt.

"Patience, babe." Raining hot, open-mouthed kisses on her neck, he ran his hands up and down her back, sending shivers of desire dancing through her.

"I don't have any patience. Don't you know that by now?"

He propped her thighs on his legs and then moved his feet apart, opening her.

"What're you doing?" she asked, her words infected with a stammer.

"Touching you."

"I want to touch you, too."

"You'll get your turn." He cupped her breasts and ran his thumbs over nipples still sensitive from his earlier ministrations. "It was infuriating today to hear that bastard call you frigid." His hands coasted down over her ribs. One arm encircled her while his other hand slid through the dampness between her legs. "Feel that?" he whispered. "That's as far from frigid as you can get."

"I hardly ever came when I had sex with him," Sam managed to say. "It made him mad."

"We know you weren't the problem, right?" he asked as he drove two fingers into her.

Sam cried out.

"Did you mess up my desk on purpose?" he asked, his fingers coming to a halt deep inside her.

Laughing, she said, "Maybe!" She wiggled her hips, begging him to continue.

"'Fess up or you won't get what you want."

"Yes! I did it!"

"That was easy," he chuckled. "Now you must be punished."

She moaned as he found the spot that throbbed for his touch.

He shifted the arm he had around her so his hand gripped her ass, holding her still for his gliding fingers. When he captured her nipple between his teeth, the combination lifted her into a powerful orgasm that stole the breath from her lungs and brought tears to her eyes.

"So hot," he whispered against her lips. "So, *so* hot."

His fingers continue to tease, and Sam was astounded to feel another climax building. Somehow she marshaled the energy to tear at his shirt, lifting it up and over his head. She ran her hand down his chest to his belly and below, dragging her finger over his steely length.

He inhaled sharply.

"Nick, *please*. I want you."

"You have me, Samantha. I'm all yours. Forever and always." He kissed her as if it was the first time all over again, exploring her mouth with deep, penetrating sweeps of his tongue.

When she couldn't stand the burning need another minute, she worked her way off his lap, pulled him up and stripped him in record time. Dropping to her knees, she took him into her mouth.

"Sam…" He buried his fingers in her hair. "Babe, wait. This was about you. Come up here."

"You said I'd get my turn," she pouted, dragging her tongue over him as she looked up to find his eyes bearing down on her.

"And you will." He helped her up, returned to the chair and brought her down to straddle him once again. "I love you."

She tilted her hips and took him in. Leaning forward she touched her lips to his. "I love you, too."

"I'm never going to get tired of hearing that."

"I'm never going to get tired of saying it."

"Promise?"

She nodded and rolled her hips to take him deeper.

Releasing a long deep breath, his eyes fluttered closed.

Sam kissed the bandage above his eye and rode him slowly, each movement taking them both closer...so close.

Suddenly, he wrapped his arms tight around her, stood up and carried her to the sofa without losing their connection.

Hooking his arms under her knees he held her open for his fierce possession. Caught up in the thrill, Sam came with a sharp cry of release that dragged him right down with her.

"Damn," he whispered a minute of heavy breathing later. "Just when I think it can't get any more perfect..."

She brushed the damp hair off his forehead. "It does."

"We're going to kill ourselves if it gets any more perfect."

Sam laughed. "Hell of a way to go."

With his eyes fixed on hers, he kissed her softly.

"I have something I need to tell you," she said, her stomach twisting as she said the words.

"Now?"

Filled with a kind of fear she hadn't often experienced, she bit her bottom lip and nodded.

"So are you going to clue me in on what I'm doing here?" Elin Svendsen said as she paced the fancy hotel room.

"I told you," Freddie said, keeping a tight rein on his libido as he watched her move back and forth. "It's for your safety."

"Are you *sure*?" Her teasing smile shot lust straight through him. He was glad he'd kept his trench coat on. "I'm starting to wonder if you made this whole thing up to get me alone in a hotel room." She sashayed up to him so that her breasts were right at his eye level.

Desperate, he said, "One of John O'Connor's ex-girlfriends was murdered."

Elin gasped. "For real?"

"Would I lie about murder?"

"I don't know. Would you?"

"I never lie about murder."

"I don't get it. He wasn't married or anything."

"Well, he sort of was."

Elin spun around. "What do you mean?"

Freddie told her about the woman and child who'd been banished to the Midwest twenty years ago.

"So you think it's her?"

"We suspect it could be, and we want to keep you safe until we find her."

Elin crossed her arms in a protective gesture that tugged at his heart. "I can't believe he had this whole other secret life."

"Apparently, no one knew. Not even his closest friend."

"I don't sleep with married guys. I know you probably think I'm easy, but I do have morals."

"I never suspected otherwise."

She tilted her head to study him. "You're pretty cute, you know that?"

Freddie cheeks heated with embarrassment. "Thanks. I think."

Smiling, she added, "We could make this little 'protection mission' of yours a whole lot more fun if you're game."

He swallowed hard. "What do you mean?"

She bent over, her top sliding forward to reveal a tantalizing view of her spectacular breasts. A hint of the Cupid tattoo was visible over the top of her low-cut bra. "Sex, Detective," she whispered. "Dirty, raunchy sex."

Feeling as if he was being tested, Freddie shifted to relieve the growing pressure in his lap. "I'm on duty."

"Who would know?"

"I would." *Sam would know. Somehow, she'd find out, and I'd be screwed in a whole other way.*

Shooting him an "are you for real?" look, Elin shrugged and reached for her bag. "I'm going to get changed."

As soon as he heard the bathroom door close behind her, Freddie closed his eyes and counted to ten. God help him, but he wanted to grab her, toss her down on the bed and have his way with her. Reminding himself that he was *working*, he willed his throbbing erection into submission.

Elin emerged from the bathroom wearing a purple silk nightgown that just barely covered her shapely ass.

Freddie suppressed a groan as she passed by him, leaving a fragrant cloud in her wake.

"Are you *sure* you don't want to have some fun?" she asked as she got settled in the other bed.

"Positive," he said through gritted teeth.

She flipped off the light. "Your loss."

Freddie fell back on the second bed and released a tortured deep breath. He was definitely being tested.

Nick grabbed a blanket from the back of the sofa and spread it over them, arranging them so they lay facing each other. He traced a finger over Sam's frown. "I don't know what's causing you such concern, but whatever it is, we'll get through it together, Sam."

She rested her hand on his chest.

Nick's heart galloped under her touch as he waited for her to gather her thoughts.

"When I was with Peter," she said tentatively, "we tried for a long time to have a baby. We were about to go for infertility treatment when I got pregnant."

Imagining what she was going to say, Nick ached for her.

"I was so excited, even though Peter and I were already having a lot of problems. I know it was foolish to think a baby could fix it, but I still had hope then."

His heart breaking, Nick wiped away a tear that spilled down her cheek.

"I miscarried at twelve weeks."

"Sam...I'm so sorry."

"It was a bad miscarriage. I lost a lot of blood, and it took me a really long time to bounce back. Peter was so devastated. He kind of retreated into himself."

"So you went through it alone."

She shrugged and sat up, moving out of his embrace. "I had my sisters, my family. Angela had Jack a short time later, and he saved me in so many ways. He's my baby as much as he's hers. She even says so."

"He's adorable."

"He's my little man." She wiped her face with an impatient swipe, as if the tears were pissing her off. "A couple of months later, the doctor told me we could try again. Things with Peter had seriously disintegrated, but we both still wanted a baby so we made an effort to fix what was wrong even though I already knew it couldn't really be fixed. For a while, though, things were better. A year after the miscarriage, I got pregnant again, but I didn't know. It was an ectopic pregnancy. Do you know what that is?"

Nick sat up, reached for her hand and tried not to be hurt when she brushed him off. "I've heard of it."

"It's when the embryo implants outside the uterus. In my case, it was in one of the fallopian tubes. I was home alone when the tube erupted. I had almost bled to death when Angela found me."

"Jesus, Sam."

"I was in the hospital for more than a week that time. It was the most painful thing I've ever been through—physically and emotionally. I lost the tube and one of my ovaries. Because of some other problems I'd had with endometriosis, my doctor told me it was unlikely that I'd ever conceive again."

All at once Nick understood what had her so worried. "It doesn't matter, Sam. Not to me. If that's what you're worried about, don't."

"But you want a family. You *deserve* a family after growing up without one."

"We'll have one. We can adopt. There're millions of kids out there in need of homes. It doesn't matter to me how we get them."

"But—"

He leaned over and kissed her. Hard. "No buts. You're the key to everything. I knew that years ago when I first met you, and I know it even more now after living without you for so long. You're what I need most. We'll figure out the rest." Caressing her cheek, he added, "You've already given me so much that I've never had before. I don't want you to spend another second worrying about the one thing you can't give me."

"I told you I'm on the pill, but I'm not. I don't need to be, but I couldn't very well blurt this whole thing out when we were about to make love the other day. I'm sorry I lied to you."

"That doesn't even count as a lie, babe. When the time is right, and we're ready to have a family, we'll work something out."

"You should think about it. You should take some time to make sure—"

He stopped her with a finger to her lips. "I don't need to think about it."

The tension seemed to leave her body in one long exhale, and when he reached for her, she came willingly back into his arms.

"Do you feel better?"

She nodded. "I felt like I was deceiving you by getting so involved with you and not telling you this."

"You weren't deceiving me. It's part of you, Sam. It's part of what's made you who you are, and I love everything about you."

She ran her finger over the stubble on his jaw. "I used to dream about you when I was married. I wondered where you were, what you were doing, if you were happy. We only had that one night together, but I thought about you all the time."

The reminder of what they'd been denied made him ache with regret. "I thought about you, too. I read the paper obsessively, looking for the slightest mention of you."

"I did, too! I knew you were working for O'Connor. I even watched hours of congressional coverage, hoping for a glimpse of you, but you kept a low profile. I hardly ever saw you."

"My profile is probably going to get even lower."

"What do you mean?"

"I checked my voicemail at the office today. Got a few job offers."

"Like what?"

"Legislative affairs for the junior senator from Hawaii, communications for the senior senator from Florida. Oh, and director of the Columbus office for the senior senator from Ohio." With a teasing smile, he added, "What do you think about living in Columbus?"

She curled up her nose. "Is there anything that wouldn't be a major step down?"

"Nope. But that's how it works in politics. Your fortunes as a staffer are tied up in who you work for. If they go up, you go up. If they flame out, so do you."

"Or if they die…"

"Exactly."

"So what're you going to do?"

"I've got some money put away, and there's that money coming from John, too, so I'm not going to make any hasty decisions. In fact, it might be time for a change."

"What kind of change?"

"I used to toy with the idea of going to law school. It's probably too late now, but I still think about it."

"If it's what you want, you should do it."

Nick chuckled as he tweaked her nose. "So you'd be willing to put up with a professional student for a couple of years?"

"Whatever makes you happy makes me happy."

He shifted so he was on top of her. "*You* make me happy."

Sam's arms curled around his neck to bring him in for a kiss full of love and promise. She wrapped her long legs around his hips and arched her back, seeking him.

As Nick slid into her, he was so overwhelmed by love for her it took his breath away. Trying to get a hold of his emotions, he stayed still for a long moment until she began to wiggle under him, asking for more. What had earlier been frenetic was now slow and dreamy. He leaned in to kiss her, managing to hang on to his control until she gripped his ass to keep him inside her when she climaxed.

"Sam," he gasped as he pushed into her one last time, unable to believe they had managed to top perfection.

CHAPTER 34

Sam was trying to shake off the sex-induced stupor and open her eyes to go back to work when her phone rang. Checking the caller ID, she saw it was Gonzo. "What've you got?"

"A bloodbath," he said. "They're both dead."

Giving herself a second to absorb the news, she said, "How?"

"Noel was shot twice in the head at close range. Just like the other one, she was tied to the bed and tortured."

"I'm on my way." Sam sat up and started pulling on clothes.

"What's wrong?" Nick mumbled, half asleep.

"Noel and Natalie Jordan were murdered in their house." He gasped. "Oh my God."

"I've got to get over there."

Reaching for his jeans, he said, "I'll come with you."

"No! There's no need. Peter's locked up, and I have to work."

"I promise I'll stay out of the way."

"You *never* stay out of the way."

"I knew these people, Sam. Don't make me stay home."

He looked so uncharacteristically vulnerable that her heart went out to him. She understood all at once that more than anything he didn't want to be alone just then. "Okay, but you *will* stay out of the way."

"I promise."

On the way to Belle Haven, Sam arranged for surveillance on Elin Svendsen's apartment building in case Patricia showed up there looking to make Elin her next victim. To Nick, she said, "Can you call Christina? I need the full list of every woman John dated during the years she worked for him."

"All of them?"

"Every one. I want names, addresses and phone numbers. Patricia has been gathering the same info we have. She's had someone digging into his past. I want to know what else she found—or rather *who* else."

"Christina might not have all that."

Sam shot him a withering look. "She was in love with him. You think she doesn't have the full lowdown on all the women he dated? Give me a break. She's probably got every detail down to their bra size in a spreadsheet. Tell her to e-mail the list to me."

While Nick made the call, Sam ordered first shift to be called in early. Rounding up all of John's Barbies was going to take some serious manpower. Her cell phone rang, and Sam took the call from Detective Jeannie McBride.

"We've checked every hotel in the city," Jeannie said. "No hits for a Patricia Donaldson. Do you want me to start checking the burbs?"

Sam thought about that for a moment. "Try Patricia O'Connor, and get some extra people on it. I need that info ASAP."

"You got it, Sergeant."

Sam ended the call, but clutched the phone as they sped toward the Jordans' house. "I can't believe I didn't get to her sooner."

"She was the love of his life. Why would you think it was her?"

"He was the love of *her* life. Not the other way around. If a guy loves a woman the way she told us he loved her, he's not banging everything he can get his hands on when he's not with her. I think maybe she was still caught up in their teen-age Romeo and Juliet romance, but he'd moved on. I'd sure love to talk to their kid. Thomas."

"He must be somewhere local with the funeral the day after tomorrow."

"If he is, we'll find him—and his mother. I just hope we get to her before she gets to another of John's girlfriends."

By the time they arrived, the Jordans' Belle Haven neigh-borhood was overrun with emergency vehicles.

Gonzo met them, his usually calm demeanor rattled. "I got here as soon as I could after Cruz called to tell me you wanted her picked up. The door was open. I saw him lying in the foyer and immediately called it in. We're getting some shit from Al-exandria, so you'll have to talk your way in."

Calling on every ounce of patience she could muster, Sam explained to the Alexandria Police that the Jordan murders were possibly tied to Senator O'Connor's killing. After some territorial squabbling and just as she was about to get ugly with them, they agreed to let her view the crime scene. They made Nick wait outside.

Noel had been taken quickly in the foyer. Sam deduced that he'd opened the door and was shot before he had time to even say hello to the caller.

"He's the number two guy at Justice," she said with a smug smile for the cocky Alexandria detective who'd tried the hard-est to keep her out. "You might want to let the attorney gen-eral know that his deputy's been murdered."

Flustered, the young detective said, "Yes, of course."

Pleased to have defused some of his arrogance, she went up-stairs to see what had been done to Natalie. She'd been bound in almost the exact same fashion as Tara. And like Tara, the blood between her open legs told the story of sadistic sexual torture. "Is that a *hairbrush?*" Sam asked, staring at the object that had been left in Natalie's vagina.

"I think so," the medical examiner said.

Sam grimaced. Judging from the ligature marks on Natalie's neck, she too had been strangled after suffering through a prolonged attack.

Patricia was exacting revenge, one woman at a time.

The Alexandria Medical Examiner estimated time of death at about three hours prior. Sam's gut clenched at the realization that Noel must've just gotten home from the polygraph when they were attacked. If she'd only pieced this together a little sooner, she might've been able to save them.

Since it wasn't her crime scene, she stepped outside after asking the detectives for a courtesy copy of their report.

Nick was once again leaning against the car, waiting for her.

"Same thing as Tara."

"Christ," he whispered. "I didn't like Natalie, but the thought of what she must've gone through..."

Sam ran her fingers through her long hair, fighting off exhaustion that clung to her like a heavy blanket. "I know."

"I've been thinking..."

She glanced up at him to find his face tight with tension and distress. "About?"

"Graham and Laine."

The statement hung in the air between them, the implications almost too big to process.

Sam tossed the keys to him. "You drive while I work."

As they flew across Northern Virginia, Nick's big frame vibrated with tension. "You don't really think..."

"That she'd go after the people she blames for ruining her life? Yeah, I really think."

"God, Sam. If she hurts them..." His voice broke.

She reached for his hand. "We may be way off." But just in

case they weren't, she gave the Loudon County Police a heads-up about potential trouble at the senior Senator O'Connor's home. She also forwarded the list of ex-girlfriends that Christina had grudgingly sent to HQ with orders to place officers at each woman's home. The officers were provided with photos of Patricia Donaldson and Thomas O'Connor—just in case she wasn't acting alone. Issuing a second all-points bulletin for both of them, Sam could only pray that the cops got to the other women before anyone else was harmed.

"Should've seen this," she muttered, hating that it had taken her so long to put it together. "So freaking obvious."

"Don't beat yourself up, babe."

"Hard not to when the bodies are piling up."

"I'll bet I know why he was killed on the eve of the vote," Nick said.

Sam glanced at him. "Why?"

"He decided the week before he was killed that he was definitely going to run for re-election. He probably told Patricia that. Maybe he'd promised her one term to satisfy his father and then it would be their time. If I'm right about that, she wouldn't have wanted him to have the chance to bask in the glow of his big victory on the bill. Not when he was screwing her over—in more ways than one."

"That makes sense," Sam said, buzzing with adrenaline as all the pieces fell into place. Certain now that she was on her way to cracking the case, she called Captain Malone and Chief Farnsworth at home to update them on the latest developments.

"Get me an arrest, Sergeant," the chief said, groggy with sleep.

"I'm moving as fast as I can, sir."

After she ended the call, Nick reached for her hand. "Why don't you close your eyes for a few minutes?"

She shook her head. "I'd rather wait until I have a couple of hours. How about you? Are you okay to be driving?"

"I'm fine. Don't worry about me."

"Too late." She rested her head on his shoulder and went through the case piece by piece from the beginning. All along she'd suspected it would be a woman, one he was close to, who had a key to his place, who he wouldn't have been surprised to find waiting for him in his apartment.

Her cell phone rang. "What've you got, Jeannie?"

"Unfortunately, nothing. We can't find them anywhere in the city."

"Damn it. They must've checked in under other names."

"That's the hunch around here. We're expanding into Northern Virginia and Maryland. I'll keep you posted."

"Thanks."

A Loudon County Police cruiser was positioned at the foot of the O'Connors' driveway when Sam and Nick arrived. He rolled down the window.

"Everything looks fine," the young officer said. "The house is dark and buttoned down for the night. I walked all the way around but didn't see anything to worry about."

"Thanks," Nick said. "We're just going to take a quick look and then be on our way."

"No problem. Have a nice evening."

As Nick drove slowly up the long driveway, Sam studied him with new appreciation. He'd handled the young cop with aplomb—thanking him for checking but letting him know they were going to take their own look—without insulting the officer. "Smooth," she said.

"What?"

"You. Just now."

"You sound surprised that I can actually be diplomatic when the situation calls for it."

She snorted with laughter.

"What's so funny?"

"You are when you get all indignant."

"I'm not indignant."

"Whatever you say."

They pulled up to the dark house, and Nick cut the engine. "I want to take my own walk around."

Sam retrieved a flashlight from the glove box and reached for the door handle.

"Why don't you stay here?" he said. "I'll be right back."

"The way you stay put when I tell you to?" She flipped on the flashlight in time to catch the dirty look he sent her way. "Let's go."

They walked the perimeter of the house, finding nothing out of the ordinary. In the backyard, Sam scanned the property. "Seems like everything is fine."

"I want to see them to make sure."

"Nick, it's two-thirty in the morning, and their son's funeral is tomorrow."

He scowled at her. "Do you *honestly* think they're sleeping?"

Realizing he was determined, she followed him to the front door and cringed at the sound of the doorbell chiming through the silent house.

A minute or so later, Graham appeared at the door wearing a red plaid bathrobe. His face haggard with grief, Sam deduced that he hadn't slept in days.

"What's wrong?" he asked.

"Nothing," Nick said, his voice infected with a nervous stammer. "I'm sorry to disturb you, but there's been some trouble tonight. I wanted to check on you and Laine."

Graham stepped aside to invite them in. "What kind of trouble?"

Nick told him about Tara and the Jordans.

"Oh God," Graham whispered. "Not Natalie, too. And Noel…"

"We think it's Patricia," Sam said, gauging his reaction.

Graham's tired eyes shot up to meet hers. "No…She couldn't have. She loved John. She'd loved him all her life."

"And she'd waited for him—fruitlessly—for her entire adult life," Sam said.

"We think he told her he was running for re-election," Nick said.

"So she assumed he was choosing his career over her and Thomas," Graham said.

"That's the theory," Sam said. "And we think she recently learned there were other women in his life."

"Why are you worried about us?" Graham asked Nick. "We haven't seen her since Thomas was born."

"Because if she's settling old scores, she certainly has a bone to pick with you," Nick said.

Graham ran a trembling hand through his white hair. "Yes, I suppose she does."

"I'd like to arrange for security for you and your wife until we wrap this up," Sam said.

"If you think it's necessary."

Knowing what had been done to Tara, Natalie and Noel, Sam said, "I really do."

Nick hugged Graham. "Why don't you try to get some rest?"

"Every time I doze off, I wake up suddenly and have to re-member that John is gone…I keep reliving it, over and over. It's easier just to stay awake."

Nick embraced the older man again, and when he finally released him, Sam saw tears in Nick's eyes. "I know what you mean."

"Yes, I suppose you do."

"I'll see you in the morning. Don't hesitate to call me if you need anything."

Graham patted Nick's face. "I love you like one of my own. I hope you know that."

His cheek pulsing with emotion, Nick nodded.

"There's something I need to talk to you about after the funeral," Graham said. "Save me a few minutes?"

"Of course."

"Drive carefully," Graham said as he showed them out.

Sam slipped her arm through Nick's and led him from the house, taking the keys from his coat pocket on the way to the car. "Are you okay?" she finally asked once they were in the car.

After a long moment of silence, Nick looked over at her. "He's never said that to me before. I've always sort of known it, but he's never come right out and said the words."

"You're an easy guy to love—most of the time."

His face lifted into the grin she adored. "Gee, thanks."

"We've got to do something about your inability to follow orders, however."

"Best of luck with that." He linked his fingers with hers as she drove them down the long driveway. "Thanks."

"For what?"

"For understanding why I needed to see with my own eyes that they're okay."

"They're your people."

"They're all I've got."

She squeezed his hand. "Not anymore."

CHAPTER 35

On the way back to Nick's house, Sam arranged for security at the O'Connor home and participated in a conference call with other HQ detectives to map out a plan for coverage of the funeral in the morning. If Patricia or Thomas showed up at the cathedral, they were prepared to snag them going in. Sam planned to wear a wire so she could communicate from the inside if need be. Because she knew Nick needed her support, she hoped she could get through the service without her job interfering, but she knew he'd understand if she had to leave. He wanted John's killer caught as much as she did.

As she followed Nick into his house, she glanced at the front shrubs, recalling once again the sensation of being hurled through the air by the force of the bomb. She shuddered.

"What's wrong, babe?"

"Nothing," she said, trying to shake off feelings that were magnified by a serious lack of sleep.

"It's going to take a while before we can walk in here and not think of it."

"I'm fine," she assured him, amazed once again by how tuned into her he was. "I just need a little more computer time."

He hung their coats in the front hall closet and then stepped behind her to massage her shoulders. "What you need is sleep."

"But—"

"No buts." He steered her up the stairs to his bedroom.

Sam wished she had the energy to fight him as he undressed her and tucked her into bed.

"What about you?" she asked, smothering a yawn.

"I'm going to grab a shower. I'll be there in a minute."

"'K," she said, her eyes burning shut.

While she waited for him, Sam's mind wandered through everything that had happened during that long night, replaying each crime scene as she tried to hold off on sleep until Nick joined her. All at once, she snapped out of the languor to discover that nearly half an hour had passed since he'd left her to take a shower.

She got up and went into a bathroom awash in steam. Opening the shower door, she found him leaning against the wall, lost in thought. Quietly, she slipped in behind him and wrapped her arms around his waist.

He startled and then relaxed into her embrace. "You're supposed to be sleeping."

"Can't sleep without you. You've ruined me." She pressed a series of kisses to the warm skin on his back. "Come on."

He shut off the water.

Sam grabbed his towel and dried them both. Taking his hand, she led him to bed. Wrapped in his arms, she was finally able to sleep.

Walking into the National Cathedral for the first time in her life the next morning, Sam gazed up at the soaring spires like an awestruck tourist from Peoria.

She wondered if staring at the president of the United States and his lovely wife like a star-struck lunatic made her any less of a bad-assed cop. In all her years on the job and living in the city, she had caught occasional glimpses of various presidents, but never had she been close enough to reach out and touch one—not that she would because that would be weird of course. Not to mention the Secret Service might take issue with it.

But as President Nelson and his wife Gloria approached Nick to offer their condolences, Sam could only stand by his side and remind herself to breathe as he shook hands with them.

"We're so very sorry for your loss," Gloria said.

"Thank you, Mrs. Nelson. John would be overwhelmed by this turnout." He gestured to the rows of former presidents, congressional members past and present, Supreme Court justices, the chairman of the Joint Chiefs of Staff, the secretaries of state, defense, homeland security and labor, among others. "This is Detective Sergeant Sam Holland, Metro Police."

Sam was struck dumb until it dawned on her that she was supposed to extend her hand. To the president. Of the United States. And the first lady. *Jesus.* "An honor to meet you both," Sam said.

"We've seen you in the news," the president said.

Sam wanted to groan, but she forced a smile. "It's been a unique month."

Gloria chuckled. "I'd say so."

Since both men were speakers, they were shown to seats in the front, adjacent to the O'Connor family. While Nick went over to say hello to them Sam scanned the crowd but saw no sign of Patricia or Thomas. Seated behind the O'Connors were most of John's staff and close family friends whom Nick identified for her when he returned to sit next to her.

She glanced over to find him pale, his eyes fixed on the mahogany casket at the foot of the huge altar. He hadn't eaten that morning and had even refused coffee. Looking back at the throngs of dignitaries, she couldn't imagine how difficult it would be for him to stand before them to speak about his murdered best friend. Disregarding her PDA rule, she reached for his hand and cradled it between both of hers.

He sent her a small smile, but his eyes expressed his gratitude for her support.

The mass began a short time later, and Sam was surprised to discover Nick had obviously spent a lot of time in church. Since she'd been raised without formal religion, the discovery was somewhat startling.

John's sister Lizbeth and brother Terry read Bible passages, and his niece and nephew lit candles. When both of them ran a loving hand over their uncle's casket on their way back to their seats, Sam's eyes burned, and judging by the rustle of tissues all around her, she wasn't alone.

President Nelson spoke of his long friendship with the O'Connor family, of watching John grow up and his pride in seeing such a fine young man sworn in as a United States senator. As the president left the pulpit, he stopped to hug John's tearful parents.

An usher tapped Nick on the shoulder. With a squeeze for Sam's hand, he got up to follow the usher's directions to the pulpit.

Unable to tear her eyes off Nick as he made his way to the microphone, Sam was swamped with love and sympathy and a jumble of other emotions. She sent him every ounce of strength she could muster.

"On behalf of the O'Connor family, I want to thank you for being here today and for your overwhelming outpouring of support during this last difficult week. Senator and Mrs. O'Connor also wish to express their love and gratitude to the people of the Commonwealth who came by the thousands to stand in the cold for hours to pay their respects to John. He took tremendous pride in the Old Dominion, and the five years he represented the citizens of Virginia in the Senate were the most rewarding, challenging and satisfying years of his life."

Nick spoke eloquently of his humble beginnings in a one-bedroom apartment in Lowell, Massachusetts, of meeting a senator's son at Harvard, of his first weekend in Washington with the O'Connors and how his exposure to the family changed his life.

Sam noticed the O'Connors wiping at tears. Behind them, Christina Billings, Nick's deputy and the woman who'd suffered through unrequited love for John, rested her head on the communication director's shoulder.

Nick's voice finally broke, and he looked down for a moment to collect himself. "I was honored," he continued in a softer tone, "to serve as John's chief of staff and even more so to call him my best friend. It'll be my honor, as well, to ensure that his legacy of inclusiveness and concern for others lives on long after today."

Like the president before him, Nick stopped to embrace Graham and Laine on his way back to his seat.

Sam slipped her arm around him and brought his head to rest on her shoulder. At that moment, she couldn't have cared less who might be watching or who might gossip about them later. Right now, all she cared about was Nick.

The mass ended with a soprano's soaring rendition of "Amazing Grace," and the family followed the pallbearers down the aisle and out of the church.

Dignitaries milled about, speaking in hushed tones as the church emptied. Watching them, Sam realized this was as much an official Washington political event as it was a funeral.

With Nick's hand on her elbow to guide her, they worked their way through the crowd. He stopped all of a sudden, and Sam turned to see who had caught his eye.

"You came," Nick said, clearly startled to see the youthful

man with brown hair and eyes and an olive complexion that reminded Sam of Nick's.

"Of course I did." After a long pause, he added, "You looked real good up there, Nicky. Real good."

An awkward moment passed before Nick seemed to recover his manners. "This is Sam Holland. Sam, my father, Leo Cappuano."

"Oh." Sam glanced up to take a read of Nick's impassive face before accepting Leo's outstretched hand. He seemed far too young to be Nick's father, but then she remembered he was only fifteen years older than his son. "Pleased to meet you."

"You, too," Leo said. "I've read about the two of you in the paper."

Nick winced. "I meant to call you, but it's been kind of crazy..."

"Don't worry about it."

"I appreciate you coming. I really do."

"I'm very sorry this happened to your friend, Nicky. He was a good guy."

"Yes, he was."

Neither of them seemed to know what to say next, and Sam ached for them.

"Well," Nick said, "the family's having a thing at the Willard. Can you join us?"

"I need to get back to work," Leo said. "I just took the morning off."

Nick shook his hand. "Give my best to Stacy and the kids."

"You got it." With a smile for Sam, Leo added, "Bring your pretty lady up to Baltimore for dinner one day soon."

"I will. I have Christmas presents for the boys."

"They'd love to see you. Any time. Take care, Nicky." With a smile, Leo left them.

"Dad?"

He turned back.

"Thanks again for being here."

Leo nodded and headed for the main door.

Nick exhaled a long deep breath. "That was a surprise."

"A good surprise?"

"Yeah, sure."

But she could tell it had rattled him. What would it be like to expect so little of your father that you'd be shocked to see him at your best friend's funeral? Sam couldn't imagine.

On the way out of church, numerous people stopped Nick to compliment him on his heartfelt eulogy. He accepted each remark with a gracious smile, but Sam could feel his tension in the tight grip he kept on her hand. When they finally made it outside, he took a deep breath.

Gonzo met them. "No sign of either of them."

Removing the ear piece she'd worn during the funeral, Sam took a measuring look around at the crowd. "I really thought they'd be here, if nothing more than to pour salt in the O'Connors' wounds. She told Cruz they were planning to attend."

"We'll keep looking," Gonzo assured her.

"Any word on autopsies on Tara or Natalie?"

"Nothing yet."

"Get with Lindsey and put a rush on Tara's. We'll have to bug Alexandria for Natalie's." Sam glanced up at Nick, whose attention was focused elsewhere. Lowering her voice, she said to Gonzo, "I need to hang with him for a while longer. Call me if anything breaks."

"You got it."

"Thanks." Taking Nick's arm, she directed him to the row of taxis lined up at the curb.

"It was a good idea you had to take the Metro in this morning," he said once they were in a cab.

"I knew security would make it tough to park anywhere near the cathedral." She snuggled into him and wrapped her arm around his waist. "Are you okay?"

"I've been better."

"You were really great up there, Nick. I was so proud of you, my heart felt like it might burst."

He hugged her tight against him and touched his lips to her forehead. "Thanks for coming. I know you had other things to do—"

She tilted her face to kiss him. "I was exactly where I needed to be. Where I *wanted* to be." Glancing up at him, she found him staring out the window. "Can I ask you something?" she said tentatively, not sure if this was the best time. But she needed to know. For some reason, she *had* to know more.

"Sure you can."

"What you said about growing up in Lowell with your grandmother…"

"What about it?"

"If you lived in a one-bedroom apartment, where did you sleep?"

"The sofa pulled out to a bed."

She bit her bottom lip in an attempt to deal with the sudden need to weep. Her every emotion seemed to be hovering just below the surface, and it wouldn't take much for the floodgates to swing open. "Where did you keep your stuff?"

"I didn't have a lot of stuff, but what I had I kept in the hall closet."

Her heart cracked right in half. "That's why you're so particular about the things you have now, isn't it? And I've made fun of you for that. I'm so sorry, Nick."

"Don't be sorry, babe. You're right to razz me. You lighten me up, and I need that."

"I had no idea…"

"How could you? But it doesn't bother me at all when you tease me about being anal. I swear it doesn't, so please don't stop." He tipped up her chin and flashed the cajoling smile she couldn't resist. "Please?"

She returned his smile with a pout. "If it doesn't bother you, that takes some of the fun out of it."

He laughed. "I love you, Samantha Holland, and all your crazy twisted logic."

Wanting to give him absolutely everything he'd ever been denied, but satisfied for now to hear him laugh, Sam closed her eyes and pressed her lips to his neck. "I love you, too."

CHAPTER 36

The cab came to a stop in front of the Willard Intercontinental Hotel, two blocks from the White House on Pennsylvania Avenue.

"The O'Connors reserved the ballroom, and the food here is amazing," Nick said, hoping to convince her to stay for a while.

"I really need to get to work."

"I know. I'm just being selfish wanting you with me."

Sam studied him. "Let me check in with HQ. Maybe I can stay for a few minutes."

Nick watched her while she talked on the phone and wished he could take her home to decorate the Christmas tree he planned to buy. He'd never bothered with a tree before, but this year he wanted the bother. This year, everything was different.

"I'll be there shortly," Sam said as she ended the call. "I'm only a couple of blocks away at the Willard."

"So you can come in?" Nick asked when she had returned her phone to her coat pocket.

She hesitated, but only for a second. "Sure. There's not much else I can do until we get a sighting of one of them."

Before they entered the hotel, Sam rested her hand on his arm to stop him. "You know it's going to be like this, right?"

"Like what?"

"I'll want to be with you, especially on a day like this, but I'll need to be somewhere else a lot of the time."

Nick smiled, touched by the hint of vulnerability he detected. "I know what I'm signing on for, babe."

"Do you? Do you really?"

Something in her tone and the expression on her face told him this too had been a problem in her marriage. He leaned in to kiss her. "I really do. I'm sorry you can't spend the day with me, but I understand you have a job to do, and in this case, I have a vested interest in you getting it done."

"Okay," she said with a sigh of relief.

"I'm never going to hassle you over your work, Sam," he said as he guided her inside with an arm around her shoulders.

"Never say never. It has a way of screwing up plans, vacations, meals, sleep…"

"I'll do my best to understand, but I'll always be sorry to see you go."

She looked up at him, a small smile illuminating her beautiful face. "I want to be with you today."

"I know, and that counts for a lot."

They checked their coats and wandered into the elegant ballroom where Graham and Laine greeted each guest as they entered the room.

Nick embraced them both.

"You did a beautiful job, Nick," Laine said, grasping his hands.

"Thank you." Nick had such admiration for the aura of dignity the older woman projected even in the darkest hours of her life.

"No, thank *you*, for everything this week. I don't know what we would've done without you."

"It was no problem."

Laine shook Sam's hand. "Thank you for coming today."

"The service was lovely," Sam said.

"Yes," Laine agreed. "I thought so, too."

"Any developments?" Graham asked.

"A few," Sam said. "I'm heading into work shortly, and I hope to know more by the end of the day. I'll keep you informed."

"We'd appreciate that," Graham said. "Nick, look me up in half an hour or so, would you?"

"Sure." With his arm around Sam, Nick steered them through the crowd toward one of the bars in the corner. "I know you have issues with them, so thank you for that...just now."

"This isn't the time or the place."

"Do you plan to do anything about them lying to you?"

"What would be the point? If they had told me the truth, it would've saved me some time. I don't have anything to gain by going after them." She glanced over at the O'Connors who were greeting the senior senator from Virginia and his wife. "In fact, I kind of pity them."

"Because of John?"

"That, too, but also for what they've missed out on with Thomas. And for what?"

"I wonder if they regret what they did," Nick said as he accepted coffee for himself and a soda for her.

"They will if we can prove Thomas's mother murdered John."

Nick shook his head. "What a tangled web."

"It amazes me that people think they're going to get away with trying to hide a baby. A secret like that is a time bomb looking for a place to detonate."

"True. I see it all the time in politics. The stuff people try to keep hidden usually blows up in their faces during a campaign."

Sam took a measuring look around the room. "I wonder where the cops who are supposed to be protecting the O'Connors are. I don't see anyone."

"Could be undercover."

"If there was a cop in this room, I'd know it."

Lucien Haverfield, the O'Connor family's attorney, approached them.

"There you are, Nick. I've been looking for you."

"Lucien." Nick shook hands with the distinguished older man and introduced him to Sam. "Nice to see you."

"Fine job you did today at the funeral."

"Thank you."

"The will is being read tomorrow at two at the O'Connor home. I need you to be there."

"Why's that?" Nick asked, surprised.

"You're a beneficiary."

"But he left me money," Nick stammered. "Insurance money, and a lot of it."

"Can you be there at two?" Lucien asked, clearly not willing to shed any light in advance of the reading.

"Yes, of course."

"Great." Lucien patted Nick's shoulder. "I'll see you then."

"Wonder what that's all about," Nick said to Sam.

"I guess you'll find out tomorrow."

"Yeah." He noticed Graham signaling to him and led Sam over to a table where Graham sat with the Virginia Democrats.

"We'd like to have a word with you upstairs, if you can spare us a few minutes, Nick," said Judson Knott, chairman of the party.

"Sure," Nick said with a perplexed glance at Sam.

"I'll, um, just wait for you here," she said.

"You're welcome to join us," Graham said. "This involves you, too."

Sam looked at Nick, who shrugged. "Okay," she said.

They followed the other men to the elevator and then to the Abraham Lincoln Suite. Nick took a moment to check out the incredible blue and gold suite, thinking he'd like to bring Sam there sometime when they could be alone. He accepted a short glass of bourbon from Judson. Sam declined a drink. Richard Manning, the party's vice chairman, had also joined them. "What's this all about, gentlemen?"

They gestured for Nick and Sam to have a seat at the dining room table.

"We have a proposition for you, Nick," Judson said.

Nick glanced at Graham and then at Sam. "What's that?"

"We'd like you to finish out John's term," Graham said.

Nick almost choked on the bourbon. "What? *Me?*"

Under the table, Sam grasped his arm.

"Yes, you," Judson said.

"But you have any number of people better suited. What about Cooper?"

"His wife was recently diagnosed with stage three breast cancer. He'll be announcing his resignation from the legislature the day after tomorrow."

"I'm sorry to hear that," Nick said sincerely. "How about Main?"

"He's been carrying on with his son's first grade teacher for years, and his wife filed for divorce yesterday. It'll be hitting the papers any day now."

"The party's having some troubles, Nick," Manning drawled. "We need someone of your caliber to step in and get us through to next year's election. We're hoping Cooper's wife will have recovered enough by then to free him up to run."

Nick couldn't believe they were serious. He wasn't the guy. He was the guy *behind* the guy. He named ten other Virginia Democrats he considered better suited to the job and was treated to a variety of disqualifying details about their personal lives that he could've lived without knowing. She's expecting twins, he's gay and in the closet—wants to stay there, he's got financial problems, she's caregiver to a mother with Alzheimer's. It went on and on.

"Listen, you guys," Nick said when he had run out of names to float. "I appreciate you thinking of me..."

"You struck a chord this morning," Judson said. "With your talk of humble beginnings. The data is highly favorable—"

"You've *polled* on me?" Nick asked, incredulous. *"Already?"*

"Of course we have." Richard seemed insulted that Nick even had to ask. "Most of Virginia and the rest of official Washington watched the funeral. You made quite an impression." Richard directed a charming smile at Sam. "Between that and your very public relationship with the Sergeant—"

"Don't bring her into this," Nick snapped. "She's off limits."

Graham rested his forearms on the table and leaned in to address Nick. "You know how this works. Nothing's off limits, *especially* your personal life. But the party is prepared to throw its support behind you if you want it. By this time tomorrow you can be a United States senator. All you have to do is tell us you want it, and we'll make it happen."

"Your name recognition is off the charts right now," Richard added. "Factor in youthful vitality, obvious political savvy, a well-known connection to the O'Connors and you're a very attractive candidate, Nick. Governor Zorn thinks it's a brilliant idea."

A United States senator. It boggled his mind. "I don't know what to say..."

"Say yes," Judson urged.

"It's not that simple," Nick said, thinking of Sam and their fledgling relationship. Could it handle the pressure that would come with a job like this on top of a job like hers? "I need to think about it."

"For how long?" Judson asked. "The governor is anxious to act."

"I need a couple of days."

"Two," Judson said. "I can give you through Christmas, and then we'll need to know."

"Why don't you want it?" Nick asked, beginning to worry about Sam's total silence and the sudden pallor gracing her cheeks.

"Hell," Judson said, "I'm too damned old to keep that kind of schedule. Richard is, too. We want to spend our spare time golfing and hanging out with the grandbabies. We need someone like you to get us through this transition. We're asking for one year, Nick. Give us that, and for the rest of your life you'll be known as Senator Cappuano."

The title sounded so preposterous, it was all Nick could do not to laugh.

Judson and Richard got up to leave. Both shook hands with Graham.

"Sorry again for your loss, Senator," Judson said.

To Nick, he added, "Let me know what you decide by the twenty-sixth."

Nick nodded and shook hands with them. When he heard the door click shut behind them, he turned to Graham and Sam.

"What do you think, Nick?" Graham asked.

"I'd like to know what Sam thinks."

"I, ah, I have no idea what to say."

He could tell by the wild look in her blue eyes that she was having a silent freak-out and decided to wait until they were alone to address it further with her.

"You seriously think I can do this?" he said to Graham.

"If I had any doubt, we wouldn't be here."

Nick studied the other man for a long moment. "This was all your doing, wasn't it?"

Graham shrugged. "I might've suggested that the best man for the job was the one who knew John the best."

"I didn't know John as well as I thought I did."

"You knew him as well as anyone."

Nick looked over at Sam, wishing he knew what she was thinking. No doubt the offer had shocked her just as much as it had shocked him. Standing, he offered his hand to Graham. "Thank you for the opportunity."

Graham held Nick's hand between both of his. "I have nothing but the utmost faith in you, Nick Cappuano from Lowell, Massachusetts. I was so proud of you up there today. You've grown into one hell of a man."

"Thank you. That means a lot coming from you."

A knock on the door ended the moment between the two men.

CHAPTER 37

"I'll get it," Nick said. He strolled to the door, opened it and gasped at the face that greeted him. John's face. Rendered speechless, Nick could only stare at the young man. He had a wild, unfocused look to him that put Nick on alert.

"I'm Thomas O'Connor. I understand that my, um, grandfather is here?"

Recovering, Nick said, "Yes. Please. Come in."

As he ushered the young man into the room, Nick experienced the same prickle of fear on the back of his neck that he'd felt once before—the day he walked into John's apartment and found him dead. Sam, he noticed, had stood up and was watching Thomas's every move as he approached Graham.

"Who are you?" Thomas asked Nick.

Surprised that Thomas didn't seem to recognize him or Sam, he said, "I'm Nick Cappuano, your father's chief of staff, and this is my girlfriend, Sam." Nick met Sam's steady gaze with one of his own, using his eyes to implore her to go along with him. Until they knew what Thomas wanted with Graham, he didn't need to know she was a cop.

"You've taken me by surprise," Graham finally said as he sized up the grandson he hadn't seen since the day he was born twenty years earlier.

"I imagine I have."

"I thought we might see you and your mother at your father's funeral," Graham said.

"She got tied up in Chicago and couldn't make it," Thomas said.

Sam and Nick exchanged glances, and he knew she was picking up the same uneasy vibe.

Thomas turned to them. "You two can take off. I came to see my grandfather."

"That's all right," Nick said, the tingle on his neck intensifying by the minute. "We've got nowhere to be."

Thomas pulled a gun from the inside pocket of his winter coat. Pointing it at Sam and Nick, he said, "Then take a seat and shut up." He gestured to the sofa.

"Thomas," Nick said, taking a step toward him, "you don't want to do this. What difference will it make now?"

The younger man stared at him, his eyes even more wild and unfocused than they were when he first arrived. "Are you serious? What *difference* will it make? My *grandfather* ruined my mother's life. He shipped her off like unwanted garbage to protect his political image."

Sam rested her hand on Nick's arm to pull him back. Nodding her head, she signaled for him to take a seat with her on the sofa.

Once they were seated, Thomas turned back to Graham. "All you cared about was yourself."

"That's not true. I cared about your father, and you, too. I sent money. For years. I made sure you had everything you needed."

"Everything except my father and my family! You took everything from us. We got him for one lousy weekend a month, and you know what he was doing the rest of the time? Fucking his way through Washington with one stupid bitch after another."

Watching Thomas gesture erratically with the gun, Nick's heart slowed to a crawl.

Sam poked his leg to get his attention.

He watched as she raised her pant leg and removed the small clutch piece she had strapped to her calf.

She pressed it into his hand and drew her primary weapon from the shoulder harness she had worn for the funeral, keeping the gun hidden in her suit coat in case Thomas turned to them. Mouthing the word "wait" she used her finger to indicate that he should go right while she went left.

Nick nodded to let her know he understood.

"You know what he told me a couple of weeks ago when I introduced him to my girlfriend? He advised me later that I shouldn't get 'tied down' to one woman. That a man needs to 'mix it up,' that 'variety is the spice of life.' It was a real touching father-son moment, and it was the first time it ever occurred to me that he'd been unfaithful to my mother. She'd waited her *whole life* for him. Ever since you banished her, she's done nothing but wait for him and settle for whatever scraps he tossed our way. And then he comes and tells us he's running for re-election! He actually expected us to be *happy* about his big news. He'd promised us one term. One term for you, his beloved father. Then it would be our turn. He lied about *everything*. Everything!"

"He loved you."

"No, he loved *you!* You were the only one he cared about."

"You killed him," Graham said in a whisper. "You killed my son."

"He had it coming! He was a fucking *whore!* I've got the investigator's report to prove it. You should see what he got done in just two weeks' time. It was truly revolting."

"That doesn't mean he deserved to die," Graham said. "Natalie didn't deserve what you did to her, either."

Thomas moved so quickly, Sam and Nick couldn't react in time to stop him from pistol-whipping his grandfather.

Graham went down hard, blood spurting from a wound on his forehead.

"Get up!" Thomas shrieked. "Get up and take what's coming to you like a man!"

"You talk about being a man!" Graham screamed back at him. "But what kind of man rapes and murders women?"

Sam held Nick back, giving him the one-minute sign.

"I made them pay for what they did to my mother. They got exactly what they deserved."

"You're a monster," Graham whispered, the blood loss weakening him.

Thomas aimed the gun at his grandfather's chest.

Sam gave Nick the thumb's up.

They rushed Thomas from behind, each of them pushing a gun into the young man's temples.

"Freeze," they said in unison.

Sam glowered at Nick. "I'll take it from here." She had Thomas disarmed, cuffed and immobilized less than a second later. With her free hand, she tugged her radio off her hip and called for back-up.

"What the fuck?" Thomas screamed, fighting the restraints. "You're a fucking *cop?*"

"Surprise," Nick said, unable to resist a smile as adrenaline zipped though his system. Watching her work never failed to fire him up. "Meet my 'girlfriend,' Detective Sergeant Sam Holland, Metro Police Department. You really ought to read a newspaper once in a while."

"Son of a fucking bitch."

"You said it, buddy." Sam tightened her hold on Thomas. "You're under the arrest for the murders of John O'Connor, Tara Davenport, Natalie Jordan and Noel Jordan. You have the right to remain silent."

Nick stayed with Graham while Sam dragged Thomas out

of the suite to turn him over to Gonzo for transport to HQ. Nick pressed a handkerchief to the wound on Graham's head.

Tears spilled down the older man's cheeks. "This is all my fault. I caused this. I forced John to lead a double life."

"You did what you thought was right at the time. That's all any of us can ever do."

"Will you find Laine for me? I need to see her."

"As soon as the paramedics get here, I'll get her to the hospital."

"Call Lucien," Graham said. "Have him send someone over to represent Thomas."

Nick stared at the older man. "You can't be serious."

"He's my grandson. What I did to him and his mother drove him to this." Graham closed his eyes and took a deep, rattling breath. "Make the call."

Even though he didn't agree, Nick said, "I'll take care of it." He rested his hand on top of Graham's. "Try not to worry about anything."

"You're going to make an outstanding senator."

"I haven't said yes yet."

"You will." The older man held Nick's hand until the EMTs arrived and whisked him away.

The moment they left with Graham, Sam returned to the suite.

"Whew," Nick said. "That was something."

A cocky grin lit up her gorgeous face. "Just another day at the office."

"For you, maybe."

"You did good—for a rookie."

"Gee, thanks." He wiped the sweat from his forehead, his legs still rubbery. "You called Chicago to check on Patricia?"

"They're on their way to her house as we speak. Thomas had her credit cards in his wallet."

"I feel sorry for her," Nick said. "She's lost them both."

"The whole situation is too sad, but his lawyer will probably mount an insanity defense."

"He was going to kill us all, wasn't he? That's why he said all the stuff he did in front of us."

"I suspect that became his plan when we insisted on staying. I just can't believe I didn't figure this out sooner. I was so sure it was a love affair gone wrong."

"Well, it sort of was when you think about it."

"Yeah, I guess you're right."

"I'm just glad we were here when Thomas confronted Graham." He shuddered. "I don't even want to think about what could've happened."

"It's probably better if you don't think about it."

Nick slipped an arm around her shoulders. "We need to talk about what happened before Thomas showed up."

"Later." She hip checked him. "No PDA in front of the colleagues."

He slapped her on the ass. "Screw that."

Sam attempted a dirty look but failed to pull it off.

"We make a good team, you know that?" he said.

"As long as you remember who's in charge."

Nick took great pleasure in hooking an arm around her and escorting her down the hallway full of hooting cops. Not even the elbow she jammed in his ribs could detract from his euphoria at having her by his side and John's killer on his way to jail.

In the elevator, she looked up at him, her clear blue eyes full of love. "Thanks for having my back in there."

Hugging her closer to him, he kissed her cheek and then her lips. "Samantha, I'll *always* have your back."

EPILOGUE

Nick got home from the reading of John's will just after five on Christmas Eve and went straight to the kitchen to dig out the bottle of whiskey he'd kept on hand for John. He poured himself half a glass and downed it in one long swallow that burned all the way through him. Pouring a second shot, he took it with him to sit in the living room where a seven-foot Christmas tree waited to be decorated. Under the tree were six festively wrapped gifts for Sam.

He hadn't heard from her all day, and after her refusal to discuss the Virginia Democrats' offer when they finally got home late last night, he had good reason to wonder if she would keep her promise to spend this evening with him. She hadn't even called to tell him that Marquis Johnson had been remanded over to trial—without incident. Nick had to hear about it on the news.

Still hopeful that Sam would keep her promise to spend tonight with him, Nick went into the kitchen to make the dinner he'd shopped for earlier. By nine o'clock the pasta was rubbery, and he had given up on her. Could she really be *that* freaked out by his job offer? Didn't she know that if she wasn't in favor of it, he wouldn't do it? Disappointment mixed with disbelief. That she would let him down like this, that she would let *herself* down like this...

He stretched out on the sofa with another shot of whiskey. The empty tree was a stark reminder of how his plans for this evening had failed to materialize. Without Sam, what did it matter? What did anything matter?

He must have dozed off because the ringing doorbell startled him awake an hour later. His heart surged with hope as he got up to answer it. He swung open the door, and there she was.

"Hey," he said.

"Hey."

"I thought you weren't coming."

"I almost didn't."

Nick stepped back to let her in and took her coat.

"What do I smell?" she asked, surprised. "Did you cook?"

He shrugged. "Nothing special."

"Did you leave any for me?"

"All of it."

"You didn't eat?"

"I was waiting for you."

Snuggling into his embrace, she said, "I'm sorry. I totally freaked, and I handled this all wrong."

Nick hugged her close, overcome with relief at having her back in his arms after a day filled with uncertainty. He brushed his lips over hers. "Tell me what you're thinking, Samantha. Tell me the truth."

She looked up at him with those blue eyes he loved so much. "I'd be a liability to you. I'm messy and loud and I swear and sometimes I even tell white lies—I don't mean to, but they sneak out before I can stop them. I'm dyslexic, infertile and my stomach runs my life. And then there're the lovely people I come in contact with on a daily basis: drug dealers, prostitutes, murderers, rapists. There's the whole fiasco with the Johnsons—and my ex-husband is headed for prison…"

Even though he was amused by her speech, Nick knew she was dead serious and fought back a smile. "That's not your fault. He tried to kill us both."

"Which will lead people to wonder what kind of woman marries a man like him. They'll question my judgment and yours for getting involved with me. They'll rehash Johnson and every other ugly case I've ever had—and there're a lot of them. It'll reflect poorly on you."

"I'm not running for office, Sam. It's being handed to me for one year, and then it's done."

Rolling her bottom lip between her teeth, she mulled it over. "We'd attract a lot of media attention after everything that happened this week."

"I can handle it if you can."

"I'd hate to be responsible for causing you trouble. I'd hate that."

"I can deal with that, too."

She rested her hands on his shoulders. "You want this, don't you?"

"My life was just fine before. If I say no, it'll be fine after."

"That doesn't answer my question."

"It's something I never dreamed of, something I never even considered before yesterday."

"My dad and Freddie think it's so cool," she said with a shy smile. "They say it would work out fine for us. My dad even thinks it could be a 'grand adventure.'"

Her skeptical scowl amused Nick. "They're very wise men. You should listen to them."

Looking up at him, she said, "Can we eat? I haven't eaten all day, and I'm starving."

He decided not to push his luck since she seemed to be coming around to a decision in her own peculiar way. "Sure."

"Oh!" she said on the way to the kitchen. "You got a tree!"

"I told you I was going to."

"When did you have time?"

"I did it this morning, along with a few other things."

"What other things?"

"A little Christmas shopping," he said with a mysterious smile as he poured her a glass of wine. "And some real estate shopping."

Her eyebrows knitted with confusion.

He served her the reheated shrimp fettuccine Alfredo and carried a tossed salad to the table. "You said you couldn't live way out here in Virginia, right?"

"Uh-huh." She dove into the meal as if she was, in fact, starving. "You never told me you could cook like this! It's amazing!"

"You never asked, and I'm glad you like it." After lighting the candles on the table, he sat down across from her. "Anyway, since you can't live here, I bought a place in the city."

"What place did you buy?" she asked, astounded.

"The one that was for sale up the street from your dad's. I looked at it on Sunday when you were at work, I offered this morning and they accepted. I'm meeting with a Realtor after Christmas to list this place."

She sat back in her chair to stare at him. "Just like that?"

"I knew you'd want to be close to your dad and to work."

"Won't you need to maintain a residence in Virginia?"

Implied but not stated was if he became a senator. "John took care of that. He left me the cabin. That's why they wanted me to come today."

Her eyes went soft with emotion. "Nick...That's wonderful. You love it there."

"I was so surprised and delighted." He reached for her hand and brought it to his lips.

"How's Graham doing?"

"Better. They let him go home today when his blood pressure returned to normal."

"That's good."

"I feel sorry for them. They've got a long road ahead of them coming to terms with all of this. And the media is clamoring for info about John's illegitimate son."

"They should just come clean at this point."

"I think that's the plan. Laine wanted me to tell you how very sorry she is for lying to you about Thomas. She said she panicked when she saw you had his photo."

"It's in the past now. I'm over it."

When they finished eating, Nick picked up their wine glasses and led her to the sofa. "John had so many secrets. Hell, I had no idea until today when the lawyer was doling out his millions how insanely wealthy the sale of his business made him. There were a lot of secrets, but he loved his father. So much. Despite everything. He loved him."

"I can understand that. There's not much my father could do to change how I feel about him."

"You're lucky to have him."

"And I know it."

He studied the face that had become so essential to him. "What're we going to do, Sam?"

"Well, tonight we're going to decorate that tree." She glanced at the tree and then down at the gifts under it. "What's all that?"

"One for every year we missed."

Smiling, she shifted to straddle him. "That's so incredibly sweet."

He pulled her in close.

"Tomorrow," she said, touching her lips to his, "we're going to Tracy's for dinner. The next day, you're going to tell the Virginia Democrats that you're their new senator."

He cradled her face in his hands. "Am I?"

"It's just a year, right?"

"One year."

"It'll be a total mess. You know that, don't you?"

"I *love* a good mess," he said with a teasing grin. "In fact, I *live* for messes."

She smiled. "We're really going to do this."

"We really are."

"I love you, Senator Cappuano."

"I love you, Lieutenant Holland. Merry Christmas."

"Same to you." She leaned her forehead against his and looked him in the eye. "It's gonna be one hell of a New Year."

"I can't wait."

★ ★ ★ ★ ★

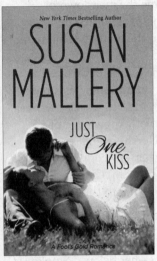

Sophie Littlefield

Of living things there were few, but they carried on

"Evocative, sensual, harrowing."
—*Publishers Weekly* on *Aftertime*, starred review

Sophie Littlefield

AN AFTERTIME NOVEL

HORIZON

Cass Dollar is a survivor.
She's overcome the meltdown of
civilization, humans turned mindless
cannibals and the many evils of man.

But from beneath the devastated
California landscape emerges a tendril
of hope. A mysterious traveler arrives
at New Eden with knowledge of a
passageway North—a final escape
from the increasingly cunning Beaters.
Clutching this dream, Cass and many
others follow him into the unknown.

Journeying down valleys and over
barren hills, Cass remains torn between
two men. One—her beloved Smoke—is
not so innocent as he once was. The
other keeps a primal hold on her that
feels like Fate itself. And beneath it all, Cass must confront the worst of
what's inside her—dark memories from when she was a Beater herself. But
she, and all of the other survivors, will fight to the death for the promise of
a new horizon....

Available wherever books are sold!

Be sure to connect with us at:

Harlequin.com/Newsletters
Facebook.com/HarlequinBooks
Twitter.com/HarlequinBooks

HARLEQUIN® LUNA™
www.Harlequin.com

LSL354TR

JULIETTE MILLER

In the midst of a Clan divided, two unlikely allies must confront the passion that binds them...and the treachery that may part them forever.

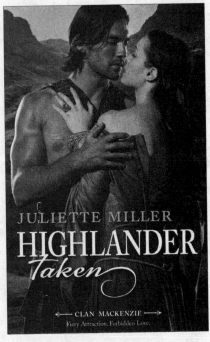

To secure her family's alliance with the powerful Clan Mackenzie, Stella Morrison has no choice but to wed the notorious Kade Mackenzie. Unable to ignore the whispers that surround him, she resigns herself to a marriage in name only. Yet as the fierce warrior strips away Stella's doubt one seductive touch at a time, burgeoning desire forces her to question all she holds as truth.

Leading a rebellious army should have been Kade's greatest challenge...until conquering the heart of his reluctant bride becomes an all-consuming need. Now more than ever, he's determined to find victory both on the battlefield and in the bedchamber. But the quest for triumph unleashes a dark threat, and this time, only love may prove stronger than danger.

Available wherever books are sold!

Be sure to connect with us at:
Harlequin.com/Newsletters
Facebook.com/HarlequinBooks
Twitter.com/HarlequinBooks

www.Harlequin.com

PHJM767TR

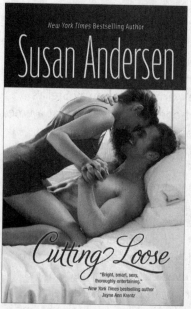

PORTIA DA COSTA

When it comes to diamonds—like their men—some women prefer them rough

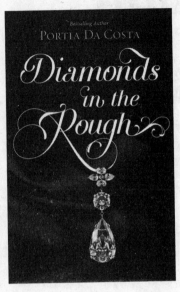

Thanks to her grandfather's complicated will, Miss Adela Ruffington, along with her mother and sisters, is about lose her home and income to a distant cousin, the closest male heir to the Millingford title. For Adela, nothing could be more insulting—being denied her rightful inheritance for a randy scoundrel like Wilson, the very man who broke her heart following a lusty youthful dalliance years ago.

Still smarting from the betrayal of his latest paramour, Wilson Ruffington never anticipates the intense desire Adela again stirs within him. Despite his wicked tongue and her haughty pride, their long-ago passion instantly reignites at a summer house party, the experience they've gained as adults only adding fuel to the flames.

Wilson and Adela are insatiable, but civility outside of the bedroom proves impossible. Determined to keep Adela in his bed, Wilson devises a ruse—a marriage of convenience that will provide her family with a generous settlement, as well as prevent scandalous whispers. Their plan works perfectly until family rivalries and intrigue threaten to destroy their arrangement…and the unspoken love blooming beneath it.

Available wherever books are sold!

Be sure to connect with us at:
Harlequin.com/Newsletters
Facebook.com/HarlequinBooks
Twitter.com/HarlequinBooks

HARLEQUIN® HQN™

™ www.Harlequin.com

PHPDC811TR